I0647816

ALSO BY KYELL GOLD

Argaea
Volle
Pendant of Fortune
The Prisoner's Release and Other Stories
Shadow of the Father
Weasel Presents

Out of Position
Out of Position
Isolation Play
Divisions
Uncovered
Over Time

Dangerous Spirits
Green Fairy
Red Devil
Black Angel

The Calatians (as Tim Susman)
The Tower and the Fox
The Demon and the Fox
The War and the Fox (2019)

Other Books

Waterways
Bridges
Science Friction
Winter Games
The Mysterious Affair of Giles
Dude, Where's My Fox?
Losing my Religion

The Time He Desires
Camouflage
Love Match (vol 1 & vol 2)
In the Doghouse of Justice
The Silver Circle
Tales of the Firebirds
X (editor)

TY GAME

by Kyell Gold

TY GAME

Copyright © 2018 by Kyell Gold

Published by Sofawolf Press, Inc.
St. Paul, Minnesota
www.sofawolf.com

ISBN 978-1-936689-68-2
Printed in the United States of America
First trade paperback edition: November 2018
Second Printing: June 2019

Cover art Copyright © 2018 by Rukis & The Neverwolf
Interior art Copyright © 2018 by The Neverwolf

For my wolf and cat

Contents

Part 3: Ty

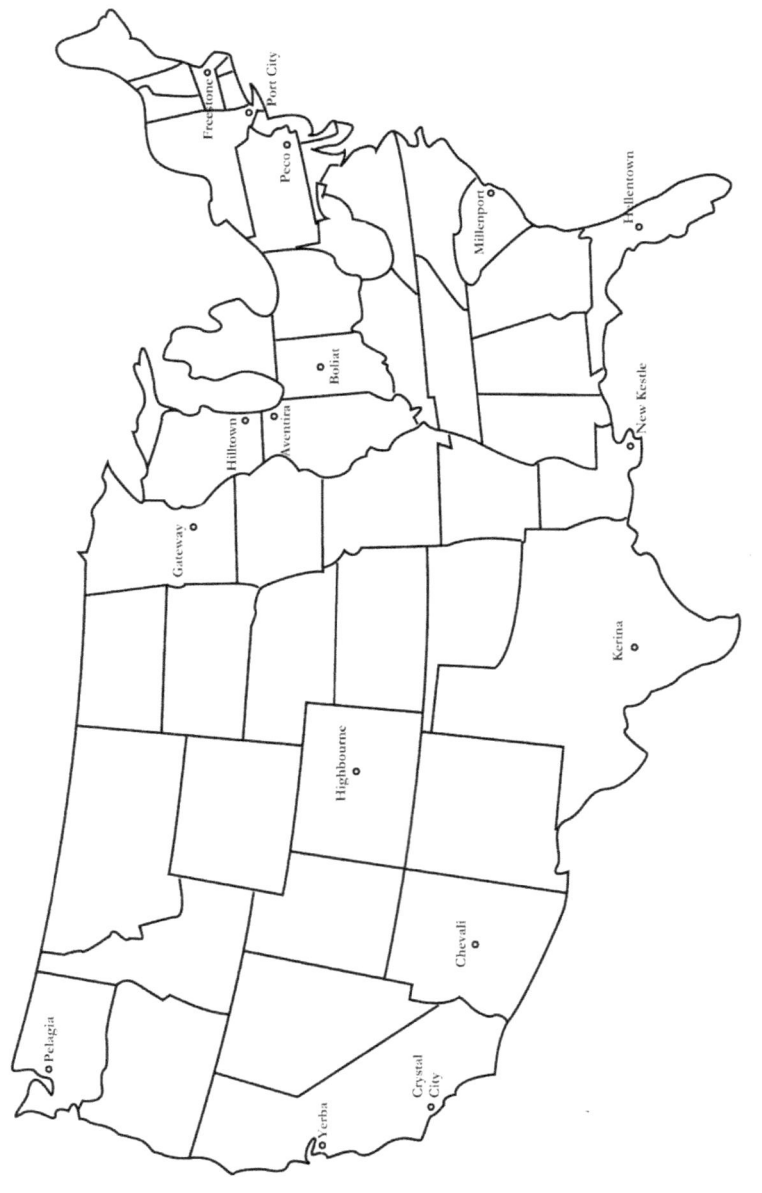

*I'm not saying the Forester Universe cities are in the United States.
But if they were, this is where they'd be.*

FOREWORD

The more I wrote in the world of Out of Position, the more the side characters took on a life of their own. I knew after writing *Over Time* that I would want to write more about Ty and his mysterious hookup that Dev and Lee catch him with. So I started this story with the idea that it would be maybe a novella.

What I didn't expect was to get to the end of that story and find that I was only halfway done with Ty's story. I'd written a short piece about the fox who writes to him and how that letter came about, and I fell in love with the world she inhabits. So went the second part of this book, and by that time it was clear that it was a novel.

I want to thank everyone who has continued to love Dev and Lee and the stories that surround them. You give me the energy and enthusiasm to write stories like this one, for which I am eternally grateful. I hope you'll also grow to love Ty and his world, and who knows? Maybe in five more years one of his friends will get their own novel too.

—Ky, December 2018

Part 1: Arch

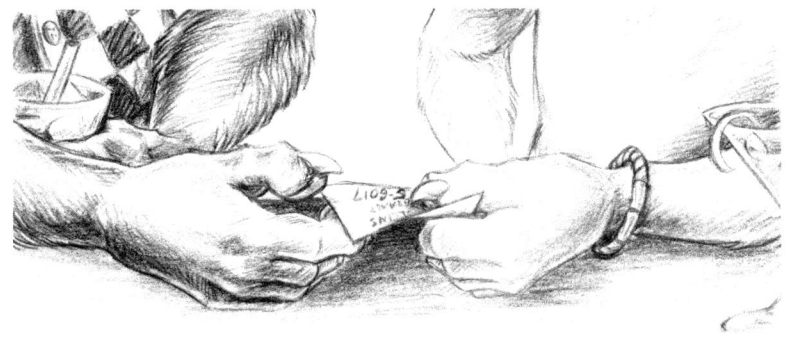

CHAPTER 1

It was weird at first, dancing without any girls around, but the bass beat drove his hips and the melody pulled his arms and tail around, and it only took a song for him to lose himself, becoming part of the music. The only thing he missed was someone to dance with, because Vonni couldn't dance for shit. Here in a gay club, though, a straight guy's options for dance partners were limited to his least self-conscious friends. Whatever. The guys back in Chevali would come out to clubs with him, but they weren't much better than Vonni so usually he ended up with whatever girl wanted to dance with a football star for an evening, and only a few of them were any good.

After a couple songs, Ty didn't even care about Vonni's shitty moves. He was dancing. The stuffy air filled with hundreds of scents, the flashing lights, the pounding trance music: he loved it. Here he could forget about football (with a little assist from the cocktails Lee'd bought) and move with the music. While he was dancing, guys didn't bother him, or they assumed he was with Vonni, a couple tall athletic red foxes cutting it up on the floor. Or at least, one athletic fox cutting it up and Vonni kind of hopping from one foot to the other, pumping his fists while his tail hung behind him. Ty looked around at the rest of the room and then turned to his right so he wouldn't have to feel bad for his friend.

There, facing him, was a wolf who could sure as shit dance. Ty lost a step to surprise, then picked up the beat again with an eye on this new guy. He looked to have plain brown and ivory fur, though who could tell under these lights, and his tank top showed off what were probably considered pretty nice muscles outside a football locker room. Heck, they were pretty nice muscles, unqualified, and the tank top hung straight down from his chest, so no gut. He wore jeans, like Ty, and a glittering pride bracelet swung around his left wrist.

Watching him gave Ty that competitive drive to tighten up his form, match and surpass the wolf. He liked that feeling, of knowing that he was doing something well. Hell, he and the wolf together were probably the best dancing team in this place (as far as he could see). The guy met Ty's eyes, and that was when Ty realized that the wolf was matching his steps and his moves, but adding his own little flourishes.

Was the wolf hitting on him? He smelled nice, no heavy perfume, no dominating scent of arousal. Seemed safe. Ty added some moves and the wolf followed them easily, again adding his flourishes. When the song changed, he shifted into a different style, more energetic, and Ty followed that one, grinning at the joy of dancing and the fun of having someone to match him.

After about fifteen minutes of this, he needed a break, so he turned to look for Vonni. The other fox was talking to some leopard chick and leaning in, like really into her, so Ty let him be. He pushed his way through to the bar, ordered a club soda, and turned to see the wolf standing right there, tongue lolling out in a grin.

Then he felt the need to raise a paw and say, "I'm straight."

The wolf tilted his head to the side, a casual grin on his muzzle. "I won't hold it against you."

Ty blinked. What was that supposed to mean? He watched while the wolf ordered a Cosmo, and then said, "I thought you'd care."

"Doesn't mean I'm gonna walk away. You got moves, and you're here with a bunch of big muscular guys, so I'm a little curious. Athletes?"

"Football players."

"Oh!" The wolf turned, and there was Dev on the dance floor. "Firebirds, right? That's Miski, the gay one."

"Right. He and his boyfriend brought us here to dance." He sipped his club soda. Definitely didn't want to get any more buzzed than he already was.

"Cool. How you liking it?"

Ty surveyed the room, lifting his nose. "It's loud." He grinned and rubbed up the side of one of his big ears. "But I'm used to that. Smells good and I love the music. Also I love dancing, you know?"

"Sure." The wolf paid for his drink and lapped at it. "You got a name?"

"Uh. Ty."

"I'm Archie. Arch for short."

"Hey, Arch." Ty extended his paw and the wolf took it, with a warm, firm grip. "You got moves too."

"Two years ballet." Arch did a little sashay with his hips. "I don't use the steps, but the coordination comes in handy. So you play football, huh? You any good?"

"Yeah." Ty couldn't help putting on what one of the girls he dated in college called his "cocky grin." Hell, he thought, if you've got something to be cocky about, why not?

"My dad made me watch football with him for a while. You know, to counteract the ballet lessons. So when I got kicked out, I swore off it. But I gotta say, between you and Miski, I might pick it up again."

"You should." Was the club soda spiked? Something in it was making him feel warm and happy. "We're going to the championship this year."

"That a fact?" Arch raised an eyebrow and finished his drink. "Well, Ty, I'm gonna keep an eye on you, then. And if you're ever back in Yerba and you wanna go dancing…" His paw was outstretched again, and a card reflected the club's rainbow lights from between his fingers. "Text me.."

Ty took the card and clasped the wolf's paw at the same time. "You taking off?"

"Heading back out to the dance floor." He folded his ears down. "I'd rather dance than talk. Maybe I'll see you there?" The wolf released his paw and backed up a step.

"Maybe." Ty looked at the card briefly and then saw Dev coming up. He shoved the card hastily in his pocket and watched the wolf's tail wag its way to the dance floor as Dev took the empty seat.

Dev was worried about Vonni, who'd disappeared from the floor, and after that Pike came up and said it was time to go, so Ty didn't see Arch again that night. But he took the card out in his room, sitting in his bed. It had microperforation marks around the edges and looked to have been printed out on a home printer. *For a good time call Archie Collins*, it read, with a phone number below it.

It was tempting to say that the guy had the wrong idea about him. But he hadn't hit on Ty at all. Couldn't a guy have a guy friend to go dancing with? Even if one was straight and the other gay? Even beyond the dancing, there was something about Arch that was different. Maybe it was that competitive urge Ty got when dancing with him. Maybe it was that the wolf had walked away. That hadn't happened with anyone, male or female, since—jeez, high school maybe.

Watch out for people attracted to your fame, the UFL had warned him and the other rookies at the beginning of the year. You can't be too careful. Don't trust strangers, and be careful even with family members trying to get closer to you now that you've got a big pro contract. Ty curled his tail up on the bed and looked at the card again, then put the number into his phone.

Chapter 2

On Sunday after the game, pretty much everyone was down after the loss: tails drooped and ears were flat everywhere Ty looked in the locker room. The rest of the wideouts grumbled around him: there was a new guy coming in, Lightning Strike, and they hadn't even had a chance to say good-bye to Ford, who'd been traded for him. So nobody was really in the mood to go out.

But Ty'd caught a touchdown, and even though he was pissed about Ford and Strike, he was already envisioning being traded to a team where he could be the number one wideout, or else hanging around a couple years until Strike left this team like he'd left all the others and Ty could take over the top spot here. Whatever happened, he was sure he'd come out on top. And he'd caught a touchdown, and he'd talked briefly to his mom and his uncle, who had both told him how great he looked out there. Then his mom had asked some questions about vixens she wanted to set him up with when the season was over, and that was exhausting because he couldn't tell her he didn't care or that right after a game wasn't the best time, even though he didn't and it wasn't. That was all done with, and now he felt like going out.

Dev had a date with his fox, which was cool that they could go out together here and people wouldn't care as much. The tiger was going through a lot of shit this season and he deserved to get out and relax. At least, relax a little; he'd still looked stressed even on Korsat Street.

The tall fox took his phone out and thumbed it open. There on the first page of his contacts was the name: Archie Collins. He rubbed his whiskers. Ah, what the hell. It didn't mean anything.

So he texted: *Sorry about your first game as a Firebirds fan.*

He'd gotten dressed and was chatting with his roommate and fellow wide receiver Rodolf (everyone called him Rodo) when his phone buzzed. Archie had replied: *What makes you think I watched? ;)*

He grinned until Rodo snapped his fingers, and then he looked up at the deer. "Sorry," he said. "Messages."

As they talked, he typed back: *Aw, I thought you liked me.*

Rodo started telling him about the terrible things this guy he knew had said Strike did while he was on the Hellentown Pilots, while Ty listened absently. And a couple minutes later, he flipped open his phone when it buzzed with the response.

"Oh, you think that's good news?" Rodo snapped. "You think you won't come in for some comment about how much better he is than you?"

"Sorry." Ty wagged his tail. "I'm sure it'll be fine."

"You ready yet?" Rodo looked him up and down. "We're going back to the hotel to have some beers and then, y'know, girls."

Tempting, but sex was over quickly, and then what did you do with the rest of the night? His teammates seemed fine with it but Ty had a lot of energy to burn off. He shook his head. "I'm gonna head out. See you on the plane."

Zaïd, nearby, swatted Ty's shoulder. "You gotta carry his bags, rook," he said. "Then you can maybe go."

Ty bristled, ready to stand up, but Rodo got between them. "He scored," he said, "and neither of us did. I'll carry my own bags."

"Hmf." But Zaïd didn't argue, and even gave a quick nod before walking away.

"Thanks," Ty said.

Rodo shrugged. "Never liked all the rookie hazing anyway. We all do it 'cause it was done to us, but you earned your spot. Go do what you gotta do."

"Seeya on the plane." Ty looked again at the message that said, *Nice touchdown :)*, and then called a cab.

•

Korsat Street wasn't nearly as crowded on a Sunday night, and the music in the club wasn't as good. Ty got a Glenlivet at the bar, savored the flavors and made a note to tell his uncle Lucas about them, and then raised his arms over his head and sauntered out onto the dance floor. He'd been tackled pretty hard a few times, but he'd had his time in the ice bath, so he ignored the soreness in his hip and danced anyway, confident that Arch would find him.

He'd been dancing for one and a half songs when the smell of wolf tickled his nose. There was nobody in front of him, so he turned with the music and there on his right Arch grinned at him and held up a paw. Ty slapped it, and they danced as if they'd come right back to the floor from taking a break two nights ago.

Arch was still good and the dancing still got Ty worked up. He hadn't really thought much about it, but it was nice to know it hadn't been a fluke, or something that he'd been remembering wrong because of the drinks. Arch could move and shake, and maybe he swiveled his hips and flipped his tail up more than Ty wanted to do, but damn, he looked good doing it.

They danced until Ty's hip protested too much, and then the fox pulled Arch over to the bar, grabbing the wolf's paw casually just like that. "A scotch and soda," he told the bartender, "Glenlivet again. And whatever he wants."

"You don't have to buy my drink," Arch said. "In fact, you lost your game. I should be buying you a drink."

Ty laughed. "Don't worry about it. Normally I'm out at a club with a bunch of guys and I drop like a thousand bucks."

Arch raised an eyebrow. "Cosmo," he told the bartender, and then, to Ty, "You go out with a bunch of guys?"

"Friends from college and home. Four of them moved down to Chevali when I got drafted there. I got them a house to live in, they support me."

"Ah." Arch's grin widened. "Around here, 'going out with a bunch of guys' means something else."

Ty's imagination took him in a flash to a half-dozen naked Arches, fucking or blowing each other or whatever. He flinched inside, but not as much as he would've thought. "That's not my scene," he said.

Their drinks arrived, and as they were sipping, a stallion came over to them. "You guys look great together," he said.

"Thanks." Arch raised a paw, and the guy headed off.

"We're not…" Ty called after him, and then shrugged. "Ah, hell with it."

The wolf grinned at him. "You and I know it. Who cares what they think?"

"If they take a picture and publish it, I'll care."

"Nobody's gonna take pictures in here. It's not cool."

Ty looked around, but nobody seemed to have a camera or even to be paying his tall, athletic body any attention other than the kind that didn't care what his name was. "I guess," he said. "But if I get 'outed' in the paper, it's on you."

"I'll deny it if they talk to me." Arch finished his drink. "How's your scotch?"

"Enh." Ty gulped the rest. "It's fine. I shouldn't get too buzzed, though. Sorry about my hip. It'll be better in a few days."

Arch nodded, and then put his muzzle closer to Ty's ear. "You ever get high?"

The words came across clearly even though the wolf had spoken softly and the music was going at full volume. Ty turned and caught rainbow sparkles flashing in dark eyes. "Back in college," he said. "Been a while. My friends don't have a source in Chevali so we mostly get drunk."

"Do they test you?"

"Yeah, but they tell us when it's coming. I already had mine this year." He waved a paw. "You got some?"

Arch chuckled. "I get these migraines, see? I really do. So I got a prescription. Got some cookies at home. You want some? Might help your leg."

The fox narrowed his eyes. "I don't get experimental when I get high."

"Settle down." The wolf put a paw on Ty's. "I read a thing about athletes using pot to deal with injuries and how it's better than the toxic drugs they give you in the training room. That's all. No," he made air quotes, "'gay agenda.'"

His hip was still stiff. In college, pot had helped him get past pain. And heck, a cab was a phone call away. "In that case," he said, "lead on."

When Arch pulled out his keys in front of a narrow three-story building on a misty street, Ty's nose counted about ten different people who'd pissed nearby in the last couple days. Piles of litter didn't help the odor all the way up to the rust-spotted gate, Ty keeping close behind Arch as the wolf tapped a code on the keypad. What kind of place did he live in? Ty looked up and down the street at the other buildings and then his gaze fell on a BMW. Brave soul, he thought, then saw another, and then a shiny new Mini standing out amid a bunch of mid-range sedans. So homeless people might piss on the sidewalks, but people with money lived in the buildings. He followed Arch through the creaking gate, tail uncurling to swing free.

The urine smell disappeared when he walked through the door into a brightly-lit foyer. Mailboxes along one wall gleamed with brass fittings and carefully painted numbers on the shiny front plates. Arch passed them all and headed for an old elegant marble staircase at the back of the building, only wide enough for one person at a time.

Ty followed the wolf up to the second floor, down a narrow hallway. "This looks like a college dorm," he said, looking at all the numbered doors and down at the worn carpeting. "Smells better, though."

"Still crowded." Arch's nose wrinkled just as Ty's did. "Used to be a small hotel, then a rabbit family bought it. Sold it off in the Depression and homeless people lived here for a while. Then a tech millionaire fixed it up to rent." The wolf turned his key in the lock of a door with number 225 on it and opened it, letting Ty in.

The room was a little larger than the hotel rooms Ty was used to, but not much. To the right, a small wooden table and two chairs bumped up against a small refrigerator and a stack of plastic crates that apparently served as a pantry, filled with cereal boxes and instant dinners. There was no sink in this room, but behind the table, an open door gave onto a bathroom.

To the left, a double bed against the wall filled most of the space of the room, sheets untidy, a collared shirt in a pile at the foot. A brightly colored pressboard dresser had been wedged between the bed and the window, and that was all the furniture the room held. There was no TV, no couch, nothing else, and no other doors apart from the bathroom. Mail and laptops cluttered the wooden table, and clothes dotted the floor.

"Home sweet home," Arch said. "Sorry about the mess."

Ty shook his head. "Reminds me of my dorm room. You live here…" He sniffed the air. "With a wolverine? Your boyfriend?"

Arch laughed. "Roommate."

"Okay…" Ty definitely smelled sex in the air. Stale, but unmistakable. "So he's not gay?"

"Oh, we jerk each other off sometimes. Sometimes more than that." Arch stopped, cocked his head, and grinned at Ty. "Depends what we're in the mood for."

Casually sexual relationship, ongoing. Weird. Ty'd had casual sex, but rarely with the same girl twice. The fox turned his attention to the fridge. "No kitchen?"

Arch stepped closer to him. "Tell me," he said. "If there was a vixen you could hang out with and sometimes sleep with, and she wouldn't ever want the relationship to be more, would you do it? If it was all about being friends and sex was just one of the things you did?"

"Look," Ty said, "I told you, I'm straight."

The wolf laughed. "I'm talking about me and Justin. You're getting all tight and judgy, so I'm putting a hypothetical to you. If Justin was Justine and we were both straight and I told you I had this female roommate who was a good friend and sometimes we had sex when we both wanted it, what would you say? Something like 'way to go,' right?"

"I guess so." Ty grinned, felt the brush of his own tail against his legs, and realized he had been getting a little tense. Nothing to be tense about, he told himself, and anyway, it wasn't like him to get worked up. He usually let the world come to him and he dealt with it as he dealt with it, a coping mechanism to survive in the uptight worlds of his family and football.

"So?" Arch stood with paws on hips, grinning.

Ty laughed and clapped the wolf on the shoulder. "Way to go," he said.

"There you go." Arch turned from the taller fox and walked over to the fridge. "Have a seat on the bed if you want."

Ty started toward the chairs by the table, and Arch caught his motion. "Not the chairs. I mean, they're okay, but what are you going to do, sit at the table and get high? Trust me, the bed's better. You can sit on the floor if you don't want to sit on a gay guy's bed with him."

What was he afraid of? "No, it's okay. I mean, I'm a fox…"

"So? You going to rub your musk all over my sheets?"

Ty shook his head and went to sit on the bed, a grin on his muzzle. This was weird, but it was also fun in a way. Here it didn't matter that he was a professional football player. He didn't have to keep thinking about the passes he'd missed in the game they'd lost or worry about running his routes or about linebackers and safeties smashing into him (though his hip still ached), or whether his teammates would mock or scold him for going to a strange guy's house and eating pot cookies. He was just Ty, a fox who liked to dance and who'd been invited by a new friend to come chill for an evening. "What if Justin comes in?"

"Then he can have some," Arch called from the fridge. "But he won't. He works graveyard, so he'll be gone 'til nine in the morning. That's why the bed works well. I sleep while he's at work, then he goes to sleep while I go to work. Sometimes we hang out in the evening."

"What do you do?"

"Data entry and customer service for a small startup downtown. It pays the bills, and it's a steady job, which is more than a lot of my friends can say. I can just about afford this place, a gym membership, and a little savings."

"How much does this cost?" Ty scooted back against the wall and curled his tail around his hips. A couple cracks ran from the corners of the ceiling, but overall the place was in pretty good shape, and it was a good sign that mostly what he smelled was wolf and wolverine—no mildew, no rot, no garbage. In that, it wasn't like a college dorm. Maybe gay guys were more fastidious.

"The place is twelve hundred a month. Justin and I split it, so I pay six."

"Holy shit!" Ty sat up and stared around. "Twelve hundred a month? That's almost as much as I'm paying for my house."

"In Chevali, right?" Arch walked over with two small cookies on a paper plate. "Middle of the desert? This is a highly desirable neighborhood here. Walking distance to Korsat, walking distance to the financial district, short bus ride to my job and thousands of other jobs. Also walking distance to about fifty amazing restaurants."

"My house has six bedrooms." Ty grinned as Arch sat on the bed and put the plate between them. "But yeah, this location is pretty cool. Apart from the piss-stained street."

"And these," Arch tapped the plate, "are legal."

The smell of pot hovered around the cookies like a cloud. Ty picked one up in his fingers. "Sugar cookies?"

"I'm not a great cook. I basically know this and chicken casserole."

"Where do you cook chicken casserole?"

Arch jerked his thumb toward the door. "There's a shared kitchen. Most of us keep a fridge and a hot pot in the rooms. I have to be careful when I'm baking these because if anyone else smells them, they come running and then cookies disappear. I usually melt some peppermint candies at the same time to cover the smell."

Ty laughed. "A guy in my college used to put Neutra-Scent over the oven vents when he made them. Once he forgot to insulate them and they caught fire. Nothing smells worse than burning Neutra-Scent."

"That's ironic." Arch picked the other cookie up. "Hey, if you're not used to these, you might wanna start with just half of one."

Ty turned the cookie over in his fingers. "It's been a while, but if I'm gonna do it, I'm gonna do it right."

The wolf nodded and raised his cookie as if toasting. "Okay. Your health, sir."

It was a good enough cookie, the sugar cutting the sharp cannabis taste. Ty crunched, swallowed, and closed his eyes. It was like college again. He leaned back against the wall and waited for it to kick in.

Movement brushed his whiskers. He opened his eyes and saw Arch pulling his shirt off. "Whoa," he said.

"Don't freak out, I'm not going down to fur." Arch dropped the shirt off the side of the bed. "I'll even keep my pants on for you. I just don't like chilling in so many clothes, y'know?"

"Sure." In a couple minutes he wasn't going to care anyway, he thought. "What do you do when you're high without a TV?"

"Movies." Arch got up and walked over to his laptop. While he opened it, Ty watched his back move. The wolf had a pretty good slender body, which made sense if he had a gym membership and went out dancing a bunch. And when he bent over and grabbed a DVD, Ty watched the wolf's tail wag. He'd looked at a lot of guys' butts—naked ones even—but he'd never thought about them sexually. And he wasn't really thinking about Arch that way either, only he knew the wolf was gay. So the wolf wanted guys to appreciate his body, right? Anyway, it was a tight, slender butt, objectively really nice. Ty still didn't want to fuck him, but he could maybe see where other guys did.

The wolf brought the laptop over, trailing a cord, and set it on the floor near the bed. "I put in this dragon-fighting movie. The dragons breathe fire and talk." Arch started the movie and sprawled out on the bed on his stomach. "It gets more dragon-y about forty-five minutes in, which is perfect timing."

"Our go-to movie was 'P.W.'s Adventure,'" Ty said, stretching out on the bed and letting his tail relax atop his legs. "But that's pretty much insane all the way through."

As the movie started, Ty grinned to himself. Lying in a dorm room watching a movie—if someone had told him that's how he was going to spend his Sunday night, he would've laughed and told them to fuck off. After all, his teammates were getting laid right now. But he found he didn't envy them. This was nice, it was chill, and he was getting used to the scent of the wolf.

The first part of the movie was a lot of setup: a nation of weasels was trying to attack a nation of deer using magic, and the deer were desperate for some way to retaliate. About a half hour in, when the young buck had reached the desert and found the dragon's egg, Ty got up on his knees and unbuttoned his shirt. He didn't really process why he was doing it; he just felt warm. Getting the shirt off felt good and cooler.

Arch turned his head, but didn't otherwise react. And it was around then that Ty started really noticing shit, like how pretty the dragon's egg was, and then when the dragon itself appeared on the screen, he said, "Holy shit," out loud. The camera seemed to linger on it, the sparkling scales and rainbow glitter around the long neck and reptilian head. When it breathed fire and the young buck only barely dove behind a rock in time, the fire danced and cascaded around the screen and looked freaking amazing.

And it turned out that the young buck had met a sarcastic dragon, but it wasn't even the dragon's lines that were cracking Ty up. It was the fact that it was talking at all. He couldn't explain it, but he just kept thinking, like, what if it wanted to talk and then accidentally breathed fire? Because that'd be hysterical.

He tried to cover up his giggles, but Arch was giggling too. "I told you this movie is fucking awesome," he said.

"Oh shit," Ty gasped. "The dragon is amazing."

"Just wait."

And it did get better. There were more dragons, and they actually set fire to a weasel army, which wasn't really funny, so they stopped laughing at that part. Arch actually wiped his eyes a couple times.

"Dude, are you crying?"

"Shut up," the wolf said.

"No, seriously, it's cool." On the screen, the weasels were retreating. "I mean, those weasels are assholes, but they shouldn't be, y'know, uh." He searched for the word. "Made to be on fire."

"Yeah. Can't they just talk about shit?"

Ty thought that was a sweet thought, and it seemed like he'd known Arch for ages. At least, the movie had been going on forever. So he put a paw on the wolf's back. And it was cool, they stayed like that until the end of the movie.

Arch turned and smiled at Ty, then rolled off the bed away from his paw and put the laptop away. "I guess you probably want to get back to your hotel."

His hotel. Oh, shit, right. Ty looked around for his shirt, and then imagined coming in and waking up Rodo. "I don't know if I should. I mean, they'll know I'm high."

The wolf came back to the bed and grinned down at him. "They won't know."

"No, I'm serious. I could get in deep shit for this. If they find out…"

"How will they know?"

Ty inhaled. "Because I'm slurring. No, I'm talking too precisely. See, I can't tell! I'll screw up, and then…"

He sat up with his back to the wall again and gripped his tail in his paw. Arch knelt on the bed in front of him. "You're not that high. You'll be fine."

"What if I'm not?"

The wolf laughed. "The alternative is that you sleep here. You wanna sleep here?"

"I kinda want to crash." There was some reason he wouldn't want to do that, but Ty didn't remember what it was right away. Then he pulled the bedsheet to his nose and sniffed. "Wait. You're gay. And you have a gay roommate."

Arch kept his smile. "You can keep your pants on. I promise I won't molest you."

"What about your roommate? The wolverine?" In Ty's imagination, he was a seven-foot tall hulking monster in rainbow suspenders. Suspenders?

"Justin's cool. He's found me in bed with guys before. He'll assume we hooked up."

"But we didn't. We won't."

Arch shook his head. "This might shock you, but I don't fuck every guy I meet, even if he is gay and wants to. Sometimes I just want to be friends. Sometimes I want to make sure the guy isn't crazy."

"Oh, shit." Ty dropped his muzzle into his paws. "I'm acting crazy, aren't I?"

"No, you're high is all." Arch put a paw on Ty's shoulder. "What time do you need to be up in the morning?"

"Uh. We're supposed to leave the hotel at nine-thirty." That, at least, he remembered.

Arch went back to his laptop. "Okay. I usually get up at eight-fifteen but I'll move it back to eight. That'll give you plenty of time."

"You sure?" Relief overwhelmed him. Arch was a great guy.

"It's fine. But *I* am going to take off my pants. You don't have to, but it's my bed, and I don't sleep in jeans."

"Okay." Ty sat and waited, calmer now that the situation was handled. He hadn't gotten high since the week before the draft, because even though he was a great believer in the general benevolence of the universe, he was also a great believer in not tempting fate, and besides, he wasn't even allowed to drink legally then. Months into the UFL routine, with his twenty-first birthday over a year in the books, he had felt more confident that one night would not result in his expulsion from the league (mainly because three of his teammates had offered him pot)—until he'd actually taken the drug.

His memories of how to handle it came back slowly. He still felt the paranoia, but remembered how to distance himself from it. It helped that Arch knew he was high and that he'd already been lying on the bed; it was strange but not too strange. He turned himself around and reclined on the side against the wall.

Ty closed his eyes and followed Arch's movements with his ears, heard the steps on the carpet and then the scrape of claws against the fasteners on his pants. The jeans slid down, making a shushing against the leg fur, and then he stepped out of them. Then the bed creaked and the wolf's weight settled onto it.

Ty braced himself so he wouldn't roll toward the weight and rested his head back. Arch pulled the covers over himself, but Ty stayed on top of them. He had his pants on, and even though he was shirtless, winter in Yerba wasn't so cold that a thick-furred red fox would so much as shiver in this apartment. He was aware of the weight of the wolf next to him, but he was unworried by it. In the deep silence of the room, the faint rhythm of Arch's heartbeat reached his ears, going at least 80 or 90, not an even 60 like Ty's athletically conditioned heart. But Arch was cool. And Ty was cool, too.

•

He came awake in a dim room, disoriented. Wolf smell filled his nostrils and the air on his nose was cool. He turned his head and Arch's muzzle came into view, peaceful in rest, smiling and handsome actually. Ty thought about waking up next to some of his college buddies on road trips, but this wasn't exactly like that. Dev was used to waking up next to a guy, but this wasn't like that either. It was feeling comfortable with someone,

He reached out a paw experimentally and rested it on Arch's hip. The wolf stirred but didn't wake. His body felt warm and solid beneath Ty's fingers.

comfortable enough to share drugs and a bed with on a second meeting, but not wanting to have sex with.

Although he did have a pretty good morning wood going on. He reached down and rubbed it through his jeans, and then imagined Arch reaching over to rub it. The idea was…interesting. In the sleepy haze of morning, when he didn't want to reject the idea just because he was straight, it didn't disturb him so much. He touched his own junk all the time.

So maybe not have sex with, but play around a bit. He'd had friends in high school who told him about skinny-dipping parties in the ocean, and one had admitted that after drinking, when there were eight guys and only three girls, some of the guys jerked each other off. Wasn't a thing, didn't mean anything.

Ty hadn't had time to do that with football and studying, even if his parents would've let him go out to the ocean late. But he'd gotten erections imagining it.

Yes, but he'd also dated girls and gotten erections from that too. And gotten erections from thinking about breasts and looking at naked vixens.

So…what? He reached out a paw experimentally and rested it on Arch's hip. The wolf stirred but didn't wake. His body felt warm and solid beneath Ty's fingers. It felt…nice. If Arch had been a girl, that touch would've been a prelude to morning sex, but here it just felt friendly.

And then, with a shrill ring, the alarm went off.

Ty yanked his paw back and sat up, and a moment later Arch did the same, rubbing his eyes. "Hey," the wolf said, and rolled over to tap the laptop and stop the noise.

"Hey." Ty scooted down and off the bed without climbing over Arch, discovering in the process that his hip felt better, if not completely so; on the way to being ready for next week, anyway. Hard to say whether it was the pot or the ice bath. He found his shirt on the floor. "Thanks for letting me crash."

"No problem. You want to grab coffee on your way over?"

"Uh." Ty pulled his shirt on. "You have coffee here?"

"There's a coffee shop on the corner. Pretty good. It'll probably take fifteen minutes for the cab to get here anyway."

Coffee would help him wake up. And fifteen minutes for the cab, and the ride to Korsat had been only fifteen…he had plenty of time. "Sure."

So Arch swung his legs out of bed and stood, and Ty saw clearly what he hadn't seen the previous night, which was that the wolf was wearing tight briefs, and also that his own morning wood was at least as prominent as Ty's, and more noticeable as it was only concealed by a thin, stretchy layer of fabric, and…

And the very tip of it was poking out of the top of his waistband. Ty was standing here looking at the tip of another guy's cock. And Arch saw him looking and didn't seem to care, nor did he smirk or offer to show Ty more, or anything like that. He yawned and stretched—maaaaybe showing off a little, but hell, who wouldn't if he had the body to?—and walked over to pull on his pants.

They got coffee, which was as good as promised, and while they were waiting for the cab, Ty said, "Hey, so thanks again. It was a fun night. Next time I'm in town, we should do it again."

"The pot and the overnight stay?" Arch smiled.

"Sure." Ty laughed. "I mean, if I freak out about being high and need to crash again."

"You didn't mind sleeping in bed next to a gay guy?"

Ty shook his head. "You didn't, like, fuck me in my sleep or anything, did you?"

Arch snorted. "Even if that were really possible, I don't paw or blow or fuck any old guy, I told you that."

"Yeah," Ty said, "I know. But would you do me?"

He'd meant it playfully, kind of the football player with an ego needing to be stroked. But it didn't quite come out as playful, and Arch gave him a sidelong look. "You asking seriously?"

"Just hypothetically. Anyway, I thought you didn't need things to be serious."

The wolf breathed in his coffee steam and then sipped from the cup. "I don't," he said after a moment. "But I'm also not interested in being some straight guy's experiment, y'know?"

"No, no." Ty sipped his own coffee, confused now, aware that he'd made he situation awkward without meaning to. "Look, I was just messing around. I had a good time—I had fun."

"It's cool. Sorry, I just had…you know, in high school there'd be guys who were like, 'hey, you like cock, wanna blow me?' and a couple times I did. I was young, I thought they'd like me after, y'know? But they…they treated me worse than the girls. So I'm done with that."

"I didn't mean—"

"No, I know you didn't. You're a good guy. Here's your cab." The green car was coming around the corner.

"Thanks." Ty held out his paw, and Arch took it, then pulled the fox into a hug. Which also felt good, again in a non-sexual kind of way.

And as he got into the cab, Arch held the door for a second and said, "Hypothetically? Maybe." And then he shut the door and stood there grinning at Ty as the cab pulled away.

Chapter 3

Brit, the cheetah who coached the wide receivers, was eating breakfast in the hotel restaurant when Ty walked in, and looked up before the fox could slip by. "Hey, Nakamura," he called, and Ty had no choice but to walk across and sit down at the table. "Out all night?"

Ty looked down at his clothes, at the cup of coffee in his paw. "Naw, just went out for coffee. Couldn't sleep." Lingering paranoia needled him to wonder if Brit could smell the pot on his breath, but coffee should be strong enough to kill it.

"If I ask Rodo, would he tell me that too?"

"Dunno," Ty said. "He was asleep when I came in and asleep when I left."

The cheetah narrowed his eyes, but smiled. "There's no curfew tonight. Whatever you need to do to get over a loss, do it and get ready for next week. You're not in trouble, but check in before you go off on your own."

"Got it, coach." Ty grabbed a piece of bacon from the cheetah's plate and munched on it. "Promise I won't do anything dumb without telling you first."

"Cubs." The cheetah watched the bacon disappear and shook his head.

"I'm an adult." Ty grinned and took another piece of bacon. "I can vote and everything."

"All right, all right, go get your own breakfast." Brit shooed him away from the table, and Ty made for the elevators, crunching the salty bacon and hoping Rodo would actually be asleep when he got to the room. Already the strangeness of the previous night was melting away in the return to the structured life he'd become accustomed to like a comfortable button-down shirt.

He was a little worried that he'd want to go lie next to Rodo, that the door that had been cracked open for him now would admit all kinds of thoughts and ideas that he didn't need complicating his football life. But, he reasoned in the elevator, Dev roomed with Charm without trying to grope the big stallion (a two-handed job, to be sure), and Dev showered with the guys without ogling them or even getting a hard-on from it, so Ty, who had merely thought about the not-very-gay possibility of a guy jerking him off, could certainly manage to partition that idea away from the rest of his life.

And indeed, when he opened the door to Rodo's snoring, the only thing he felt was the memory of having been woken up by the deer's snorts so many times. He threw a pillow at Rodo's head and said, "Breakfast in fifteen," and then jumped in the shower before the deer could retaliate.

•

That Monday, they were introduced to Lightning Strike, the team's new receiver, and even Ty's balanced, positive personality was tested. The presence of Strike reminded the rest of the wideouts that they were at best a number two, and although Ty bounced back well, not everyone else did, so he had to endure grumbling and sulking from the guys he usually had a good time with.

For a week, he lost himself in the world of football: practice, curfew, teammates. Now that he was back in Chevali, the whole night in Yerba felt dreamlike, the more so because he'd been high and watching a fantastical movie, sleeping in a stranger's apartment. He went out to strip clubs and discovered that he still liked looking at female bodies, and he went out to clubs and discovered that he still liked fucking them too.

His friends lived their own lives for the most part, but they acknowledged that he paid their room and board by dropping whatever they were doing whenever he wanted to go out. Paul, another red fox, was studying for an advanced law degree, Kimi, an otter, was working on writing a video game, and Kellen (swift fox) and Morshin (goat) didn't seem to be doing much of anything. Not that Kimi had accomplished much beyond a demo either; Paul was the only one who'd actually done anything productive with his time.

But they'd been there for Ty through college, Kimi and Kellen as backups on the football team, Paul his friend from high school, and Morshin… Morshin had been someone's girlfriend's roommate's boyfriend maybe? Or he'd shown up to a party one night. None of them really remembered, but he'd gotten friendly with them and had stuck with the group.

Anyway, it didn't cost Ty that much to support them here: the house, the food, the occasional night out. One part of his head realized that five grand a month was a lot even for five people to live on, but another part of him reasoned that it was less than a third of what he was making every *game*, let alone the one point five mil he'd gotten as a signing bonus and signed over to his parents to manage for him. So he didn't really sweat it; he focused on working hard and making sure that when this rookie deal ran out, he'd be making three or four (or ten) times as much every game. His parents, as well as the UFL, had drilled financial responsibility into him, and so he'd bought a modest house and had taken out a mortgage because the interest rate was low and he could earn more return on his cash.

And then he'd let the money go to do whatever money did. His friends weren't crazy extravagant and they were a good group to come home to, so they were worth five grand a month, and the occasional new piece of technology. In fact, he liked going to the electronics store with them. Two grand for a laptop? Six hundred for a game system? A thousand for a video camera? No sweat, guys. And he'd exaggerated his club bills to Arch; they'd run up nearly a thousand only one night, and otherwise they kept it in the low hundreds.

It wasn't until Thursday night that he took out his phone and called up the texts from Arch. He kind of wished the wolf lived around here; then again, Arch was so closely connected with Yerba that Ty couldn't imagine what the wolf would do in Chevali. He had his own life and his own place, and that in itself was cool and different. Thinking about it reminded Ty that there was a world outside the structure of his life.

So he texted Arch then: *Been busy. Fun time Sunday. Thanks much.*

And he held the phone, thinking, he probably won't text back right away. I shouldn't even expect it.

He was just about to put the phone down when it buzzed.

Arch: *You're sweet :)*

Ty grinned. His tail hit the bed, and he realized he was wagging it. "Well," he said softly, "why are you so happy? He's just a cool guy."

But his tail wagged on regardless. So he texted Arch again and told him in general terms that the week had been stressful and that he was looking forward to getting on the field against Freestone that weekend. And Arch texted and told him that someone had yelled at him on the phone and that he'd had to stay late Tuesday and Wednesday because a big work project needed to be done.

Ty asked him about the club and Korsat Street, and Arch said he hadn't been out there since Sunday. *Going out again tomorrow tho*, he typed. *Wish you were here.*

Yeah, me too, he typed. Rodo and Zaïd were headaches and Strike was a migraine; without Ford on the team, Ty didn't have a real friend in the wideouts. He could use a night cutting loose and dancing. But not here; if he went to a club, he would end up sitting around and drinking with the guys, maybe hitting on some girls, and that was it.

In fact, that's what happened Friday night. Kimi asked if Ty wanted to go out, and Ty almost said no, but it was Friday night and the game wasn't 'til Sunday, and Chevali was favored by 6.5 and would probably win by more than that. And anyway, they were allowed to go out and cut loose Friday nights.

So Kimi, Kellen, and Morshin went out with him and the otter and goat got roaring drunk, while responsible Kellen kept the car keys. Ty got buzzed, and there was a cute otter there who was ecstatic to dance with a Firebird, and she was kind of a shitty dancer but she rubbed her chest up against him pretty nicely. And while he didn't feel like taking her home, there was a corner of the VIP lounge in this club that was curtained off and not on the security cameras, so Kimi and Kellen parked themselves in front of it and Ty took the otter back there and let her suck him off.

He enjoyed it, of course. She had a nice tongue and a piercing that felt good on his cock, and she'd obviously done it many times before. After he came, he sat back in the chair and let her play with his junk, his whole body relaxed. His mind turned to Arch, and he thought, see, femmes still turn me on. I don't want to sleep with Arch, I want to dance with him—he's way better than anyone at this club—and hang out with him. He's not like my other friends, and I'm only having these thoughts because he's gay and he's interested in me.

The otter girl stroked him and then cleaned some drips off his length and licked them slowly off her fingers. "I'd love to give you another bath." She lowered her muzzle to his cock and flicked her tongue across the tip, making him shiver. "Or a full ride, if you like."

"Sure," he said, reaching down to rub her ears. "If we run into each other."

"I can give you my number."

He slapped his hip with practiced ease, the wide black paw against the red and white bare fur. "I don't have anything to write it down on. Friend's got my phone." He gestured outside. "Speaking of which, I should probably get back to them."

She pouted, but she'd been around the block too, and she got the hint. While he was pulling his pants up, she made a point of spraying her mouth with Neutra-Mint and then pushed her way out.

Ty stretched and flicked his tail. If he stood near the curtain, he could hear his friends talking. They weren't saying anything really interesting, although Kimi was jealous that the otter hadn't given him a second glance. Kellen said, "When you're a UFL star, dude, you'll get the otters and the foxes."

With one paw on the curtain, Ty paused. There was a difference. If he hadn't been born with physical talents—and, to be fair, worked really hard—and if he hadn't been lucky enough to be chosen early and gotten playing time for a UFL team, he wouldn't have gotten blown by an otter tonight. But he had done that work and he had gotten blown, so he might as well enjoy it, right?

With that in mind, he put a smile on his muzzle and parted the curtain, wrapping an arm around each of Kimi and Kellen's shoulders, the otter and the swift fox. "Thanks, guys," he said. "I asked if she wanted to stick around for seconds, but she didn't seem excited about that."

Kellen pointed out a couple of raccoons in low-cut dresses at the bar. "Those two been giving us the eye. Hang out for a bit, I bet they'll come over."

So they sat around and talked, and sure enough, the raccoons came over, but they didn't want to go behind the curtain. So Kellen drove everyone home in his SUV, one raccoon rubbing her paws over him from behind while Kimi made out with the other in the far back. Morshin sang their college fight song all the way home, and every time Ty turned around from the front passenger seat to talk to him, he said, "You're such a great guy, Ty. You're great. You're really great. I wanna hang out and talk with you. Just talk."

It was nice, and obviously heartfelt, but when they got home and Kimi and Kellen took their girls to their rooms, Morshin collapsed on the couch snoring. Ty made sure the goat was sleeping on his stomach in case he threw up, and then went to look for Paul.

The fox was asleep, so Ty retired to his room. He needed to get to sleep anyway, but as he undressed, he kept looking at his phone on the dresser. Finally, down to his boxers, he picked up the phone and texted Arch. *Good Friday? I got a blow job.*

The wolf didn't text back until Ty was in bed, and then his phone buzzed. *Hey, me too. Wolf. What was yours?*

Otter, Ty typed, grinning.

You get pics?

What? He laughed out loud and typed back, *No, can't have that out on the Internet.*

It took a second for the wolf to answer. *Me, I don't give a shit, want to see?*

Ty stared at his phone. He didn't know what to type. He didn't really want to see Arch's junk in some other guy's muzzle, but he wondered if refusing would endanger the friendship they had going. Was it traditional for gay guys to exchange pics of each other having sex? He pictured the otter's muzzle bobbing up and down on his cock. Would Arch want to see that?

His phone buzzed again. *j/k :)*

Whew. He grinned. *I'll get one next time*, he typed.

It's cool, just razzing ya, Arch typed.

But when Ty lay back on his pillow, he put a paw to his crotch and wondered what kind of picture Arch would take.

•

The Freestone game was the first time Ty and the other wideouts had really seen Strike in person. Watching in practice was different, and he'd never really gotten loose during the Port City game when they were playing against him. Against Freestone, he broke free for a touchdown and Ty, trailing him on the field, pulled up with a big grin on his muzzle and a feeling in his chest like opening a present at Christmas and finding the game system he'd been longing for for months. There wasn't even any jealousy; Strike was so clearly in a league of his own that he might as well be jealous of a basketball player.

"Fuck," the Freestone corner who'd been tailing Ty said, and walked off to the sideline in disgust.

Not all the wideouts shared Ty's enthusiasm, but Dev, getting ready to go out on defense, did. He slapped paws with Ty and left the fox bouncing on the balls of his feet.

They won the game, not that there was any doubt, and for the first time Ty started to think of this team as an elite team. He went out to celebrate the win, and in the middle of the celebration, Arch texted him. *Congrats :)*, the wolf said. *Even though you didn't score.*

Don't care, Ty wrote back, *I scored Friday night.*

Inside he was happy Arch was watching the games and paying attention, but that was only one happiness piled on to all the rest. It was going to be a great season, maybe even a championship season, and Ty Nakamura, rookie wide receiver, was going to be part of it.

•

He and Arch continued to text back and forth for the next couple weeks, though Ty's opportunities were sporadic due to travel and practice. The Firebirds found themselves in the hunt for not only a playoff spot, but a first-round bye, and though they won their game at Kerina easily, the Hellentown Pilots kept pace, going into the final week with the same record as the Firebirds, 11 and 4. The good news was that the way the league was shaping up, 11 wins already guaranteed them a playoff spot. If they beat Hellentown, though, they would win the division and maybe have an out-side chance at getting a week off if Boliat lost to Hilltown. The coaches kept saying the week off was "in play," but nobody Ty talked to actually thought that would happen, mainly because Hilltown was terrible and was already sitting most of its good players in an attempt to fall behind Pelagia for the first pick in the draft next year.

In any case, he didn't go out at all between the Freestone and Hellentown games, worried about losing an edge in concentration. Kimi kept pestering him to go to a club because it would help him relax, and Ty finally snapped that they had his credit card and they could all go without him, and then the house was uncomfortably quiet until they all went out to dinner and he went to bed early.

Kimi apologized the next day, and Paul later told Ty he'd had a talk with the otter and reminded him that Ty's job paid all their bills and had to come first. Ty thanked him, but that didn't make him feel a whole lot better about having snapped at his friend.

And then they went out and lost to Hellentown, and there went the division title and the week off (Boliat beat Hilltown, so they wouldn't have gotten the bye anyway). They were still in the playoffs and it didn't matter, only it left a sour taste in Ty's muzzle. They were going to have to go *to* Hellentown and play them *again* in their home stadium, and then if they won that they would be on the road again, and it was going to be basically three weeks away from home.

He griped to Arch about it on his phone, and Arch said, *Why does it matter where you play? You beat them in Hellentown already.*

How, Ty wondered, can someone know so much about the season and not understand home field advantage? And yet, Arch's naïveté was refreshingly cheering. He said, *It sucks to lose.*

Sure, Arch typed back, *so mellow out, have a cookie.*

Ty couldn't do that, not here, but he could go out and get drunk. Rodo often had parties at his house to which dozens of people found their way, and all the wideouts had open invitations. The party was going to be more somber because of the loss, but that didn't mean that some of the team didn't need the comfort of booze and babes.

Kellen came along to be his designated driver, and Ty announced his intentions before they even got into the house, dropping his car keys in the swift fox's paw as soon as the beep of the lock sounded. "No drinking for you," he said.

"I know, I know." Kellen peered around Ty's shoulder at the house. "I better get some action, though."

"Just tell them you're front office, or tell them you're my best friend and if they blow you, they can do me later."

"That is what I tell them." Kellen snorted. "Remember that bunny from after the New Kestle game?"

"She did you first? Huh." Ty grinned and patted his friend.

"What?"

"Oh, just she told me I was the best cock she'd had in her mouth."

"Shut up, she did not."

Ty strolled through the door as Kellen held it open. "You weren't there, were you?"

The swift fox grumbled, and Ty grinned, and they walked into the noise and chaos.

Rodo had told Ty he'd bought his place specifically to be able to throw parties in. The ground floor living room and dining room connected to what the deer had described as a "banquet hall," which was where the pizza and chicken was spread out. Music blared around the different rooms and professional colored lights cast red and gold highlights on the crowd that stood around chatting.

One of the rooms had been cleared out for dancing, but nobody was dancing, and that was fine because the dancing at Rodo's parties was even worse than at the clubs. A few of the second-string wideouts were playing a game of tossing chips up and catching them in their muzzles. A cluster of groupies stood talking casually without the desperate looking around the room that they often had at busier parties, and there were fewer of the ladies than Ty had seen previously; many of them probably stayed away because the mood would be down after a loss, the party not as much fun.

Still, there were enough. Ty was pretty pent up at this point and so they all looked good to him, from the coyote in the tight blue strapless dress to the goat in the red and gold tube dress. He generally liked coyotes best because they were close to foxes but he didn't have to worry about getting them pregnant if it proceeded that far, which it rarely did anyway. But still, he'd been attentive during the UFL's rookie symposium, when old player Teema Olinata talked about his six illegitimate children. Officially, the line was "be safe." Unofficially, afterwards, veterans told the rookies, "leave it in the mouth and don't go south."

Couple of Ty's fellow rookies said they didn't like the mouth, scared of teeth, and if you stayed with other species you'd be fine. Others said they only liked their own species, so they had to stay with blow jobs. Ty liked vixens, but really he felt good with any canid, and coyotes had big ears and a similar scent.

So the coyote would be his first choice, and then he'd move on down the line. First, though, he sought out Rodo, and found the deer leaning against one of the pizza tables with a beer in his hand talking to Shane, a bobcat who'd been slated to start at wideout until the Firebirds had drafted Ty.

"Ty!" Rodo slapped him on the shoulder. "Good to see ya. Thanks for coming by. Help yourself to whatever. Who's this?"

Ty introduced Kellen, who shook Rodo's hand and thanked him for hosting and didn't mention that Rodo had met him twice before. "He's my DD," Ty said as Rodo offered the swift fox a beer. Shane watched the three of them, not moving, not offering his paw or any courtesy.

"I can have one now, and I'll be fine in an hour and a half." Kellen walked over to the cooler to rummage around in the ice.

"Guess you're staying an hour and a half." Rodo grinned at him.

"I'm gonna get some beer too," Shane said, and followed Kellen over to the cooler.

Ty watched the bobcat go. "It's been a season. You'd think he'd get the fuck over it."

"Sucks when you lose your job to someone better," Rodo said, "like that fuckin' cheetah. But it's worse when you never get a chance because the team keeps picking up people better than you. He was saying he's barely played this year and he feels like why the fuck are they keeping him around, but he doesn't want to push for a trade because he's afraid he'll get stuck on another team's bench too. The coaches here know him, he says."

"So he sticks around hoping one of us gets hurt. Sucks to be him." Ty held out a paw as Kellen returned with two beers and handed one to the red fox. Shane lingered by the beer cooler and then wandered into the next room.

"Why, because he's a backup?" Kellen twisted off the beer cap and put the bottle to the end of his muzzle. "So he gets paid a couple hundred thousand a year to sit on the bench. Can I have that job?"

Ty and Rodo exchanged looks. "It's not about the money," Rodo said, even though he and Ty both knew it was to some degree. Your salary was how much you were worth: more salary, more worth. Ty was on a rookie deal so getting a little under a million a year; Rodo was on his first post-rookie contract and stood to make three mil. Lightning Strike was getting eleven million this year.

"I know." Kellen elbowed Ty. "Ty told me. But I think he should be able to look on the bright side, y'know? I mean, hell, I woulda liked to have been a quarterback, but I'm friends with an awesome guy who brings me to parties and pays for my house. I'm pretty grateful for that."

"This is why I keep him around." Ty draped an arm over Kellen's shoulder and grinned. "He keeps me grounded."

"Don't get too grounded," Rodo warned.

"Nah," Ty said. "I was just telling Kellen I was going to blow off some steam tonight, get a little buzz going, get some action. Looks like there's enough here to go around."

Rodo nodded toward the other side of the room. "See the mink in the green dress, no shoulders? Try her. She's got experience."

Ty raised the beer to the end of his muzzle and let the cool, carbonated malt trickle down over his tongue. "Y'don't say," he said.

It wasn't until an hour later that he actually approached the mink. He chatted with Rodo a while longer, then ran into Vahir, a gazelle who, despite being a backup wideout, didn't cop an attitude about the starters. Also he played Xbox and was pretty good at Halo. After Ty excused himself to refresh his beer, he saw the backup tight end, a friendly guy he'd worked out with on occasion, and so it wasn't until he was on his way to get his third beer that he found himself standing next to the mink.

"Hey," he said, and she turned to look at him. "Ty Nakamura."

"I know." She had a soft, throaty voice and a warm, calculating smile.

He wondered for a moment what she was really like when she wasn't trying to hook up with a football player, and then he decided he didn't care. "Wanna go upstairs?"

That was all it took. Three minutes later, she was undoing his pants while he closed the door to the small study (leather couches, two video game consoles, 48" TV—not bad for a secondary study). He sat on the couch, already stiff by the time she yanked his underwear down. She spent a little time exploring his length with her fingers, giving him that smile again, and then she said, "I'm gonna be the best you've ever had."

He doubted that, honestly, because his memory of being sucked off in the bathroom at his friend Joel's party held a special place in his heart reserved for first times and a sixteen-year-old fox's enthusiasm, but he was certainly willing to let her try.

So she held his base and licked up the shaft with tiny flicks of her tongue, washing up to the tip and around. Then she applied more of her tongue, and more, and with a coquettish look at him, pursed her lips around his tip.

It was such a lovely image that he thought of Arch and the blow job pics, and reached for his phone only to remember that it was in the pocket of the pants that the mink was currently bent over as she sucked him off.

Easily remedied. "Hey," he said. "You think you could reach in my pocket and get my phone?"

She stopped and opened her mouth, letting his cock flop against his belly. "What?"

"I want to take a picture." He gave her his best vulpine grin. "To remember this by."

She still looked dubious, so he said, "And to show my friends," because she was a jock-chaser and she knew very well who his friends were.

"Oh," she said, and showed her teeth with a little dainty lift of her cheeks and whiskers. "Where is it?"

"Left hand pocket. That side." He pointed.

She found it and passed it up to him. While he called up the camera, she took him in her mouth again and smiled into the little lens on the backside of the phone. "Say cock," he murmured, and centered the picture and snapped it.

Then he set the phone aside, closed his eyes, and let her lips and tongue work their magic.

When she'd swallowed the last drop, she licked her lips and got up. "So?"

Ty panted against the back of the couch. His tail flicked erratically; he wasn't really controlling it anymore. "So?"

"Best you ever had, right?"

He lifted one paw and made an "O.K." sign. "Best I ever had."

She believed the lie at least enough to leave him alone, which was what he was after. Once the door clicked closed, he rested his head back on the couch and closed his eyes again. It had been pretty good, but sixteen-year-old Ty still insisted that the bathroom blow job had been the best thing ever (having to go home afterwards and having his parents ask how the party had been, having that secret to keep to himself—that was the extra spice that he just couldn't get anymore).

The nice part was that he was still slightly buzzed, so he kept remembering how into him the mink had been. Even so, that feeling wasn't anything new. It was a different party but the same situation, a different girl but the same result. And it wasn't a bad result—Ty had never had a really bad blow job—but it wasn't the same as walking into a college party and having all eyes turn to him his freshman year. Now he expected eyes to be on him and his teammates.

It was only when he finally pulled his pants up that he remembered his phone, sitting beside him on the leather seat of the couch. When he turned it on, the first thing that came up was his shiny cock disappearing into the dark brown muzzle of the mink, her blue eyes gleaming back at the camera. Oh yeah, she'd been into him. Those eyes were really blue, too. Contacts, maybe. He examined the picture again and grinned. His equipment came out looking pretty impressive. Maybe it was the perspective, but the way her mouth was positioned made it look huge.

Definitely he'd take this downstairs and show people. But first…he called up Arch's number and, with a little fumbling, texted him the photo. *Got lucky tonight*, he texted along with it.

The photo was a hit downstairs. "Holy shit, she let you take a picture?" Rodo laughed. "You gotta send me that."

"Is that your junk?" Vahir's eyes widened. "Seriously?"

"Jesus, Ty," Kellen said, laughing as he took the phone. "Don't show that around." He was about to pass it back when it buzzed, and Kellen's eyes slid downward. "Hey, you have another…"

The swift fox looked at the phone, his smile vanishing. "Who'd you send this to?" he asked.

"Just a friend." Ty took the phone back. "Wh—"

The incoming message had flashed onto the screen with a thumbnail of the picture sent, and the picture was of Arch, from the side, his muzzle around someone else's thick shaft. The flash overexposed it and washed out his fur, but what was going on was unmistakable.

Kellen grinned. "Looks like you're not the only one who got lucky. Sorry, though: your friend's even more impressive than you are."

"He's not really a friend." Ty pressed the phone's screen until the image went away. "He's just a guy I ran into, and we were talking about blow jobs and he said we should share pics. I didn't think…"

Kellen put a paw on his arm. "Relax," he said. "You took one, he took one. What's the big deal?"

"But look," Ty said, "I didn't think he was gonna take one like that." He licked his lips, trying to figure out how to explain or lie to Kellen so his friend wouldn't wonder about this gay guy sending him blow job pics.

"Like what?" Kellen stared at him.

"Like…of himself like…doing…" Ty flattened his ears. Hadn't Kellen seen the picture?

The swift fox's ears went down too. "Wait, was your friend the girl?"

The incoming message had flashed onto the screen with a thumbnail of the picture sent, and the picture was of Arch, from the side, his muzzle around someone else's thick shaft.

What girl? There hadn't been a girl in the picture. "No," Ty said, and then his brain asserted itself through his fading buzz and he finally understood what Kellen had been assuming. "No," he said, "no, he's the guy, I was just surprised. That he was getting a blow job at the same time. And that the picture was from the side, the way…it looks like he had the, uh, the girl take the picture himself. Herself."

"Oh." Kellen scratched his ears and perked them up. "Can I see it again?"

That was the last thing Ty wanted, but he called up the picture and passed the phone across. Kellen examined it. "I think you're right," he said. "Pretty baller, getting the girl to take it."

Ty took the phone back and hid the picture. "I'm about ready to go home," he said, even though now he felt stone cold sober.

On the way back, he stayed quiet while Kellen talked about the blow job he'd gotten, from a leopard girl who'd made him promise to point her out to Ty next time. "Sure, sure," Ty said absently.

What the hell was he doing, sending a picture to a gay guy? And getting one from him? It had seemed like fun when he'd done it, but now it seemed insane. What if someone grabbed his phone and took a closer look? What if someone asked him why this girl was named Arch? What girl's name could that stand for? Archietta? Archanna? Were those even names?

When he got home, he thanked Kellen for the drive and the company and scurried back to his room. There he flopped down on his bed, called up his photo, and deleted it. He navigated to Arch's and started to delete it, then hesitated, looking more closely. The wolf was smiling around the shaft, and the far eye, which was almost out of sight with how his head was turned, was closed.

Ty sat up. Arch was winking at the camera? He didn't know what that meant. But now it felt like he and Arch had gotten away with their secret. They'd put one over on all his teammates and friends, all those guys who had looked at the picture and not figured out that Ty's friend was the one with a cock in his mouth.

Even though Ty'd gotten off an hour ago, he was getting hard looking at the picture. If Arch's jaw could fit around that cock (Bear? Stallion?), then certainly he could handle Ty's as well as the mink had earlier.

But no, no, he didn't want Arch in that way. He wanted him as a friend. Unless Arch *wanted* to suck him off.

No, Ty'd made it clear where his preferences lay. Arch had teased him a bit, but they were friends who teased each other, the way Ty would tease a female friend about cute guys and she'd tease him about cute girls.

But if a female friend had sent him a picture of herself sucking off some guy…what would he think?

Jesus Fox, what was going on here? He kept staring at the picture of Arch, and then he saw that another message from the wolf had come through. *All done now*, it read. *How was yours?*

Great, Ty typed back numbly.

Another photo came through. It was a better picture of Arch's muzzle. He was licking his lips and had a thumbs-up partly out of frame of the camera. *Me too.*

The curl of his tongue was cute, the darker pink underside and the ridge that bisected it before disappearing an inch below the tip. His nose glistened, and behind his tongue, his whiskers shone white in the flash of the camera. Because he was looking to one side, not at the camera, his eyes didn't shine; instead Ty could see the brown irises and grey-yellow flecks in them.

He turned the phone off and put it on his nightstand. Tomorrow he was going to have to fly to Hellentown, and he would spend a week preparing for this game that would be the most important of his young career. He didn't have time to worry about Arch and why he was still hard, stretching out in bed, or why his mind wouldn't let him forget the picture of his friend the wolf with his muzzle stretched wide.

The next morning, he thought of what he should have written to Arch the night before, so he texted it as Paul drove him to the airport. *So that was a special guy?*

Arch didn't text back until he was on the plane, sitting down next to Rodo. *Sort of, it was Justin.*

His roommate. Ty nodded, and then he frowned. *I thought Justin worked nights.*

OK, you got me, Arch typed. *It was an old photo, I didn't get lucky. :)*

Ty chuckled. *You had me going*, he said.

Rodo leaned over. "You're not texting that mink, are you?"

"No." Ty shielded his phone.

"Good."

The fox let his tongue loll out as he grinned. "Thanks, Dad."

The deer blew a snort out of his nose and closed his eyes. "You don't seem the type to get serious about anyone."

Ty thought about that as Arch typed back, *In what way? ;)*. "I'm going to have to eventually. Mom wants me to get married and have a family. She's already got a parade of vixens for me to look at when the season's over."

"Surprised she hasn't shackled you up already." Rodo cracked an eye.

"She introduced me to a few last year, but when my agent told her I'd be drafted high, she decided to see how my team did. The better we do in the playoffs, the more prestigious the vixens."

Rodo laughed, and then turned toward the fox with both eyes open. "You're serious."

"Uh-huh. Mom takes marriage seriously."

The deer patted his knee. "You'll always have the road, and you'll always be welcome in my place."

"Thanks." Ty grinned. "I'm not worried. It's just a thing I have to do. Mom and Dad's marriage was arranged and they're happy together."

Rodo leaned back and closed his eyes again, so Ty turned his attention back to the phone. *In a couple ways*, he typed.

Pics or it didn't happen, the wolf responded.

Later, Ty typed. *On plane now*.

And then he put the phone away and stretched his legs out. His mind kept going back to that picture, though, Arch with his mouth open, superimposed on the picture Ty had taken of his own cock. Would Arch go down on him? It wasn't like no-strings blow jobs were hard for him to come by, so what kept this image in his mind? Was it the novelty of it? The secret? Was it that scary and yet compelling mingling of the worlds of friendship and sex? What if, for instance, Kellen followed him up to his room and wanted to blow him? How would he feel about that?

Somewhere over Kerina or New Kestle, two thirds of the way through the flight, Ty had an epiphany. It didn't make a lick of difference (ha ha, so to speak), really. He happened to be thinking that it was weird that Dev wasn't on the plane, and then that Colin and Herzon and those guys must be happy about it, and *then* he thought, *if only they knew that there's still a guy who's been fantasizing about getting a blow job from a guy.*

But really, how weird was that? Half the guys on the plane were fantasizing about getting blow jobs, probably right now. Did it really matter from whom? If Ty truly believed that it didn't make a difference whom Dev was in love with, then he also had to believe that it didn't matter whom he was fantasizing about slurping on his cock.

After all, he reasoned, who else's business was it? Nobody's. It was between him and Arch, and it wasn't like he was going to marry the guy, after all. He didn't owe anyone an explanation, he didn't owe anyone his fidelity yet, and he'd already done a bunch of things he wasn't going to tell his parents about. He'd done fewer that he wasn't going to tell his teammates about, but certainly they all had secrets too.

So when he landed, he typed, *How about I show you?* For a few seconds he stared at the words, and then he hit the Send button.

Arch didn't reply until later, while Ty was in practice, so he got the message on his way back to the hotel. *You sure, Mr. Straight Fox?* the wolf had typed.

If you want, Ty replied.

Arch sent back a picture of himself, muzzle open, tongue hanging out in a big grin.

"What are you grinning about?" Rodo asked.

"Nothing," Ty said, and slipped the phone into his pocket.

CHAPTER 4

They won the Hellentown game, and they went to Boliat the next week and won there, too, with Strike shining in both games. Ty didn't mind; he got a pretty impressive touchdown in the Boliat game, a nice play drawn up by their offensive coordinator that was a fake to Strike and designed for Ty, and he ran his route like clockwork and Aston threw it perfectly.

In Boliat, the day before the game, Ty had brought up the question of other gay guys on the team with Dev, to see if anyone maybe noticed anything or if anyone thought about it. He passed it off as being interested in the gay clubs because the dancing was fun and it was cheap, and nobody seemed to care about or remember the conversation later.

After winning the game, Ty shared the excited high with his parents and uncle and then went out and got trashed with his teammates. He only remembered the evening in flashes: Vonni singing off-key, Zaïd doing some kind of dance on the tabletop, and even Strike hanging out with the guys, everyone wanting to be near him after his great play, the last play of the game on the onside kick. "Going in the trenches," people said of him, "when you make all that money."

"Whatever it takes to help the team win," Strike said, and even though Ty and Rodo had both gone out to help the team on that last play too, nobody cared. They were going to the championship in Crystal City.

For Ty, it was like a dream: in his college career, he'd never gotten to a really important game, but here in his first professional season, he was going to be playing in the championship. He texted back and forth with Arch, but didn't send any more pictures, and they didn't talk about the blow-job pic exchange at all. Arch said he'd had to answer questions about why he was cheering so loudly when the Chevali fox scored a touchdown, and had made up something about putting down a bet on a fox scoring. His friends, no more conversant than he was with sports betting, had believed it, although then it had cost him thirty bucks when they insisted he buy them two pitchers out of his "winnings."

Ty said he'd pay him back, and Arch said he didn't have to. Ty told Arch about the heavy practices and the tension of the championship game, and Arch told Ty about some minor drama in which Justin's ex-boyfriend had come back and tried to break into the apartment while Arch was there (and Justin was not) and the police had been called. Cops always made him nervous.

From the time he'd been a star athlete in high school, Ty had never had problems with the cops. Friends of his had gotten stopped, even arrested once or twice, but they were out making trouble and Ty'd felt they deserved it. In his experience, the police had always been one of those forces he'd never dealt much with but respected and appreciated. *Why nervous?* he asked.

Arch's reply came quickly. *Back home, the cops used to beat me up.*

Ty was sitting on the bed in his hotel room in Crystal City, and he stared at the phone. "Used to." Like the way he might say, "Back home, I used to go to the ice cream shop." Like, more than once. Finally he typed, *Why?*

Because I was a faggy little wolf, Arch said. *I think my dad asked them to beat some sense into me.*

Jesus, Ty said. He tried to imagine his father asking someone to beat him up, and that refused to come together in his head. Even if he did something terrible, something so bad that his parents didn't want to associate with him anymore—even if he did something with Arch and they found out about it, it wouldn't be that bad; they would just ignore it as if it never happened—the worst thing that could happen was that he'd be excluded from the family, cut off from his history and all the traditions they'd shared over the years. And that was bad to imagine, but then on top of that Arch had had cops come after him? Beat him up? Because he was gay and his dad didn't like that? Fuck.

It was years ago.

As though that made it all right, as though time could erase that betrayal of authority and the trauma of being victimized by the people who were supposed to keep the harm away from you. *Shit, I'm sorry.*

It's cool, Arch said.

The weird thing was that Ty read so much into those words, that it wasn't really cool, but it was cool enough for him to live with, and that he didn't want Ty to worry about it, not because it wasn't Ty's problem, but because there was nothing any of them could do about it. He couldn't say how he felt that so strongly, but he did.

Kinda want to hug you right now, he typed.

I'd settle for a dance :)

Sure. When?

I hear you'll be in Crystal City in a week or so…

He laughed aloud, a sharp bark, and typed back, *I'm there now, but a little busy.*

Arch came back with, *We can celebrate after the game maybe, or you might need to unwind before.*

Unwind. Oh yeah. The thought of getting high wasn't as appealing right now as it had been after the loss, but for sure he could blow off some steam dancing. *You know any clubs in C.C.?*

I'll find some.

Done, then. :)

And just like that, he was making plans to meet up with Arch again. A wag built up in his tail and he let it out, grinning. He hadn't even made plans for his friends to come out, though he was sure they would, and he was already excited about meeting this wolf.

He thought about the pic again and wondered whether Arch was going to expect anything this time. The question stilled the wag in his tail, but didn't get rid of his grin. It would be easy enough to ask, but then again, if he asked, he'd get an answer.

•

The practices and the Media Day and all the other circuses around the championship game kept him occupied for the next eleven days. He thought of Arch, but mostly with vaguely positive anticipation, and it wasn't until the Friday night before the game that he gave the matter much thought. Charm kept telling him about this strip club, and they got Dev to come along (the tiger had been mopey lately, which Ty kept reminding himself to ask Dev about when he got a minute and he never did), and the coyote Zillo came with them at the last minute.

Arch would get into town Saturday morning. Ty had bought him a hotel room and as the rigorous movement of practice fell away from him that evening, he thought more and more about the wolf checking into the hotel. Guys bought rooms for their local gals all the time, but there wasn't much question what those rooms were used for. Sometimes guys did bring in family or good college friends, and Ty's friends also had a couple hotel rooms he'd paid for.

But Arch didn't fit neatly into that category either. This was about dancing. There'd been nobody Ty could share a really good dance with since that one girl in college—what was her name? Shawla? Shana? Zhala? Anyway, he was seriously jazzed about finding a club and getting to dance again. And after that? Who cared? Maybe Arch would want to take things further; the wolf had been aggressively flirting with him and he'd flirted back, but that didn't mean anything. Freed of meaning, he'd been excited about it, but he found he couldn't quite let it go that easily. So he was somewhat relieved to find that he was getting hard watching the dancers at the strip club, and at the anticipation of Charm getting them one or two of the waitresses to play with.

After an unexpected conversation in which they asked Dev about sex with guys and Charm confessed to getting a blow job from a guy, Charm did in fact get two waitresses to play with. He took one for himself and left the other for Ty and Zillo, and Zillo was so drunk that he needed help to get to the back room, and then before Ty could say anything, the coyote had his pants down and the fennec was blowing him. After that, she asked him to fuck her, so he did, with the half-conscious Zillo sitting leaning against a wall.

Seeing Zillo's cock, even in a sexual situation, didn't make him want to blow his teammate, and that lessened his anxiety over Arch. At the same time, his curiosity about what might happen after the dance didn't go away.

•

Saturday was exhausting and nerve-wracking even though they barely worked out at all. Nobody actually said, "shit gets real," but everyone joked less, and the coaches drilled them on their routes with a grim intensity that reminded Ty of CPR training. Teammates called each other out on the small stuff, not in a bad way, but helping, everyone getting each other's back, the team pulling together.

By the time the day ended with a "get a good night's sleep" speech from Coach Samuelson, Ty was completely drained—mentally, at least. Some of the guys were going to go back and play FBA '09, and video games sounded pretty good. But Ty had a couple messages on his phone from Arch, who'd landed and made his way to his hotel, and dancing also sounded like a good way to turn off his mind. *I can't dance too long*, he typed, *because I need to be fresh tomorrow.*

You don't have to come dance at all, Arch had typed back. *If you need your rest, take it.*

And Ty'd said it would be good to take his mind off things, so he called a car service and hired it for the night. "Picking up an old college buddy," he said, and the driver, a llama, said nothing. Probably didn't give a shit. Ty cursed himself mildly for being over-talkative and then leaned back in the car seat, smiling, and thought about Arch.

At the hotel, the wolf stood out front in a tank top and a light pink collared shirt hanging open over it, thumbs hooked into the pockets of a pair of distressed jeans. Ty's ears perked at the sight, and he grinned as the wolf's eyes lit on the car. Arch frowned slightly, so Ty rolled down the window and stuck his muzzle out. "You coming?"

Then the wolf lit up with a grin too, and he hurried past several pedestrians to the car door. Ty slid over to let him get in, and a moment later they were crawling through traffic down the street.

Arch grabbed his forearm and Ty clasped the wolf's in return. "Hey, good to see you," Arch said.

"You too. Where we going? Tell the guy." Ty gestured forward.

The wolf grinned and leaned toward the front of the car. "Jamz, on West Ivy and Santa Monica."

"You know it?" Ty called forward.

"Yes, sir," the llama said.

Arch looked good, smelled good, solid and real. "So," the wolf said as Ty was looking at him, "you guys ready for the game?"

"Sure," Ty said automatically.

The wolf laughed. "Sorry, stupid question, I guess. You've been practicing all year for it. You wouldn't be going dancing if you weren't ready."

"Nah, I know what you mean." Ty wagged his tail. "Honestly I dunno. But there's only so much you can do. I've been working my routes, I've caught a million passes, I've blocked…at some point you gotta relax or you drive yourself crazy."

"Blocking?" Arch asked. "I thought you just caught the ball."

"Yeah, but if the play's going to someone else then I gotta keep the defenders occupied if I can. Or sometimes there's trick plays where I pretend to block and let them get by me, then they think the play's going to someone else but it frees me up." He shook his head. "I was a number one option in college so I never ran it too much."

"La di da."

Ty laughed. "We never needed to. I could shake free whenever I wanted. Pros are way way faster." When Arch tilted his head with a look that might have been interest, Ty went on. "There's something like thirty-five hundred football players in college in any given year—like, thirty-five hundred freshmen, thirty-five hundred sophomores, and so on. And every year, only about two hundred fifty get drafted into the UFL. So pretty much every pro team is a college all-star team. Imagine a college team playing against a bunch of guys off the street."

"Okay." Arch laughed. "I get it: you're pretty good. I knew that already."

"Not as good relatively, is what I'm saying."

"No, I get it." The wolf grinned. "I was a top ten student at my high school and then when I got to college, I started getting B's and C's. It was pretty scary for a while."

Ty perked his ears. Grades had never been a real issue for him, but he wasn't going to admit that to Arch. "So what'd you do?"

"Cracked down on myself." Arch leaned back into the seat. "Told myself I could do better, that I knew I was better. Ended up putting a lot of work into it and brought my GPA up." He grinned sideways. "What'd you graduate with?"

"A degree," Ty said. "Bachelor of something in Communications."

Arch snorted. "What GPA, I mean?"

"Oh." Ty waved a paw. "Shit, I don't know. Enough to graduate. Probably not a lot more."

"Man, the life of a college athlete." Some bitterness crept into Arch's tone. "Fuck."

"Look, I had the chance to get through college that way," Ty said. "I took advantage of the system."

"Yeah, but…" Arch closed his eyes. "You know what, you're right. I'm sorry, it's completely not your fault and I wanna have fun tonight."

Ty waited a second, not sure what to say, but then Arch turned to him and smiled. "I'm serious. I'm frustrated with the system, but it's not your fault."

"All right," Ty said. "Let's talk about something else. How's your roommate?"

"Ah, still freaked out about the ex. He bought a can of mace, like that's going to do anything."

"He's a wolverine. What would he be afraid of?"

Arch snorted. "Sure, in a naked fight with Delmond, Justin would kick his ass. But Delmond carries knives around. He says he's worried about fag-bashers, but come on, in Yerba?" The wolf's ears folded back. "How's that tiger doing in your locker room?"

"Dev?" Ty tilted his head. "Dev's cool. I mean, everyone's used to it, nobody messes with him."

"Cool." Arch leaned back in the seat. "That's the impression I get, but you never know what the media's not reporting, y'know? It's good to hear."

Ty nodded, and for a moment felt excluded. Arch and Dev had kind of a family bond, and though Ty was friendly with both of them, he wasn't one of them. He thought again about the pictures Arch had sent him, and rested his paws on his tail as the car went on through Crystal City to the dance club.

At the club, Ty told the driver he'd call when he needed a ride back, and then he and Arch walked down the sidewalk to the unassuming entrance. He wouldn't have known anything was going on in there if there hadn't been a big crowd hanging around.

"Come on," Arch said, and pulled Ty to the back of the line of people waiting to get in.

"Y'know," Ty said quietly, "we could just—"

"You wanna be discreet, right?" Arch grinned and elbowed him lightly. "Don't worry, big shot. It won't take that long."

They spent fifteen minutes waiting, joking about the other people in the line, talking about the Crystal City weather, and when Arch started a little dancing there on the sidewalk, Ty joined in.

"All right, you two, do it in the club," the bouncer growled, waving them inside. Ty paid the cover charge, and they walked together into the hazy atmosphere, deep blue and red lights, and pulsing techno music. This club had a main floor and then two smaller rooms up off the second story where other music was going, one kind of a country remix and the other a constant throb of trance.

Arch pulled Ty to the trance room, where they found space on the floor and let loose. Two weeks of practice and meeting, of media pressure and teammate pressure and coach pressure, of tension and worry from inside that built up no matter how much Ty believed he was good at dismissing it, all of that melted away as he threw his arms up, hopped his feet back and forth, and swished his tail around. Across from him, Arch matched his moves, led him or followed fluidly as they danced, and sometimes spun off to do his own thing like Ty did. They kept track of each other when they weren't dancing together: what Ty used to call his "dance buddy" in college.

A slender mouse in a tight-fitting low-cut dress danced her way up to him as he spun away from Arch. She put her paws on his hips and grinned up.

Earlier in the season, or back in college, Ty would've draped his paws over her shoulders and pulled her close, and later he would've gone into a back room or back to his house with her if she wanted. Tonight, though, he gently disengaged her with a smile and a shake of his head, and she shrugged and danced off elsewhere.

He didn't think Arch had noticed, but when they took a break to grab a beer, the wolf said, "Why'd you push away that mouse?"

Ty sipped. "Don't want to get into anything tonight. I need to be loose tomorrow."

Arch chuckled. "Doesn't sex loosen you up?"

"Maybe. Sometimes." Ty looked out onto the floor. "Didn't want to leave you hangin', though."

The music washed over them. Arch settled back against the wall. "How d'you mean?"

Oh, Ty realized. Arch was thinking about their blow job texts. He had been too, but the joy of dancing had pushed that to the back of his mind. Well, two could tease. "Oh, you know," he said. "Not really fair for me to go off and have fun and leave you with nobody, is it?"

The wolf snorted, a soft sound that Ty's ears still picked up. "I can amuse myself," he said.

"Yeah," Ty shot back, "but I hear if you do that too much, you go blind."

Arch had lifted his beer and now sputtered around a mouthful of it. "Goddamn it, warn me when you're going to say something funny," he said, setting the beer down and licking his muzzle.

Mmm, that tongue. Ty looked away from it and tipped the beer back. This was fun.

Once more a girl came up to them, interested in Ty, but this time Arch took the initiative. He slid around behind Ty and clasped his paws over Ty's chest, grinning at the girl from around the fox's shoulder, as he wasn't quite tall enough to get over it. She got the hint and moved on with a smile, and Ty turned, still dancing, and tried to shove Arch gently in the chest.

But the wolf kept his arms around Ty and grinned up. "What?" he mouthed.

It was kinda nice being this close to him. It felt naughty, out in public like this, even though he knew nobody cared if he was gay or straight or whatever. And Arch's paws held him, bounded him, and that too gave his tail a tingle. So he put his paws on Arch's hips and kept dancing.

They got close enough that the fronts of their bodies touched, and even though Ty was trying to keep his sheath from brushing Arch's, the music was too fast and their dancing too close to keep that from happening. When it did, though, it wasn't a big deal; it was a pleasurable touch, but Arch didn't change his dance or expression, and so neither did Ty.

They danced close until the next break, and then Arch said, as though they'd just been doing something very normal, "When do you need to get back?"

"What time is it?" Ty checked his phone. "Ah, dammit. Probably not too long now."

"I'm ready to go." The wolf panted with a grin. "Was a fun night."

So Ty called the car, and they piled into the back, sitting closer together than they had on the way to the club. Arch's scent mingled with booze and beer and sweat, and Ty sagged back against the seat, letting his tail flop out alongside him. "Thanks for coming out tonight," he said as the car pulled away into traffic.

"Thanks for inviting me." Arch paused. "And for paying for the hotel."

"Ah." Ty grinned and leaned against the wolf. "I got lots of money. Don't sweat it."

"Uh-huh." The wolf leaned back. "I appreciate it. It was a lot of fun."

"Great music there," Ty said. "Whoever recommended it to you knows his stuff."

Arch laughed. "I'll be sure to drop the Crystal City Trib's Society Editor a note."

They talked about the club for a bit and then about the people at the club and a little about the game. "I'll watch from a bar or something," Arch promised.

"You don't have to," Ty said.

"I like watching you work." The wolf stretched out.

"Maybe I'll come to your office next week."

"Oh, god." Arch snorted. "Come to think of it, people might be impressed if I had a football player come by. I bet I could get out early."

The car slowed, and out the window Ty saw Arch's hotel. "Maybe I'll do it, then," he said. "Anyway, thanks again. I needed this."

"You can thank me in your speech," Arch said. "Or on second thought, don't."

Ty grinned. "I'll figure out something."

Arch opened the door, put one foot out, then hesitated. "You want to, uh…" He inclined his head toward the hotel.

"Oh." Ty had been thinking about it, of course, and part of him did want to come up, did want to see what the wolf could do with his tongue, did want to see how far he'd go. But he was also still keyed up, thinking about the game, he was tired, and he knew how late it was. "I better not."

"Yeah, okay." Arch turned. "Good luck tomorrow."

He said it naturally, not angry or disappointed or anything, but Ty still felt guilty, like he was leaving the wolf blue-balled. He hated feeling like a cocktease, but in this case he had to. Still… "Hey," he said.

Arch turned his muzzle back, and Ty leaned forward to kiss his whiskers. "Thanks."

For a moment, the wolf didn't move or respond. Then he smiled big and bright, and licked Ty's nose back gently. "I'll be watching," he said, and got out.

It was crazy, Ty thought as he pulled away, that he should feel so good about having brought that smile to Arch's muzzle. What made the wolf so special? For a moment, the thought that he might be gay like Dev surfaced, and with it that tingle of excitement over having a huge secret. Then he reminded himself about the mink and the fennec and all the other girls he'd undeniably enjoyed and wanted to be with. Ah well, he thought, leaning back and closing his eyes, better start worrying about those Sabertooths cornerbacks.

Chapter 5

Game day: crazy, tense, and a little scary. Ty kept telling himself that it was just another game, the same as all the coaches were telling them, the same as Fisher said loudly to anyone listening. But his stomach buzzed like it never had, even in the bowl game in college (although that had been a mid-tier bowl, and it wasn't really a big deal). The playoff games had been easier somehow, because there was nothing to lose and they weren't even expected to be there. But that logic had stopped working sometime during Media Day when it sunk in that they were here, that everyone was taking them seriously, that if they won this game, he would be part of a team that would never be forgotten.

When he'd been drafted, a bunch of his then-friends had laughed at him. "Firebirds," they said. "Great. Pile up stats for a couple years then get yourself a fat contract with a good team." At the time, he'd considered it as a strategy, and though his agent wouldn't say anything so blunt, Ty'd read between the lines. "The better you perform," Delino had said, "the better your next contract, wherever it is." But he'd also stressed that it was important to work well with the coaches and be known as a "coachable" player, because that lengthened your career.

Ty had done all he could, but sitting in the locker room half-dressed, his paws clasped together, he looked back and saw mostly his mistakes, his missed opportunities. The ball that his slid past his fingertips in the Gateway game (sure, Aston could've thrown it better, but maybe Ty was a step off); the many times he'd struggled learning the playbook early in the season and had screwed up a route; the time he'd returned a kick and had juked left instead of right, directly into a block; the times he'd turned a second too late; the times he'd turned a second too soon. Even the touchdowns now seemed to him lucky, unrepresentative of his ability. He had to get some chances in this game, had to prove that the rest of it wasn't a fluke.

"Hey." Brit sat next to him. He had on his Firebirds polo and khakis, and his spotted tail switched back and forth. "You doing okay?"

"I'm fine, coach." Ty closed his eyes, took a breath. The locker room smelled the same as it always had, all his teammates and the uniforms and the weird soap from the shower that they used here in Crystal City (some guys said that the soap in the visitors' locker rooms was old, or weird, or purposely scented to throw teams off their game, but to Ty's nose, all soaps and even sometimes the water in different cities were different and weird and none of them was particularly worse than another).

Brit nodded. "It's okay to be nervous. Big game. You're starting in your first year and you're in a championship. Not many guys can say that. It's a lot of pressure."

"Thanks," Ty said. "I hadn't thought of that."

"You know why you're starting?"

Ty turned to see the cheetah grinning at him. His chest loosened, just a bit, and he smiled back. "Because I'm the third best wideout you got."

"Because you're good." Brit squeezed his shoulder. "You can do all those things we want you to do. You know we drew up about six new plays just to take advantage of your talent?"

The fox perked his ears. The pressure in his chest loosened further. "Which ones?"

So Brit told him, and he asked if any of them were going to be run today, and Brit said they would see if the occasion presented itself. "Depends how you play, doesn't it? You ready?"

"I'm ready." Ty was pleased to find his voice firmer, his chest loose, his body jumping, in fact, with eagerness to get out there.

Brit stood. "Then get dressed, rook," he said. "Show us what you can do."

He got his pads on, threw his jersey over them, and got his knee wrapped by a trainer. "You want the ankle, too?"

Ty shook his head, bouncing from one foot to the other. "Ankle's fine. Knee's fine, too. It wasn't hurt."

"Coach says keep it wrapped for the game. Don't want you twisting it again."

"I didn't even get on the injury report."

"So go tell Coach that." The trainer, a slight rabbit, cocked one eyebrow up at him. "Or shut up and live with it."

"Yeah, yeah." He flexed his knee. The restriction was very slight, same as always. He'd have to get used to it. It hadn't stopped him from scoring in the Boliat game, after all.

Everything went very slowly, seconds crawling by as they waited for the introductions, and then the opening ceremonies dragged on and on. Even when they were on the field, there were announcements and special guests and then Aston and Gerrard went out for the coin toss.

And then time sped up. Ty went out onto the field and tried not to look at the stands full of blue and gold, the section of red and gold, but it was hard not to. He blocked and ran his routes to draw the safeties away from the action, and then a pass came to him and he stretched his arms up as far as he could and it skimmed over his claws.

"That's on me," Aston came over to tell him as they jogged back to the sideline. "I'm jazzed up. I'll get you next time."

And he did, on a short pass to get across the fifty. Then he was blocking for a long pass down to Strike that went incomplete, and Aston went back to him for a short gain. Ty caught the ball, turned, and saw daylight. *Touchdown* flashed through his head. He took two steps and weight closed around his legs and the ground came up to meet him.

He got up with the help of fifty-five, the coyote linebacker, flipped the ball to the ref, and jogged back to the huddle feeling like he should've gotten the score. But nobody said anything to him; they were already on to the next play, and the only other time Aston threw to Ty in the half, a Crystal City corner had jammed him and thrown him off his route, so he was a yard from the ball when it fell.

At halftime, Coach praised their effort even though they were behind, and then Brit came and talked to the wideouts. "Stay sharp," he said. "Stay on your routes. Focus on the ball and block when you can. We're getting to their D and we'll get more chances in the second half."

Halftime, when he wasn't playing, dragged on (though of course it was also twice as long as a normal halftime). By the time they went out onto the field again, Ty's paws and tail were twitching with the need to get back out there.

He caught a ball and broke to the outside, getting a nice gain to give Aston a manageable third down, and then Aston took a sack and the drive was over. Ty jogged back and had to watch the defense go out. Dev was doing great, and so was Vonni, but the Sabertooths offense was doing a little bit greater.

And then it was the fourth quarter and the Firebirds were down 21-16. Ty had caught a few more passes, but they just couldn't put a drive together. Watching the defense, he thought again about how he'd actually grown closer to Dev and Vonni and Zillo than to most of the guys on offense (except Rodo, who was his roommate, after all). Rodo stood with him, both of them muttering with all the guys around them that they just needed a break, just one lucky break, and they'd be right back in this, and then they saw what they'd been waiting for the whole game: the penetration of white jerseys into blue, the quarterback dropping under a defender—Dev, holy shit it was Dev, he got the sack!—and Carson was scooping the ball up and running to the end zone and they were all leaping up and down, barely restrained by the sideline, craning their necks out to watch and then screaming as the PA said dully, "Touchdown Firebirds."

All of a sudden, anything seemed possible. The defense had to go out again, and they stopped the Sabertooths with two minutes left which meant that Aston and Ty and the offense had to get two first downs, twenty measly yards. Dev yelled at Ty as they jogged out and Ty waved back to tell them, *No problem, we're fucking doing this!*

He knew full well that they were going to run, run, run, to chew up clock, and mostly what he'd be doing was blocking. But to his surprise, on second down, Aston motioned to him. "Firebirds X," he said, which was a double crossing route designed to shake close coverage. "They'll be collapsing for the run, it's a low-risk pass."

But if the pass drops, it stops the clock and helps the Sabertooths, is what Aston didn't say because they all knew it. Ty knew this route, lining up on the right and then sprinting to the left, leaving the linebacker across from him (a coyote again, but fifty-two, not fifty-five, a step slower and less intuitive). And here, for the first time, the world slowed down. He heard the snap count, timed his start, and broke cleanly across the middle. And there was the ball—shit, no, it was too high and behind him and the coyote was right on his tail, and he wasn't going to make it but he had to make it—he leapt and turned, and stretched his paw out with nothing but intuition, and there, miraculously, was the ball.

He came down still on his feet, pulled the ball to his body, and a moment later he was down with it on the turf, fifty-two on top of them both. Clock still ticking, two yards to go.

Lightning Strike, the huge speedy cheetah, got them the first down. Ten yards to go. Jaws ran it for two, then around for four, and that took them to the two-minute warning. So it was third and about four, and in the huddle again Aston looked to Ty, and Rodo beside him. "Strike's going to draw a double," he said. "Four yards across the middle, that's all we need. S to C." His finger went from Ty to Rodo. "One of you will be open."

Ty and Rodo looked at each other and in the deer's eyes, Ty saw his own determination. "Fuck that," Rodo said. "We'll both be. Just get us the damn ball."

This thing right here, this was the most important play of Ty's life. Make it and he'd be a hero. Miss it…well, it'd be giving the Sabertooths life, not necessarily dooming the Firebirds. But for everyone who'd mocked his team, for all his friends who'd played their hearts out on defense, for all his friends watching: Kimi and Paul and Kellen and Arch, he squeezed his paws closed and opened them, and then trotted out to line up.

He ran it perfectly, leapt across when the ball was snapped, but the coyote bumped him, shadowed him to his spot in front of where Rodo was waiting and there was the ball, leaving Aston's paw, fluttering towards him. The coyote had a paw on Ty's arm, but the fox could still jump, and he kept his eyes on the ball the whole way, stretching his arm up, and the ball dropped—

—just past his fingertips—

—and hung in the air as Rodo and the other coyote dove for it—

—and it fell to the ground and the pass was incomplete. The Sabertooths were going to get the ball back. Ty looked at the refs to see if somehow the grabbing of his arm was enough for an interference call, but no flags came out.

"That was too close," the coyote, fifty-five, said as they got up.

"You guys are good," Rodo replied. "Scuse us if we don't wish you luck."

Fifty-five laughed. "You took a hell of a shot. Now it's our turn."

"Great coverage," Ty said to the other coyote. "Fucker."

Laughter all around, and then they were trotting to separate sidelines and Ty didn't want to go back. He yelled ahead to the coaches, "Let's do it again! Come on!"

"Get off the field." Rodo took his arm. "It's back on the D now."

"I'm going." The fox looked down at the white line as he stepped across it, off the field and out of the action. The punt team was already out there, preparing. "We should've had it there."

The deer lowered his voice. "If it was a better thrown ball, you'd have caught it."

"He was under pressure."

"You think McCrae flutters that throw under pressure?"

"We got here with Aston." Ty felt the need to defend his quarterback, because the fault was clearly his own. If he'd jumped a second sooner, run a little farther back…

"It's okay." Rodo changed the subject. "Our guys can stop 'em."

Ty hoped so too, but it soon became clear that they couldn't. A little here, a little there, exactly what Chevali hadn't been able to do when they needed to. And then they were on the edge of field goal range and they called time out, and Ty and everyone stood around trying not to listen to Coach talking to the guys. The worst feeling in the world wasn't not being able to do anything to help; it was knowing you'd had the chance to help and had blown it.

They went back out and Ty found his paw in Rodo's hand, squeezing, and every one of them straining to watch except for Aston, who sat on the bench with his head down. They saw their teammates line up, felt the determination in the lines of their bodies as they crouched and braced.

The ball snapped. The play sprang into motion.

"We're blitzing," Rodo breathed.

Six Firebirds came forward, but McCrae, the Sabertooths' wolf quarterback, didn't stumble or panic. He whipped the ball over Dev's shoulder right to a jackrabbit, down the Sabertooths' sideline, for a first down and more, easily in field goal range now.

And they made the kick, of course, and now Ty was going back out and Strike went with him as the two best catch-and-runners on the team. "I'll get it if you block for me," Strike said.

"Whatever it takes," Ty replied, too focused on cutting loose the desperation. His college coach had told him: don't worry about whether it's been done before. Worry about doing it now. He flexed his fingers and trotted out. He'd be the lead returner with Strike behind him; if they kicked deep, Strike would get it. If they squibbed it, Ty would get it first.

Beside him, Zillo came out: backup linebackers and safeties and wide-outs and tight ends all played on special teams, and Zillo's contributions there kept him on the team. He was a good runner but a better blocker, with a knack for knowing how to get in someone's way.

They lined up. Ty knew somehow that they were going to kick it on the ground, that it was coming at him, even before the line went into motion and the kicker ran at the ball. It bounced fast along the ground, but he read its path and stepped into it, fielding it cleanly—

—look the ball into your paws first—

—and then looking up to see where his running lanes were—

—then look at the field—

—and there was space, two possible lanes. He darted forward to the one on the left, behind a block by Zillo, but it closed immediately in a wall of navy and gold. He spun—

—that fox can change direction on a dime and give you eight cents change—

—ran behind Zillo looking for room, there must be room somewhere else—

—don't run backwards unless you're sure you can make something happen—

—and pressure closed around him. His right eye caught a flicker of white in its peripheral vision, but right in front of him was Zillo with his paws out, and Ty didn't even think, just tossed it backwards to the coyote as the pressure pulled him off his feet and the weight of a cougar (he knew from the smell) flattened him to the ground.

But he could still hear, and the roar of the crowd erupting was a noise he knew well, though he hadn't heard it in over a month. They'd silenced crowds in Hellentown and Boliat, had lost their last game in Chevali, but this, this was the sound of a crowd whose team had won. Ty closed his eyes and wished he could close his ears.

The player on him, whoever it was, leapt off and ran to celebrate. Ty lay there for another few seconds, and then one of the backup safeties came over and reached a spotted paw down. Without a word, Ty grabbed it and got to his feet. Their eyes met, and the other guy clapped him on the back. Together, they walked the vast distance back to their sideline, to the flat ears and lifeless tails marching joylessly into their locker room.

Zillo caught up to him at the entrance to the concrete tunnel. "Sorry," he said. "I tried—I couldn't—it just fell out—"

"Not your fault," Ty said, and cheering above him, out of tone with the rest of the stadium, drew him to look up.

Over the tunnel, a small family of possums in red and gold had their fists in the air and broad smiles on their faces. "We love you!" a little kit, probably no more than eight, shrieked down. "We love you!"

Ty waved up, forced a smile, because that's what you did for fans, but all he could think was, *I let them down.*

A lot of the guys sat around the locker room, not wanting to take their uniforms off, not wanting it to be over. Ty knew how they felt, but he also wanted to get in the shower and lie down, and if he didn't think about the game, the prospect of someone rubbing down his sore muscles sounded heavenly.

He had his shirt off and was picking at the laces on his pants when Vince, the media liaison, ran into the room with a laptop in one arm and a phone against his ear and yelled for Dev.

"I don't know what's going on!" Dev yelled back.

Ty perked his ears. Dev had a phone in his paw too. And then Vince said, "Polecki just said he's gay," and everything else in the locker room stopped. "They want your take on it."

Polecki? That was the coyote, fifty-five. He'd tackled Ty, had helped him up. He was a hell of a player. Someone asked, "Did he feel you up when he tackled you?" but Ty ignored him, heading to Dev's side where Charm was already dispensing his usual wisdom.

"You only did it in a room of fifty people," the stallion said. "This guy did it in front of seventy thousand."

"Seventy million, counting the TV," Ty added. Dev, dazed and hurrying to dress, wasn't really paying attention to him, and who could blame him? This was huge. This was a game-changer. The tiger was lit up and fumbling with his clothes, and Ty thought it might be a little like finding out you had a long-lost brother or something. Or some kind of family member.

And then guilt swamped him as Dev fled the room. He could've made Dev feel that way. He could've come to him the night before and said, "Hey, you're not alone. I kissed a guy. I thought about doing more with him. Hell, I was out all night dancing with him."

But would that have been fair? Dev would've said, "So are you gay?" and Ty would have to have said "no," or at least that he wasn't sure, because first of all, he did still like girls, and maybe it was just this one wolf that did it for him, and for another thing, there was absolutely no way in hell that his family would let him be with a guy. Anyway, he wanted to have cubs he could share his traditions with like his parents had done with him, those comforting rituals that were sometimes dumb but that he loved, like the particular kind of tea you drank before every birthday celebration. So what would he tell Dev? "I like this one guy but I'm still going to marry a vixen and all, but hey, maybe we can talk about sex in private sometime"?

Ugh. He stripped his clothes off and padded to the shower, letting it soak through his fur. As he washed with the Crystal City soap, he looked around at his teammates. What would Arch pay for a snapshot of this shower? And yet for Ty, it did nothing. Even Zillo, whom he'd seen drunk and fucking, didn't turn Ty on. But the thought of Arch did, enough that he banished the thoughts lest he get hard in the shower.

He stepped into the fur dryer and let the warm air soothe him, then brushed himself down and walked back out to his locker and got dressed. Most of the guys were waiting for a bus to the hotel, but Ty walked past them and out into the sunny, jubilant street.

Chapter 6

"I'm at this brew pub called McSmokey's," he told Coop, the team assistant. "Send a car over."

"Sure," the coati said. He didn't ask where it was, or if Ty was drunk, or anything. The only thing he asked was, "When do you want it?"

Ty examined the remains of his beer. "Ten minutes."

"It'll be there in nine."

"Thanks, Coop." He hung up the phone and swigged the last of his beer. The brewhouse was full of raucous, shouting fans who thankfully hadn't recognized him. He'd thought he would get a beer and then go, but perversely, he couldn't stop looking at the highlights of the game on every TV in the bar, everywhere he looked. The touchdowns, the stops. That final play, the ball sailing from his arms to Zillo's, and then to the ground.

Even so, after one beer, his fur itched and his feet kicked at the bar and he had to go, and he knew where he wanted to go. Whether the beer had loosened him up or just provided enough buffer space between the game and the evening didn't matter. He was ready.

He picked up the phone again. He'd already talked to his parents and that had been less help than he'd thought. He'd expected some kind of "sit for three years on a rock" parental shit about enduring the hard times, but his mother had said, "even the kappa gets washed away in the river," which implied that he'd been in over his head, overwhelmed by the game, and he hadn't, so even though he knew the saying and knew exactly what it meant, he'd said, "What the fuck is a kappa?" and his mother had very properly ignored both the profanity and the question and asked him when he was flying home.

He didn't want to talk to anyone, but he didn't want to be alone. Grumbling under his breath, he scrolled through the messages from his agent, from Kellen and Kimi, from Uncle Lucas, from his college coach and some of his college teammates. He'd replied without putting any thought into the words. *Thanks. Fine. Yeah, it sucks. Thanks. Next year.* Now he brought up another one of the texts, *You looked great*, and replied: *Can I come over?*

Arch replied quickly. *Sure. My hotel?*

Yeah. Be there in

He stared at the *in*, tried to calculate how long the car would take and gave up, erased *in* and wrote *soon*.

Arch texted back his room number and asked if there was anything he should have ready. Ty thought about it as he got up and dropped a fifty on the bar. The bartender picked it up and said, "I'll get you change."

Ty waved him off. "You deserve it," he said. "Congrats."

The chinchilla's thin fingers closed around the bill, and his fluffy face seemed to puff out as his eyes widened. "Thanks," he said, and then as Ty turned around, "Hey…"

But Ty didn't look back as he strode to the door, and then he was outside leaning against the corner. He typed to Arch, *Those arms*, just as a Towne Car pulled up to the sidewalk and a jaguar hopped out of the driver seat.

"Mr. Nakamura?"

Ty nodded, stepping forward. She held the door for him and then closed it when he was in. He read Arch's reply, *Done*, as she slid back into the driver's seat. "Back to the team hotel, sir?" she asked, her eyes on him in the rear-view mirror.

"Different hotel," he said, and gave her the name of Arch's.

"Yes, sir." She pulled away into traffic, and Ty leaned back and closed his eyes.

When she opened the door in front of Arch's hotel, Ty thanked her and said he'd call when he was ready to come back. Three minutes later, he was standing in front of Arch's door. This is it, he thought, this is the threshold. If you're not going to step over into the gay world, turn around and walk away.

He stared at the door, and then it opened and Arch's smile greeted him. "Generally the knocks work better when you don't just think them."

"Seems to have worked pretty well."

The wolf flicked his ears. "I was waiting, and I heard you, and came to the door and smelled you, then looked through the peephole…" He cleared his throat. "Are you coming in?"

"Yeah," Ty said, and stepped through the door.

It swung closed behind him, and then the wolf's arms were around him and his were around Arch, and the wolf's head rested against his shoulder. "You played pretty well, from what I could tell," Arch murmured. "I watched in the bar…"

Ty reached up and took the wolf's muzzle in his paws, pushing it back gently until he could look into Arch's eyes. "I don't want to talk about the goddamn game," he said, and then he leaned forward and touched his lips to Arch's.

The wolf's were warm, and his sweet, fresh breath washed over Ty's whiskers, definitely masculine, but that didn't matter. He was Arch, and Ty could kiss him, could make the wolf's body tighten at the touch of his lips. The power to spur that reaction excited him, and when they parted and Arch panted before pulling his tongue back into his muzzle, Ty grinned.

"Uh," Arch said, "you want to, uh, talk about something else?"

"Yeah." Ty just held him. "Remember those texts from a few weeks ago?"

"Hmm." The wolf was regaining his composure. "Sort of, vaguely."

His paws felt nice above Ty's tail, and Ty liked the feel of the wolf's slender body in his arms, too. Eventually he would want to move to the bed, but he didn't have to just yet. "All right," he said. "We can start the conversation over again."

It was Arch who nudged them toward the bed, after another kiss, after their breath mingled among their whiskers and the flicker of their tongues. At the edge of the bed, Ty pulled his shirt off over his head in a single motion, and Arch, already sitting, mimicked him. The shirts fell by the bed, and Arch reached up to put one grey-brown paw on Ty's white, taut stomach.

Ty smiled down, and Arch said, "You know how hard it was, that night in my apartment, not to do this?"

"You could've."

"Then? I was worried you'd freak out and leave."

"Maybe I would have."

"You're pretty gorgeous, you know?" The wolf smiled. "Normally it's against my principles to say that to a fox, so you know how exceptional you must be."

Ty's response was to unfasten his pants and let them drop to his ankles, tail wagging. "Was it hard not touching me while we slept?"

"Not once I went to sleep." Arch's eyes traveled down the fox's body. "Mmm. If I'd seen this, though…" His paw slid down, hesitating above the waistband of the tight briefs, and his eyes met Ty's.

The fox let his lips curl up in a smile and kept his paws at his sides. Arch's fingers slid delicately down over the cloth, claws teasing through to the sheath and barely hidden erection below it. "You sure you're okay with this?"

Ty shivered and nodded. "I don't think I'm gay," he said, "but I'm pretty sure I'm not straight."

The wolf's paw cupped Ty's sac and then returned up to squeeze his sheath more firmly. "Good. Because I don't want to be some straight guy's experiment."

"You're not." Ty closed his eyes. "You're a…not-straight guy's friend."

"With benefits." It wasn't a question.

"Yeah."

"All right, then." Arch grinned up at him, and one claw flicked at Ty's waistband. "So what are you ready for tonight?"

"Do whatever," Ty said. "I don't want to think. I'll tell you if you start something I'm not ready for."

"Oh ho." Arch closed his paw around the thin fabric around Ty's shaft. "Whatever, eh?"

Ty swished his tail back and forth. "I trust you," he said.

"Aw, dammit." Arch leaned forward and pressed his nose into Ty's stomach. "You hadda go and make it all trusty."

"I'm serious." Ty reached down and played with the wolf's ears. "I don't know shit about doing stuff with another guy. You're the expert and I trust you."

"Mmmkay then." Arch exhaled warmth into Ty's stomach fur and licked around his navel. "Promise you'll tell me if you feel uncomfortable."

"Promise."

Ty had a pretty good idea what Arch would do first, and he was right. The wolf eased his briefs down over his shaft, pushed them down his legs, and then drew his tongue up Ty's pink flesh. The fox inhaled and steadied himself, bracing his legs, and moved his paw down to Arch's shoulders.

He'd had blow jobs before, of course, and as he'd expected, getting one from a guy wasn't all that different from getting one from a girl. Arch's tongue curled around him just as warmly, his lips pursed over Ty's tip just as

Ty had a pretty good idea what Arch would do first, and he was right. The wolf eased his briefs down over his shaft, pushed them down his legs, and then drew his tongue up Ty's pink flesh.

nicely, and if he could get rather more of the fox's cock into his mouth, that was more because he was a wolf than because he was a guy.

And even the paw on Ty's rump holding him steady, the fingers holding the base of his shaft and squeezing his knot as it grew…there was gentle affection in them, but when Ty'd had a girlfriend in college (before she broke up with him for seeing other girls), she'd been affectionate too. Most of the girls he'd had sex with recently had been more interested in the sex than him—or at least, more interested in the sex *with* him.

But Arch was a friend, too, and getting a blow job from a friend was nice, Ty decided, no matter what gender the friend was. Especially after a fucking rollercoaster of a day that had filled him with so much tension he was about to collapse as it left him, shaking and panting.

Arch stopped sucking him and slid his muzzle back, holding Ty by the hips. "You okay?"

"Yeah." Ty squeezed his shoulder. "Really good. Just…it's been a hell of a day."

"I know. C'mere." Arch pulled him onto the bed, up on top of the smaller wolf, and wrapped his arms around Ty. The fox's damp cock pressed into Arch's pants, but the wolf didn't seem to care, just stroked along the fur of Ty's back and nuzzled him.

And it was nice, lying there naked on top of a friend. Arch radiated warmth and smelled refreshing and familiar, and his paws stroked soothing patterns in Ty's fur and his muzzle and warm breath tickled the fox's neck. Ty played his paws down Arch's sides until they got to his pants, and then he brought them around front to fumble with the snap there.

Arch let Ty take his pants off, and the underwear under them, and it was no surprise to find the wolf's cock as hard as Ty's. It was a surprise that Ty didn't mind it so much when they pressed close again, that he liked taking that cock in his fingers and rubbing it, exploring the differences with his own, feeling the swell of the knot.

"Hey," Arch said after a little while.

"Mm?"

"You meant it when you said you were up for whatever?"

Irritation flashed that Arch would keep asking him, but of course the wolf was being cautious, like Ty would be if he, dunno, brought the wolf to a football practice or something. Then he curled his tail, because he thought Arch might want to get on top of him, but he'd said 'whatever,' and if Arch thought it would be okay, he wasn't going to go back on his word. "Yeah," he said, and nipped the wolf's ear.

"Hey." Arch squirmed and grinned, wriggling free. He rolled across the bed and off, hurrying into the bathroom.

Does he want me to pee on him? Ty wasn't sure he could, all hard like this. But a moment later, Arch reappeared with a little foil packet and a small bottle. "All right," he said, and tossed the packet to Ty. "Let's see how you ride a wolf."

Ty's ears perked. He took in Arch's body: nicely built, a little more padding than an athlete, but not more than the girls he was used to seeing. His fur was shaggier, not kept short like most athletes (to show off their muscles), but Ty thought it gave him a neat natural look. And his tail was wagging, so he was about as excited as Ty was. "All right," he said, so Arch wouldn't ask him again if it was okay.

While he tore open the packet and put the condom on, Arch flipped the cap of the bottle and squeezed out some liquid into his paw, then rubbed it back behind him. He hurried back into the bathroom, got a towel, and came back out.

Ty stroked himself through the condom as Arch spread the towel out on the bed and then got up on all fours facing Ty. He squeezed out some more lube onto the fox's wrapped shaft, then spread it around with the same paw. "Now," he said, "I need a little prep before you just shove that in."

"Okay." Ty took the bottle of lube Arch was holding out. "What do I do?"

"Start with two fingers. Try not to scrape me with your claws too much. Then work in three. You'll be able to feel me relax. When you can get three in, then," he nodded at Ty's cock, "go for the main event."

Stick his fingers in…? Well, if Arch could stand to have fingers stuck in, Ty could stand to do it, he guessed. He started to move around behind the wolf.

"Oh," Arch said, looking over his shoulder. "And you might want to keep pawing yourself if you don't find that sexy."

"Right." Ty shook his head and situated himself behind the wolf.

The bushy tail was arched out of the way, and the wolf's balls hung down between his legs. Ty reached under there to cup them. The feeling was odd, but not unpleasant; he'd cupped and rubbed his own balls enough that he knew it felt good, so he played with Arch's for a little while, then slicked up his fingers and took a breath.

From experience, one finger was about his limit, but the wolf took two easily, his passage already slick. Ty worked his fingers against the muscle and Arch made appreciative noises, his tail flagging over Ty's arm. Just as Arch had said, Ty felt the wolf's clenching muscles ease as he worked his fingers around. "Try three," Arch said, and he hesitated and then tried.

It was pretty amazing to him that he could fit all three fingers in. He pulled them out and looked at how thick that was, and it was definitely thicker than his cock. After a little more working around to make sure the wolf was ready, he got up and pressed his hips against the fluffy white rear.

"Ready," Arch panted, "if you are."

"What do you think?" Ty positioned his cock and pushed forward.

Tightness gripped him, the sensation different from making love to a girl and yet similar enough that he thrust forward and back in a familiar rhythm, leaning his weight atop the wolf. His arms came around naturally to circle the wolf's chest, but it wasn't until he met the muscular, flat chest that he remembered where at least one of his paws should go.

He reached the slick paw down to Arch's hardness, gripping it and finding its warmth familiar. It was kind of like jerking himself off while he was fucking someone, which was a hot thought and helped him get more excited.

Time blurred into motion and desire, and the game fell away from him, his worries about what he was doing fell away, and all that remained was the body below him, his cock pushing into it, another cock in his paw, and the noises in his throat as his body gathered itself. His legs kicked back into the sheets, and his knot strained against the wolf below him. It wasn't usually this hard to push in, he thought dimly, not realizing why that would be until he'd worked it in and everything was lighting up, sparking, exploding out of him in a rush and his muzzle was buried in wolf fur, yipping and moaning muffledly through it. The wolf below him squirmed, twisted, and Ty closed his grip around the lithe body, hips locked to the jerking rear and still pumping into it.

And then he was spent, and the energy left him in a long, shaky breath, and he blinked, realizing that he was biting the scruff of Arch's neck. Below him, the wolf shook a few more times, and the smell of his seed drifted up to Ty, and then the two of them collapsed flat to the bed. Ty shifted his muzzle to mouth at the wolf's ear, and Arch whined.

"You make cute noises," Arch murmured. "Big tough athlete."

Ty wriggled. "Little wolf," he said, and then added, "sexy," because it seemed appropriate.

"Heh." Arch's tail, trapped, wagged feebly. "I guess that answers my question about whether you're still okay with this."

Heedless of the mess on his paw, Ty pushed it under Arch's chest to hug the wolf. "I'm generally okay with sex, y'know. It helps that I have a teammate who apparently does this all the time and still manages to be a regular guy somehow."

"I guess he's doing this tonight, too." Arch chuckled. "Letting off steam."

"I dunno." Ty rested his muzzle atop Arch's head. "Never really asked Dev about his sex life. But yeah. It also helps that…I trust you, like I said. I like you. I like making anyone squirm under me, guy or girl."

"Good." Arch had his arms under him, resting on his elbows. "For what it's worth, you feel pretty good on top. I, uh, wasn't going to ask you to tie, but there really wasn't time to stop you."

"Oh." Ty tugged, but his knot was still firmly lodged.

"Don't worry about it. I like it, even if I might be a little sore tomorrow."

"Am I that big?"

"Ha." Arch clenched around him. "Don't flatter yourself. Any canid knot is pretty big."

"Really?" Ty nipped Arch's ear again, because it made the wolf twist under him. "How many knots have you had?"

"Uh, including you? Three. Including a toy I have at home? Four, but a bunch of times."

"Oh-ho." Ty chuckled. "Am I bigger than your toy?"

"I'll show you sometime…" Arch trailed off. "Uh, if you want. I mean, if you want to visit."

Ty puffed a laugh into Arch's ear. "I'm lying here knot-deep in your ass and you wonder if I want to see you again?"

"Do you see most of the girls you fuck again?" The fox stayed quiet. "I know you pro athletes have tough lives, and you're not always going to have free evenings."

"Do you want to see *me* again?"

"Aw, fox, of course I do." The answer came without hesitation, making Ty feel loads better.

"Okay. Then we'll see each other again. And I'll fuck you again if you want. Or you can blow me. Or…" He hesitated, but the warmth of the wolf around his cock broke down any barriers he might have. "I'll try blowing you."

"All right, all right, slow down, big guy." Arch turned his head and grinned. "You going back to your hotel tonight or can you stay here?"

"I can do whatever the fuck I want. But I do have to be on a plane first thing in the morning."

The wolf's paw reached down to clasp his, beneath both of their weights. "I understand if you have to go," he said. "But I'd like it if you'd stay."

•

While Arch was in the shower, Ty called the car service directly so Coop wouldn't know what he was doing. "Pick me up at seven a.m.," he said, and gave them the hotel address.

The call to Rodo was a little trickier. "Come hang out with the guys," the deer pleaded. "You gotta be with your teammates. We all feel it."

Hearing his voice reminded Ty of the game, and he wasn't entirely lying when he said, "I feel like I let everyone down. I just want to be away from it all."

"Come on, Ty. I know it's hard, your first year and all, but nobody blames you. Nobody cares what Strike said."

"What did he say?" His ears flattened over the phone. "Never mind, I don't give a fuck. No, look, a friend of mine flew in for the game. I'm going to hang out with him and get drunk. He's got a spare bed so I'll crash here. I've already got the car picking me up in the morning."

"You sure?"

"Yeah. Hey, thanks. Let's get together in the off-season."

"For sure. Miranda wants to meet you."

"Looking forward to it." He smiled, though his chest tightened at the mention of Rodo's wife. He was going to have to go home to Pelagia, sit through dinners with vixens, feel the pressure from his parents to pick one: another reason he wanted this evening with Arch.

The wolf rubbed a towel over his naked body in the bathroom doorway as Ty hung up. "Teammate?"

"Rodo," Ty said. "My roommate when we're on the road."

Arch nodded and grinned. "Spare bed, huh?"

Ty waved toward the still-pristine bed from the rumpled one he was sitting on. "Technically true. Especially if you don't want to sleep in a smelly haze of wolf musk."

"Smelly, is it?" Arch stepped closer.

"Isn't it?"

The wolf grinned. "Yeah, I guess it is. Nothing to fox musk, though."

"Oh, like you'd know."

"I sniffed your condom in the trash in there."

"Ew, gross."

Arch laughed. "I've offered to swallow it, but sniffing it is gross?"

Ty patted the bed beside him. Arch sat and put his arm around the fox, claws ruffling damp russet and white fur, trailing down to Ty's bare hip. "So what do you want to do with the night?"

"Mmm." Ty tossed his phone onto the bed and draped an arm over Arch's shoulder. "Dinner. Sit here with you." He pointed at the bed. "Lie there with you. Sleep."

"Uncomplicated. I like that. Dinner here in the room or downstairs or out?"

"Here in the room. It's on my card, I'll pay for room service. Besides, I don't want to get dressed."

"Fair enough." Arch rested his head against Ty's shoulder. "Can I text Justin a picture of you?"

Ty stiffened, and then he felt the wolf shaking against his side and heard the hiss of laughter through his teeth. "Oh, fuck you," he said, and turned to nip at the dark tip of Arch's ear.

"Hey." Arch grinned and pressed closer to him, his tail thumping the bed. "What about just your cock?"

"Come on," Ty said, but then Arch got up and picked his phone out of his pants. "Wait, you really—when did you—?"

"When I was sucking on you. I wanted it for me, but Justin likes seeing them sometimes." He scrolled through his pictures. "Martz too, actually. There you go."

And Ty looked down at a small, grainy picture very much like the one he'd seen a few weeks ago, Arch looking at the camera with his muzzle wrapped around a long pink cock, glistening with a white streak down its length to the slight curve of a growing knot. *That's mine*, Ty thought, and his sheath pulsed in response. "It's not a great pic," he said.

"The light'll be better in the morning."

Ty met Arch's eyes. The wolf grinned with the tip of his tongue protruding from his black lips below the white fur. A returning smile pulled at the fox's lips. "Use my phone," he said. "Camera's better."

Arch laughed silently, his tongue lolling out as he took his phone back. "Deal," he said.

"But if it doesn't work out," Ty said, "you can send that to your friends. And one to me too."

"Will do." Arch set the phone down on the dresser and walked around to the other side of the bed, where he lay down and stretched out, throwing one arm across the side of the bed where Ty sat. The fox, who'd turned to watch him, leaned back and stretched out as well, pushing his arm behind the wolf's head.

Arch rolled to lie against him, bringing his other paw around to rest on Ty's bare stomach, his fingers smoothing down the white fur. His breath ruffled the fur of the fox's shoulder and chest.

Ty leaned his muzzle against Arch's eyebrows. The wolf blinked against Ty's short fur. It felt odd, this closeness, the both of them naked, especially with Arch's fingers so close to his sheath, with Arch's own sheath lying against his thigh. But it wasn't unwelcome, and it wasn't strange because Arch's paw and muzzle and rear had all been around his cock already, and if that itself was a little strange, it was now a fact of his life. He'd done many things in his life that were at least as odd as fucking a guy, including fucking a strip club waitress after watching her blow a friend of his.

To distract himself from thinking about whether it was weird and allow himself to just enjoy the moment, Ty's mind drifted back to the game. He chuckled. "So that makes two firsts for today. First time I lost a championship, and first time I slept with a guy."

"Excuse me," Arch said, his fingers sliding down Ty's thigh and back up, "but it's the second time you've slept with a guy. With this guy, anyway."

"Okay, first time I fucked a guy," Ty said.

The wolf's fingers reached over to pat the fox's warm sheath. "That I'll believe." His fingers trailed down Ty's balls and then went back to the fox's stomach, resting flat. "Want to talk about the game?"

The weight of Arch's paw lowered as Ty exhaled. "I saw a kid on my way out of the stadium, Firebirds fan, screaming his heart out." Arch shifted closer and then went still. "And I felt bad for letting him down. It was like he was all the fans, all of them who'd been hoping for me to win the game for them."

"I don't know football that well," Arch said. "But it looked like there were a bunch of other guys in Firebirds uniforms out there with you."

"Yeah, but…I had it at the end." He gripped Arch's shoulder, flushed with guilt that he wasn't with them, commiserating. "I know, everyone on the team feels the same way. The point is, though, that kid—he's not going to stop loving the team. Or me."

Arch chuckled, a warm movement and a soft breath, a fresh minty smell; he'd brushed his teeth. "Why would you think he would?"

"You know that the fans will always be there for you. I mean, you don't play crappy one week and come out to an empty stadium the next. But seeing it like that, especially that kid…I mean, it's okay to not win some of the time, isn't it?"

"Speaking as someone who almost never does…"

"Yeah, yeah." He exhaled. "What I mean is, it hurt so much to get that close. But that was still pretty good. I mean, there's fourteen other teams of fifty-two guys in the league who would cut off a finger for the chance to lose the championship."

Arch made a face, squirming against Ty. "I don't know about that."

"You haven't heard about this guy Fisher told us about. Never mind. I'll save the story. But the point is, we get all this 'win win win' shit in our heads, and you know what? We got the championship and we played a damn good game."

"One of the sports talking guys said, 'instant classic.'"

"I dunno about that." He snorted. "But it does kinda feel nice to think I was part of that. And I've got a whole career to get back, right?"

The wolf nodded and resumed the slow movement of his fingers through Ty's fur. "The talking guy said stuff about you, too. Like 'talented' and 'promising.' I got the feeling that I could brag about having slept with you."

Ty laughed. "You figured you were going to sleep with me while you were watching the game?"

"You did ask if I would blow you, and…well, I know you're formerly straight, but you were flirting with me. And I knew I was willing to sleep with you. So I figured there was a pretty good chance."

"You're smart."

"Experienced," Arch said.

"And warm."

Arch breathed in and slid his paw over Ty's sheath again. "You're hot."

Ty didn't answer. The wolf squeezed lightly. "Does that make you feel better?"

"Not really."

"But a little?" Arch's fingers rubbed. "Come on, I can feel that it's making you a little happier."

Ty breathed out. "Are you going to jerk me off now or blow me in the morning?"

The wolf's fingers kept rubbing. "Oh, blow you in the morning for sure. Do you want me to jerk you off now? Or want to just go to sleep?"

If he didn't answer, the wolf's fingers would answer for him, or rather, they would discover an answer by themselves. Already his pulse was quickening and his mind was racing with the primitive urge of *I wanna come again could I come again I want to and he's going to jerk me off*, and so by the time he opened his muzzle, he was already hard, and Arch's fingers had curled around his shaft, pushing the fur of his sheath down. "I guess you can jerk me off," he murmured.

The wolf laughed and pressed closer to him. "Got anything left in the tank?"

"Pff. I've gone three times in a night before. Ain't no thing."

"Oh, to be twenty-two again," Arch murmured. His erection pressed against Ty's hip, and the fox wondered idly if he was going to be expected to take care of Arch again, but let that care float away in the building waves of arousal and the warmth of the paw around him.

When he came, it felt slower, less urgent. The build took longer and even his release, quick though it was, faded more slowly. Arch lifted his paw away as Ty lay back panting, brought his dripping fingers to his muzzle, and licked them clean. Through half-lidded eyes, Ty watched, his own musky smell strong in his nostrils. "Ew," he said.

Arch grinned and licked his lips. "Again with the ew. You never came in your own mouth?"

"Not for years." Ty folded his ears back. "Anyway, it was always more gross when it was cold like that."

"It's not cold." Arch held out his paw.

Ty stared down his muzzle at it and then sleepiness and languor led him to flick his tongue out, across one of Arch's fingers, and lick away the sheen of his seed on it. It tasted like him, familiar and strong, and a little unpleasant. He licked again and then the texture got to him. "Ugh. Is that enough?"

"Sure." Arch finished cleaning his paw, then rested it again on Ty's hip. He didn't make a move to clean Ty's stomach fur, nor did he push his very hard shaft against the fox's leg.

Sleep seemed to be coming up quickly. Ty thought about reaching over to take Arch's shaft, but he'd have to reach across his sticky stomach, and he'd have to lift his arm, and it was far too heavy for that. So he rested his muzzle across the wolf's and pulled him closer with his arm, and Arch snuggled into his side.

Chapter 7

Morning arrived with the blare of the iPhone's alarm, and traffic noises when Ty's paw found the phone and turned it off. He and Arch had drifted apart in the night, but at the noise, the wolf yawned and stretched beside him. "Morning," Ty said.

"Hey." Arch gazed steadily at him. "You're not freaking out."

Ty shook his head. "Should I?"

"I dunno. First gay sex, right?"

The fox shrugged. "If I freaked out, I'd have gone last night." He leaned closer and breathed in Arch's scent, mingled with the fur shampoo from the hotel. "I still like you, and I like dancing with you and getting high and watching dumb movies, and flirting with photos I guess, and now I know one more thing I like doing."

"Okay." The wolf grinned. "How much time do we have before your car?"

"Half an hour." He scratched at his dry, matted stomach fur. "Got to rinse this off though."

"Hm." Arch scooted closer. "If I'm going to make good on my promise, I'll have to be fast, then."

His paw slid under the covers toward Ty and encountered the fox's side, brushing down his side, smoothing the fur. "If you're ready," he said, and then, as his claws brushed Ty's morning erection, he grinned. "Oh, you are."

Ty leaned over to lick the wolf's ears. His body thrummed with anticipation and the memory of Arch's skilled muzzle the night before. The wolf didn't disappoint him, diving under the covers and going to work quickly. Ty closed his eyes, and within moments he was shuddering, coming into Arch's warm muzzle while the wolf's paw squeezed his knot gently.

He lay back gasping as Arch raised his head and the sheet with it. "Mm, you've still got twenty-some minutes to shower," the wolf said, and licked his lips.

Ty stared down his chest and stomach at his erection. "Plenty of time." His eyes slid over to Arch's underside, where the wolf's erection hung heavily below his hips. He reached up with a paw, his claws barely able to brush it.

"Let me get the lube," Arch murmured. "It'll go faster." He moved obligingly closer anyway, letting Ty get his paw around the stiff cock.

Ty rubbed gently. "What if I put it somewhere else?" He tugged until Arch scooted up, but with his hips still a foot away from Ty's muzzle, the wolf looked down and stopped.

"I mean it." Ty pulled again, and the wolf grinned.

"I know. But you don't have time to blow me properly, and I don't want you to do a half-assed job your first time."

"My first time is the best time to do a half-assed job."

Arch laughed. "You have eighteen minutes."

"So?" Ty raised his eyebrows. "How long does it take you to come? Four minutes? Five? I can get rinsed and dressed in ten." The wolf still hesitated, so Ty said, "At least let me give it a few licks to get used to it."

"All right, all right." Arch straddled Ty and moved forward. "Can't believe I'm arguing so much about getting a blow job."

Ty grinned and held the wolf's tip to his nose. A small bead of pre formed at the tip, and that almost put him off. Then he told himself, Come on, Arch just swallowed a whole load of yours, and before he could second-guess himself, he leaned forward and closed his lips around it.

The musky, lupine taste wasn't unpleasant, just weird. Ty stopped thinking about it and licked it the way he used to lick himself, back before he could get other people to do that for him. The weird part was not feeling it when he moved the cock through his lips. He could imagine it, though, and when he glanced up and saw Arch swaying above him, dancing almost, he could really put himself in the wolf's place. Having just had a pretty good orgasm, it pleased him to be able to return the favor.

And Arch was happy to make it easier for him, pushing with his hips, but not too hard. "Mmm," he said after a moment. "Okay, maybe...maybe you do have time...uh...I'll tell you when I'm close."

"Nn-hnn," Ty responded.

"Which will be...in a minute...you don't have to take it...in your mouth..."

If Arch could do it, Ty could do it. But then he imagined himself talking with Rodo and Vonni and those guys and the stuff they'd said about Dev—"You think he lets his boyfriend come in his mouth?" "I could never fuckin' do that."—and for a moment his resolve faltered.

But what else was he going to do? Let the wolf come on his chest? In his paw? He didn't have time to clean up that much. He didn't have to swallow, after all.

And then Arch gripped his shoulder and said, "Unh…close…" And it was too late to do anything else.

The wolf tried to pull away, but Ty gripped his hips and butt and pulled him closer. Arch's paws left his shoulder and slammed into the wall as the wolf gave in, and his squirming orgasm felt remarkably to Ty like any female he'd gotten off, with the rather significant difference that the wolf's cock spurted fluid into his muzzle.

Not a lot, though, and Ty easily held it in his muzzle while Arch finished, panting, and leaned over him. "Okay," the wolf said, and leaned down to nuzzle between Ty's ears. "Go spit and clean up. You've got thirteen minutes."

"Mmmf," Ty nodded to him and smiled, heading for the bathroom.

Ten minutes later, fully dressed, Ty grabbed the naked wolf and hugged him. "I'll be in touch. For sure."

"Okay." Arch touched noses and then pushed Ty away. "Go. You've got three minutes!"

Ty laughed. He picked up his phone. "They'll call me, I'll say I'm on my way down, it'll be fine. Have a safe trip back home."

In the car, he picked up a bottle of water from the side of the door and cracked the top, gulping down a few swallows. The taste of musk lingered in the corners of his mouth. He found he didn't mind it so much.

•

On the plane, he kept thinking back to that morning. Rodo gave him a rundown of what Strike had said, something about how if someone with experience had had their paws on the ball at the end of the game blah blah blah, and Ty laughed it off. "Did you expect anything else?" Rodo snorted and punched the fox's shoulder. Ty punched him back and they discussed the offseason again.

When Dev boarded, the big tiger sat behind him and they talked about being on rookie contracts, about keeping the team together, which they both knew was futile but pretended it wasn't, and all the while Ty kept wanting to tell him, *Hey, I fucked a guy last night and blew him this morning. How do you get the taste of come out of your mouth?*

It was a symbolic question because they all had beers and he could no longer taste Arch. And anyway, Rodo was right there and what would he think? And Charm, Dev's friend, and all the other guys. It wasn't any of their business and wouldn't ever be.

Dev could bring Lee to events and have him meet people, but Ty wasn't ever going to have Arch—or any guy—as a permanent partner. Maybe when he and Dev had some time together, and had a few drinks, he might confess his adventure (maybe plural adventures by that time); maybe if Kellen pressed him, or Paul, he'd tell one of them (with the proviso that nothing like that would happen between them, of course; he couldn't think of his friends in that way any more than he thought of his teammates in that way). But for the moment it was his secret and he only let it show in the slight widening of his smile, an extra wag in his tail.

So he chatted warmly, comfortable in the embrace of his teammates, and before he knew it they were landing and walking out into cheers. His muscles tensed and his fur rose, waiting for the cheers to die down when they saw him, the one who couldn't get the ball to the end zone at the end. But when he emerged, they cheered even louder, they called his name, and his fur settled and a brilliant smile bloomed on his muzzle as he waved to them. Dev had a cub come up to him and thank him for coming out, and that was a sweet moment, and there was a banner on the wall of the terminal that Ty went and signed his name to.

Cars waited outside the terminal, and people got into them and left, not even taking one last moment with the team. Just like that, they all went their separate ways. A few had wives and partners waiting for them; most simply got into their own cars. Kellen and Paul and Kimi and even Morshin were flying back to Chevali that afternoon, so Ty got in his car alone and drove back to his big empty house.

He texted Kellen, but the swift fox didn't respond. Paul didn't respond either; they were likely on the plane. So Ty texted Arch: *Thanks for last night. And this morning.*

The wolf responded quickly. *Thank you too. :) You feeling better?*

About the sex or the game?

Were you feeling bad about the sex?

No.

Then the game, fox. :)

Ty grinned at the phone and reclined in his couch. *Yeah*, he typed. *I am. Thanks.*

Anytime you lose a championship, I'll be there for you to fuck, Arch typed back.

I hope other times too, because I'd hate to never fuck you again.

Ty didn't even think about the words as he typed them. He just knew he'd liked the sex and he couldn't imagine getting up the nerve to try to meet another gay guy who'd understand his situation. Anyway, if he slept with two guys, that was more significant than one, wasn't it? And he hadn't done everything with Arch, not yet. He wondered about taking it up the tail. He'd never really played with himself that way, and yet Arch had really gotten into it. But Dev had said he was on top like it was an either/or thing, not both, so maybe Ty didn't have to do everything.

Arch still hadn't answered, so Ty started up FBA '09 and lost himself in the meaningless games on the screen. There when the crowd moaned their disappointment at a loss, he could shut the game off and they'd be gone.

But when he won, it was the same thing: they lasted only as long as he kept the game going. He shut it off and stared at the TV, and then laughed at himself. Fucking philosophical thoughts. That's what happened when he had too much time by himself.

As if on cue, his phone buzzed to life. Kellen, then Paul, both telling him they'd landed and were on their way home. Ty's ears and spirits perked up, and by the time they got home, he was kicking back with his feet up on the coffee table and a beer in his paw, watching *Boompocalypse 2* on the 60-inch plasma.

"Boom boom," Kellen said as he walked in. The others filed in silently behind him.

"Yup." Ty got up and clasped paws with all of them.

They murmured things like "you were great," and "fuckin' Sabretooths," and Ty held up a paw.

"I appreciate it," he said, "but you guys have an idea why Shitsplosion 2 is on instead of SportsCenter?"

That broke the tension. Kellen laughed and said, "Hang on, I'll get everyone a beer."

They sat around and watched the goddamn explosions and Ty asked what they did in Crystal City and they told him about the restaurants and the stores and the beach, and when they asked what he did ("besides, you know," Paul said with flattened ears), he said, "Went to a club with the guys one night, got drunk and passed out in the hotel one night."

In the middle of it, his parents called. Ty saw the number and said, "Hang on guys," as he walked out of the expansive living room through the kitchen and out onto the back patio into the cool Chevali evening.

He took a breath to prepare himself for platitudes and reassurances about the game, but his mother started by asking, "What time are you coming in tomorrow?"

He'd already told her at least three times, but she wasn't asking because she didn't know the time. "Around nine, but it's okay, I'll take a car from the airport."

"We'll pick you up. When exactly are you landing? What's your flight?"

"I've already reserved a car, Mom," he lied. "It's fine, I'll be home around ten."

"You don't have to spend the money…"

Family picked you up at the airport: this was one of Mom's dictums. The only way to win this argument was to repeat, "I've reserved the car, it's fine," over and over, through her question about whether he could cancel the reservation, then how much money he was spending, then about what would happen if his flight was late. Finally she moved on to warning him about the two areas of construction between the airport and their house, and the places where his father had seen speed traps, and he repeated them back to her so she could be sure he'd understood them. Then, finally, she got to why she'd called.

"Make sure you pack that suit you wore to your press conference," she said. "Not the one yesterday, the one where you were introduced to the team. I scheduled a dinner for you every night this week. There was one for tomorrow night, but you're getting in too late, so don't worry about it. I'll reschedule for Sunday night. Also on Thursday there's a visit to the Children's Hospital, and on Friday morning we're meeting with a lawyer to talk about setting up your foundation."

He leaned back against the stone of his house wall, ears perked to the sounds of the movie inside and his friends talking, and to the sounds of the Chevali evening around him. "Great," he said. "Nothing Wednesday?"

"Nori is coming to visit and I was going to make sushi. Your cousin Mattieu started college this year and your Aunt Brigitte wants you to talk to him about applying himself. He isn't very disciplined."

Mattieu, named for his Gallic grandfather, was a scrawny fox whom Ty remembered for the last few years being mostly drunk or stoned. It wasn't much surprise that he wasn't doing so well in his first year of college, and even less surprise that his mother had criticized his lack of discipline. Had Kendo been her younger brother and not his father's, this marriage to a non-Yamatese hot-blooded un-*disciplined* vixen would never have happened, and whatever imaginary cousin they would be entertaining this weekend would certainly have been top of his class. "Sure," he said. "Will Uncle Lucas be there?"

"Of course he will. Now, I thought you could talk to Mat about that time your second year in college when you were failing your English class and you studied hard and got your grades up."

"Uh, yeah. What about when I was benched my freshman year and came back and practiced hard?"

"He doesn't play sports."

"No." The thing about that English class was that the coach had gotten him a tutor who basically wrote the paper that got him a passing grade. Not one of Ty's prouder moments. "But sports lessons are applicable to life. That's why they're so universal."

"Not everyone understands sports."

You don't have to remind me, he thought. And then Kellen called out, "Hey Ty, get in to see this part!"

"Mom, I gotta go," Ty said. "I'll see you tomorrow, okay?"

"I'll email you an update on the construction. They might be done by the time you land, but you should still be careful. And we might get rain tomorrow, though it shouldn't get down to freezing."

"Bye, Mom."

She said good-bye and Ty clicked the phone off with an exhalation that left him sagging against the wall, his tail uncurling and hanging limp. He slid the phone into his pocket and went inside to watch the rest of the movie.

In retrospect, he was kind of a dick that night, forcing everyone to watch another shitty action movie when Kellen clearly wanted to go out; when Paul tried to go upstairs to study, Ty said, "Fine, I guess I'll see you again when I get back from home in two weeks," and the other fox slunk back down the stairs to the corner of the couch and stayed there with his tail curled around his knees.

Morshin didn't care where they were drinking as long as there was beer, and Kellen and Kimi tried to keep the conversation going. "Send us a capsule of each one of the prospective wives, like last time," Kimi said, and Ty said he would. Morshin said he better pick a wife this time because otherwise people would start saying he was gay like his teammate, and Kellen asked if his mother had sent him a by-the-hour weather update this time and Ty said she hadn't. The otter and swift fox rather determinedly dragged Ty along through one painful conversation after another.

Until Morshin got drunk enough that he forgot they weren't talking about the game, and he pointed at Ty, belched, and said loudly, "Hey, fuck the fuckin' Sabretooths, right? Don't let them ruin tonight. Don't let them ruin…this fuckin' year was awesome, fox, you're awesome, and it don't matter if those bunch of cocksucker buttlickers came out like one point ahead or whatever because you are awesome."

At which point Kellen shut him up and started to say something to Ty, but Ty cut him off. "You ever licked someone's butt?" he asked the drunk goat.

"There was this sheep…" Morshin laughed. "No fuckin' way."

"Then don't knock it. And one of my teammates is a cocksucker, so just shut the fuck up with the gay shit, okay?"

They all stared, and then Kimi said, "Shit, sorry, Ty."

"It's not…" Morshin belched again. "I'm not, like…look, he's cool, just don't…" He set his beer bottle down and stumbled toward Ty and then back to the couch. "You should…you should drink more."

"Yeah." That was where Ty stood and walked up the stairs, pausing halfway to tell them to clean up the beer bottles.

He lay in his room, a huge king bed surrounded by dirty clothes and football posters, plaques from his college career and a nice display case with his six game balls, five from college and one from this past year. Room for more, he thought, and stared at the empty space.

What the fuck would his life be like if he got married? Would his wife want to live in a house with his college buddies? Or would he leave this house to them? Not all of them, obviously. Paul would be the most responsible, but Kellen was still his closest friend, and Kimi had actually been a great guy this past year. Morshin, who'd been so much fun to get drunk with in college, was not making the transition to adult life as well.

Shit, he could buy another house. He could buy a house a block away and come visit the guys whenever he wanted. Maybe his wife would stay in Pelagia and it wouldn't matter who the fuck he married.

Maybe Arch would want to move down here.

Nah. Ty waved the thought away. He wouldn't want to be taken away from all his friends and the clubs and Korsat Street and all that. He certainly wouldn't do it for Ty. Just because he'd been Ty's first didn't mean anything. To Arch, Ty was desirable not because he was a star, but because he was unusual, not part of the "scene." If he took Arch out of the scene, then Arch would miss it and things would be all different and the few times Ty wanted to dance or sleep with him, well, that wasn't a life Ty would pick.

He closed his eyes and sighed. He ought to get ready for bed, to undress and brush his teeth and everything, but he was just too tired.

CHAPTER 8

He got about three minutes with Uncle Lucas on Wednesday. Ty was adjusting the uncomfortable collar of his shirt and wondering how long he had to wait before taking off the thick warm sport coat when Lucas, almost Ty's height but wearing a much better fitted shirt and coat, strode up to him. "Great game," the older fox said, clasping Ty's arm and pulling him into a hug. "So proud of you."

"Yeah—"

"And don't you go griping that you lost. You played your heart out, that's what matters."

Warmth in his chest forced a grin up to Ty's muzzle. "Okay. Thanks."

His uncle's muzzle brushed his ear. "Also you beat the spread and I won enough to get a new bike. Don't tell your mom."

Ty laughed and replied in the same low whisper, his muzzle against his uncle's tall black ear. "She doesn't keep track of your bikes. Don't worry."

"She notices. I'll tell her I got a good annual bonus at work." Lucas pulled back with a grin that showed off his missing left canine tooth.

"Sheesh. Oh, speaking of." Ty released his uncle's paw and beckoned him over to his bag. "I got something for you."

Lucas followed him and when Ty pulled out the souvenir program book, his uncle took it with reverent paws. "Wow."

"Open the cover." Ty grinned, tail wagging.

"Holy shit, Ty." Lucas stared down at the black scrawls of signatures. "Is this the whole team?"

"Nah, just most of the offense, and Dev and Gerrard and a couple of my other friends. But Aston's there," he pointed, "and Jaws, and—"

"Lightning Strike."

"Yeah, I think signature pens have a special scent that he homes in on. Couldn't keep him away."

Lucas closed the book and hugged Ty again. "This is great, thanks."

"And if you want to sell it, I'll understand," Ty said. "Your name's in there a few times, but—"

"No, no. I'm keeping this one. Until you go to the next one. And probably even then." He winked. "It's terrific, thanks."

"Ty!" His mother found them then and dragged him off to sit with Matthieu over warm cups of futsu-mushi sencha green tea, whose fragrance filled the room.

Ty tried dutifully to tell Matthieu his story, but his cousin sat with his ears at different angles and stared past Ty, though at least he was listening. He said, "Uh-huh," in all the right places and at the end of it said, "Thanks, Ty, that's helpful."

"So," Ty said, "did you watch the big game?"

"Yeah." Matthieu's eyes flicked back to him with a bit of interest. "You did pretty good, I guess. The announcers said nice things about you, anyway."

"Thanks."

"Did you see the commercials? There was this one directed by Ernst Zwift."

Ty blinked. "No, we were pretty focused on the game."

"I know, but it's on YouTube now…" Mat shrugged.

"Who's Ernst Zwift?"

The younger fox's eyes bugged out. "Are you serious? *Furless Dawn*? *All That The World Must Lose*?"

Ty shook his head. "Movies? I don't get to see movies very much during the season." He briefly considered telling Mat about the dragon movie he'd watched with Arch. Probably not a great idea.

"Oh, you gotta see *All That The World*, it's so brilliant. It's like this post-apocalyptic drama where all the world's been devastated by a plague and the only survivors are on an island and there's only six species left: there's tribes of fox, wolf, white-tail, rabbit, rat, and this one guy who says he's a ringtail but it turns out later he's a lemur—anyway, they're talking about all the different species that are gone now and some of them want to remember the species by taking on their traits and some want to go find other survivors." He shook his head. "It's beautiful."

"Okay." Ty nodded. "I'll look it up."

Turning the conversation to movies kept him barely engaged. Matthieu liked horror, but not what he scornfully called "slasher-gore bullshit." "Anyone can dump gallons of corn syrup around a set," he said. "Real horror makes you *think*."

"I don't want to watch a movie to think," Ty said, maybe too honestly.

But as hard as he'd tried to convince Matthieu to study, his cousin now tried to convince him to open his mind to the beauty of literate cinema, as he called it. Ty knew it better as "pretentious art-house crap," but he kept that opinion to himself.

There were more cousins, Matthieu's mother, Ty's own parents, as though he wasn't going to see them enough, his sisters, and then finally he got a little more time with Lucas, sitting out on the back deck while his uncle smoked a cigar.

Lucas indicated Ty's beer bottle. "You should drink wine, not beer. Better for your heart."

"I like beer, and I'm sick of tea."

"I'll send you a case of wine. Collect, of course."

Ty laughed. "Go ahead. I've got a goat in my house who'll drink whatever I don't."

"I'm serious," Lucas said. "Beer is fine for college students, but you're out of school now and when you and your new wife entertain, you're not going to have coolers of beer. Maybe for your teammates, but the people backing this foundation you're doing, some of the upper manager types, those guys drink wine."

"All right."

"And you're going to want to impress them. You could be in this league a long time. You could write your name in the books."

"I'll do my best."

They were quiet for a moment, and then Lucas said, "So if I send you wine, does that move me up on the house list?"

Ty laughed. "You're already second. You want to get ahead of Mom and Dad?"

"Did they watch the championship?"

"Of course. Mom gave me the Yamatese kappa story." He rolled his eyes, fleetingly annoyed all over again.

"Ah, the Yamatese." Lucas cast a sharp eye at him.

"I know, I know," Ty said. "I'm a sport."

"You're a good sport."

The joke completed, they chuckled together and watched the sun crawl down the cloud bank. "Mom and Dad keep saying they don't need a new house," Ty said.

"I'm inclined to agree with them."

"So you might move up the list anyway. But I still feel like I have to buy them one."

"Dutiful son. You're at least that Yamatese."

Ty stared down at his paws. "I hope I'm Yamatese enough to get through these dinners."

Lucas elbowed him. "Ask your friends how terrible it is to have people go find a bunch of beautiful vixens for you to go on dates with."

"Not really dates." Ty leaned back. "More like auditions or something."

"Whatever. There's a bunch of them, right? One of them is sure to be nice, and your parents won't care as long as she's one of their choices. Then you can have a nice wedding and stop worrying about that." Lucas puffed on his cigar. "Take it from an old bachelor who would've liked to have that settled a long time ago."

The wedding would be nice. Even over the cigar smoke, Ty smelled the tea and the scent of family. This was a place he belonged, and soon he'd meet a vixen and he'd get to introduce her to his family and their customs, and then they'd have cubs. He'd moved up in the world, so this group had to be better than the last bunch. Right?

(It didn't even matter that much; this wasn't going to be his whole life. Like his teammates, he could "have fun" when he was on the road, if he wanted.)

"Thanks," he said to his uncle, his tail uncurling. "I guess I should try to look at the bright side of this."

That was as peaceful as Ty felt before his parents called them all in for the tea ceremony.

•

To: Kellen Grindle, more…
From: Ty Nakamura
Subject: First evening

Okay, guys, the first one was actually pretty innocuous. Her name was Shizuko and she didn't say a word. I mean that almost literally. Her father accompanied her to the dinner, and he ordered for her, and he answered every question I asked while she sat there with her head bowed.

My parents loved it at first: so proper, so demure! Exactly what a Yamatese vixen should be! But by the end of the meal, Mom was trying to get her to talk, and we did get her to say three words, in Yamatese, which Mom said were, "I am most honored," but Dad thought might have been, "I am very tired."

On the way home, Mom said, "I liked her," and neither Dad nor I said anything. But all in all, still not cracking the top two worst dinners.

Miss you guys. Stay out of trouble. Don't break anything in the house.

Ty

•

To: Kellen Grindle, more…
From: Ty Nakamura
Subj: Dinner number two

Okay, this one is a lot more entertaining. First I have to tell you what kind of restaurant we went to. Shigeko's is very traditional, a sit-cross-legged-on-bamboo-mats, hot sake, proper tea service kind of place. Well, Keiko and her mother were already sitting down when we arrived—that's a no-no, first of all, because we're all supposed to sit at the same time.

Then Keiko tried to get up to meet us, and her mother had to grab her wrist and pull her back down, and she bumped the table and spilled the tea. She didn't seem mortified at all, though.

She was enthusiastic about everything. She complimented my clothes, my parents' clothes, my mother's jewelry, my mother's Yamatese, my fur (when I took her paw), the tea, the sushi, the feel of the chopsticks, the scent of the restaurant, the scent of the hostess, the color of the plates…and so on and so on. Mom even brought up our championship game loss (thanks, Mom) toward the end of the evening, and she told me something like, "I'm sure you played as hard as you could and it's just wonderful that you're a professional ball player. It's so hard, I can't imagine how you do it, you must be the most wonderful athlete."

As you may imagine, Mom was not very pleased with her. We tried to talk about her prospects and her interests, but anything we mentioned was the most wonderful idea, the most fabulous adventure. As best I can tell, she loves to sing, study chemistry, sew, drive motorcycles, sail small craft, travel the world, feed homeless people and animals, bake cookies, dance (ballroom and rave), play video games (but not the violent ones where people die because that makes her sad), write letters to her political representatives (I can only imagine), and let me see, I feel like I'm forgetting something…oh yes, she also writes reviews of girls' magazines on a blog.

The thing is, I get the feeling that she actually has the energy and enthusiasm to do all those things. She primarily wants a husband who can afford them and who will give her pretty cubs to sweep up into her whirlwind life, I think; at any rate, nothing I said seemed to dissuade her. Being away from home nine months out of the year, being physically beaten up every week, the uncertainty of where we'll live from year to year, all of that was exciting or an adventure or an obstacle to surmount.

Mom and Dad and I didn't talk all the way home. We were all exhausted.

Miss you guys,

Ty

•

To: Kellen Grindle, more…
From: Ty Nakamura
Subj: Three down

Friday nights are supposed to be fun, right?

I met Hideyo tonight and her parents. She's a short vixen, shorter even than Mom and Dad, and when we were introduced I thought, If I ever propose to her I'm going to have to lie on the floor.

But she was nice enough. Her father worked with Dad at Boeing five or six years ago, and she's only seventeen, but she's pretty sharp. She reads more than I do and she's never seen the Boompocalypse movies, but you know, that's not a deal-breaker. At this point I was thinking that I just wanted to find someone semi-decent to get this whole ordeal over with. If the parents like her, I can sleep with her enough to have a family, I can put her up in a house and she can even have a boyfriend if she wants, and we'd be fine, right?

Hideyo seemed like she might be on board with that. She was applying to colleges, so even before I got to say that I'd be on the road a lot, she was telling me that she'd be attending a college that wouldn't be in Chevali, so we'd be apart for four years while she got her education degree. She talked about all the cubs she wants to have, and Mom perked right up at that.

The problem came when she started asking me about myself. She asked what I'd majored in, and I told her I never actually finished my Communications Degree. Mom pointed out that I was making a better salary than any of my classmates, and Hideyo said, but what about after football? I said that I would make more in a short career in football than she would make in a lifetime.

Everything was awkward after that. She got a little snippy and said she'd be improving lives, and I didn't say anything to that because Mom kicked me under the table. But not talking wasn't any better, because then she thought I was judging her. Even when we told her about Mom's foundation, she kept asking me questions about it and Mom kept answering them, so she figured I didn't actually care about the kids. I tried to explain how busy I was, but by that point she was letting us know that football players didn't really work, we were all paid for playing a game, you know. So I finally told her off, told her how hard we work, but of course it didn't impress her. Needless to say, it ended badly and by the time we were putting on our jackets, our fathers were the only ones talking.

I'm supposed to go to another dinner tomorrow, but I'm tired of this. If you don't get another letter from me, then I bailed.

Ty

CHAPTER 9

He'd gotten into the habit of hunching while in public spaces like at the airport. When he stood up straight, his ears stuck up over a crowd and people noticed him and came over to ask for autographs, or sometimes to harass him, if it was cities he'd recently beaten.

Pelagia's airport wasn't so bad, and Ty reclined in first class for the hour and a half flight down to Yerba. But when he got out, a red fox cub who'd been on the plane and must have been watching him the whole flight came running over to him and said, "You were in the championship! You lost!"

His parents came over and apologized, but Ty had to admit who he was, and then more people came over and there were autographs and smiles and it was nice, but over it all hung questions like, "What was the difference?" and "Came up a little bit short, huh?" They were well-meaning; nobody here was a Crystal City fan and they'd been rooting for Chevali, but still it was wearing. When he finally broke free after the last autograph, he darted through the crowd to get to the outside, where he sucked in lungsful of the chilly, humid air, the sun already low in the afternoon sky.

Landed, he texted Arch as he waited in line for a taxi. When his turn came, he got into a standard, unremarkable sedan from Mission Point Cabs. The driver, a pangolin, had scales that made clicking noises as he turned. "Where are you going please?"

"Uh. The Six Stars Hotel?" That was one of the chains the team booked frequently, and Ty was pretty sure they'd stayed in one in Yerba.

The pangolin consulted his GPS. "The Six Stars Marina or the Six Stars Soldier Hill?"

Neither of those sounded familiar. "Marina," Ty said, just as Arch texted him.

What hotel are you staying at? the wolf asked.

Six Stars Marina, Ty replied, and leaned back.

This was definitely not the hotel the team had stayed at, but it did have a nice ocean view—bay view, the hotel clerk corrected him—and though they'd initially said they were full, Ty said he would be happy to take a suite if that's all that was available, and the rabbit behind the counter, her eye on the hundred dollar bill casually resting under Ty's paw, booked him right there and gave him the key.

Ford had taught him that trick before being traded away to Port City. Ty hadn't realized how much he liked having the older fox around until Ford was gone. Rodo was his roommate and Dev a good friend, sure, but they were both around his age. Ford had taken the time to mentor Ty on and off, and then he'd been traded for a cheetah who had pontificated about the responsibility of wideouts and then sold out Ty when things went bad. Not an even trade from Ty's perspective, though he couldn't deny that Strike was contributing to many more Ws than Ford had. Port City had lost their first game post-trade, to the woeful Hilltown Dragons, and Ford had sent him a bitter text saying, *Hell is frozen.* But Port City won their last two and were going into the offseason with some optimism, having only missed the playoffs by one game. Good for Ford. Maybe they'd meet in the playoffs sometime.

It felt like he'd barely stretched out on his bed in the top-floor one-bedroom suite when his phone buzzed again. Arch, saying, *What's your room #?*
2208, he texted back.

About five minutes later, the wolf knocked at his door. Ty opened it and smiled broadly as Arch stepped through. "Hey," the wolf said, and then his eyes rose over Ty's shoulder and his jaw remained hanging open.

Ty closed the door. "Pretty nice, huh? Their other rooms were all full. I guess it's a touristy area." His tail wagged, and he smiled at the sight of Arch's eyes and the wolf's expression.

"You, uh." Arch cleared his throat and set the small paper bag he was carrying down on the counter. "You have a bar. And a chandelier."

"And check out the view." Ty dragged him over to the window, where the fog was rolling in over the ocean—shit, no, the bay.

Arch slid a paw around Ty's midsection and looked out. Ty returned the embrace, steadying himself as the wolf's weight came to rest against him. "Wow, beautiful," Arch murmured. "How much does this place run a night?"

"Oh, I dunno," Ty said carelessly, and then he felt a shift in Arch's weight and remembered the wolf's annoyance at his pro athlete lifestyle. "I mean…it was like five hundred but she said there were hotel fees and tax on top of that."

"That's not too bad for a suite."

"I'm a rewards member." Another thing Ford had taught him. Ty grinned at their reflections in the glass. "What'd you bring?"

The wolf's glance flicked up at him. "Just some stuff. In case you want to, y'know." He sighed and his tail brushed Ty's leg. "I'd love to just stay here with you all night and look out at this."

"Well, I want to go dancing."

"Sure," Arch said. "Korsat's about fifteen minutes away by cab."

"Cool. Sorry I couldn't get here earlier. I was trying to get out first thing in the morning, but couldn't get away from the family, and then the first flight I tried to get on was full."

"Couldn't buy your way on?" Arch's smile broadened. "What was going on with the family?"

"Oh…" Ty sighed. "Parade of wife candidates. They were all terrible."

"How terrible?"

"Nice people, I mean. One of them was giving me a hard time about being a professional athlete, and one was super chirpy and excited about everything, and one was so quiet I thought she had laryngitis for the first hour of the dinner. And my parents were at dinner with all of us, and at least one of the vixen's parents too."

"Were they attractive?"

Arch's smile had faded into more earnest interest. "Yeah," the fox said, "two of them were hot. The other was pretty, at least. But I can't just sleep with them. I have to live with them, too."

"Not most of the time. Didn't you say you're on the road a lot?"

Ty leaned down and brushed his muzzle against Arch's ear. "You're hot, too."

The wolf squeezed. "I wasn't fishing for a compliment."

"I know. But I came down here to get away from them. So I'd rather not talk about them. How was work?"

"Work's work." Arch waved a paw and returned his attention to the fog and the ocean. "It doesn't change much."

"All right." Ty grinned. "Let's go dancing."

The wolf didn't turn back toward the door when Ty did. "You okay?" Ty put a paw on his shoulder.

Arch's breath fogged the window as he leaned his nose closer to it. "Yeah. I mean, this is cool and all and I want to go dancing, but I feel like I should ask…you going to want me to come back here with you after? You didn't really answer, before."

"Sure." Ty set his shoulder against the glass and looked at the wolf's profile. "That okay?"

"Course." Arch's tail wagged once, then fell still. "Okay, okay. I just wanted to know if this was a dance call or a booty call."

"Both." Ty leaned closer. "You're free to say no if you're busy."

"It's not that." The wolf grinned. "We just haven't been texting much since we slept together and I wasn't sure how you felt about it."

"I was home," Ty said. "Sorry about that. No, I'm fine."

"Okay."

He wanted to kiss Arch to reassure him, but as he decided to do that, the wolf turned and said, "All right, did you eat?"

Ty hadn't, so Arch took him to a small Middle Eastern place and they had kebabs and curry with pita bread. The conversation was fun, easy, and relaxed, but in the back of Ty's mind he kept seeing Arch's uncertainty.

Of course the wolf knew that this relationship couldn't go anywhere. He and Ty could hook up, and maybe they'd both end up with open relationships that would allow that, or else maybe they'd both feel okay cheating on their significant others. Ty at least wouldn't feel that bad about cheating on his arranged spouse. Women who married athletes knew that came with the territory, and it was the athlete's job to be safe, not pick up diseases or leave behind cubs. A lot of guys Ty knew didn't believe that freedom went both ways—one of his college teammates had gotten in trouble with the cops because he hit his girlfriend when he found out she slept with a lacrosse player (and if Ty hadn't already known the guy was an asshole, hitting his girlfriend would've clinched that). But as far as Ty was concerned, if his future wife didn't pick up any diseases or have someone else's cub, she was free to fuck around as much as she liked.

At The Floor, there wasn't much of a line, but Ty walked up to the door anyway and said, "Hi, Ty Nakamura, Chevali Firebirds. I think I'm on the list," and even as Arch grabbed at his sleeve, the big cougar at the door told them to go ahead in.

Ty flashed a grin back at Arch and the wolf grinned back, shaking his head. "Fucking athletes," he said, and Ty grabbed his paw and pulled him out onto the dance floor.

The music pounded through him, driving his legs and arms to match the rhythm while Arch did the same. Stress flew away as though Ty were shaking it off with the dance, and after just a minute or two, he'd relaxed into a happy smile.

A bit later, over the wolf's shoulder, Ty saw a pair of male cheetahs kissing, and he remembered Arch's uncertainty. He pulled the wolf close by his cheek ruffs and planted a warm kiss on his lips.

Arch stiffened and then returned the kiss, resting his paws on Ty's hips. After their muzzles parted, his eyes searched the fox's. "What was that for?"

"Because you're a good dancer. Because you dropped everything to come out with me tonight."

"It's not like I had other plans." The wolf smiled.

"Yeah, but…" Ty sighed. The thing about Arch was that he wasn't impressed with Ty's job, with his performance on TV, with anything but the fox himself. And Ty was happy to be the wolf's friend, but he also knew Arch was looking for more than a friend, was looking for a lover and companion, while Ty was pretty much looking for someone to dance, sleep, and joke with. Right now those searches were aligned. They wouldn't always be.

He draped his arm across the wolf's shoulder. "Let's take a break."

They turned toward the bar. Ty scanned the crowd absently as they walked toward it, and his attention settled on a big tiger who was staring at him. He put on his automatic public-places smile, but then he recognized the tiger and the fox sitting beside him. "Ah, shit," he said.

"What?" Arch followed his gaze. "That guy? Don't worry, just tell him you're not interested."

"I…don't think that'll work." Ty wanted to laugh. What were the odds? Pretty good, considering this was the place Dev's boyfriend had taken them both. If they were both in town at the same time, it made sense they'd go back here too. He hadn't even thought about that, hadn't worried that someone else might come back, because which of the Firebirds would be in Yerba this week? Everyone was at home, which for most of the guys was Chevali.

Arch nudged him. "You know him?"

"He's one of my teammates. The tiger who was here with me the night we met? The gay one with the boyfriend?"

"Oh." Arch's eyes widened. "Oh. Miski, right? And he didn't know—"

"Nope."

"But he does now?"

"I'm assuming he saw me kiss you, so yeah." Ty took a breath. "All right, let's head over there."

He kept his eyes on Dev to let the big tiger know he was coming, because he could see Dev tense and figured if he bolted for the exit, there'd be a movie-worthy chase scene. Arch's figure and scent and movement accompanied Ty, reminding the fox of how amazingly awkward this whole thing was. He could claim to be drunk. Or he could claim to have done it on a bet.

But no, Dev deserved the truth. And as he got closer and could make out the tiger's puzzlement and hurt, Ty felt even worse about not having told his teammate right away. Wouldn't Dev have been happy to know?

So he played it casual and cool. He grinned as he got up next to Dev and reached out to clasp the big tiger's arm. "Hey, Dev."

" 'Hey, Dev'? That's it?" Dev gripped him back and then released him, still glaring. "What the fuck is—"

Ty cleared his throat and reached over to shake Lee's paw. "Lee, good to see you again. This is Arch."

Arch shook paws while Dev said, "Ty—Come on—"

"Okay, sorry," Ty said, and held up a paw. "Do you mind if me and Arch get a couple beers, and then I'll tell you all about it?"

"That'd be fine." Lee put a paw on Dev's arm.

Dev kept staring at Ty, and then turned to Lee. "Fine," he grumbled. "We'll be over there." He pointed to an empty table and marched off toward it.

"Pyramid Hefeweizen," Arch told the bartender, and then turned to Ty. "What do you want? You doing okay?"

Ty tracked Dev and Lee over to the table they'd indicated. "Yeah, I think so. Uh, same as you." His stomach still buzzed, but it wasn't bad. Survivable.

"Good. I thought he was going to rip your throat out when you gave him that, 'Hey, Dev.' " The wolf chuckled and rested a paw on Ty's back.

"Nah, Dev's cool." Ty gathered his glass as Arch picked up his. "I guess, well, you know. I mean, what if one of your best friends suddenly turned up at this club kissing another guy?"

"All my best friends are gay."

"Well, fine." They threaded their way through the tables. "So say you have a co-worker—that guy, what's his name, the one who invites you over all the time, Ronnie."

"You don't have to keep up the analogy. I get it." Arch smiled and walked closer to him. "He's gonna be upset because he thought he was the only gay one and now he knows you're messing around on his side and didn't even tell him."

"Something like that." Ty took a breath. "All right. Here goes."

Arch held him back with a paw on Ty's elbow. "Anything I should avoid saying?"

Ty shook his head. "Shit, I'm not worried about that. If anything, talk more. I think when he sees how cool you are, he'll get it."

At the table, nobody seemed to want to talk first, so Ty jumped in again. "Hey, Dev. Didn't know you were in town."

"We're looking for apartments for Lee." Dev still sounded angry. "I didn't know you were here, either."

"Right." Ty felt again the weight of guilt. "You won't tell anyone else on the team, will you?"

Dev's sigh fluttered against his whiskers. "I'm not here with anyone else on the team." Ty looked up at him, and the tiger said, "I won't tell them."

"Thanks." Ty exhaled, felt his chest loosen. He could talk to Dev. So he opened up about Arch, how they'd met, and how they were, you know, trying stuff.

"Trying being gay?" Dev wanted to know.

Ty still wasn't sure he was out of danger. Lee seemed very relaxed, but Lee probably couldn't hold back Dev if the tiger got really mad. "I'm not gay," he said. "Maybe a little bi. I like girls, but it turns out I don't mind doing stuff with the right guy either. Arch is pretty cool, and I haven't been, like, checking out guys or anything here."

"Oh, my fluttering heart," Arch said, and Ty kicked him under the table, making the wolf grin.

And then Dev wanted to know how long it had been going on, and Arch had to tell them about how Ty asked if Arch would blow him, and Dev still had that wary feel, though his boyfriend was smiling broadly. "I can't believe you didn't come talk to me," Dev said.

"To be fair," Ty replied, looking at the other fox, "you got a boyfriend. I figured he wouldn't be too happy if I asked *you* to blow me."

The joke was off the cuff, but it worked. Lee giggled, and when Dev didn't, Ty leaned in. "It's a joke." The tiger still didn't react. "Hey, seriously, look, I'm sorry, but you were—we were all up to our fuckin' ears in playoff shit and I figured I'd sort it out myself and then I promise I was gonna come talk to you about it. I mean, I can't really talk to the other guys about this nice piece of ass I found if there's a cock on the other side of it, right?"

Arch folded his arms at that and said, "Oh, is that how it is? Maybe I'll go back to my own place tonight."

"Yeah, maybe," Ty said, not too worried because the wolf's foot was rubbing his leg under the table. "Until I remind you about the fluffy robes and the bread pudding and the view at the hotel."

"God dammit." Arch turned to Lee. "Rich guys, what the fuck are you gonna do?"

So Arch and Lee went off to chat about gay guy stuff, or maybe football-player-boyfriend stuff, and Ty was left alone with Dev. The tiger wasn't talking, so Ty took a breath and dove in. "I promise I would've come to talk to you," he said again. "I was actually thinking that when I get through with all the shit happening with the folks that I should look you up in Chevali. This all happened kinda fast."

"Over months," Dev growled.

"Yeah, but…" Ty replayed the memories in his head and grinned. "At first it was just teasing around. I hung out with him, he was cool, and I said, 'so would you do me?' And he was all coy about it. He's not really impressed with football at all. So I kept texting, and he texted back, and it was fun, like this little secret life. We exchanged blow job pics, you know? And then after that game, that fucking game, I didn't want to be around anyone from the team."

"Being around the team helped, sort of." It looked like Dev was finally starting to relax. "I mean, everyone felt the same way."

"That's what Rodo said. But you know, none of them had the ball on the last play." It was getting easier to say. To his surprise, he found he could think about the game without the searing guilt now. It was another game and he'd moved on, and he'd be ready for the next one.

"I kinda fucked up toward the end, too."

"Ah." Ty brushed Dev's attempt at humility away. "You did what the coaches told you to. You sacked McCrae! You did good."

"You were fine on the plane home."

"Yeah." Ty had to look away. "Kinda wish I'd talked to you then. But… thing is, y'know, I know this can't be serious. I can't be gay like you can."

Now Dev was relaxing for sure, and maybe the beers were helping. He closed a paw around Ty's wrist. "Sure you can. I'd like to have another friend who's out."

"No, I mean—" Ty sighed. "I ever tell you about my folks?"

Dev shook his head. "I know they're Yamatese, right?"

"They came over when they were very young cubs, with their parents. Keeping that connection back to their families and their homeland is really important. Like, the most important thing. And getting me married to the right family in the right way with all the right customs around it is part of that. I can't say no."

The tiger got this serious look. "You think you can't, but my parents weren't too thrilled about me and Lee, and they've come around—"

Ty held up a paw to stop him. "I've got Christian friends. It's different. There's such a long connection stretching back hundreds of years…and beyond that, you know, I want to have a cub too. I want to do all those stupid traditions with them that my parents did with me. We have rituals for New Years, a special tea we drink on birthdays. It's terrible, but…it's birthday tea. When you get to drink it, you feel…" He spread his paws. "Great. Special."

"Mmm." Dev stopped talking, and Ty hoped that meant that he got it, at least enough to stop arguing. "So…why go out with him at all? If you like girls too, I mean. Aren't you just leading him on?"

"He knows it's not serious. But…" Ty looked out to the floor of the club, at all the dancers there. His feet tapped in time to the music. "I love to dance. And I've never met anyone who can dance like he can. I just want a dance partner. Who is also willing to fuck, you know, and who's fun to hang out with…it's relaxing. With girls, the sex always has these expectations around it and with him it doesn't."

"So," Dev said, "you're on top, right?"

"Hell yeah." Where was this coming from?

"It's just…you asked me that when I came out. I was just…" The tiger waved his paws, looking all awkward.

"Oh." Ty snapped his fingers. "I did, right?" He hesitated, and then the beer and warm camaraderie of the moment loosened his tongue to something he'd barely even admitted to himself. After all, if Dev had done it, he'd be able to coach Ty a bit. "You know, to be honest, I'm wondering about that. He gets so fuckin' into it, I'm starting to wonder. You, uh…you ever?"

"I told you, no."

Whoops. Dev was still a little sensitive about who was on top. Out here in public, Ty sympathized. Letting another guy stick his dick in you felt like it would be emasculating. Only he'd done it to Arch, and if he felt like that, then that meant he felt Arch wasn't masculine. That feeling didn't ring true to him. So if Arch could take a cock and still be a guy, then why couldn't Ty? "I know you said that in the locker room, but I mean, I get it now, it's not…it's not a big thing."

"Look." Dev leaned back, paws up, defensive. "For the first year we were dating, I wasn't even sure how to do things with a guy. He had to teach me how to give a blow job. And then we only saw each other every week or two, with his schedule and mine, so we just…y'know, stuck to what works."

"Makes sense." Time to change the subject. Ty grinned. "You do suck him off, though?"

"Uh. Yeah." He was embarrassed, but he'd already admitted it.

Now Ty could make him feel better by admitting he'd done it too. He was obscurely proud of having sucked off Arch, his first time having sex with a guy, too. Well, first visit. Technically second or third time. "That was weirder than fucking him, for me. I mean, I put my own in my mouth when I was growing up, but someone else's…feels weird."

"It is. I mean, it was. It's totally natural now."

"Cool."

They rested comfortably across the table, and Dev said, "You guys want to get coffee or something later?"

"Sure." Ty took another drink and smiled. "We cool, then?"

"Yeah, sorry. It was just…I wasn't expecting it."

"Sorry. I know you were going through a lot of shit. I wish I'd been able to help more. Better late than never, though, right?"

"On the bright side, I never had a teammate I could talk to about blow jobs before."

Ty laughed. "Really? Charm didn't want to hear about them?"

"He didn't want to hear about giving them. You remember him in the club."

"Yeah. That guy. You know he wanted both waitresses?"

"Doesn't surprise me." Dev finished his beer. "Wait, so did you end up with the other one or did Zillo?"

Ty cast his mind back to that night and hesitated, not sure he wanted to share with Dev that he'd watched Zillo have sex, but he was rescued by the reappearance of Lee and Arch. "Come on," Arch said, holding out a paw. "We'll see them after. There's only another couple hours of music left."

"Yes, sir," Ty said, and saluted the fox and tiger, then let himself be dragged out to the dance floor.

They slipped back into the rhythm of the music without a word, but in the space between songs when only the beat kept driving, Arch said, "Lee's pretty cool, I guess."

"You guess?" Ty called back as the music picked up again, his feet moving along with the new melody line.

"Kinda wordy. Thinks he's pretty smart. But maybe that's a fox thing. You think you're pretty smart too."

Ty laughed. "What'd you guys talk about?"

"You, mostly. His boyfriend some."

"I hope you said nice things."

"I didn't lie." The wolf grinned at him.

"Yeah, well, I told Dev about how you sent me a picture of you blowing a guy."

Arch kept dancing with no visible reaction. A moment later, he said, "So?"

"So what?" Ty was already feeling a little regret about the remark because it didn't seem to have gone over as the joke he'd intended.

"Did he think it was gross?"

Ty lost a little of the dancing rhythm and had to pause to pick it up again. He breathed in and out and let the music carry away the snappy remark he was going to make. "We didn't really discuss it, y'know? I just said you sent me pics and I wanted to do more with you."

"So the pics were enticing?" The wolf's expression remained neutral.

"Come on," Ty said. "I told you that, didn't I?"

"No." There was a hint of a grin on the wolf's muzzle. Or was it a trick of the light?

"Well," Ty said, leaning closer, "I slept with you. I thought that sent a message."

Arch did smile at that, so maybe he'd been mollified. "They seem like a nice couple."

"Dev's cool, and I like Lee."

"Of course. He's a fox."

"It's not just that. There are some foxes I can't stand."

"Really? Are they not smug enough about their species? Do they not talk enough?"

"Some foxes are assholes. Some wolves are assholes. Some wolves are being dicks."

"You're the dick, foxy. I'm the asshole."

The dance floor was not the place to bring up his curiosity about reversing those roles, so Ty swatted the wolf's tail and then grabbed his paw and pulled him around in an improvised two-step that Arch followed along with easily.

They danced together so well, Ty thought. Dev and Lee had a relationship; he could maybe have something with Arch, like a permanent on the side thing when he was in Yerba. Sort of like a lot of the guys had a permanent on the side thing in every city—Gerrard in Hellentown and Port City (and a couple others from what Zillo'd said). It wouldn't be serious, only maybe a little more serious than he'd been treating it up to now. It'd be like having a friend you went dancing with when you were in the same town, only in addition to dancing you'd have sex after. It wasn't that big a deal. He'd be safe and he wouldn't have any other cubs to pay support for.

There was no guarantee Arch would go for it, but the guy'd come out to see Ty a couple times and hadn't blown him off (ha ha), so maybe.

Dev and Lee came over to say they were worn out and going for coffee. "Text me where you are when you get there," Ty said, because he and Arch were nowhere near done dancing.

For a while, Ty was able to set aside his prospective wives, his worry about the team, and all the questions about Arch from the far future to that very night. There was nothing but the thrum of music in his muscles, the slap of his paws on the dance floor, which he didn't even care was sticky, the beat in his ears and his bones. It was like being in a football game, better because there were no routes to run, worse because there were no touchdowns to score, no plays to complete.

And different because you could do it with just one other person.

Kimi and Kellen were great with parties, Paul and Morshin were fun to hang out with and good to talk to about his family, and all of them had been with him through college, so they knew him. But none of them could dance the way Arch could.

Also none of them would put his cock in their mouth.

Would it be so different if Arch lived with them? The wolf could do his own thing like Ty's friends did, and he and Ty would go dancing and have sex sometimes. When Ty got married, he'd work out some arrangement. There wasn't really any reason Ty couldn't have everything.

He would work that out later.

Chapter 10

They danced until they were worn out and then Ty texted Dev and found the tiger and fox at a coffee shop. Dev told Ty that Fisher was going to retire, and hinted at something else going on, but in front of Lee and Arch they weren't going to talk about it more.

They parted with promises to get together again before Dev left town. As Ty and Arch walked away down the street, Arch reached out and took the fox's paw in his.

Ty pulled it away reflexively, but when he looked down, Arch was grinning. "Lots of gay guys on the street here," he said. "Nobody's going to care."

"That's what we thought in the club." Ty glanced back to the coffee shop, but he took the wolf's paw anyway.

Arch let his paw go once they were in the cab. Ty leaned back against the headrest and let his tail flop onto the seat between the two of them. Arch's tail rested over top of his a moment later.

Back in the hotel room, Arch stopped to look out the window again. Ty shrugged off his shirt and then walked up and put his paw on Arch's back. The wolf leaned closer to Ty, and his eyes flicked to the reflection. "I feel overdressed," he murmured.

Ty rubbed at the small of the wolf's back. It was funny how some moves worked both with girls and guys. "You look sexy in that shirt," he said, wondering if some lines did, too.

Apparently so. Arch smiled and reached over to press his paw through Ty's stomach fur. Ty stood closer and breathed in the residual scent of the club, the cab, and beneath it the smell of Arch himself, the wolf—the masculine wolf, no doubting that—and thinking about taking the wolf into the bedroom was getting him hard.

"How long do you want to stay and look at the view?" he asked.

Arch grinned and slid his paw downward. Ty's pants were loose enough that the wolf's fingers got down into his boxers with ease. "A little eager, foxy?"

"A little." Ty let his own paw slide down to cup the wolf's rump. "Little warm in these clothes after all that dancing, don't you think?"

"Well, it was chilly out, but the room is warm…" Arch's paw found Ty's sheath and curled around it with a squeeze. "We could move to the bedroom."

Ty grunted and pulled the smaller wolf against him, leaning down to bite one perked ear. Arch squirmed and lifted his muzzle, and they kissed right there in front of the window.

Their clothes came away quickly after that. Ty tried to pull the naked wolf to the bedroom, but Arch twisted out of his grip and hurried to get the small paper bag he'd left on the bar counter. "Some stuff we'll need," he said, and Ty's nose caught the scent of the pharmacy as Arch rejoined him.

Both naked, both aroused, they tumbled to the bed together, Arch on his back and Ty atop him, arms around each other, bodies pressed close. Ty's tail flicked and his breath came quickly; below him, Arch made soft pleased noises and licked around Ty's collarbone.

"So what's in the bag?" Ty murmured when the urgency of his erection demanded more than just cuddling.

"What do you think?" Arch grinned up at him. "Stuff. You said you wanted to fuck me again."

"Uh-huh." Ty slid his hips down so his cock poked below the wolf's sac and thrust forward. "So…?"

Arch spread his legs and his smile grew wider. "Let me just grab that, then." He reached over to the bag and slid his paw inside. "Something for you, and…something for me."

Ty raised himself onto his elbows as the wolf shook the paper bag off of his paw. His fingers held a box of three condoms, from which he extracted one, and a small bottle marked, "CanidGlide," which he dropped onto his stomach.

While Ty rolled the condom over his shaft, Arch popped the bottle top open and squirted out lube onto his paw. He lifted his hips and pushed two fingers down under his tail, his expression settling into a blissful smile. Maybe he'd insisted Ty do it last time to get the fox used to poking around down there.

"Mmmkay," Arch said finally, and squirted a little more lube onto his paw. "Let's see that fox cock."

"You going to stay on your back?" Ty raised his hips so Arch could reach down and slicken his wrapped cock.

"We can do it this way. Trust me. Unless you don't want to look at me while you're fucking me."

The glint in the wolf's eye probably meant he was teasing. "I can always close my eyes," Ty teased back, and then stiffened as Arch squeezed him and pulled him forward. "Nnf! Okay, okay, I'll look."

The wolf laughed. "If you don't like it, I'll roll over onto all fours again. Promise."

"Let's just see." Ty positioned himself and then hesitated. "Hey, can I have some of that?"

"The lube?" Arch looked up at him. "Yeah, sure. Why?"

Ty held out his paw and Arch squirted lube into it. "Just, ah, want to try something."

But then Arch was looking at him and he didn't want to reach around behind himself with the wolf watching, so he pushed his cock forward.

That worked. Tightness surrounded him; he pushed through and in, and Arch closed his eyes and huffed out a breath as though Ty'd pushed it up through his throat. And that was when Ty reached behind himself and rubbed the lube over his own hole.

He couldn't bring himself to put fingers in at first, worried about his claws, worried about pushing in at that awkward angle, so he just rubbed the lube, which felt surprisingly good, and focused on getting his cock all the way into the wolf below him. Arch had meanwhile rested a paw on his own erect shaft and was holding it, not stroking, as Ty entered him.

They fell into a steady rhythm, Arch bracing himself and pushing forward as Ty thrust against him. Ty kept his paw under his own tail only for a short time before bringing it around to slide up and down Arch's cock. In this position, he almost felt like he was jerking himself off, only with a really nice lube and not the liquid soap he'd had in college (that dried up so you kept having to get more).

And it was nice to be able to look down at the wolf's blunt muzzle, the tooth-baring grin as he pressed his head back into the pillow, the broad chest and fluffy white stomach, the balls hanging down over where Ty's cock pumped back and forth. Ty leaned forward and kept his paw moving as he licked at the wolf's muzzle, and then Arch reached up to grab the fox and hug him, pressing their muzzles together.

A moment later, the wolf made some noises in his throat that vibrated against Ty's teeth, and his body started squirming. Ty held onto him tighter, enjoying the feeling of restraining the wolf's struggles. Soon enough, though, he himself was panting, licking at Arch's whiskers as the wolf moaned, claws digging into Ty's back, and the fox's hips thrust forward harder as his arousal surged. His muscles clenched all over, bracing his hips as he strove to bury himself in the smaller wolf.

"Ahh," Arch gasped under him. "Ah, ah shit, nnnnff!"

Ty's knot encountered resistance, so he pressed harder. Arch's cries melted into breathy grunts, getting louder and louder, and as Ty forced his knot in, the wolf squeezed him, tensing all over. A moment later, his hips jerked, yanking Ty's with them, and warmth spread slick between them in spurts that Ty felt against his stomach fur.

The fox wriggled and panted, emptying himself into the wolf just as Arch's shudders died down. The wolf kept moaning, "Ah, oh god, oh fuck," as Ty clenched his teeth and whined through them, forcing Arch's legs up so he could get deeper into the wolf, his hips shaking as he came.

"Nnnnf." Ty collapsed atop Arch.

The wolf set his legs down, knees bent so his thighs framed Ty's hips. He buried his muzzle in the fox's neck and murmured something.

"What?" Ty flicked an ear.

"I was just making noises," Arch said. His breath came in warm pants on Ty's fur, reaching down to the skin. "But I think if you translated them, they would mean, 'holy shit.'"

"Yeah." Ty pushed his paws farther under the wolf and hugged. "That was, uh, pretty good."

"Yeah, I, uh." Arch exhaled. His claws raked Ty's fur gently. "Glad you thought so too."

The glow of sex suffusing him, Ty closed his eyes. "Is…" He nuzzled the wolf's ear. "Is the knot uncomfortable?"

Arch's rear contracted around him and then relaxed. He squirmed, making the wolf whuff in amusement. "Not any more than last time."

"Right." Ty flicked his ears.

The wolf's paws reached down to his rear. "You curious about it?"

"Uh." Ty's tail swished across Arch's paws.

"Is that why you wanted the lube on your fingers?" Arch squirmed around, getting one of his paws under Ty's tail.

"Hey," Ty said, but he couldn't move easily, tied as they were. Arch's paw found his entrance and rubbed at it.

"Ah, yep, it's lubed up here. You fingered yourself?"

"Kind of." The fox tensed and then jerked forward as Arch's finger probed into him.

"Like it?"

"Ahhhh…" Ty gritted his teeth. "It's—no, it's—it's weird."

"Feels like you have to go?"

"A bit, yeah."

"Uh-huh." All the while, Arch's finger was rubbing smoothly, in and out but never fully out.

"Look, I don't know if I want to…" He breathed heavily out over Arch's ear. "Enough!"

"Okay." The finger withdrew, and Arch rested that paw on Ty's rear. "We can play around with that if you want, sometime."

"I gotta think about it."

"Mmm." The wolf nuzzled him. "Sometimes it's better if you don't."

The pressure in Ty's knot had lowered enough that he could slip out with only a little tugging, and he rolled off Arch to lie side by side against the wolf. They didn't talk too much, just traced claws through each other's fur as warmth and sex lulled them into a half-doze.

What would it mean if he did let Arch fuck him? He'd never be able to say he hadn't had a cock in his ass, for one thing. But he'd already had one in his muzzle. Was this all that different? He wasn't a girl, but neither was Arch, and he looked like having a cock in him was about the best thing ever. So what if Ty was missing out?

Arch's arm twitched, draped over him, and the wolf's breath ruffled his chest fur. Ty nuzzled the little ears and rubbed his fingers over Arch's arms.

The wolf would be gentle, he was sure, and his finger had felt—weird, but not bad. But still, Ty didn't know. Guys who let themselves get fucked… it wasn't what a professional athlete should do. That thought, far from discouraging him, enticed him further. It wasn't what an athlete would do, but Ty could do it.

•

In the morning, he woke next to Arch, his nose full of their scents and the lube and Arch's jizz. He draped an arm over the wolf, but Arch just yawned and snuggled against him and kept sleeping.

Ty didn't really want to lie in bed doing nothing, so he disengaged himself, grabbed his phone, and walked out to the living room. The curtains here had remained open, and he could see the soft blues and pinks and golds of the sunrise over the hills beyond the bay. He plopped his naked butt down into an armchair facing the windows and checked his messages.

Two from his mom asking when he was coming home. One text from Dev saying they couldn't get together Monday but how about Tuesday? That made it easy. Ty sent his mother an email saying he'd be back Wednesday, and Dev a note saying he'd be around for dinner Tuesday.

And then when he looked at his public email, it had 159 messages in it. What the fuck?

They all had subjects that either said, "Consider me for your wife," or something along those lines, or Yamatese characters he couldn't read. He picked one of the English ones at random and read it. "I understand you are looking for a wife. Please consider my qualifications. I am nineteen years old and was born in Shokuro." It went on like that.

Another one had a picture of the vixen attached. She wasn't bad-looking. Her message was similarly unhelpful. Had his mother arranged this?

The third message provided the answer. "I saw the report on TMZ that you are looking for a wife."

Ah, shit. He pulled up TMZ Sports and searched on his name, and there it was: "Firebirds Rookie Lookie for Nookie." Jesus fuck. "I'm not even a rookie anymore," he said out loud.

He went back to his mailbox to delete the messages, but he didn't know how to delete them all at once, so he went through one by one, and there were a bunch with pictures, and two of the pictures were of the vixens naked.

"Hey," Arch's voice said from the bedroom doorway. "Nice morning wood."

"Hey." Ty blinked up at the wolf. He was naked too, and his cock was about half hard.

"Or are you looking at porn?"

"I just…" He turned the laptop around. "Look."

Arch frowned and came closer. "Oh. Amateur porn."

"There are a hundred fifty girls who want to be my wife."

"And they're sending you naked pictures of themselves?" The wolf shook his head. "You poor thing."

"How do I delete all of these at once?"

"The pictures or the emails?"

Ty flicked his ears. "Is it wrong to keep the pictures? I kinda want to."

"Yes, it's wrong." Arch leaned in and closed the pictures. "If you want to jerk off to girls, do it when I'm not around."

His sheath hung right near Ty's muzzle and his erection had actually gone down. Ty nosed at the wolf's thigh. "What if I just think about them and don't tell you?"

"Whatever." Arch was playing with Ty's email client. "Hey, check out this message. She says she's copying her mom."

"Don't care," Ty said, but Arch had already opened the email. "Don't look at that."

"What?" Arch grinned. "It's not private; she doesn't know you. You were just going to trash the letter anyway. Listen: she starts with 'Hey' and not 'Dear.'"

"I can read," Ty growled, and because Arch was reading, he read the letter too.

Hey, Ty,

I'm writing because my mom is making me. And she's going to see a copy of this letter, too. Hi, Mom. So anyway, I guess I'm writing because she saw in this article that you're looking for Yamatese foxes to marry and we're Yamatese. I mean, I was born in this country, so I'm a Union citizen like I guess you are, but we came from the same place.

I'm a supervising software engineer at Shirokaze Games. If you've ever played Over Water (affectionately known as Boat Chase) or the Boliat Bill or Federal Treasure games (I'm sorry), then you've played some of my code. Right now I'm managing a team at Shirokaze and we're under deadline for Jumbo Bubbles X, but everyone tells me I need to go out more.

So anyway, it looks like we're both getting pushed around by our Yamatese heritage. If you'd like to get a drink sometime and commiserate, I'd be happy to spend an evening with you. Drop me an e-mail—I'm not going to give you my phone number without meeting you.

Best,

Tami Tachibana

"Tachibana," Arch said. "Over Water was pretty good."

"Never played it." Ty glanced up at the wolf. "I've heard of Shirokaze, though."

"What games do you play?"

"Sports games mostly." Ty grinned as Arch rolled his eyes. "I'm in the new UFL '09. You could like, run me around on the field if you wanted."

"I like sports games only a little less than I like actual sports." Arch paused. "I'm sorry. What a shitty thing to say. I like your sport. I just mean…uh."

Ty didn't say anything, just kept staring, and Arch reached a paw up behind his ear. "Not gonna let me off the hook for that, are you?" When the fox shook his head, Arch smiled. "Um…you can fuck me again?"

"You mean I wouldn't have been able to otherwise?" Ty raised an eyebrow. "Do I have to wait until you say something douchy to have sex?"

"I don't think that would be a good arrangement for either of us." Arch's smile wavered. "Seriously, I'm sorry. I mean, if someone said he didn't like what I did…"

"You wouldn't give a shit, because it's just a job, right?"

"Well…"

"It's okay." Ty put an arm around the wolf's waist. "Seriously. You like me, don't you?"

"Not really." Arch leaned into the embrace. "But you take me to nice clubs and nicer hotel rooms and you're pretty good in bed. Also you don't show up at my office with flowers after our first date."

Ty rubbed his nose into the wolf's stomach. "Nobody does that." Arch didn't say anything, and Ty looked up. "Seriously?"

The wolf held up two fingers. "Twice. There was a posting on some Yerba gay dating board about how that was a really romantic thing to do, and so for a while a lot of guys thought they should. It's always the tops, too, y'know? I mean, not that I let a guy top me on a first date." He coughed. "Usually. Mostly. Anyway, yeah. One day it was this lemur with a dozen red fucking roses, and last month there was a possum who showed up with daisies. And they were both just casual dates, and we hadn't even set up a second date."

"Last month?" Ty said.

"Yeah. Wes had gone out with him and thought we'd hit it off, and he was fine, but you know, he spent the whole dinner talking about plays and theater and these books he likes, and we liked a couple of the same books, but he hadn't been to a movie theater in months, he said, and…what?"

"What?" Ty tilted his muzzle.

"You're looking at me funny."

"I am?" He composed his face and made sure his ears were up. "No, I was just…you know, was this possum one of the guys you let top you?"

The wolf bent his head closer to Ty's. "No. We did blow each other."

"You didn't send me pictures."

"Didn't have my phone there." Arch set a finger on Ty's nose. "And you were having lots of sex in the last month, if I recall. Not to mention," he gestured to the screen, "interviewing wives."

"Yeah," Ty said, bumping Arch's nose with his finger. "So?"

"So…" Arch leaned down to kiss the fox. "So you can't be jealous."

"Mmf." Ty broke the kiss. "Jealous? Ha. Who's jealous? I just wanted pictures. I heard things about possum dicks."

"They're interesting." Arch returned his attention to the computer screen. "You want some pics of us doing it?"

Ty watched the wolf save the message from Tami, select out another two or three with interesting subjects, and then delete the rest. "What, now?"

"Or we could put clothes on. There's a good diner not too far from here and I'm hungry."

"Mm." Ty slid his paw down the wolf's waist. "You going to stay here tonight?"

"Well…" Arch tapped the top of the laptop screen. "You done with this?"

"Yeah."

The wolf closed the laptop. "I was thinking that we could do some shopping, and then maybe see some sights in the afternoon, then go back to my place and get high and watch a movie. But we could bring the cookies here, too. I just don't know how to get a movie player here."

"Check the TV," Ty said. "If there's something on pay per view that you're interested in, we can buy it."

"I'm going to need to go home Sunday night for sure, because I have to work Monday." Arch padded over to the TV and looked.

The wolf's tail swishing over his nice butt brought back memories of sex, and with them the stirring for more. Ty rested a paw on his sheath and brushed the fur. If Arch was going to stay with him all weekend, they could have sex that night and he didn't have to have one last roll now. "Let's get some food," he said.

"Okay." Arch pointed to the movies. "There's a couple that'd be fine."

"Right," Ty said. "Breakfast, shopping, cookie, movie, and then bedroom?"

Arch turned and grinned. "Sounds like a day."

And it was. Arch took him to a terrific little diner with a view of the Bay, and then they walked down to the shopping district, where the wolf pointed out three nice collared shirts for Ty to wear in brighter colors than he normally would've selected. Aquamarine, magenta, and canary yellow all promised to set off his fur nicely.

They dropped off the shirts at the hotel and then walked around the marina by the water. Where Ty had grown up, he was used to being near water, but the marina here was full of tourists and shops and a different sort of history, Eastern immigrants coming to make a life, war fortifications, and huge businesses that rose and fell like whales breaching. Pelagia sat on a large bay as well, but inland; here you could turn from the Bay westward to the ocean and the water went on and on and on, broken only by the blocky shape of a tanker on the horizon or some big military boat out on maneuvers.

Leaning on the railing and looking out at the water, Arch pointed down to the beach below. "Hey. Check out that cheetah down there."

Ty followed his finger down to a tall, well-muscled cheetah wearing nothing but a white speedo that did little to conceal the bulge of his sheath, even from thirty feet above. "I'm in better shape than he is," he muttered.

"Wait for it," Arch said. "He's going to turn around."

The cheetah did, giving them both a view of a perfectly sculpted rear that the speedo covered only the top third of. "Ahh," Arch said.

"Hey." Ty elbowed him. "You're with me and you're looking at him?"

"I'm only gonna get one dinner at the restaurant tonight, but that doesn't mean I can't drool over the whole menu." Arch grinned. "Anyway, that's not the point."

"What restaurant? What is the point?" Ty looked down at the cheetah again. The way the guy was strutting around, he must know he was drawing eyes. Ty looked back at Arch's muzzle, still pointed down.

"The point is that you should be appreciating him too."

What if there were someone around with a cell phone ready to send a picture to TMZ? "Fox Looks at Cocks," the headline might read. Nobody around them seemed to be paying attention, but you could never tell. "I like that snowshoe hare better." Closer to them, lying out on a towel, a hare's white fur showed off the curves of her red bikini.

Arch's nose wrinkled. "I get it, you're not gay. At least can you admit that the cheetah is hot?"

"He's hot." Ty scanned the beach for another guy to point out. A fox in a tight swim trunk with a flower pattern stepped out of the water, his fur slicked to his form, the suit tight around his sheath as well. "What about that fox?"

"Not bad," the wolf said, "if you like foxes. But he's not gay."

Arch wasn't smiling, but Ty was pretty sure the wolf was fucking with him. "Yeah, well, if you don't like foxes, you can go see what that cheetah's up to tonight."

"He's way out of my league." Arch kept staring down. "You could maybe land him, though."

"How do you know that fox isn't gay?"

"I dunno. He doesn't look it."

"Because he's not wearing a speedo that barely covers his sheath?"

"Yeah, partly that." Arch's tail flicked against Ty's leg. "How do you know that hare is straight?"

"Because there's a guy standing lookout over her, for one thing." The other hare could only be her boyfriend or husband. He glared at every guy who turned an eye on her, while she lay there oblivious.

"But there's more than that."

"Probably." Ty was still looking at the wet fox. He'd joined a crowd of guys, all looking young from the way they moved; at least, they reminded Ty of his friends. Most of whom were straight. Maybe Arch was right. "But," he said, "I told you *I* was straight."

"Huh?" Arch turned to look at him.

"That fox." Ty gestured with his nose.

"Oh." Arch nudged the fox with his elbow. "You want to invite him up for a three-way?"

"No."

"If you want to do that, I know a guy…"

"No." Ty checked to either side of them, but nobody was close by. He lowered his voice. "How the fuck would that even work?"

"Easier to show you."

He stuck his tongue out. "One thing at a time, okay?"

"Sure." Arch grinned. "I'm hungry. You hungry?"

"Yeah." Ty didn't say the thing he'd been thinking, which was that as hot as the cheetah and fox and hare were, he much preferred just looking at Arch's muzzle and seeing him smile. "Let's—hang on." His phone was ringing. "Ah, it's Vonni. I should take this."

Arch nodded as Ty brought the phone to his ear. "Hey, fox."

"Hey, fox. You find a wife yet?"

"Fuck." Ty put his paw to his eyes. "Everyone saw that goddamn article?"

"Pretty much. Daria told me I should call you 'cause she knows a couple Yamatese vixens. One of them's already married, but not happily, so ya know, she'd totally drop him for you."

"Are any of them a—a video game developer?"

Vonni's voice rose. "You're seeing a vix who makes games? Marry that, Ty, right fucking now."

"It's not that easy."

"If you don't, I will." He paused. "I mean, I—"

Ty grinned. "She's not the kind who'd be waiting outside the stadium after a game, either."

"What kind is she?"

"I dunno, Von, I haven't even met her. She wrote me a letter and Arch—" The wolf's ears perked at the sound of his name, and Ty turned it into a cough. "Ahem. I mean, it sounded good, but that's it."

"All right. Would you at least look at one of Daria's friends? It'd help me out."

"Sure, send 'em along." Ty rolled his eyes at Arch and shook his head.

"Hey, speaking of dropping husbands, you hear about Gerrard?"

Ty perked his ears and turned away from Arch, out toward the sun and ocean. "No. What happened?"

"Angela kicked him out. Caught him cheating."

Ty whistled. "Fuck, dude." He paused and then spoke low into the mouthpiece. "You worried?"

Vonni laughed. "Last time I checked, you can't get another species pregnant, especially from coming in her mouth."

"Daria's out, huh?"

"Hell yeah. I'm in her—our back yard. Somewhere. Unless I'm on someone else's property. You gotta come out here and visit, this shit is off the fuckin' hook. And I can afford something like this. It's crazy. I wanna buy her a house bigger than this one just so she sees I'm better than her parents."

"But wait, so Gerrard got another coyote pregnant?"

"Yeah, way Zillo told it, he had a cub and he'd been supporting them for years. Angela found out last week, dropped the hammer. Boom."

"Harsh." He couldn't think of a way to say that he couldn't imagine Gerrard being upset by the loss of his family as much as he'd been upset by, say, losing the championship. Ty didn't deal with Gerrard much, but he knew the coyote, of course, the unflappable presence on the field and sidelines, first to workouts, last to leave. "Is he—I mean, is he doing okay?"

Vonni laughed, shorter. "He's Gerrard. Long as he can have a football in his paws, he's fine. I think he'd rather scrimmage than fuck his wife anyway, to be honest. You know, there's a few guys like that."

"None we got on offense. There was a guy in college though."

"Yeah. Anyway, I'll shoot you a couple pics along. Thanks; it'll make me look good for Daria. *I* like fucking my wife."

Aware of the proximity of Arch, Ty just said, "I hope one of them is as hot as she is," and then they hung up.

"Trouble with…" Arch paused. "Friends?"

"It's okay that you listened." Ty smiled, putting the phone back in his pocket. "My teammates saw that TMZ article and that was Vonni. He's a cornerback…uh, the guy who tries to stop guys like me from catching the ball. Anyway, he's a fox, his wife wants to send me pictures of some of her Yamatese friends."

"I got that much." The wolf smiled. "Do you need some private time to look those over tonight?"

"Hell no." Ty snorted. "Let's go get some food." And then, because he still wasn't sure if Arch was upset, he lowered his voice. "Cookies, movie, bedroom."

"All right, all right, straight fox," Arch said. "I'm not offended."

•

The movie Arch chose was a dumb comedy that got way funnier when the cookies kicked in. They were roaring at some dumb gag when Ty's phone rang. "Ah, it's my agent," he said, wiping his eyes. "Hee hee. I should probably see what he wants."

Delino's sharp voice came through the phone. "Sorry to call so late. Just saw the TMZ thing. You need any help with anything?"

"It's not late," Ty said. "Sorry. No, I mean. I'm fine. I'm pretty sure I'm fine. Am I fine?"

Arch said, "I think you're fine," and they both broke into laughs again.

"Who are you talking to?" The ram's voice got deeper and more stern, more parental.

"Just a friend." Ty leaned against Arch. "No, I don't need anything. I mean, can you make my mom just chill the fuck out about this?"

"Sorry, I can't—"

"Oh, wait! Do you know a vixen who works at Shirokaze Games? She's supposed to be pretty cool. What was her name?" Arch shrugged. "Never mind. I got her email, I'm going to write her. You don't have to do anything."

It occurred to him then that he was talking too much, so he shut up. Delino took a few seconds to answer. "Ty, are you…high?"

"I am…" Ty had to think for a minute. "Not."

"Okay. Before I hang up, I'm going to remind you that the UFL does random drug testing even during the off-season, and that if you're caught with drugs in your system, you can be suspended for four games. That's about a hundred thousand dollars. Is getting high worth a hundred thousand dollars?"

"No sir," Ty said.

The ram exhaled. "That shit stays in your system, Ty. Just…just cut it out, okay? Trust me."

"I promise I will cut it the fuck out." Ty had to clamp a paw over his muzzle to keep from giggling.

Delino sighed again and hung up. For a moment, guilt washed over Ty, but then Arch asked if everything was okay and he said, "Sure, sure." And then the rabbit in the movie was pretending to be a gerbil for some reason and it was hysterical, and everything was okay.

They ended up leaning against each other on the couch and giggling, and when the movie was done, neither of them really made a move to get up. Ty, larger, had the smaller wolf leaning into his side, his arm lazily around Arch's shoulder and rubbing his chest, and he himself was wedged back into the corner of the couch. The movie channel switched to previews of other available movies, which was entertaining enough, and Ty felt sleepily mellow and content.

"Was this different stuff than last time?" he asked.

"Yeah." Arch yawned and rested a paw on Ty's thigh. "More mellow, less…silly, I guess."

"I was still pretty silly."

"We were watching a funny movie." The wolf's head felt nice and warm on Ty's shoulder, the way he might've relaxed with one of his friends, if one of his friends was open to cuddling on a couch like this without thinking it was gay. Though of course, it was gay in this case, so that wouldn't work. He tried to imagine Kellen leaning against him, the swift fox's slender build and bushy tail, his foxy scent in Ty's nose the way Arch's was. But it didn't really do anything for him. Of course, he was only about half-aroused in his current state anyway. But he didn't think of Kellen in that way.

"You still awake?" Arch squeezed his thigh.

"Mmm. Sorry. Thinking about stuff."

"What kind of stuff?"

"Just…" Ty tried to figure out how to explain it. "I never really thought about being like this with anyone. It's like…it's a whole big world. I was trying to imagine my friends…if they'd want to watch a movie like this. But I don't think I even want to. This is the way I'd watch a movie with a girl, only this is different, you know?"

"Wow," Arch said. "You know, I never thought about all the ways I'm different from a girl."

Ty turned to meet the wolf's eyes because he thought for a moment that Arch was serious, but the wolf was grinning, and that started Ty giggling again, and pretty soon the two of them were laughing there together on the couch. And then they were quiet, and then Arch kissed Ty's collarbone and Ty closed his eyes with the weight of the wolf on him.

When he opened his eyes again, Arch was breathing evenly against his chest and the TV was showing a preview he'd already seen. He stretched his free arm and then leaned up to nuzzle Arch's ears.

"Hmmmf." The wolf shifted, pressed his nose into Ty's chest ruff. One eye opened. "Fox."

"Wolf."

"Urg. What time is it?"

"No idea." The windows were dark and the room quiet.

"Should we go to bed?"

"Mm." Ty shifted, and the wolf sat up.

They stumbled to the bed, shedding clothes along the way, but when they crawled under the covers in their underwear, neither made a move. "If you wanna do something," Arch mumbled, and trailed off.

"I'm here tomorrow night, too." Ty yawned. "And tomorrow morning."

"Mmmkay." The wolf turned his back to Ty and scooted back, spooning against the fox. Ty rested his arm across Arch's chest.

When Ty woke to golden light suffusing the bedroom, both of them felt obviously differently. Ty's erection pressed up against Arch's rear, and the wolf murmured back to him, "You awake?"

"Mm-hmm." Ty squeezed the wolf.

"Okay. I'ma go get the lube and condoms. We're gonna get that thing inside me and then I gotta go to work."

"Such sexy talk." Ty grinned as Arch slid out of the bed and pushed his underwear down. Moments later, as promised, his slick condom-wrapped shaft thrust under the wolf's tail as Arch moaned happily. He came in Ty's paw, his whole body shuddering so that Ty would've slipped out of him if he hadn't pushed his knot in by then, and the motion itself was enough to send Ty over the edge as well.

They lay together panting for several minutes, Arch clenching around Ty's knot and shaft, until finally the fox had relaxed enough to pull free. Arch turned and kissed him, wrapping both arms around him, but only stayed that way for a moment. "Shower's big enough for two," he said. "Want to join me?"

And Ty did, and that was fun too, soaping each other and rubbing paws all through each other's fur, his winter coat coming out in clumps in Arch's paws even from the places where he kept his fur trimmed. "You wolves shed too, right?" Ty said, combing claws through Arch's belly.

"Not as much as this. Are you sure it won't clog the drain?"

"Ah, I'm paying a 'scent equalization surcharge' anyway. Might as well get my money's worth." He grinned and turned. "Now do my tail."

After the shower, they had time for a quick breakfast in the lounge and then Arch said, "I really have to run. I'm sorry."

"You have to work." Ty grinned. "Hope it's not too bad a Monday. I hear people hate those."

"Athletes," Arch grumbled, and flicked his tail at Ty as he left.

The day stretched ahead of him, so he figured he'd start by actually paying attention to his email. Predictably, there were several messages from his mother, beginning by asking if he would come back Monday instead of Wednesday, the last one telling him that she had had to break a date with a girl for Monday night because he hadn't responded to her to tell her when his flight on Monday would be.

He sighed and put that one aside. Kellen had written him asking how the wife thing was going and where he'd bailed to, and he thought for a moment about telling him the truth. The swift fox would probably—maybe—understand, and as long as Ty made it clear that it was only this wolf, that it wasn't anything he wanted to do with Kellen, probably things would be cool. But he didn't know about the others, specifically Morshin (Kimi and Paul would probably not give a shit), so he sent Kellen a note saying he'd run into a teammate down here and had been having fun playing tourist for a weekend.

And then there was that message Arch had saved, from the vixen named Tami.

Ty pulled it up and read it again. She sounded cool, actually. Of course, there was no way—no way in all the world—that she would pass his mother's suitability test. And yet…her mother wanted her to meet a Yamatese fox. So her family was at least somewhat traditional.

If this were a way he could end the parade of uncomfortable dinners, not to mention articles on TMZ about his love life, then it was worth at least taking an hour or so to write a letter.

An hour proved optimistic. At that point he had exactly two sentences, not counting the greeting: "Hi, Tami. Thanks for your email. You sound interesting." What the fuck should he say after that? He'd tried, "I think my mom would like you," but that sounded too much like someone who cared what his mom thought. He'd tried, "Let's go out when I get back," but that was kind of too casual, the kind of thing he'd say to a girl he wanted to sleep with. He'd written out, "You sound different from all the other vixens my mom is fixing me up with," but that sounded stupid *and* contained too much mom.

He'd written most of a letter to Paul, who was good with words, asking him how to write to a vixen who sounded interesting but whom his mother might not approve of even if Ty didn't care if his mother approved of her but he wanted to warn her that even though he was interested in her it might not work out, not that he was that beholden to his mom's wishes except that he was, when it came down to it. Then he read through the letter again and erased it. He needed help from someone Yamatese, and he didn't have any Yamatese friends (as his mother liked to remind him).

But he did have an uncle. Even if Lucas wasn't Yamatese himself, or technically related to Ty, he'd been included in all of Ty's family traditions growing up. He definitely had enough experience with Ty's family to be able to dispense advice.

So he wrote to Lucas, and this one was a lot easier: "Lucas, I got a ton of emails from Yamatese vixens after that TMZ story. One of them is actually interesting, but I'm not sure Mom will approve of her. How should I write back to her?"

The other emails Arch had saved were not as interesting as Tami, though one of them claimed to be a fashion model. He deleted those and then he answered a few emails from teammates, catching up with Ford who wanted to know if he'd be attending the wide receivers camp in Taysha in March, writing to Rodo about getting together in Chevali when he got back, and then he found an email from Zaïd.

Hey all,

(It was addressed to all the wide receivers, Ty saw, all except for Lightning Strike.)

In advance of the free agency period, I think it would be helpful if we presented a united front to management regarding whether we want Lightning Strike back with the team. I of course have not had any contact with them because that would be illegal, but if we have all our opinions together when communication opens up again, that'll be most helpful to them. Please email me privately or text me and let me know how you feel about Strike.

Enjoy your vacations and I'll see you in a couple months.

Ty's first thought was, that's awfully together of Zaïd. His second was, of course he's talked to management. The cheetah and his wife went out with Brit and his wife all the time. So this was a coded message probably indicating that management wanted to know how much their wideouts could tolerate Strike being around.

It was an easy call for Ty. He shot off a note to Zaïd saying, "Keep him on the team. Can you imagine having to play against him?"

That cleared out most of the emails he cared about. He shut the laptop down and leaned back in the chair. The door to the bedroom, hanging ajar, revealed rumpled sheets and sparked a memory of that morning.

Once he went back to Pelagia, even if things didn't work out with Tami, would he see Arch again? He rested his muzzle in his paw, rubbing one of his canine teeth. The way Arch loved having a cock in him…this might be Ty's last chance to feel that. The wolf had seemed willing, if not enthusiastic, so Ty's reluctance was probably the only thing stopping it from happening.

Ty did have access to an expert who could advise him, and he'd be meeting him for dinner that night. He lifted his muzzle, the decision made, and that cleared his spirit. So he grabbed a light jacket and went out into a foggy morning to enjoy the city.

Chapter 11

Dev and Lee picked an Etruscan place that smelled amazing, and Ty beat them there, so his stomach demanded an appetizer of bruschetta before they arrived. When Dev parked himself at the small four-top beside Ty, with Lee across from them, the waiter said, "I can find a bigger table if you'd like."

"Dev, switch with me," Lee said. "Then you two huge football players aren't crowded around one side of the table."

"But then our legs bump into each other."

The waiter cleared his throat. "There's a larger table over here. It's no trouble at all."

Ty smiled and pushed his chair back. "Thanks, then."

Once they'd moved and gotten drinks, Lee wanted to know what Ty'd been doing in Yerba, and he said, "Mostly shopping and sightseeing. I walked over the bridge this morning."

"Any museums?"

Ty grinned. "I'm not really a museum kind of guy."

"But shopping?" Dev arched an eyebrow.

"With Arch, yeah. He cares about what I wear."

"Nice shirt, by the way," Lee chimed in.

"He picked it out." Ty adjusted the shirt cuff self-consciously. He wanted to talk to Lee and did not think he would have a problem, but Dev in real life was much more real, much more his friend than the Dev in his imagination who was mostly up on gay advice. This Dev wanted to talk about teammates, which was about as far from gay sex as Ty could imagine any topic being, unless it was about teammates' wives, and of course, because of Gerrard, that came up too.

Dev had heard, but not from Gerrard, which Ty thought curious because he'd always assumed the linebackers were pretty tight like the wide-outs were. Certainly if Rodo had gotten kicked out of his house, Ty and Zaïd would be the first ones he'd call, and vice versa.

(Though Ty hadn't talked to either of them about his gay experimentation, but that was different.)

And then they were wrapping up dinner and Ty still hadn't gotten up the nerve to ask Lee for his advice. Finally Dev got up to use the bathroom and Lee was going to go with him, but Ty coughed, and it came out super awkward.

They both stopped and stared. "Uh, Lee, can I talk to you for a couple minutes?" he said, his ears self-consciously flat.

"Sure." The other fox stayed seated. Dev hovered at the table, and Lee glanced in his direction. "I'm warning you, though, Dev and I don't keep secrets from each other."

"Yeah, uh." It was uncomfortable having Dev stand there waiting. Ty looked down at his paws. "I'll tell Dev tomorrow or Friday, I promise, just…I need to ask you something."

"All right." Dev ruffled Lee's head. "I can always work it out of Lee later."

When he'd left, Lee leaned forward. "He can't really. Well. Probably not." Which of course meant that Dev would know maybe even before Ty told him. "What's up?"

There wasn't anyone with sensitive ears at the nearby tables, and the restaurant was loud, but Ty thought about the TMZ article and pitching his voice the way he used to when he and Paul were sitting together in high school and didn't want to be overheard. "I was thinking about trying… uh…letting him fuck me. I wanted to ask how your first time was, and, y'know, any tips?"

Lee perked up at that and slid his chair closer to Ty. "Oh. Well, basically, use lots of lube—*lots*—and go really slow."

The other fox's confidence gave some to Ty. "Did you like it right away?"

"Well, yeah." Lee smiled, his whiskers lying back, looking a little abashed. "But you gotta understand I'd played with myself a lot before I had a first time."

Ty sipped his wine. "You think I should wait?"

"Nah. Trust me, if I'd had anyone in high school willing to play with me, I'd have done it. But also, some guys like that more than others. Polecki says he and his boyfriend—" He hitched up there, maybe searching for the name or something. "They switch back and forth. Dev and I don't. You might try it once and think, eh, not for me."

"Yeah." That was comforting, the idea that he might not like it. He realized that he'd been thinking there might be something wrong with him if he didn't, and he was worried he might end up being gay a hundred percent if he did. "I kinda feel like that's what's gonna happen. But you know, looking down at him when he's taking it, and he gets…" The memory of that morning came back in force, getting him a little hard. "He gets loud like a girl, and I'm thinking, wow, I should try that at least once."

Lee laughed and nodded approvingly. "Good luck. I mean, I like it, but I know it's not for everyone."

Ty hesitated before asking the next question, but Lee was another fox, and he was mellow from the dinner and wine. "Dev never wanted to?"

"Nah. We're pretty happy the way things are. And honestly, the first couple years we were going out, I think we had maybe one week of vacation together. That was early on and he still wasn't even calling what we had a relationship then, so he sure wasn't going to try that. After that, we were seeing each other weekends and it was more important to stick with what works."

"That's what he said, too." Laid out so matter-of-factly, it sounded completely sensible and Ty felt silly about having been so worked up about it. "I'm probably an idiot."

"You're exploring. It's cool." Lee smiled and his tail wagged. "How are things going with him?"

"Good. But you know, it's not really a relationship or anything. I mean, I'm gonna have to get married and have cubs; that's how my family is."

"He knows that?"

Ty nodded. "Yeah. He doesn't want anything long-term or serious either. So maybe this is it."

"Who knows, maybe in ten years your wife will be kicking you out because she found out about him."

"Ah, shit, I hope not." Ty grinned, now back on ground where he was more confident in his expertise. "I'm better at keeping secrets than Gerrard. Dude lives football year-round. Probably he sent the cub a football or something. But that's the life, you know? You get laid on the road because there's all this tail hovering around waiting for you. Like," he waved a paw at the smells of tomato and basil and the old Etruscan song playing on the speakers. "Say you're on a diet and you walk into this place and they tell you that you can have anything on the menu for free. And you think, well, I can cheat on my diet this one time and nobody will care."

"But eventually you get fat," Lee said. "And also then you're only cheating yourself, not someone else who trusts you."

Was Lee worried about Dev cheating? Ty tried to reassure him. "We took Dev to a strip club once. Charm and I banged a couple waitresses there," and so did Zillo, who'd had a girlfriend at the time, but that probably wasn't Lee's business, "but he just went home. Didn't really care about any of it. Don't know if that's because he's gay or because he was thinking about you, but…I don't think he ever did anything. Not that I heard about, anyway." He hurried the end of it because he spotted Dev coming back from the bathroom.

"Thanks." Lee smiled and relaxed, and Ty thought maybe he'd read the other fox right.

"I took as long as I could," Dev said as he plopped down into his chair. "Secret fox conference over?"

"Yup." Ty punched the other fox's shoulder, lightly. "Lee's helpful."

"Ask him about running your routes sometime," Dev said. "He's helpful like that too."

"I don't watch the wideouts." Lee's ears went back.

Ty put his paws up and laughed. "Don't worry. I've got plenty of coaches. Practically got one for every wideout. And Rodo keeps on my case, and I still talk to Ford."

"Plus you've got Lightning Strike," Dev said. "That's like having three more coaches right there."

"Yeah." He was about to tell Dev about the email, but remembered at the last minute that Lee worked for Yerba now and probably that kind of thing would at the very least be frowned upon and at most might cost him a lot of money. If he was going to be fined, it wasn't going to be for saying the wrong shit to the wrong guy. "He actually reminds me of this coach I had in college, an assistant coach who'd played for the team for four years and stayed with the program when he graduated. He was a cheetah too and he had so much energy we used to say his blood-coffee level was over the legal limit."

"Are all cheetahs hyper?" Dev growled. "One of the guys on the Dragons was that way too."

"Zaïd's cool, but he's also pretty religious so maybe that mellows him down."

The waiter returned then, and Ty and Dev both wanted dessert, so they ordered the tiramisu. When he'd left, Dev said, "Zaïd's religious? I never see him hanging out with Colin and the Christians."

"Well, he's Muslim, that's probably why."

"Really?" Dev rubs his chin thoughtfully. "What do they think about gay people?"

Ty spread his paws. "I can ask him."

"No, no, it's okay."

"I mean," Ty said, "if he hasn't given you shit then he's probably fine with it. I dunno if he'd want you to fuck him, y'know, but other than that, don't worry about it."

Dev laughed, but it was more a polite my-friend-made-a-joke laugh. So Ty said, "Our conditioning coach is Muslim too. That's the only reason I know. The two of them observe Ramadan and they go off to pray together."

"Which one?"

"Poriq. The fennec."

"Oh, right." Their tiramisu arrived, and both Ty and Dev dug in, with Lee taking only a dainty taste. It was sweet and rich, espresso and chocolate and cream all blending together on Ty's tongue, and he wanted to take a piece to the hotel for Arch, but by the time he thought of it, there were only a few bites left.

"I've never seen them pray," Dev said.

"They have a room they go to. When there's a game they might have to skip the full one, but Zaïd said he always knows which direction to pray in and his imam gave him special permission to pray shortly in those cases. I don't think Poriq is all that religious, but he observes the prayers to keep Zaïd company."

"Cool," Lee said.

"Yeah, that's great." Dev rubbed his fork around in the remains of the tiramisu, making trails of chocolate through the islands of cream left on the plate. "I don't care if someone's religious as long as they're not a hypocrite."

Lee put a paw on Dev's arm and the big tiger shut up, but Ty didn't have to think too hard to figure out who that remark was about. He only knew Colin because the foxes on the team had gotten together during training camp and Ty'd met him as the other fox rookie. He'd thought they might bond over that, but they played different sides of the ball and came from different sides of the country and that was too many differences to be bridged by a mere genetic coincidence in that case.

Vonni, by contrast, even though he also played defense and came from the east coast, had befriended Ty more than Colin had either of them. In Vonni's case, maybe it was that the young rookie cornerback was seen as his future replacement, or maybe it was that Vonni had actually gone to a west coast college in Ty's conference; Colin had attended a heartland school. So Vonni and Ty knew people in common and had gone out for drinks, which Colin hadn't been inclined to do, and so even during the year, Ty had hung out with Vonni when he wanted a friend. And Vonni had led him to Pace and Norton, Gerrard and Carson, and eventually Dev.

The other guys on offense, though a tight group of friends who welcomed Ty, also had families to go home to and viewed Ty more as a kid brother than a peer. Which was fine, but sometimes you didn't want to be a kid brother.

He insisted on paying the bill, and when Dev tried to protest, Ty said, "I was a first round pick. I might not've scored a beer commercial yet, but…"

"All right, all right," Dev said.

"Anyway, you're buying a house."

"You'll get a commercial," Lee put in. "I'm surprised that you haven't, after that championship game."

"I might have," Ty said. "My agent just called to ask about the TMZ thing."

"What TMZ thing?" Dev asked, so Ty told them briefly about the article and they both shook their heads.

"Maybe you could get an endorsement for a matchmaking service," Lee said.

Ty laughed, and held his credit card up for the waiter. "And another tiramisu to go, please."

The tiger and fox both looked at him as the waiter left, and Ty folded his ears down. "For Arch."

"Awwww." Dev grinned and poked him. "That's so *sweet*."

"Yeah, well. I'll still get half of it." Ty grinned back, both embarrassed and pleased to be able to be honest with the two of them.

Outside, he found a way to tell them that. "Great to see you guys," he said. "I'm glad you came to the club."

"Me too." Dev squeezed his paw.

Lee shook next, and Ty smiled down. "Good luck with the house and all."

"Thanks." The fox grinned up. "Good luck to you too."

Ty flicked his ears back, curling his tail self-consciously down and then realizing he was doing it and letting it swing free. He waved as they got into their car and sped away, and then gripped the paper bag containing the tiramisu and raised his arm to hail an approaching cab.

On the way back, the idea of letting Arch top him segued into the idea that this would be their last night together, and as much as he kept adding, "for a while," it bothered him. What if Arch wasn't free next time Ty was in town? What if Arch found another dance partner in the meantime? Ty didn't need a commitment, but he wanted to know that he'd be able to see Arch again. To dance, mainly, although the sex afterwards was fun too. Wait—was that a commitment? No more than he'd ask of a friend, right? His friends in Chevali were always available to go out with him. Oh, but he was paying for their house. Well, maybe he could pay Arch's rent…no, wait, that started to feel like paying for sex.

When he opened the door to the hotel room, he smelled wolf right away and slid the privacy locks shut on the door behind him. "I brought dessert," he called, and set the bag down on the bar.

The TV was on in the bedroom. "Good," Arch called. "This movie is terrible."

"What are you, uh." Ty had crossed the room in several steps and stopped in the bedroom doorway. Arch grinned back at him, his long grey muzzle and black tipped ears leaning back from the long stretch of his completely nude body, the ivory chest and stomach fur down to his creamy white sheath and brown-grey legs, darker where they creased with the muscles. His tail wagged against the golden-brown sheet of the well-made bed.

"I figured," Arch said, resting one paw on his thigh right beside his sheath, his brown eyes gleaming and dancing along with the smile of his muzzle, "that I'd jump ahead a little bit."

"Yeah." Ty swallowed, the conversation about their future forgotten. "I feel overdressed. You want something to drink? Wine? Beer?" He kept looking down the wolf's body, and damn, it looked nice.

"I'm good. But get yourself something if you want."

Ty nodded. "Be right back."

He poured himself a glass of water in the bathroom, which was open to the bedroom so he could watch Arch out of the corner of his eye. The wolf's back was to him, watching the TV, tail wagging over the curve of his rear.

It was no longer so strange to imagine himself sliding under that tail, wrapping his arms around a male wolf and fucking him. Was that what he wanted now, another challenge? He drank the water and reached around under his own tail, rubbing there through his pants, remembering the feel of Arch's finger.

Ty set the glass down on the counter and Arch's ears flicked back. He was listening to Ty, not the TV. The fox grinned; his tail wagged, and he unfastened his pants.

Arch turned off the TV and rolled onto his back as Ty approached the bed, his eyes taking in the fox's nude form and partially-exposed cock. "Mm," he said, stretching out a paw. "You look gorgeous."

The compliment felt warm and enjoyable even though Ty was the one used to telling girls they looked good. He knelt over Arch and breathed in wolf, and as fingers rose to brush his balls, he touched his nose to the broader black one. "You too," he said.

The wolf's paw rose to press against his sheath, and his lips rose to meet Ty's. The kiss warmed him and sent waves of arousal to his groin, or maybe it was Arch's paw, or maybe it was both. His tail swung back and forth and he closed his eyes.

It didn't take long for both wolf and fox to be fully erect and panting against each other. And then Arch reached for the lube and said, "One for the road?"

Ty thought again about going back home, about getting engaged and how quickly training was going to start up again. "Hey," he said. "I don't want this to be our last night."

The wolf's eyes sparkled with the reflection of the moon outside the window. "Sure, fox," he said.

"I mean it."

"Yeah, I know. Look." Arch lost his smile. "I know you got another life. Trust me, the night after the championship game? This little visit? Means a lot. I'm sure I'll see you, and maybe we'll dance, and maybe…" He reached down and gripped Ty's cock. "We'll play. But you've got a busy life to get back to, and I've got my own life too. I'm not going to fool myself that this'll lead to anything. So maybe we'll see each other again and maybe we won't."

Ty exhaled across the wolf's ears, leaning into the warm grip. "I know it won't be easy, but maybe…" He touched his nose to Arch's. "Whatever relationships we end up in, maybe we get to be each other's exception?"

The wolf looked steadily up at him. "Yeah. I don't know if I work that way. Or if I'd want you to cheat with me."

Cheating wasn't such a big deal, Ty was about to say, and then he decided that maybe it was to Arch, and maybe it was more to him than he wanted to admit, and that most of all, he didn't want to have this conversation when he could be having sex. "All right," he said. "But I want you to know that whatever happens, I want to come back."

"I do appreciate that." Arch smiled and squeezed Ty's cock. "So let's get this all warm, huh?"

The fox cleared his throat. "Actually, uh." He grinned, ears folding down slightly. "Would you want to warm this up?"

His fingers grasped the wolf's cock and slid along it. Arch's eyes widened with more surprise than he'd shown when Ty'd said he wanted to keep seeing him. "You want me to top you?"

"I want to try." When Arch stayed silent, Ty stroked him again. "Come on, what if this is my last chance?"

Arch barked a laugh. "You walk into any gay club in this country and you've got yourself another chance. But sure. I mean, I don't know how good I am, but, uh."

"How 'good' am I?" Ty let go and trailed his claws up the wolf's stomach. "I mean, you stick it in, you pump it back and forth, right?"

"Ye-es…" Arch shook his head. "I mean, you're good. You stay hard, you feel nice inside, you don't take forever. Oh, don't get all puffed up about it," he said, and Ty supposed the enjoyment of the compliment must have shown in his ears and whiskers. "It's not like you're writing a symphony or—"

"Or playing professional football at the very highest level?" Ty asked smugly.

"Yeah, yeah." Arch poked him in the stomach. "So yeah, if you want me to top you, I'll give it a try. First thing," he said as he held out the lube to Ty, "is lots of this."

So Ty squeezed out a lot of the slick gel and hesitantly reached around under his tail. "Around, or inside, or what?"

"Anywhere this is gonna go." Arch rolled a condom down over his cock and winked.

Ty took a breath and pressed. "Cold," he murmured, but rubbed it around and pressed one finger into himself. Didn't feel too bad. He pushed the finger in and out, trying to imagine what the wolf's cock would feel like. His finger felt pretty darn big, but when he took it out and held it next to Arch's cock, the cock was at least twice as big around.

The wolf saw his measurement. "Oh yeah, you want to get at least two fingers in and comfortable first. I can do that if you want."

"Let me try first." Another squirt of lube, the fur on his fingers slicked down. The smell of the lube overwhelmed the smell of his musk and his rear. "It's tricky with the claws."

"Keep your fingers straight going in and out and you're fine."

He pushed the one in again easily and then tried to force the second in alongside it. It stretched him with a sharp pain so that he pulled both fingers out. Arch watched, stroking his shaft easily up and down. Ty tried again with his fingers and this time the pain was less. It was uncomfortable but there was also some pleasure to it.

"Give me a minute," he murmured.

"Starting to like it?"

"Starting to not hate it."

The wolf nodded. "Fair enough."

It took another three insertions before Ty felt stretched and relaxed enough to nod. And then Arch lay on his back as the fox got to all fours. "Nope," Arch said. "Get up here and straddle me."

"Okay." Ty lifted one knee over the wolf's body and settled down atop him.

"This way's a bit easier for your first time." The wolf's ears flicked. "Unless you want to be on all fours with me on top of you."

"No. I mean, that'd be fine but this is fine too."

"So reach back and get me into position." Ty's fingers found the warm length, the slick latex, and pulled it upright. Arch closed his eyes for a moment. "Good. Now just push yourself down on it when you're ready."

When you're ready. The moment crystallized in Ty's chest: he was about to have another guy inside him, to get fucked, to be a bitch.

Except…he wasn't. He was on top, he was in control. The wolf lay passively below him, and Ty was the one dictating the pace. He already felt warm under his tail from his fingers, and the shaft was right there. It was so easy just to let himself down, to feel the pressure against his entrance increase and then stretch him wider than one finger, wider than two, but smoother, and then oh shit, the wolf's cock was inside him.

He pushed down slowly. It seemed to take forever before his rear rested on Arch's hips. The wolf grunted and curled fingers around Ty's cock, sliding them up and down with some lube to help. "Go at your own pace," he breathed. "Don't worry about me."

Right, because it wasn't just about being inside, it was about fucking, about the rhythm. In a way, he had to think about Arch, because then this was just like jerking off the wolf, only using his butt instead of a paw. And while he felt disorientingly full, it wasn't unpleasant, and as he raised and lowered his rear and the cock slid back and forth in him, the sensations actually became enjoyable.

It helped that Arch was stroking him as he did, and though at first he'd thought he would never come from having a cock inside him, it took surprisingly little time before the familiar sensations crested in his groin, before he gasped and hitched his breath and then convulsed, spattering Arch's paw and chest with his come. His rear clenched around the wolf's cock, a little painfully, but Ty barely felt it.

He met Arch's eyes, his tongue lolling out of his muzzle. "Uh," he said.

"Felt good." The wolf teased his dripping cock.

"Nnnf. Yeah, it wasn't bad." Ty wiggled his rear. Discomfort was taking over again. "Did you, uh…?"

"Nah." Arch reached down to Ty's hips and lifted them, and the fox obliged. The feeling of relief as the cock slid out of him brought another gasp, and he sat back on Arch's thighs.

The wolf reached for his wrapped shaft, but the fox stopped his paw. "Let me."

He worked a claw under the condom, taking some time to tease the wolf's knot while Arch squirmed under him, then slid the latex off and dropped it to the side. Arch's shaft rested against his tail, so Ty stayed astride the wolf, pinning the smaller canid down while behind him his paw worked up and down the thick, warm shaft. To his surprise, he liked the idea that this had just been inside him; looking down at the wolf's panting muzzle,

He was on top, he was in control. The wolf lay passively below him, and Ty was the one dictating the pace. He already felt warm under his tail from his fingers, and the shaft was right there.

he imagined that the shaft sliding through his fingers was sliding into him, that he was actually going to make Arch finish the way they'd been before.

It didn't take long, because Arch was pretty wound up, and from the way he squirmed, he liked being pinned down by a muscular fox. Even when he came, bucking up and down, he couldn't budge Ty very much, and he yelped as he spattered the fox's tail and paw with warmth.

Then he lay back and closed his eyes, arms falling open on the bed. Ty fell atop him and Arch licked at his muzzle, and then they kissed and rolled onto their sides, claws ruffling through each other's fur.

The wolf regarded him through sleepy eyes. "So?" he murmured.

"I'd do it again," Ty said. "But like once for every five times the other way."

"I don't know that I'd want to do it that often." Arch nuzzled him. "But glad we did it this once and you're not freaking out."

"Why would I freak out?"

"Oh, jocks, masculinity, getting fucked in the ass…you know."

Dev had seemed pretty touchy about it, but then Dev was uptight about a lot of things. If Ty let himself, he'd probably be just as wound up. Like what if someone at the hotel took a picture of him and Arch the way they had of his dinners in Pelagia? Or someone at the club? What if his parents found out he'd been out with a guy, much less sleeping with one? "You know," he said, "if people heard I'd slept with a guy, I don't think it'd matter whose cock went where so much."

The wolf laughed and licked Ty's whiskers. "You're cute. Hope you wind up with a good wife."

"That's—that's way off in the future."

Arch's fingers played at Ty's side and down his hip. "It's tomorrow potentially, right? You're going back and you're going to have dinner with more of them, and you're going to end up with one."

"Maybe." Ty laid his ears back. "I'll still come see you when I'm in Yerba."

"I'll look forward to it. But I won't wait for it. You know?"

Ty pulled back, scooting up to a sitting position where he could look Arch in the eye. "If I say I'm gonna come back, I will."

"Okay."

"I'm serious."

Arch nodded and tried to tug the fox toward him. "I believe you."

"No you don't. You're just saying you do so I'll stop talking about it."

"Yes." The wolf sighed. "Because this might be our last night together, so I want it to be nice and pleasant. You can text me about your wives when things happen and we can have this conversation then."

"I'll see you again," Ty insisted. His chest felt tight; his tail curled around on itself.

"I'm sure you will." Arch smiled and pulled him again. "Just lie down with me tonight, okay?"

How could he make the wolf understand that he could do what he wanted, that if he said he was going to come back and see Arch in this very hotel room, even, that it would happen and the only way it wouldn't was if Arch changed his mind about wanting to see Ty? Arch said he didn't understand the world of professional athletes, and maybe Ty needed to remind him. "I'm not just a dance club hookup," he said.

The smile on the wolf's muzzle faded. "Then what are you?"

"I'm a friend of yours. With benefits. And I want those benefits to go on."

"If you want it, then I guess it'll have to happen, won't it?" Arch rolled onto his side, supporting himself by an elbow, and he was no longer smiling at all.

"Yes! That's what I'm saying."

Arch glanced toward the living room. "Let's get high," he said.

"Sure." Ty folded his ears back, confused, and then remembered the call from his agent. "Well…I'm going back to workouts in a month, and my agent's right, I mean, that could cost me like a hundred thousand dollars."

"Uh-huh. But you want to do it."

"I do, but it's not worth it. If you really want to…"

"No." Arch sighed and rolled off the bed. "I was proving a point."

Ty scrambled off and after the wolf as Arch found his pants and pulled them on. "What point? Hey, where are you going?"

The wolf pulled his shirt on and turned to Ty. "I should probably go. I need to be up early to go to work in the morning."

"I'll buy you a cab." He gripped the wolf's wrist.

"You can't buy your way out of everything."

"I get it, okay? I get the point you're making, but it's different! It's not the same. They can't test me for—for wolf come."

For a moment, he thought the joke had salvaged everything. Arch laughed, and Ty laughed too, and he loosened his grip on the warm wrist. But then Arch pulled him close and hugged him, kissed him on the nose, and stepped back. "This was a lot of fun, Ty. I like you a lot. I really hope I'll see you again."

Ty followed him to the bedroom door and leaned against the frame as Arch walked closely past the windows without even looking out onto the hazy lights of the city. The wolf's tail hung limp behind him and his ears were down. He got as far as the counter near the door before Ty said, "Arch."

The wolf stopped and half-turned with a paw raised. "Don't," he said. "If I stay, it'll just mean we have to go through all this again in the morning. Might as well say good-bye now."

If Ty promised to be good in the morning, maybe Arch would stay. But his promises hadn't meant anything before and there was no reason to assume they would mean something now. He could offer to pay Arch's rent, to fly him to Chevali or Pelagia, but those ideas felt desperate and, worse, irrelevant. "I was just going to say that I like you a lot. And I had a really good time, too."

"Thanks." Arch moved to unbolt the door.

"And if you're free next time I'm in town, I'd like to do it again."

The wolf nodded once, said, "Me too," so low that even Ty's cupped ears barely caught it, then pulled the door open and stepped out into the hall.

The door shut with a slam. Ty closed his eyes, exhaled, and went to the bathroom to clean himself off.

Chapter 12

His mother was less than pleased when she called him the following morning to confirm his travel details. "Who is this Tami Tachibana?"

"A bunch of vixens wrote me after the TMZ article. I liked her letter."

"Where are these letters? I want to read them."

Ty sat next to his packed suitcase on the bed, the smells of the night before still in his nose. "I deleted them all, Mom. They were boring."

"Tchah! I know you don't really want a good Yamatese wife, so at least you could do me the honor of allowing me to choose her. Since you do not care."

Tami had responded to the letter Lucas had helped Ty write with a wary acceptance of a potential dinner sometime in the future. He'd put Arch out of his mind as much as possible that morning, but the effort of doing so made him shorter of temper than he cared to be. "You can choose the candidates, Mom. I just added one to the list."

"You add one of yours so you may say no to all of mine. No. You will have dinner with only the vixens I choose."

"Mom," Ty said, "If you don't want to come on our date with us, that's fine, you don't have to."

"I won't approve of you marrying her."

"Then I'll elope." Probably Ty wouldn't talk to his mother like this face to face, but sitting in the hotel room whose emptiness weighed on him, staring at his reflection in the window, he didn't care.

"Taiyo!"

"What?"

"Apologize to me right now."

"I'm sorry, Mom." Before she could voice the words he heard her gathering breath for, he went on. "Of course I won't elope. You'd be invited to our wedding."

She was silent. He knew she was waiting for him to apologize for real. He'd gone along with this whole wedding thing with very little complaint because it had been impressed on him since he was a little cub that he'd have a good marriage arranged to a good family. Of course if he were to bring someone into the family, it had to be someone his parents would approve of; you couldn't just pick any old girl you liked. Some of his friends had made fun of him, talked about those catalogs of vixens from Platania and told him to just order one, but the idea of a structured life had been a relief through college. Someone else was going to take care of his love life so he didn't have to, and he had a ready-made excuse to keep out of a serious relationship. He could devote his energy to football.

Only now was he realizing what a difference it would make if his wife were someone he also liked. He'd assumed all through college that his parents would pick a vixen he'd be able to build a life with, but his own preferences had barely come into play in the choices he'd been given so far.

"I'm sorry, Mom. But I am twenty-two," he said when she remained silent. "This Tami is Yamatese so I'd be marrying a Yamatese vixen just like you said. And she's interesting. Why are you so sure you won't like her?"

"I know all the good Yamatese families in the area and all their daughters of marrying age."

"Maybe she moved there recently. I don't know. But please, Mom. I really want to meet her. I already wrote her back."

He held his breath through another long several seconds of silence. Finally she clacked her jaw. "I will come along on this dinner. And if she is not suitable I will not permit you to consider her."

"Thank you, Mom."

Ty made a mental note to send Tami a letter detailing all the things his mother was going to ask about. If that scared her off, then this wasn't the right family to marry into anyway, and Ty would be stuck with his mother's choice. It wouldn't be Hideyo, he vowed, purely out of spite because his mother liked her best. Maybe the bubbly one wouldn't be too bad in small doses.

At least his friends would be around, and maybe he could still live in the same house with them. He could buy his wife the house next door and she could have her group of friends live there. They could sleep together when she was in season and otherwise they'd leave each other alone.

Of course he could make that work out. He could have anything he wanted.

PART 2: TAMI

CHAPTER 13

Jumbo Bubbles X had been submitted to the publishers only two days late, which Tami considered a victory. Devin and Axel dragged her out to celebrate, but half an hour later she went back to her cube to review the meeting notes for the known outstanding issues that they were still working on while the publishers reviewed the game. Never stops, she muttered. Never stops.

Her email pinged, and she sighed. Nine-thirty at night and she was going to kill Jaden if he was emailing to tell her they'd discovered a problem with the build. They'd rushed QA because they had to, but he'd signed off on it and that should've been the—

She'd opened the email program while she thought, and her thoughts juddered to a halt when she saw who the email was from. Ty Nakamura? Spam—no, it was that football player.

Holy Mother, he'd written her back. And the subject line was "Hey, how about dinner?"

For a moment her brain locked up as though it were in an infinite loop. "How about dinner?" she kept seeing, and how weird was it that this guy was asking her out without even having met her, based on nothing but her email? And yet she had sent him a letter based on even less, based on just, what, that he was looking for a Yamatese vixen? That was how relationships started in Yamatese dating sims, the kind of improbable setup that people loved in movies and books that never actually worked in real life. Real life was neat, orderly code; it was project plans and a progression of steps and deadlines and penalties.

But of course, this wasn't a marriage proposal at all. It was dinner, no more. And she'd asked for it, so she couldn't very well back out now, couldn't send back a message saying, "Whoa, sorry, didn't think you'd actually accept."

If she did reply, if she did accept, what did that do to her plan? It wasn't that she didn't want to date; it was that there would always be guys around, now or in twenty years when she'd been running her own game studio for a while and was ready to ease off the throttle. Her parents kept their own separate lives and sure, they'd raised her and her two younger brothers, but despite her mother's assurances (and Marci's pregnancy and Ada's marriage), Tami had not yet felt the urge to reproduce.

So what was the point of even going on a date with this guy if her best case scenario was that she wasted one evening and had a story to impress her few male co-workers who liked football? What were the odds that this Ty Nakamura was going to become so famous that when she was trying to make connections, people would be impressed that she'd had dinner with him? There were hundreds of football players; how many could the average guy name off the top of his head? She'd have to ask Axel, whose knowledge of sports was limited to video games.

Connections, though…she rubbed one finger along her left fang. Famous or not, he'd be worth millions in five or six years, which was right around the time her plan called for her to be looking for funding to run her studio. A football player wouldn't be a bad guy to know. Notoriously careless with money, childlike and impulsive…

Now that she'd taken some time to think about it, her heart slowed and the fog cleared from her mind. She hit Reply and typed out a quick letter saying that his schedule was probably more crowded than hers, so she'd make time whenever he could. Then she added that she had a deadline coming up in six weeks, so probably the sooner the better.

She stared at the letter and then deleted all the bits about her deadline. There was no point in telling him that his schedule was more important and then telling him all about hers. If he picked a day near her deadline, she'd work around it. It was dinner, after all. It wasn't going to last five hours. Three max, and she could work after it was over if she needed to.

•

At work the next day, she grabbed Axel to walk off the company campus over to the Halberd Square Sandwich Company. "My treat," she said.

"You know how to get a guy to lunch." The marmot stood from his desk. "Should I grab Devin?"

"If you want," Tami said, and then, "No, actually, just you and me."

Axel's eyebrows rose. "Okay." And he didn't say another word until they were out of the building.

Under the grey skies and light drizzle, Tami opened her umbrella, but Axel barely acknowledged the rain apart from cinching his trenchcoat's belt. "You're leaving the group," he said, not looking at her. "You got Destiny's Angel."

"They haven't announced that yet."

His eyes widened. "You're leaving the company? Take me with you."

"Calm down. It's not job-related."

He splashed through a puddle and fixed her with a stare. "In the submission period, you want to have a non-work-related conversation? Are you sick?"

His muzzle had such a wrinkled, worried expression that she said, "I'm fine." They navigated through a crowd of umbrellas, Axel patiently remaining at her side as she twisted and turned hers to avoid getting stuck on other people's. They took shelter under a large department store awning while waiting for a light to change.

Tami breathed in the cool, moist air and exhaled. "I don't want this to become company gossip yet."

Axel opened his mouth to say something, closed it, and then when Tami didn't go on, he grabbed her wrist. The worry vanished into a huge smile, "You got a date."

"Sort of."

The smile widened. "Oh! Is it that guy your friend Ada was trying to set you up with? That's so cool. Look, take it seriously, don't look at it as like a break from work. But you don't have to dress up or anything." He brushed his whiskers back over his round muzzle, inspecting her. "But dress up more than this."

Tami flattened her ears, smoothing down her hoodie. "Fatima keeps saying the same thing."

"Course." Axel smiled. "If you want to be promoted, you can't dress like a coder. You have to dress like a manager. And if you want a date to go well, you have to dress like someone who wants to be on a date."

"Ugh. Okay, that's a whole other topic, though." She ran a paw over her ears, letting them come back up as her paw slid over them. "I wanted to ask you to explain football to me."

His little ears flicked around. "Why, does he like sports? You really need to steer the conversation to topics of mutual interest. Don't pretend to like something…" Then he stopped dead on the sidewalk so abruptly that the person behind him bumped into him and muttered before moving on. "Oh, no. No!" He slapped her arm, looking like a cub at Christmas. "That football player?"

Despite herself, Tami smiled because she loved surprising her friends. "Yeah. He wrote back. I guess he likes me."

"Aah!" Axel clapped both paws to his muzzle, cutting off his exclamation. "Oh my god, Tami, you're going to dinner with a football player!"

"Uh-huh." People around them turned their heads. She realized that the light had changed and was red again. "Anyway, it's probably not going to lead to anything, but I don't want to go in not knowing anything about what he does."

"Of course, of course. Did you want to do this over lunch? Maybe two lunches? There's no football going on right now but we could probably get a video of the big games from last year. Oh! I can get you the championship game which he was actually in. Not over lunch, though."

"I wasn't thinking it would take more than a lunch. Wait, you watch actual football?" The light changed, and Tami herded Axel toward the curb, raising her umbrella again.

"Just the playoffs. Mialo likes it and I've gotten into it a bit."

More conscious of the crowd around them, she lowered her voice. "Good. I was hoping you could explain the basics and then I could grab one of the video games. Which one's the best?"

"Well," Axel said, "there's really only one game that has the official teams. A couple years ago I would've said the Pro Football Complete franchise was more playable as far as learning the game, but UFL '09 fixed a lot of the issues and got really good ratings. Mialo played it for like a solid month when it came out." They splashed across the street, and Axel brushed water off the sleeves of his coat. "Actually, he could probably explain football better. You want to come over and play one night?"

"Maybe." Tami hurried forward to the awning of the sandwich place. "Let's see how this goes."

They placed their order and found a table against the wall. Axel draped his coat carefully over the back of his chair and sat while Tami leaned her umbrella against the wall and swept her tail to the side. When she sat, Axel leaned forward. "All right," he said. "Now, football. How much do you know?"

"I, uh." She scraped her claws over the plastic table surface. "I know what a football looks like. And I know that it's called a touchdown when they score."

"Okay." Axel tapped his whiskers. "You know that most sports are sublimated expressions of war, right? So the teams are two armies fighting over a piece of territory, which is represented in the case of football by the field." He pulled a paper napkin from the chrome dispenser and laid it between them. "The idea is you've conquered the whole field when you get to the end, called the 'end zone.' They get seven points when they get the ball there. Well, six, and then they have to kick it through the goalposts for one more, but even that's too complicated for now. Following so far?"

"Simple." Tami nodded. "I've heard 'end zone' before, too."

"Great." Axel's buckteeth showed prominently in his smile. "They move the ball one play at a time. A play starts with the center giving the ball to the quarterback, and it ends when either the ball hits the ground or the player holding the ball is tackled to the ground, or a player gets to the end zone with the ball. Generally. Sometimes the ball can hit the ground and players can grab it, but again…" He waved a paw. "Too much detail for now."

"I can handle some detail," Tami said. "I'm not an idiot."

"I know, but I'm just trying to go over the basics here. So the quarterback can either throw the ball—generally forward, but he can go backwards for some plays—or he can run it forward or give it to another player to run forward."

"So if he throws it, the player who catches it can't run?"

"No, no." Axel's claw traced the arc of an imaginary throw. "The guy who catches it can run until he's tackled, too. It's just that if the play starts with a throw forward, it's called a pass play, and if it starts with running then it's called a running play."

"That doesn't make a lot of sense."

Axel looked up, a smile still crossing his muzzle. "What did you say to him? What did he say back?"

She tapped the table next to his napkin. "You haven't finished explaining the game."

"This is back and forth, boss."

"Ugh." She rolled her eyes at the title.

"I tell you some things about football, you tell me some things about this date."

She turned back to the counter in time to see two sandwiches come up. The harried ringtail server grabbed them, looked at the ticket, and after scanning the room, came over to their table. "You guys need anything else?"

"We're fine." Axel reached for his sweet pepper and mushroom sub. When she'd gone, he raised his eyebrows. "So? Come on, tell."

Tami took a bite of her tempeh and pesto sandwich. "Well, I said… okay, my mom got on me about him too, after you guys told me about him. So I wrote him and said my mom was making me write him, that I worked for a video game company, and that…I don't even remember. I specifically wrote it so he wouldn't want to write me back, just so I could tell my mom that I wrote him."

"Uh-huh. And what did he say when he wrote back?" Axel ripped another bite off his sandwich. "I have no idea what football players talk like."

"Oh, it wasn't…It was just an email. He said, I dunno, I sounded interesting and did I want to have dinner."

"You haven't memorized the wording?" The marmot shook his head. "Tch tch."

"I don't know how to do this stuff—" Tami caught herself, noticing Axel's smile. "Har har. Okay, that was one for you. Back to the football. What does this guy do?"

Axel's cheeks bulged as he chewed, and then he swallowed his mouthful. "He's a wide receiver, one of the guys who catches the ball. This was his first year and he caught a touchdown in the playoffs and did pretty well in the championship game."

"What's 'pretty well'?" Despite herself, Tami found herself intrigued by the rules. She still didn't want to join the crowds of people who wore colors like gang members and painted their fur and lived and died by the actions of a few guys playing a game. But she also didn't really like the fan communities that sprung up around video games. The games were their own little worlds, with their strengths and flaws, and she could see the appeal of football as a game like that. The fans were people, and they all viewed the games through their own lenses of whatever color and thickness. How many times had she heard complaints about the main character of a game being one of the more common species? And on the few occasions when a game went out of its way to make models of a less common species—Tami had worked on one game with bat-eared fox models—the wolves and foxes and otters complained that too many resources had been wasted on species that "nobody would ever use," rather than taking the chance to try out being someone else for a change.

Axel had been talking for a good fifteen seconds while her mind wandered. She snapped back to him. "…but a touchdown is pretty good, regardless of yardage, so any game where a receiver catches a touchdown is probably a 'pretty good' game."

"Points win the game," Tami said, to make him think she was still processing that information. "But it sounds like Nakamura didn't catch a touchdown in the championship? You said he caught one in the playoff."

"Yeah, he didn't catch a touchdown in the championship, but he caught a few balls to advance the team. I forget exactly how much." He took another bite and tapped the table. "So where's he taking you for dinner?"

"This place called Aquitaria. I looked it up online. Pretty fancy."

The marmot's eyes widened. "Wow. It's so fancy I haven't even heard of it."

Tami affected surprise. "Maybe I should ask Devin about it."

"Hah." Axel ripped at his sandwich. "If it doesn't measure the dinner entrees in pounds, Devin won't know about it. Hey, so you have to order a Negroni there. That's how Bradley Warner judges the quality of a bar."

She eyed him. "What's a Negroni supposed to taste like? If I don't know, I won't know if they do one right."

Axel stared at her, his expression growing more mournful as he chewed his sandwich. He swallowed, and heaved a sigh. "All right. What night do you want to go out with me to Vince's?"

Chapter 14

Armed with the taste of a Negroni cocktail (a little sweet, a little bitter; she liked it quite a bit, actually) and an evening of playing UFL '09 with Axel and his boyfriend Mialo (mostly watching them play and listening to Mialo talk about football), Tami only realized on the night of the dinner that she had completely neglected the third aspect of the evening when she opened the door to her apartment and found her mother waiting there.

"Tami, where have you been?"

"Mama?"

"I called you three times today." Her mother stood and smoothed down her immaculate silk dress, a gesture Tami found herself imitating sometimes even with pants. Her ears came up at exactly the correct angle as her eyes met Tami's. "I've told you how I feel when you don't answer."

"I was trying to get work done so I could take tonight off!" Tami tossed her laptop bag on the couch and folded her arms. "I talked to you last night and I told you I'd pick out a nice outfit."

"And I called you this morning to tell you that I found one of your old formal dresses in the house and to ask if you wanted it. And you didn't answer, so I just brought it over." She held up a plastic-wrapped yellow… thing, with frills around the short sleeves and the hemline, and white flowers adorning the belt.

For a moment, Tami couldn't speak. "That's…" she finally managed, "that's my junior high school dress. It doesn't fit anymore."

Her mother glanced down at her chest. "You've haven't grown since junior high. Maybe an inch or two. It will fit."

"It was hideous ten years ago. It's worse now. And my fur itched all night and it smelled bad. No, I have a sensible blouse and nice pants—"

"Pants!" Mama reacted as though Tami had suggested going naked to the dinner. "Pants? You want them to end this dinner before it even begins? No pants."

"I'm not wearing that dress."

The older vixen sighed and lay the dress carefully along the couch. "Fine. Let me see what skirts you have."

"Uh—" Tami got no more than that syllable out before her mother was in her bedroom. By the time she followed, the closet door was open and her mother's paws were on her hips, her tail curled behind her like an upside-down question mark.

"Where are the rest of them?" she demanded, pointing at the two skirts Tami called 'the brown one' and 'the blue one.'

Tami leaned against her door frame. "Hopefully being worn by some poor people who need them more than I do."

"You gave them away? Those were gifts from me."

"You bought them for me every time we went shopping even though I told you I'd never wear them."

Her mother turned back to the closet. "And now it's too late to go shopping. We have to leave in twenty minutes. All right." She took a deep breath and turned, trailing a paw down her side. "You may wear this dress. I'll wear one of those skirts, and they will not care because I will be judging, not judged."

"I'm not wearing that dress." But Tami had to admit that if forced to wear a dress, the one her mother had on was a pretty attractive one.

Her mother reached around behind herself to undo the zipper as if Tami hadn't spoken. "It feels lovely on the fur, it's attractive, and it smells like me. I hope that is not objectionable."

"He's a football player," Tami said. "He's not going to care if I wear a dress, and anyway," she hurried on because she had no idea what kind of girls football players liked, and it was possible that her mother had done research on that topic, "what is the point of dressing like someone else to go on a date? He should be meeting me, not some dressed-up version of me that—thank you—all right."

Her mother had slid delicately out of the dress. Tami averted her eyes, reaching out to take the silk dress. "It's not for him to meet you," her mother said, unconcerned about standing in front of her daughter in her underwear. "It's for his parents to meet you. If they like you, then you may meet him later wearing a filthy sweatshirt and torn jeans if you must." She sniffed and took the brown skirt down from the closet.

"If he shows up completely by surprise at the job where I wear jeans and a hoodie insisting we go out to dinner right away, then I'm sure I will." Tami took the dress into her bathroom and closed the door.

If the dress were too small for her, then she could insist on wearing something else, perhaps, but her mother's yoga and aerobics apparently equated to her own missed dinners and lunches when work took over her life, and the dress fit quite well. Catching sight of the mirror, Tami grimaced; she looked, in fact, more like her mother than herself.

It didn't help that her mother had chosen the blouse and skirt Tami wore to her important meetings at work, even though she looked uncomfortable in them. For a moment, Tami had the odd impression of staring into a future mirror, her eyes slightly narrower, her ears and muzzle with touches of grey.

And then her mother stepped forward, shaking her head, and adjusted Tami's collar and pulled the sides of the dress down until it hung straighter. "All right. Now, what do you have to put behind your ears?"

"Pencils," Tami said, adjusting the dress.

"Stop." Her mother swatted her paws away.

"It's going to get wrinkled in the car." Tami let her paws drop to her sides. Already this whole evening had become far too much of a production, a preparation for a role in the theater rather than a pleasant dinner out.

Her mother strode briskly out to the living room. "Less so if it doesn't start that way," she said.

Tami followed to find her mother pulling two small red flowers out of her purse. "Here. Clip these on."

They perfectly matched the red trim on the silk dress. Tami took them and clipped them to her ears without a word.

•

"Negroni, please." Tami ignored her mother's look of surprise and kept her eyes on Nakamura—Ty, he'd insisted she call him, over his mother's objections. He was one of the most athletic foxes, or males of any species, that she'd been this close to, and her first thought when she'd shaken his paw had been that she understood the hyperbolic analogies in sports articles comparing athletes to gods. Maybe this Ty wasn't a god, but he certainly looked like one of his parents might have been.

A moment later, when she met his parents, she reconsidered that thought. Both stood a foot shorter than their son, and Mr. Nakamura had a doughy, unathletic figure to go with his nearly-silent personality. Mrs. Nakamura, thin and sharp, engaged in verbal sparring with Tami's mother, feeling each other out during the first few moments of the evening.

"So nice to meet you." The mother of the prospective bride made the first greeting; she'd told Tami she would have to, and that each family would basically have to downplay their own worth to the other. "It certainly is an honor that you have selected our humble daughter to meet your worthy son."

"We are delighted that your family accepted the invitation. It's truly gratifying to meet with you."

The greeting seemed fine to Tami, but her mother's ears flicked back—just a quarter of an inch, nothing that anyone not looking would have noticed, nothing anyone could have taken offense to, but enough to tell Tami that her mother felt offended.

"The pleasure is all ours, truly. And it is quite the honor to meet the parents of such an accomplished young fox. How lucky the two of you must be."

"We do feel that we have been blessed by the gods in ways that few parents are," Mrs. Nakamura had replied smoothly.

"May we share in each other's blessings," Tami's mother parried.

"Nothing would delight us more."

And then Mrs. Nakamura went on. "It is such a shame that Mr. Tachibana was not able to join."

"As I said in my letter to you," Tami's mother said, to her credit without a trace of stiffness, "Mr. Tachibana resides in Port City where Tami's younger brothers attend university."

"Of course. So he looks after the sons while you look after your daughter."

"Quite." They hadn't been sure how Ty's parents would feel about a divorce. Tami had said that it was 2009 and if they couldn't handle a divorce then she didn't want to be part of their family. Tami's mother had insisted that there was no reason to make waves, and had pointed out that one could always reveal the divorce later, but it couldn't be concealed again once it was told. There was always the question of why they had concealed it in the first place, but there were enough things to argue about and Tami had let that one go.

So they moved to the table without Tami ever getting a chance to say hello to Ty. He smiled at her and she smiled back, feeling fake and uncomfortable in the dress, and then her mother herded to a seat across from him at a six-person table and took the seat to her left, while the Nakamuras sat on her right.

When she ordered the Negroni, Ty's ears cupped her way with interest, ignoring the waiter's attention to look at Tami. "That's interesting," he said. "You like Negronis?"

"I always order one at a place I haven't been to before. It's a way to take the measure of the bartender."

At most of the bars she was accustomed to, the waiter or waitress would have stepped in at that point to assure them that their bartender was top-notch, but this tuxedoed rabbit stood stiffly silent, like an automaton awaiting the proper set of code words. "Good idea," Ty said. "I'll try one as well."

This activated the waiter, who said, "Very good, sir."

"And my parents will have a vodka martini and an Old Fashioned."

"Yes, sir."

Was Tami supposed to order for her family? She shot her mother a panicked look as her mother said, "A glass of the house red."

"Ma'am," the waiter said, "I'll ask the sommelier to come over."

Even Tami couldn't miss the tension that descended over the table following that remark, though she had no idea where it came from. Her mother's ears swept back and then came forward. "There's no need. Tell them I'd like something fruity, not too dry, full-bodied."

"Yes, ma'am." With that, the rabbit turned on his heel and was gone.

Tami met Ty's eyes again and almost giggled out loud at his startled look of incomprehension. She mimicked it and gave him a quick nod, and then her mother kicked her leg and she composed herself again.

"Oh, shoot," Ty said. "Mom, I'm going to make sure they use Grey Goose in your martini. I forgot to tell him."

"It doesn't matter," his mother said. "I'm not particular."

But Ty stood anyway and patted her shoulder. "Won't take but a second. Why don't you ask Mrs. Tachibana to show you her bank account statement?"

Then he was gone, leaving his parents to stare uncomfortably at Tami's mother. "Of course we won't ask—" his mother began.

"Please don't worry about it. Children can be so wilful." Her mother didn't even look at her as she said it.

Mrs. Nakamura leaned forward. "Yes! And unappreciative. We have brought him to nine dinners this winter alone."

"Nine! I would have expected many more."

"As you say, children can be wilful." Here Mrs. Nakamura quieted herself, which was a shame because Tami wanted to hear why nine wasn't enough dinners and how Ty had somehow avoided going to more.

He came back a moment later. "All set." He patted his mother's paw.

"It's really not important. I don't know what's gotten into you. Any vodka they serve here will be fine."

"Mom has her favorites," he said to Tami. "She doesn't like to put people out, but if they didn't make it with Grey Goose, we'd hear about it all the way home, right, Dad?"

"What nonsense you speak." Mrs. Nakamura pulled her paw away, but despite her tone her ears remained properly up. "You make it sound as though I'm some kind of overly particular harridan."

"Goodness, no!" Ty affected shock. "I meant only that you know what you like, and you're determined to get it."

His mother sniffed and turned to Tami's mother. "Where was your family from originally?"

Tami's mother began to recount her family history, which Tami knew, and so she studied Ty. He seemed quite pleased with himself, leaning back in his chair with both paws in his lap and smiling at her. She tried to convey her approval of his teasing his mother, and she thought he understood, but then she was pulled away from that conversation as her mother asked her to recount her accomplishments at primary school.

The pointless list was thankfully interrupted by the arrival of the cocktails, each one in the perfectly appropriate glass upon a white cocktail napkin. "A toast," Ty said cheerfully, and raised his glass. "To future alliances."

Everyone raised their glass in turn, said, "Cheers," and drank. When Tami caught Ty's eye again, he was fiddling with his napkin. He looked directly at her, then down at a corner of his napkin, then back at her before dropping the napkin back on the table.

Odd. Her eyes went automatically to her own napkin. There was nothing unusual about it. She looked back up at him while telling the Nakamuras about her high school debate team championship (she hadn't won an individual award, but had contributed), and he gave an encouraging nod.

So she picked up her drink with the napkin, contriving to slip her finger between the layers of the corner, and caught a glimpse of writing on her napkin in light pencil, hidden under the top layer.

She put the glass down again, and when the conversation had shifted away from her, she idly played with the napkin and folded the corner back. Below the top layer was a phone number and, printed in lowercase, "text me."

She looked up into Ty's eyes. He smiled and looked down into his lap—where, she realized, he must be holding his phone. Could she even get hers out without anyone noticing? Her mother had warned her about having her phone out at the table when it was just them at dinner, let alone a formal engagement like this one.

But her lap was hidden, and she spent half the time looking demurely down anyway. So how to forge an excuse to go into her purse?

She took another drink of her cocktail—it was superb, too, better than any of the other ones she'd tasted. She would have to tell Axel about it. And when she put it down, she had an idea. Nobody was looking right at her, so she tilted the glass and tapped it on the table, letting a little of the drink spill out over her paw.

"Oh, I'm so sorry!" She shook her paw, and then reached for her purse. "So clumsy. Er…" Her mother was staring at her. "I must be so nervous in the presence of such an honorable family. I'm sorry. I'll be right back."

Before anyone else could say anything, she grabbed her cocktail napkin, pressed it to her fingers, and fled.

The dampness on her fingers had soaked into the paper, but she could still decipher the phone number written there. In the bathroom stall (in case her mother came in after her), she entered it, saved it as a contact, and then texted, *I can't believe you did that.*

She hadn't left the bathroom before he texted back. *I can't believe you did THAT. Ballsy!*

I'm a girl.

So? Girls can be ballsy. You want me to say you were ovariesy?

Are you really texting at the table?

Sure. They're talking about some dead people from back in Yamato and seeing if any of them know the same ones.

God this is horrible.

Really? It's the most fun one I've been on so far.

That reminded her that he'd been on eight others. Or maybe nine. His mother hadn't specified whether this one was included in the nine. *You don't do this with all the girls?*

Just you. :)

She stared at those words, trying to overcome her disbelief. *I'm really pretty dull*, she typed, and then imagined what Marci would tell her to say and erased it. *I'm sorry those other girls were so dull*, she wrote instead, and sent that.

Hazards of the family. So would you go out with me sometime?

She laughed, the sound echoing off the glossy marble floor and elegant porcelain. *What do you think we're doing now?*

This? A meeting with better food and drink.

It does remind me of a meeting. It's missing a Powerpoint preso tho.

Don't suggest that to my mom or she'll make me do one, and I haven't done one of those since freshman year of high school.

Don't worry, she typed, *I do them all the time.*

Would you help me with it?

Of course.

Great. Hey, you'd better get back to the table. Your mom keeps looking toward the restroom. I think she's about to come get you.

Omw.

Her phone expanded that into *On my way!* and she hurried out of the stall, washed her paws, and made her way back to the table.

She and her mother insisted that the Nakamuras order for them, emphasizing Tami's vegetarianism as a health choice rather than a moral choice (another of the battles Tami had chosen not to fight her mother over). The meal was delicious when it came, though Tami had seen the prices and knew that she could get food ninety percent as good for about thirty percent of the price at any number of restaurants she'd previously thought of as fancy. She kept her phone in her lap and exchanged texts with Ty about the food and conversation whenever she dared, which wasn't as often as he dared. She had no idea how he got away with it; it seemed obvious to her when he was typing something, but maybe that was because she was looking for the little movements of his shoulders, the downward glances of his eyes. She was a better typist, but didn't dare look down as often, so their messages contained equal parts errors, something that as the night wound down she found herself grateful for, and she even texted him about it when afforded a little more time by her mother and Mrs. Nakamura's verbal sparring over the bill.

"I insist that you allow me to pay for this privilege," her mother said.

I'll go out with you, Tami texted. *I think we're compatible enough to warrant an actual date.*

"Under normal circumstances, of course we would accept your generous offer. But the extraordinary good fortune our son has enjoyed allows us to step outside the normal bounds of propriety. Please accept this meal as a token of our thanks, and as a way for us to thank our ancestors for the fortune they have bestowed upon us."

Great, Ty texted back. *What did it? Was it the joke about the salmon roe?*

"Your generosity certainly speaks well of your good nature and your devotion to your family," Tami's mother replied. "But my daughter also enjoys quite a fortunate career and has worked hard all her life. In addition, I am most happy to pay for this meal as a measure of my hope that our two families may enjoy a long and happy association."

No, Tami texted. *It's that you make about as many spelling mistakes as I do. I don't think people with a wide disparity in typographical competence will ever do well together.*

Fasinating, he wrote back, misspelled, of course. *I'll call you.*

"What a lovely offer!" Mrs. Nakamura smiled. "Allow me to propose a solution. We will pay for your dinner and your daughter's, and you may pay for ours. In that case, both of our families will have shown sufficient gratitude for our respective fortunes."

Ty got up then, sliding his phone casually into his pocket. "Shall we go, Mom, Dad?"

His parents looked at him. "Ty," his mother said, "we haven't finished settling the question of who will pay the bill."

"I paid it fifteen minutes ago." He smiled at Tami. "Meeting adjourned."

There were more discussions outside about when they would be in touch to schedule another dinner, during which Ty and Tami stayed very quiet. He stood politely, ears cupped toward the conversation, but his eyes indicated his mind was elsewhere, so Tami felt comfortable letting her mind wander as well.

This ritualized courtship felt as though she'd stepped into a movie, cast in a role that wasn't quite right for her. The dress fit well enough, and the silk didn't bunch up at all (unlike her underwear, which she had not been able to un-bunch by wiggling her hips discreetly), but it was her mother's dress and her mother's world, not hers.

It was past nine-thirty according to the time on her phone when she'd last texted Ty, and that meant she'd be home by ten. If her mother didn't linger to talk about the evening, she'd have three or four hours to review Gri's code, set the agenda for tomorrow's team meeting, glance over the documents Fatima had sent out to all the team managers, and maybe—maybe—watch an episode of "Game of Thrones" before going to sleep.

"Tami-chan." Her mother almost never called her that anymore. "The Nakamuras are departing."

"Oh," she said, looking around at the two politely expectant foxes and their foot-taller son standing just behind them. Before her mother turned back, Ty caught her eye and made a quick comical face, rolling his eyes and sticking the tip of his tongue out. A moment later, he was perfectly composed again and waiting for his parents to bow to her and touch whiskers before leaning forward and down to brush his whiskers against hers, left side, then right side.

"It's been a pleasure, Miss Tachibana," he said.

"Tami." She had a good look at his amber-brown eyes up close, pretty and playful, and that and his expression reminded her that he was young, three or four years her junior, and that he played a game for a living. "I've enjoyed this quite a bit as well."

He pulled back from the embrace with a smile, and then the valet arrived with his car, a sedate four-door luxury sedan that she wouldn't have thought a young jock would buy. Ty held the door for his mother in front and his father in back, raised his paw to wave to Tami, then climbed into the driver's seat. She waved back, and a moment later the sedan pulled smoothly away.

"What did you think?" Her mother wasted no time.

Tami started the three-block walk to where they'd parked, making her mother hurry to catch up to her. "He was nice, I guess."

"I was worried that a football player might not have any manners, but he certainly did. His parents were so stiff and formal, don't you think?"

"I don't know." Tami tugged at the dress, finally able to smooth down the patches that annoyed her. "You kept up with them very well."

Her mother took the intended insult as a compliment. "I haven't had proper Yamatese company in a long time, but you know, you never forget such things. Your grandmother used to give dinners where I had to wear uncomfortable dresses and sit stiffly and never talk unless I was spoken to."

"I can't imagine." Tami reached around her tail to unbunch her underwear.

"Tami! Don't—in public—"

"Oh, Mama. It was only for a second, and nobody noticed but you." That probably wasn't true; there were a number of people walking toward them and a few behind who'd probably seen it, but Tami didn't care. Her thighs felt blessedly clear of bunched fabric and the underwear now hung as it should over her fur. She wondered briefly if Ty could afford to get that forty-dollar underwear that was supposed to lie with the fur and not ride up. Even if she didn't like him, it might be worth going on another date with him for that.

"The true measure of a person is how they behave when nobody's watching." Her mother lifted her muzzle primly and marched on ahead.

After a silent block, honesty won out over irritation. "Thank you for making me email him, Mama."

Her mother's muzzle lowered slightly, and she looked up at Tami out of the side of her eye. "I told you you should."

"I know." Irritation claimed another foothold. "He seems very nice." She'd been about to tell her mother about making the date with Ty, but now she didn't want to give her the pleasure.

"He paid for that whole dinner without even thinking about it. I'm glad, you know." Tami knew her mother had been waiting for an opening to go on about the dinner. "I would have paid for their dinner, but did you see how expensive that tuna was? I can get tuna in a can for three dollars. Of course, that was the finest tuna. Did you know there are seven grades of tuna? I'm certain that was the top grade. It's very expensive."

"Do they call fish eggs 'roe' so they can charge more for them?"

Her mother laughed and put a paw on her arm. "Maybe so. If you change the name of your video game, maybe they can charge more and then pay you what you deserve."

"They pay me fine." Tami was pleased that her mother had laughed at Ty's joke, then annoyed again at the implication that she was settling for less than she could make elsewhere—mostly because it reminded her that she probably was settling for less than she could make elsewhere. But Shirokaze had a lot of potential, she had friends there, and besides, she didn't have time to look for another job.

To change the subject, she asked, "Would you really be happy if I married him?"

"Oh, Tami." Her mother smiled, a little sad. "Of course you're not going to marry him. We aren't the kind of family they're looking for. But it was nice to have the dinner, wasn't it?"

On the way home, her mother took advantage of having Tami trapped in a car to tell her about the last few weeks in life at their temple, making it sound more like a bright, welcoming, engaging party than the repetitive, monotonous gossip circle Tami knew it to be. She listened, her mind already on the meeting notes she was going to have to prepare.

When she got home, she checked her phone and found a text from Ty. *Did you really have quite a good time?*

Her mother was still chattering on, though she'd switched subjects from the temple to her neighbor, whom, she was sure, was reading her newspaper every morning and then putting it back. Tami nodded while texting back to Ty. *I might have been exaggerating for the benefit of the parents.*

Mine are still talking about you.

My mother is talking about her crazy neighbor. He keeps birds.

"Tami! Who are you texting with? I'm talking to you."

"Sorry, Mama." She put the phone down. "It's work. One of my coders just checked in a project and I need to review his code."

"You work so hard, and they pay you so little—"

"Thanks for loaning me the dress." Tami kissed her mother on the cheek. "I'll dry clean it and give it back at our next dinner. Have a safe drive home."

"All right, but next week I'm having Aya and Kumi over for dinner and you will come too. They ask about you all the time." Her mother kissed her back. "Get to sleep at a reasonable hour. And don't forget to brush your tail out."

Ty Game

"I brush my tail every night." Tami hurried her mother out the door before she could start in on the litany of personal hygiene lessons.

In the meantime, Ty had texted back. *My parents have a bird.*

She opened her laptop, checked her auth key to log in, and pulled up Gri's code. While it was opening, she texted, *This is birds, plural, like plural plural, like you could make a pillow every day from the shed feathers…*

Chapter 15

The texting didn't help matters. It took her half again as long to review Gri's code as it should've, and she only skimmed the notes for the meeting, so she was wholly unprepared for it. Fortunately, she wasn't too far behind everyone else, and it would be at least another week before they got the first round of bugs from the publishers; everything else was under control.

When she got back to her desk, there were half a dozen IMs from Marci, all variations on "How did it go and what was he like?" Tami sighed and tried to answer quickly with one message, but Marci kept badgering her for details until she agreed to meet for drinks that night even though she didn't really have time.

Axel and Devin, at lunch, were almost worse. "How hot was he?" Axel wanted to know.

"Very."

Devin leaned across the table. "Did he talk about the game at all?"

"No. It was a very proper Yamatese dinner."

The marmot rested a paw under his chin. "Did he keep his shirt on the whole evening?"

"Dude." Devin flattened his ears, his muzzle wrinkling in a mock grimace.

"Come on, I can dream. Don't worry." Axel patted Tami's arm. "I know he didn't take it off. But there wasn't an unfortunate wine spill or something?"

"No." She laughed. "I can ask him for a shirtless pic if you want."

"Wait." Devin held up a paw. His whiskers twitched. "You…you got his number?"

"Okay, so…" She told them the story of the texting during dinner, which made Axel laugh until he clutched his sides and gave Devin a grin that went all the way up the wolf's muzzle to his cheek ruffs.

"That's great," he said when she finished. "So he's cool *and* handsome *and* talented *and* rich."

"Don't be jealous." Axel grinned across at the wolf. "You're only three away."

"Fuck you," Devin said amiably, and then, "Wait, which three?"

"I wouldn't kick you out of bed."

"I wouldn't be in bed with you in the first place."

"It's an expression."

"And mine was an actual sentiment expressed in my own words."

"Boys." Tami held her paws up. "Flirt on your own time."

"The point is," Devin said without missing a beat, "you're going to see him again, right?"

"I think so. I mean, he wants to, and I sort of said yes, but…should I?"

They both stared at her. "Are you seriously considering not seeing him again?" Axel said after a long pause.

"I agreed to a date, but…" She sighed. "His parents probably don't like me, and anyway, you know what this next month is going to be like."

Devin stabbed a finger at her. "This is a goddamn unicorn."

"Wait." The marmot held up a paw. "A unicorn like 'too good to be true'? Like therefore he must be hiding something? Or a unicorn like 'a once in a lifetime miracle'?"

"That second thing." Devin glared at Axel, then back at Tami. "You don't let a guy like this get away."

Axel folded his arms. "For a straight guy, you sure know a lot about dating guys."

Tami rolled her eyes. "I mean, look. It might be a few laughs, sure, but I'm—we're trying to do something cool here, and it really feels like it might end up being awesome. Am I right?"

The wolf and marmot exchanged looks. "Are you talking about your dating Nakamura?" Devin said. "Or about Jumbo Bubbles Fucking X?"

"I know you have to say those things, but do you really believe it?" Axel leaned forward. "Or is it an excuse?"

Tami flattened her ears. "It's not an excuse. Okay, I know it's not going to be game of the year, but there are a lot of kids who really love the franchise. It's important to them, just as important as Destiny's Angel would be to us."

The marmot sighed. "Maybe what you could have with him would be really important too."

She laughed. "Right."

"At least sleep with him," Devin said.

"Oh, definitely," Axel agreed. "If you forget how to do it, I can point you to some websites."

She swatted him away. "It hasn't been that long."

Devin reached over the table and lowered his voice. "This isn't about the guy. You know that, right? JBX is under control, and I can cover for you any evening you want. This is about you, and—"

"Spare me." She put the lid on the remains of her hummus salad. She didn't really feel like finishing it. "I've got to get back. I have a one on one with Gri to talk about their bugs and then I have to touch base with the PMs and start looking at Paul's bugs and you guys are late with your timesheets again, so you'd better get on that."

"Slavedriver," Axel said, but they let her get back to work.

That evening, Marci met her at their favorite bar, an upscale place with fabulous cocktails, fifty beers on tap, and passable hors d'oeuvres. The rat wore her suit, so Tami suspected she'd also come directly from her office. She didn't get a chance to ask, though, because Marci launched into the same questions Axel and Devin had.

Tami gave her a slightly longer account of the evening. "He seems like a neat guy," she concluded, "but I don't know. I mean, I'm going to see him one more time. I promised. But he lives in this whole other world."

"You can make it work." Marci sipped some pale blue drink that smelled of rum. Tami hadn't caught the name. "Look at me and Djardino. He works for a non-profit," she sniffed.

"Little bit different." Tami held her fingers half an inch apart, smiling. "But besides that, I mean, what do I do if he wants things to get more serious? Say 'great, I can see you for an hour during the week, and maybe for a couple hours on weekends'?"

"You're not that busy." Marci checked her Blackberry absently.

"I really am, though."

"You're as busy as you want to be. I work for a law firm and I have time free."

"You're working right now," Tami said.

The rat didn't even look up from her little screen. "I'm not working, I'm checking work. We're still having a conversation, right? When Djardino and I go out, our Blackberries come with us. Well." She rolled her eyes. "His Paw Pilot."

"But you're both where you want to be," Tami persisted. "I'm not. If we nail this release, Fatima said her boss is considering me for the lead developer on the next Destiny's Angel title."

That got Marci to put her Blackberry down. "You didn't tell me that."

"I didn't want to type it over the work IM, and it's, you know, it's not definite or anything, but I've been there longer than any of the other candidates and I told her I want it, and I did QA on that first one when I started here."

Marci grabbed Tami's paw. "So Lead Developer means that you'd get a say in what goes into the game? You could put some Easter eggs in."

"I'm not putting you in the game." Tami's chest and stomach unclenched. She'd been wanting to tell someone about this for so long, and to be able to share it with Marci now relaxed her even more than the beer she'd gotten halfway through.

"Fine." Marci released her paw and leaned back. "Just a female rat lawyer will be fine. Maybe if they visit all eighteen fuel stations, it unlocks a nineteenth and I'm—I mean, the rat is the station owner."

"I'll propose it. But seriously, I've seen a couple of the mockups and it looks amazing. This could be, y'know, *the* game."

"There's always another game." Marci finished her cocktail. "Oh, don't give me that look. I know what you mean. But that's what they tell us at the firm. 'You might think this case is going to make your reputation, but there's always another case.' Until there isn't, but that's what one of the partners said when he retired last year." She waved a paw. "I'm not worried about that part yet. The point is—"

"I know, I shouldn't put all my hopes into this. But your cases last, what, months? I'm gonna be on this game for a year at least. And it'll be available…" She rapped her knuckles on the table. "For people to play for years. They still talk about Dynodeer 2, you know, and Super Tojima Brothers is legendary."

Marci signaled for another drink. "You want calamari?"

Tami's willingness to count seafood as a vegetable depended in large part on her mood and on where it lay on the spectrum from fish to mollusc. "Sure."

The order in, Marci leaned over to her. "Okay, I get that you need this thing. That's your priority. So make sure he knows that, and it'll be, what, a few months? Then you'll get the job and you can spend more time dating."

Tami shook her head. "His parents want everything done officially and they want him married soon, I'm pretty sure. They didn't say it in so many words, but his mother said they're anxious for him to settle his home life so he could go to work on his job. His 'job.'" She made air quotes around it. "I wish I could play a game for a living."

Marci gazed steadily at her until she said, "I don't play games. I make them. It's different."

"Thin ice, darling, and that's from a lawyer." The rat leaned back. "Tell me, do you like this guy more than Destiny's Angel?"

"No." Tami sipped her beer and thought about Ty making a funny face at her, about him texting to ask if she'd really enjoyed the evening. About his physique. God, she didn't want to be shallow, but he was in terrific shape. She'd thought Jason had been good-looking, and he'd been pretty good in bed, but Ty would send Jason scurrying for the corner with his bushy fucking squirrel tail between his legs. The image was so appealing that she wondered briefly if she could convince Jason to show up somewhere to see her with Ty.

Marci snapped her fingers in front of Tami's nose. "That was an awful long pause after that 'no.'"

"Not yet," Tami admitted.

"All right. I'm going to solve your problem for you. You ready for this murine wisdom here? Go on a couple more dates with him. Squeeze out the time. Kalia and I can muddle through our bar sessions without you. You should tell her, by the way. She'll be excited."

"She'll be annoyed at me for same-speciesing it."

"For a football player, she'll make an exception, I'm quite sure. She didn't like Jason much even though he was diff-species."

"Nobody liked Jason."

"Except you, but you told us why and it was acceptable up to a point." Marci licked around her lips and Tami folded her ears back. "Speaking of, how long has it been?"

"Since Jason? You know how long."

"Yes." The waiter brought Marci's drink and the calamari, and Marci smiled at Tami. "I also know how long it's been since what I was really asking, unless there's been someone since that stag seven months ago."

"It—it wasn't seven months," Tami stammered, and then sank her head into her paws. "It was after the July 4th barbecue. Oh, God, it has been seven months."

Marci patted her paws. "He's an athlete. He's probably down for a quickie. And it'd do you good. I know your next season is a month or so away, but you should wear condoms with same species anyway because of diseases. I have a pack if you need one."

"Why are all my friends so interested in my sex life?" Tami grumbled, taking a piece of the calamari in her fingers. The greasy breading almost stopped her eating it, but the spicy smell of the marinara sauce overcame her misgivings. She dunked it and tossed it in her mouth.

"Nature abhors a vacuum, darling." Marci took one of the tentacle pieces, dipped it in the sauce, and chewed it with relish.

Chapter 16

Ty didn't text her again for two days, during which time she decided that at least she should live up to her promise to go out on one more date. If she wanted to sleep with him, she'd probably have to do two more, unless customs had changed since she'd been dating Jason.

She meant to text him to set up a time on Wednesday, but Tuesday they got the first bugs back from the publisher and everyone scrambled to fix them. That night as she was going through Paul's bugs, she found a problem—Paul was writing a bug fix that relied on changing one of the modules that had been locked down before submission, and that could potentially create a bunch of problems.

So Wednesday morning was an emergency meeting with Paul to brainstorm a different solution, and then a check-in with the PMs to make sure everything else was on track, and then a call to Fatima to assure her that they were handling the bug reports from the publishers but she still wanted to change her project status from green to yellow just in case, and by 7:30 she was so frazzled that when the text came in on her phone, she stared at the name "Ty" and thought, "I don't know anyone named Ty."

The fog cleared when she saw the short message. *If you haven't forgottn me, how about tonight?*

"Forgotten" was misspelled intentionally, she was sure, and it made her smile. She rubbed at her ear where the flower had clipped on that night and typed out a response. *Can't tonight, work is crazy. How about…*

She paused, trying to think of a night that would work. Tomorrow she would be prepping for the Friday meeting. Friday night she was going to dinner with her mother. Fatima had asked for a status report on Monday morning, when they were expecting to start submitting fixes to the publisher-reported bugs. Tami had done nothing to pull the report together, figuring that the weekend nights would work for that, and she'd promised Paul she'd be available to review his code over the weekend he was going to work. More bug reports were sure to come in from the publisher, and though the first batch hadn't been too bad, you could never tell when a big one would surface.

If she pushed it to Monday night, would he think she wasn't really interested? More to the point, did she want to push it to Monday night? She'd been avoiding leaving the office because that meant a half hour break in her car with a stop at Jack in the Box and then back home to work. But she could get up early and prep for Axel's one on one. He always said she over-prepared anyway. And apart from that, all she was going to do was look over the note Hadley had sent her asking for her help with a coding issue—which could wait until next week. There was no reason Tami needed to look at it tonight except that the next few days were all so busy, and anyway the date would probably be over by 11. She'd have two hours to look at it after that. And to prep for Axel's one on one, and start pulling together the Friday meeting stuff.

But Fatima was watching her on this project and had dropped hints that higher-ups were watching her too. The lead job on Destiny's Angel was still open and Tami was so close to getting it that she had had stress dreams about it. What if this date was the one black mark that sank her below the other candidates?

Her gut roiled, and she shook her head quickly. No, that was crazy. Everyone in the company had a life outside work, as Axel and Devin kept reminding her. Fatima was married with kids. Devin had a semi-steady girlfriend. Axel and his boyfriend went out to concerts all the time. Tami could go on one lousy date with a guy who was fun, attractive, and probably down to break her seven-month dry spell in another week.

She erased her refusal and typed instead, *Tonight works fine. Where?*

You know Jack B's on the Hill?

Her fingers brought up Maps in a second. There it was, about a fifteen minute drive. In the opposite direction from her house, but whatever. *Got it*, she typed back. *When?*

ASAP. I'll save you a seat.

I'm not dressed for it. I should swing by home.

Come as you are. :)

She straightened her hoodie. At least the zip-up looked a little more professional than the torn Olympic U. sweatshirt she'd almost thrown on this morning. *On my way.*

Even without the Maps printout, she could've found Jack B's. It blared its name in bright red letters across the front of the restaurant, dwarfing the stores to either side. Beside the front door, a cartoon of a female jackalope greeted her, naked, but in an underground-comic-hippie-Earth-mother sort of way, not in a Hooters kind of way. She hadn't had much experience with in-your-face hippies, but when she opened the door she smelled beans, olive oil, chicken, and fresh-baked bread that made her mouth water.

"Tami!" Ty raised a paw from a corner booth where a glass of beer stood in front of him. He looked like a grownup sitting at a children's table, more so because of his white collared shirt with purple pinstripes, open at the collar. As she approached, she caught the pleasant scent of lemon verbena.

He'd positioned himself on one side, so she took the back: near him but not next to him. "You're sure they don't mind us having only two here?"

Ty shook his head. "Didn't seem to. Does it bother you?"

"It's not efficient, is all." But there were plenty of empty tables around the restaurant. "I guess it doesn't matter."

"That's what I thought." He raised a paw to signal a waitress.

The décor captured Tami's attention while Ty was doing that. About half of it was made up of street signs, local and otherwise, with some fishing tackle and some old produce box labels tossed in. The other half was all jackalopes.

She knew some of the pictures, of course: the still from *Curse of the Jackalope*, the picture of Ronny Dole as Jeremy the Jackalope in the TV show *Jack of All Lopes*, the jackalope character from *X-Files*, the Saturday morning cartoon character Jack T. Lope. But there were many more she didn't know, and she was studying them when she realized Ty was watching her patiently.

"Sorry," she said. "It's just…it's a lot of jackalopes."

He laughed. "This is a local chain. Each Jack's has a theme. This one is jackalopes. I would've taken you to Jack D's, because that's video games, but that's way down in Verra."

"Maybe some other time." Tami smiled. "So you know this place? Did you grow up around here?"

"Nah." Ty shrugged. "I looked around for places nearish to your office and this one looked good."

"You know where my office is?"

"Uh…" His ears flattened. "I looked it up. I don't know which one's yours, just where the Shirokaze building is. Sorry if that weirds you out. I didn't mean it to be creepy, honest. I just wanted to pick a convenient place and I didn't know how else to do it."

"You could've called and asked me what was convenient."

"Yeah, maybe I should've, but…" He looked away. "I guess I just wanted to…I dunno, it seemed easier."

"It's okay." Tami laughed. "If you'd shown up outside my office without calling, I would've been upset. I like to find things out too."

His ears came back up. "I wouldn't come by your office. I know for sure that's creepy."

She thought again of Jason. "Some guys are creeps."

"Not me." He poked his own chest.

"Good to know." She smiled again, feeling guilty that she'd put him on the spot right away.

Fortunately the raccoon waitress came by at that moment to get her drink order. When Tami, trying to be friendly, commented that her fake rabbit ears and antlers looked cute, she gave a rote and unenthusiastic, "Thanks."

"So what did your parents think of me?" she asked after the waitress adjusted her fake ears and left.

Ty smiled. "Don't care."

She frowned. "I mean, what did they say?"

He waved a paw. "They liked the ones they chose better. Why? Did you want to go on a date with *them*?"

"Doesn't it make a difference? I mean, if you're doing this for their benefit?"

"I'm doing it for my benefit," he said, fingers tapping the back of the cushion inches from her head. "I'm doing the dinners for their benefit. I get to make the final decision. I already had an argument with Mom about that."

His grimace kept her from asking more about it. "Okay."

"But I won't send them pictures of this date, because that might really make her dig her heels in."

Tami shrank into her hoodie. "I told you I wasn't dressed."

Ty laughed and tugged at her shoulder, and she didn't resent the touch, though she did stay hunched inward. "Come on," he said, "I like the hood-ie. It's fine, it suits you more than that dress the other night."

She felt stupid. This guy was a millionaire, a multi-millionaire, and the shirt he wore so casually in this barbecue place probably cost a hundred dollars or more, considering the stitching around the cuffs and the little embroidered logo she didn't even recognize. And here she was wearing a twenty-dollar grey hoodie with one frayed hood pull and the logo of some clothing company on the front that she'd liked because it sort of looked like the biohazard symbol. They'd texted back and forth, sure, but they lived in different worlds; just because neither of them belonged in the world of their parents didn't mean they belonged in the same one.

"Hey," Ty said. "Look. Tami, c'mon. Look."

She lifted her eyes from the sleeve of his shirt, which he had moved any-way. "Whoa, wait!" Panic overcame her self-consciousness, and she reached out for his arms. "Don't—you don't have to—"

He grinned at her and kept unbuttoning his shirt as though she weren't even touching his arm, his…wow. His steel-hard muscle, which flexed un-der her fingers (he was showing off for her, part of her mind told her). She lifted her paw and let him unbutton his shirt. For a moment, she thought he was going to leave the shirt on and open, but he shrugged out of the shoulders and pulled his arms out of the sleeves.

"What are you doing?" she asked, and she couldn't stop staring at his chest and shoulders and arms. His fur was trimmed short, so all his mus-culature was on display. Axel is going to be so jealous, she thought, and the best part was that Ty probably looked even better than Axel was imagining.

"Making you feel better." He balled up the shirt and dropped it on the seat next to him and then raised his paw.

To judge by the waitress's reaction, Tami wasn't the only one who'd nev-er seen an athlete in person with his shirt off. The raccoon turned, gave an automatic polite nod to let him know she'd seen him, and then did a literal double take, eyes wide. She dropped the rest of the drinks at the table of mice she was serving and came directly over to theirs.

"Yes, sir?"

Ty smiled pleasantly. It occurred to Tami that he was very much aware of the effect he was having as he pointed bare-armed toward the front of the restaurant. "I think I saw some "Jacks" t-shirts on sale up front?"

He laughed. "All right. I wanted us to be on an even keel, that's all. Anyway, I'll have a shirt on in a minute. Unless you'd like me to keep it off?"

"Uh. Yeah. Yes, we have logo shirts and ones with the jackalope on them."

"Could you bring me an XL of whichever one comes in white or yellow? And add it to the bill?"

She nodded and stood there staring. Ty inclined his head. "Could you grab it right now? And I believe the lady hasn't gotten her iced tea yet."

"One comes in yellow," she said, trying to recover herself, "and the other comes in white. Are you—are you with the Manticores?"

Ty shook his head. "I'm afraid not. I'll take the yellow one, then, please."

"Yes, sir." After another moment the waitress hurried to the front desk.

Ty smiled at Tami. "Still feeling underdressed?"

"No, but." She let her eyes travel along his chest, down to his stomach, back up to his arms. He was trying to get her off balance and she had to regain control of herself, and then she'd have control of the situation again. "Maybe you should?"

He laughed. "All right. I wanted us to be on an even keel, that's all. Anyway, I'll have a shirt on in a minute. Unless you'd like me to keep it off?"

"No, that's okay." In that moment she had no doubt that if she asked him to, he would eat the rest of his meal shirtless, even in a restaurant. Where probably there were rules about being shirtless, but the waitress hadn't brought them up, hadn't even asked why he needed a new shirt. She glanced toward the front, where the waitress was talking with another waitress and the hostess, all three of them staring openly at Ty. At her date. When, she wondered, was the last time she had been on a date who'd had other females staring at him? Had she ever? She was surprised to find that she liked the feeling.

"So how have you been since our meeting?" He sat back, both arms stretched out over the back of the booth. The smell of verbena grew stronger with the closeness of his short, dark-furred paw.

"Fine. Work is crazy. I've got this project that needs to get done, and I'm in the last month or so and trying to keep everything from falling apart." She paused, rubbing one paw down her hoodie's zipper. "I'm a bit on edge. Sorry for being weird just now. I promise I'm not always that dramatic."

He shook his head. "No worry. I don't usually take my shirt off in restaurants. Ah, thank you."

The raccoon waitress came back with Tami's iced tea and the shirt, a yellow tee with the name "Jack's" on the front in red. She'd recovered her composure; she held the shirt out but didn't give it to Ty. "You sure you have to put it on?"

"Don't you have a policy?"

"We do, but…" She indicated the other waitress and the hostess, still gawking. "My manager said it was okay."

He picked up the shirt anyway, shook it out, then pulled it over his head. Even an XL clung to his upper arm muscles in a very aesthetically pleasing way. "I appreciate it," he said, "but I think out of deference to my date, I'll put the shirt on."

The waitress gave Tami a look which said that if Tami preferred his shirt on to off, then she was insane, and which also might have said that if Tami were to step away from the table, the waitress would gladly take her place, but she didn't say anything except, "Are y'all ready to order?"

Ty glanced at Tami. "Oh," she said, "I haven't looked at the menu yet…"

"It's no trouble." The waitress was about to walk away, but Ty stopped her.

"What's good here? It's our first time, and the lady is a vegetarian."

"Oh." The raccoon smiled. "We got lots of good vegetarian entrees. The Portobello burger is really good, done with our house barbecue sauce, and I personally like the veggie skewers."

"The Portobello will be fine," Tami said. "Do you know what you want?"

"The half-pound house burger." Ty collected the menus and gave them back to the raccoon.

"Soup or salad to start?"

"Green salad," Tami said, and Ty ordered the same.

The waitress's eyes lingered on Ty, probably wishing he would take his shirt off again. "Thanks," Tami said deliberately, drawing the raccoon's eyes back to her. "That's all."

"Sure thing." The waitress's ears flattened. She turned and walked quickly away.

Tami couldn't help a smile at the waitress, and encouragingly, Ty smiled too. "So," he said while she searched for something to talk about, "why'd you go vegetarian?"

"Oh. Usual story, I guess. I mean, a couple of my friends did too around the same time. One of our teachers was a boar. Mister Dalembert, I even remember his name. And we were learning about food and how, y'know, domestic pigs are killed, and…we were kids, you know? Full of empathy for poor animals more than for each other."

Ty laughed and nodded. "Yeah, I don't think I ever stopped eating meat, but I asked about that for sure. And you stuck with it?"

"We're Buddhist, so Mom let it go. I mean, a lot of her friends were vegetarian too. And it's easy. You just end up hanging out with herbivores a lot."

"Yeah." He leaned back again. "If I'd ever wanted to go veg, I think that would've been knocked out of me in junior high when I started playing football. Coach was all about meat and protein to build muscle."

"What about soy protein?"

Ty made a face. "You ever tried that shit?" He caught her eyes and his ears snapped back.

It took her a second to realize that he might be worried about cursing. How adorable. "I've had tofu and soy *beans*."

"Not the same." He shook his head, ears coming back up. "The soy protein shit is gritty and they always put crappy chemical flavor in it. Anyway, Coach was a leopard and said 'if you've got fangs, you eat meat.' So you do it on a kind of a 'animals are too much like us' grounds?"

"Yeah, I guess. I mean, at this point I know that they're not intelligent and that nature includes predation and all that jazz. It's more habit than anything else. Maybe a little bit health related. I mean, some meat is made in really poor conditions."

"I heard about that." He nodded. "I think that's pretty cool. Of you, I mean. I don't know if I'd be able to do it. Mostly because I have to eat a ton during the season, and meat's the most efficient."

"I've read about these protein concentrates…" Tami stopped herself. "You know what, you have your diet and I have mine, and yours seems to be working pretty well for you, and mine works for me."

Ty laughed again, his ears perking up. "One of my teammates, Lightning Strike, he's on this organic diet and he can't shut up about it."

"I promised myself back in high school that I would never be one of those people." She picked up her tea and sipped it: watery but not too bad. "So, um, you're on vacation now? When do you go back to—" She didn't want to say "work," but "play" and "game" also sounded wrong. "Things?"

"Oh, not for a couple months. My agent will put it on my calendar, I'm sure." He waved a paw. "Last year, the draft was at the end of April and then we started orientation in late May and mini-camps in June. But I'm not a rookie this year, so we've got voluntary workouts starting in April, I think, and I'll be on and off with the team until June, when things kick into gear for real. I got invited to a practice camp for wide receivers next month, but I'm not sure I'm gonna go."

"And the championship was…January?"

He nodded. "Last week of January."

She did some figuring in her head. "So you get two months off, and two months partly off. Not bad."

His smile flickered a bit. "It's pretty hardcore when it's on, though. Pretty much seven days a week."

"Oh." Her ears flattened. "I didn't mean—I'm sure it's really difficult. There aren't many people who can do it." To make up for her gaffe, she went on before he could answer. "So what's the hardest thing about it?"

He gave her such a long look that for a minute she thought she'd said something wrong. Then he laughed. "Nobody's asked me that in years. Mostly people want to know what I do with all the money, or what certain players eat…little things like that. But the hardest thing…" His eyes drifted away from her. "You know, a month ago I would've said it was getting beat up every week. You ever work out so hard that you can't lift your arms, taking a step is an effort?"

"Uh…no."

"Oh." He raised his eyebrows. "You should sometime. It's great. Anyway, it's like that every week. And I thought that was the hardest thing, that you have to be pushing yourself physically all the time. You see these guys around you doing the same thing, and that makes it easier because you're all in it together, but also harder because you have to live up to those standards. And plus," he waved a paw, "you plant your foot wrong once, tear an ACL, you're done for a year."

"ACL?"

"Uh." His ears folded back again. "I don't know what it stands for but it's this really important thing in your knee. It tears a lot. Hang on." He brought out his phone, and here where he wasn't trying to hide it from his family, it was clearly one of the new iPhones. "I think I can get to the web from here."

"But you were saying that's not the hardest?" Tami wanted to tell him not to bother looking up the acronym, but it seemed important to him to know.

"Oh, yeah." He tapped the phone a few more times. "I think the hardest is letting things go. Only you don't know that right away."

She took another drink of her tea. "What do you mean?"

"Anterior cruciate ligament," he said, and put his phone away. "That's what ACL stands for."

"I'm going to leave it at 'important thing in your knee,'" Tami said with a smile.

Ty laughed. "Okay, good." He tilted his head. "So I don't know how much you even know about the championship game."

"One of my friends is a fan. He told me you guys lost." She remembered too late that that wasn't what she was supposed to lead with. "But that it was a great game and you should've won."

"Nah." Ty waved a paw. "I appreciate that. But 'should've' is the kind of thing I'm talking about. There's guys who let that 'should've' get into their heads, and they start thinking about the loss as an injustice instead of a game with some lucky breaks and some unlucky breaks."

"So you're good at letting things go?"

His smile tightened and his ears dipped, though they didn't go all the way back. "I'm getting there. It's a bit different when the ball was in your paws at the end of the game, and if you could just get past that one guy… did your friend tell you how the game ended?"

Tami nodded. "We watched the highlights. But I thought it ended when Crystal City got that last field goal." The words came casually, easily, and she patted herself on the back for being able to talk about football so easily.

"No, they had to kick it off to us. It came to me, and if I could've run it back to the end zone, we'd have won. I've done it a couple times before. But they closed in, and I tossed it to Zillo—one of my teammates—and he didn't score either, and then the game was over." His paw clenched. "I know that I'd have to be extremely lucky to score on that play. But then there are all the other times. If I'd slipped a tackle, or if I'd landed with slightly better balance…"

Tami blinked. She'd been thinking of Ty as this carefree kid, but when he talked about the championship game, he tightened up, his smile disappeared, and he looked a lot older. "It's a team sport," she said. "There are lots of other guys who could've made a difference."

"Yeah." His eyes met hers, and she was struck by their lovely sienna color and the emotion in them. *It'd be nice to have someone care that much about me*, she thought, and then slapped herself mentally, focusing back on the words he was saying. "But I'm one of the guys who's supposed to make plays."

That feeling she knew. That feeling she could sympathize with. "I don't know if this will make you feel better, but I'm a team lead on this game we're developing, and so I have a lot of responsibility for it, more than the guys who are coding. But what we learn in project management is that everyone needs to do their part, and it's the responsibility of the managers to make sure everyone's prepared to do their part. So…you have managers, right? Coaches, I mean."

"Yes." He smiled. "It's not quite the same, though. I know you guys write your code or test or whatever, but when I'm out on the field…that's *me*. I know technically it's the same thing, but you don't have TV cameras turned on you. You don't have millions of people screaming at you to win or lose."

"We have boards of directors who can take away a lot of money if we don't get the game out in time, or if it goes out with bugs."

"Yeah." His eyes got that faraway look again. "It's still not the same, but…it's okay. I thought I knew what it'd be like. I used to dream of playing in the championship game, and it was nothing like I imagined."

"How was it different?" she asked.

His ears came up. "For one thing, every time I imagined it, I won."

It wasn't what she'd meant, but she felt bad all the same. When she didn't say anything, he gave a small laugh and reached out to touch her shoulder. "I'm sorry. The whole point was that I'm learning to let things go. I guess I haven't completely let go of that yet. But it's fine, really."

"I have a pretty good imagination," she said slowly. "But…I think you're right. I can't actually imagine what that would be like."

The waitress came over with their salads, and Ty perked his ears up. "That's enough about me. Tell me about your games and your team."

"My two best friends are Axel—he's a marmot, and he's gay. He kind of knows football and his boyfriend explained it to me this week. Oh, also he wanted me to get pictures of you with your shirt off. Sorry, I didn't think of that earlier."

He laughed and gestured for her to go on. "And Devin is the other one, and he's a wolf, and he's straight, but he's a sports fan too, and he wanted me to ask you something about the game, but I forget what it was now. I think you've probably covered it. Anyway. We were all three coders together, but I had seniority and so now I manage a team that includes them and four other coders. Axel is a UX guy—sorry, user experience. He works on the parts of the game that you'd interact with, the controls and all that. Devin is a graphics guy and he's my second on this. He's got a little team of his own…"

She rambled on for probably a good ten minutes about the frustrations of working at Shirokaze and then caught herself the way she usually did. "But it's great, actually, I mean, their benefits package is really good, and they're pretty good at staying out of our way. My boss has weekly check-ins for me to report my progress, but as long as I keep our project green, she doesn't bug me otherwise. And yeah, we're moving to yellow this week but that's precautionary and she'll understand."

"What's that mean?" His ears cupped forward.

"Oh—projects have color status. Green means everything's running as expected. Yellow means there are some problems and we're in danger of slipping our dates. Red means we're definitely going to slip the dates."

"Got it." He kept his eyes on hers. "Is it harder for you because you're a vixen?"

"I'm a fox," she said, and then looked away, angry at herself. "Tch. I'm sorry, it's just—I prefer to be called a female fox. 'Vixen' is—"

He raised a paw. "No problem." He didn't seem offended; that easy smile still stretched across his muzzle. "If that's what you want to be called, that's what I'll call you. Do you object if other female foxes want to be called vixens? Or if I call my mother a vixen, for example?"

"Uh." She blinked. "You know, you're supposed to be a jock."

He raised an eyebrow. "I can find footage of my career if the championship game didn't convince you."

"No, no, I mean—aren't jocks supposed to be all, uh…"

"Stupid?"

Her ears flattened. "I was thinking more like 'unenlightened.' You're not stupid."

He laughed. "I prefer to think of it as specialized intelligence. I could show you our playbook, which every player on the team has to memorize, and not only do we have to know twenty to a hundred and forty plays—yes, even the guys who mostly run into other guys, the linemen, because they have to know which guy to run into, and which way to push them—but we have to be able to read the other guys on the field and adjust on the fly. So yeah, we may not know what 'UX' stands for, but I bet it'd take you or your coders a little while to come up to speed on the playbook, too."

"I didn't mean—"

"That said—sorry, I'll let you finish in a second, but I wasn't done." She nodded. "That said, a lot of the guys basically don't have any curiosity about anything outside of football or getting laid. I don't know many coders, but I'd guess that you probably know some coders who don't really pay attention to anything outside of coding, maybe some specialized hobby. So yeah, a lot of them are dumb relative to society, and a lot of them probably wouldn't understand why you don't want to be called 'vixen.'"

"And you do?"

He smiled. "I didn't, but I sort of get it, and I'll listen if you want to explain it."

"Okay. I was going to say that I didn't mean that jocks were dumb, just that they live in their own world, and that it's a world in which there aren't a lot of females, and the ones that are there fall into very specific roles, like family, girlfriends, or wives."

"Or one-night stands."

"Or that. So I guess I would've been better off saying, 'rather unsophisticated as regards female rights.'"

He grinned. "That does sound better than 'stupid.' Sorry for assuming you were going right to 'dumb jock.'"

"Yeah…" She sighed. "Honestly, I probably was. But your speech gave me time to course correct."

His smile widened. "So we've established that I don't want to be called 'stupid' and you don't want to be called 'vixen.' So how about my original question? Is it harder for you?"

Tami was about to answer when the waitress brought their dinner. The Portobello smelled pretty darn good, and the meat scent from Ty's burger did too. The raccoon lingered after setting down their plates, fussing with the silverware. "Y'all need anything else?" she asked Ty.

He checked with Tami, who shook her head. "We're good," he said. "Thanks."

As she walked away, swinging her rear and her ringed tail (Ty didn't obviously stare, to his credit), Tami picked up her burger. "Mind if I postpone your question until we're done? I'm pretty hungry."

"Sure. It all smells great. You get the basil and the cracked pepper in the barbecue sauce? And I think…" He made a show of sniffing at the bun. "I think I get local grocery store plastic off the buns."

She laughed, and leaned forward herself. "Definitely," she said, and found to her surprise that she did smell the faintest touch of that distinctive plastic. It was fun having dinner with another fox and being able to talk about the smells. Devin was like that, his nose more sensitive than hers if anything, but he wasn't really interested in talking about the smells or being funny about them. If she brought one up, he'd say, "Oh yeah, I smell that," but he wouldn't go on about it.

So they finished the burgers, drank up their drinks, and then Ty lowered his voice. "Mind if we go for a walk? I'd rather not sit still, and the waitress keeps staring at us."

At him, Tami was sure, not both of them, but he was kind enough not to assume that or say it out loud. "Some people have no manners," she said.

"Do you, uh, do you dance at all?" He kept his tone casual, but his ears were perked and his eyes bright. "There's a club about half a mile over."

"I don't, sorry. Not since—I think I went to a dance in middle school once. My coordination is—it's not great."

The brightness dimmed, but he kept his smile up and his ears perked. "No problem. Anywhere nice around here to walk to?"

"Sure. There's a nice park not too far."

So Ty signaled, and the waitress hurried over as though there were no other diners in the restaurant. Tami briefly argued that they should split the dinner, but Ty said it was easier for him to take care of it, and then Tami remembered every romantic comedy movie she'd seen in which the guy would expect sex if he paid for the dinner, and she shut up because she still wasn't sure how to ask him to go to bed, and it might be easier if he expected it.

All the way out of the restaurant she tried to imagine how he'd ask her. Would he invite himself into her place for "coffee"? Would he ask if she'd like to have breakfast with him? Would he put a paw on her shoulder and look into her eyes with a smoldering, masculine gaze? None of those seemed quite right for Ty. In fact, given his forthright behavior so far, the most likely scenario seemed to be that he would smile and ask her, "So, feel like having sex yet, or should we wait?"

"Are you thinking about my question?" he asked as they passed the iron gates into the park.

"Wha—what? No!" She gulped. "I mean, which question? Did you ask me—sorry, I was thinking about a problem."

"About your sex?"

This was it. This was how he was going to ask her. She stopped beside a bush and stared at the fountain ahead of them and thought about what she wanted him to—wait, no. He'd asked about her *job*, how her job was different because of her... "You mean my gender?"

"Yeah. Sorry."

"Oh." She sucked in a breath. "It is, actually. It's really hard being female in a tech environment. I'm constantly being asked to justify my position. I get interrupted in meetings. I lucked into working for another female, which insulates me a bit from all the bullshit, but—god, I've had people say to my nose that I must count on the guys on my team to do the heavy coding. That I got moved up to management because I couldn't hack it as a coder. This from people who never saw a line of my work, who assume they know me because of my gender."

"Do people think you slept your way to your position?"

"You know, I haven't had that one, actually. Maybe it's me." She snapped her muzzle shut too late to stop those words from coming out. What if he thought she wasn't interested in sex?

But he didn't pursue the remark. "I guess that's good. At least they recognize that you have the ability to do your job."

"If I couldn't do my job, I'd be out the door." Tami recovered a little of her poise. "Does your teammate get treated differently because of his orientation?"

"Ah." He paused, then kept walking along the sidewalk. She had to take three steps for every two his long legs took, even though she suspected that he was walking slower than usual for her benefit. "He did at first, but pretty much people figured out that he still plays as well as he used to, and whatever he does off the field is his own business."

"Very open-minded."

"Have I not changed your preconceptions about athletes yet?"

When she looked up, his eyes were sparkling with the reflection of the city lights around them. "Not entirely," she said.

"All right. Give me a little more time." They reached the edge of the fountain, where one couple sat on a bench, a pine marten and grey fox holding paws. Ty waited for her direction, so Tami chose the unoccupied bench across the fountain from them and sat down.

Ty sat beside her, a few modest inches between them, but close enough that she could feel his presence. She wondered if he could feel hers the same way. "I wish I'd had more dates in high school," she blurted out.

He laughed. "Why?"

"Because then maybe I'd know what to do on one." She exhaled. "I'm sorry. My last boyfriend I met through my previous boyfriend, who I met in a class in college. In high school I mostly read books and talked about games with my nerdy friends, and none of them knew what to do on dates either, so we never went on any."

Ty reached out and put an arm around her shoulders. "This is one of the things people do on dates. This okay? I promise my fingers won't move from here," he said, tapping them on the front of her shoulder, "if you're worried about this being a 'move' or something."

She'd stiffened at the touch and now tried to relax. "Okay. That's okay." Tentatively, she leaned against him. He felt very solid. "Have you had many girlfriends?"

He exhaled. "That depends on what you mean by 'girlfriend.' Like, someone I maintained a relationship with? Yeah, back in high school, but we both knew it wouldn't go anywhere. She was a binturong. Very flexible." When she looked up at him, he winked. "She was also a terrific basketball player. Went to Storrs on a scholarship."

"Is that good?"

"They won two titles while she was there. We keep in touch a bit here and there. Don't worry, I haven't seen her in person in years."

"I'm not worried. I'm not even sure—" She stopped. "I mean, we're not at the 'don't see other people' stage yet, right?"

"I don't think so. I'll ask my mom."

She laughed with him. "What else should I know about you?"

"What else do you want to know?"

"Well…what about the other definition of 'girlfriend'?"

"Ah." He cleared his throat. "What do you want? A number? A list? In the interest of being honest, I'd do my best, but also in the interest of being honest I'd really prefer to save that for a later date."

"So there'll be another date?" She pounced on his words.

"Ha." He looked down at his lap, not enough to conceal his wide smile. "I meant—but yes, I've had a good time. I'd like to keep seeing you."

"Me too," she said. "So what else would you like to know about me?"

"Hm. Favorite movie, album, book."

"Oh gosh. Movie is probably the last Lord of the Rings. Album…it really depends on my mood, but I love Flogging Molly."

"I don't know them."

"I'll send you some. And book…" She shook her head and looked up at the city-lit cloud cover. "You might as well ask me my favorite star."

"Okay," he said. "What's your favorite star?"

She laughed and smacked his knee lightly, not even thinking about it until after. He didn't seem to mind, and he didn't try to get closer to her. "Aldebaran. Do you have a favorite star?"

"Angela Priestley," he said, "but that's recent and based mostly on her being nude in 'Private School.'"

"Oh, god, you liked that?"

His ears flattened. "It was funny."

"It was moronic."

"Wait, you saw it?"

"Sure." She grinned at him. "Axel and I watched it to make fun of one night because Devin liked it."

"You see those guys after work a lot?"

She shifted against him. "I told you, Axel's gay. And anyway, that was at work. We were coding late. He, uh, found it online and we watched it at the office with a couple other coders." That had been a good night, fun and relaxed. Why didn't they do things like that anymore?

"Oh, okay." He was quiet. "I didn't mean—I mean, I know you're not seeing anyone else seriously."

"Even if I were seeing someone casually, we're not talking about your girlfriends so we shouldn't talk about my boyfriends."

"Not girlfriends," he said. "I told you about my girlfriends. Just… hookups."

"Right. Hookups." She had been breathing in his scent up close for a while and was aware of the strong masculinity of it. Would it cheapen their date to have sex? Would that turn their date into a "hookup"? "What other movies have you seen lately?"

It turned out they'd seen very few of the same movies; "Private School" and the acclaimed "Mortimer's Child." At least he shared her opinion that the latter had been overrated. "But it was time for Jake Weathers to get an Academy Award, I guess," Tami said.

"I think 'Bright and Clear' was a better take on that story, personally."

"I love that movie." She pressed her paws together. "I still think about it sometimes." Not recently, though. Ty mentioning it reminded her of her favorite scene, the heroine standing on the threshold of the doorway of her house, silhouetted against the morning light, and then taking one tentative step out.

"That was when Kylie Morgan was hot."

She looked up, sure he was joking, and indeed he was grinning at her. "Kidding," he said, paws up.

"I figured. So why did you see it?"

"Parents took me. It wasn't one of the movies I talked about a lot in college. I don't want to reinforce your prejudices about jocks, but not many football players saw it. And if they did, they sure didn't say they cried at the end."

"You cried?" She raised her eyebrows. "Or is that a line you use on girls?"

His smile widened. "I didn't cry exactly, not like hot tears soaking the fur of my muzzle crying, but I got choked up and I stayed quiet. Honestly, I don't think about the movie a lot, but back then, seeing someone break her way out of a bad life and go on to be happy—"

"Presumably."

"Presumably happy, it was a big deal to a sixteen-year-old kid. For a while I didn't want to admit it because it was a girl's movie. But lately I find I don't give as much of a shit what people think."

Tami smiled. "It helped that she was a fox, for me."

"Yeah, same here. That's why we went to see it. When I was growing up my parents went to see any movie starring a fox. We saw some terrible ones."

"'Golden Tails'?"

He grimaced. "Saw it. And the sequel."

"Ouch. I missed that one. What about 'The Fox Is an Angel'?"

"Goddammit, I hadn't thought about that movie in a decade. Stop this game now."

She laughed and relaxed on the bench. The cool crispness of the winter air stung her nostrils just enough to be invigorating, and Ty's scent was slowly easing from interesting to familiar. "I do need to work in the morning," she said. "I suppose I should get home before too long."

"I don't want to keep you." He didn't move his arm, and she didn't move to escape it. "How about you pick the place for our next date? Then tell me how to dress. Sorry I didn't do that this time."

She played with her hoodie's drawstring. "No, it's silly. I shouldn't have worried about it. But I'll come up with a good place." She'd have to ask Axel for a good restaurant to take a date to, because Ty probably wouldn't be impressed with Jack in the Box, even if the teenaged otter behind the counter knew Tami's name.

"Just text me. And, uh." His ears flicked, and he looked away from her, then back. "You can text me other times, too. If you want to vent about work or something."

"I certainly have a lot to vent about." Was he even going to ask her to bed tonight?

"Sounds like it. Just remember what you're working toward." Now he did lift his arm away from her. "And how lucky you are that you get to have something finished to point to every time, a game with your name on it that might not be perfect, but at least it's something."

"Yeah, but…not having a championship doesn't change all the hard work you did. Not everyone can win one. Right?"

The evening light turned his eyes dark brown. "Are you asking to make me agree with you or because you really don't know?"

She laughed, and he laughed with her. "I know not everyone can win one. So I'm asking you to acknowledge my point."

"Okay. Acknowledged." He rose gracefully and extended a paw down. She took it and stood next to him. "I'll walk you back to your car."

So he wasn't going to ask her. Or was he waiting for her to ask him? They walked side by side but not holding paws, the cool evening air creating misty halos around the streetlamps and bringing all sorts of smells to them: restaurant food, people, car exhaust.

It was already after ten. There was the thing Hadley'd sent her, and as it had been simmering in the back of her mind, she thought she knew how she wanted to handle it. And there were a couple things she wanted to look up for her one on one with Axel, and if she waited 'til tomorrow night to prep for the Friday meeting, she'd be frazzled. Really she should start pulling things together tonight.

But.

But, she told herself, he's not just handsome, he's sweet. Even if it hadn't been seven months, if this were just a routine date, she'd want to sleep with him. So…why not?

.

Chapter 17

They were two blocks from her car before she got up the nerve. "Can I ask you something?"

"Of course."

She drew in a cool, damp breath of air. "You've talked about all the hookups you've had…" His ears splayed out to the sides. "But you haven't…well, I don't think you've come on to me. Unless I'm really dense about those kinds of things, which is very possible, so if you did, then that's why I didn't respond."

"No." His ears came up and he reached out and took her paw. "I didn't."

"Why not?"

A moment later, she wished she could take that back. But Ty didn't seem offended. "I thought about it, but to be honest, you know, those hookups were…they were just that. I don't know if this is going to lead anywhere, but we met through a very deliberate search by my parents to find me a wife, so it'd be…" His ears flicked out to the side again. "I mean, we can't pretend that's not in the mix. If things go well."

"Right." She liked the feel of his paw, secure around hers as he tried to explain himself. "But I assume you would, you know, have sex with your wife." The image of herself in a wedding gown standing across from Ty in front of an alter flashed across her mind; she dismissed it as ridiculous even though intellectually she knew that was one of the endings of this trajectory.

"I'd hope so." He flashed that grin again. "But that'd be a ways off."

"Several meetings still to go to?"

Her attempt at humor caught him off guard and then he laughed and his ears came back up. "At least. So I dunno. I've hooked up a lot, but that's mostly, you know, girls who want to hook up with a ball player. Not really girls who want to date one long term. So I didn't want to spoil this by coming on too strong too soon."

It all made sense, if your idea of dating came exclusively from '90s movies. "What if you'd spoil this by *not* coming on to me?"

His smile vanished and his tail curled up against his (very nice) butt. "Uh." He swallowed. "I didn't think that would be a possibility."

"It's nice to know if you're sexually compatible before getting married, right?"

"Sure…"

"So?" She held onto his paw and swung around to face him. The street corner smelled faintly of garbage, outside a restaurant that had closed for the night and a bookstore with a light on in the back and faint scrapings coming through the metal grille in front. A lone ferret hurried along the sidewalk across the street, and ahead of them, a possum couple strolled away. In that moment, though, they felt very alone.

His paw held hers in a good, strong grip, but not too tight; strong, but not needing to prove it to her. He studied her eyes. "You're unusual. In a good way, I mean."

"Why? Because I'm interested in sex? You just told me about aaaaall these other girls who came on to you."

He smiled. "No. Because you're as smart as you are attractive."

She released his paw and folded her arms. "So a female can't be smart and attractive?"

Again, the smile vanished. "No, I didn't mean that. I meant—of the ones I've met—I mean, the ones who come to parties aren't usually—"

"You're pretty unusual too. You're a jock who can hold a conversation."

Ty snapped his jaw shut and stared at her. "All right, all right," he said. "Point taken. How about: you're unusual because you're the first female fox I've met that I want to sleep with and talk to before and after."

"I'll take it." She smiled and reached for his paw. "Come on. I'll drive."

"Wait, what—" He allowed himself to be pulled along after her.

"You just said you want to sleep with me. I want to sleep with you, too. So let's do it. Why not?"

In another minute they were at her car, Ty standing at the passenger side. "Are you sure?"

She wasn't, but she knew she should be. "Worst case, we get one awkward night of sex and then it saves us a lot of dates and meetings, right? When you start a new project, you have to evaluate all the risk factors."

"Very practical of you." He gave her a smile and opened the door.

On the way back, she second-guessed herself at least a dozen times, often losing track of the conversation with Ty. The football player either wasn't worried about what they were going to do or was very good at multi-processing, because he asked her a bunch of questions about her neighborhood, and patiently asked again when she missed one because of the questions she was asking herself.

Like: Is this really the right thing? What if he thinks you're too easy? Or: Your place is a mess. He's going to hate it. Or: What if Hadley tried separating out these two functions so he could address them separately and then called just one from that point that was giving him the problem? Or: Have you really thought this through? About Ty, not about Hadley's code?

It was this last question that prompted her to ask him, stopped two blocks from her house at a light, "Oh, do you have any…protection?"

"Not on me. Don't you have any at home?"

"I don't think…" Wait. Had Jason left a box of them? And if so, were any left in it? "Maybe. I'll have to check when we get there."

"We can stop at a pharmacy or something. I think we passed one a ways back."

"There's a 24-hour place over that way." Tami and Jason had made an emergency visit there for just that purpose.

At the pharmacy, she turned to insist that he stay in the car, but he was already getting out. "I'll buy," he said. "You can come along if you want."

"I'll stay. Thanks," she said hurriedly as his door closed.

She watched that nice butt and the tail swinging over it walk into the brightly-lit pharmacy, tapping her paws on the wheel. If she weren't so self-conscious about buying condoms, she wouldn't have minded walking in with him. But then the people in the pharmacy would know that they were going to go off and have sex.

Who cared if they did? Well, she responded reasonably to herself, it wasn't any of their business. Ty was handsome and she wouldn't mind being seen with him. But her private life was her private life. Axel would say that was cute. Devin would say that was ridiculous.

That sent her back to thinking about Devin and his offer to cover for her. She couldn't give him Axel's one on one, nor Hadley's request, but maybe have him brush up on the project to back her up for Fatima…

Someone in the pharmacy stopped Ty, a snow leopard in a hoodie even rattier than hers, with a paunch and a bit of a hunch to his shoulders. His ears were up, eyes wide and tail flicking, a huge can't-believe-this-is-happening grin as he took out his pocket camera to ask the clerk to take a picture of him and Ty.

Now she was glad she hadn't gone in. She'd have had to stand awkwardly to the side while the guy got his picture. Was that what life with Ty would be like, if it got that far? People in late-night pharmacies taking pictures with him, people in shopping malls or restaurants? It was a miracle they'd gone on two dates without anyone recognizing him. Though—probably the waitresses at Jack B's had. They just hadn't taken pictures.

"Everything okay?" He came back into the car, a brown paper bag in one paw.

"Fine." The snow leopard was driving away. "Met a fan?"

"Oh, him? Yeah, he recognized me. No biggie, just wanted a picture."

"That must feel good." She pulled out of the parking lot and headed for her house.

Ty leaned back in the seat. "You get used to it. I used to be surprised in college. Now it feels like…part of my job, I guess. They told us that, that we're 'ambassadors' of the UFL."

She slid her fingers over the wheel as they went around a corner. "Do you ever get disappointed when you're not recognized?"

He laughed, relaxing. "Not any more. Now it's a relief to be able to go around and do normal things like," he patted the paper bag, "this without being stopped. But Ford—he's the older wideout, got traded mid-season— told me that I should appreciate every guy who stops me to ask for a picture, always be grateful, because these people are investing a lot of their life and energy in you." He folded his paws over the bag. "Sometimes that's hard to remember when you're just trying to buy condoms and this guy insists on a photo."

"You seemed to do okay. From what I saw."

His slender muzzle turned toward her, his smile getting longer. "Thanks. I think he left happy."

"Did he comment on the, uh." She inclined her head toward the bag.

"Nah. Sometimes people do that. Like, they want to ask you about what you're doing and all. But this guy didn't even look at what I was holding."

She turned onto her block and then into the alley behind her building. "Thanks for going in and getting them."

"Hey, it's the guy's responsibility, right?" Ty looked around, ears perked, as she guided the car into the garage. "Nice building."

"Thanks." Tami wondered what he'd say about her apartment. It was… reasonably clean. She kept it presentable not because she might have company over, but because having everything in its place was the most efficient way to live. And hey, it was a reflection of her and her life, so if he didn't like it, to hell with him.

But she thought he would. Ty was pretty easygoing, and what's more, he didn't seem like the kind of guy who would say something disparaging about her apartment when she'd brought him over specifically to sleep with him. Wasn't that one of those "rules" Devin had told her about? Say something to knock down the lady's confidence so she'll be more likely to want you? "Baby, your fur's a mess, but I don't care, I like you anyway," stuff like that.

No, Ty hadn't done anything like that. He was actually interested in her, at least as far as her limited experience could tell. Disappointed that she didn't want to go dancing, maybe, but that was a minor issue. What was the other thing Devin had warned her about that guys would try? Something about sex, but not the old "all they want is" because she knew that one. In any case, it wasn't likely to be terribly relevant, because she was the one driving the date at this point, literally for another thirty seconds until she got to her parking spot.

"How long have you lived here?" he asked as she locked the car.

She led him to the elevator. "Six years? No, seven. Well, six and eleven months."

He sniffed the air. "They keep the garage pretty well Neutra-Scented."

"Yeah, they're good about odors in general. The garbage is over there, away from the elevators."

"God, my dorms in college…" All the way up he told her about the numerous complaints lodged by the canid students in the dorms about the location of the garbage right near one of the main hallways, and about the friend of his who had to switch rooms twice because they kept putting him near machinery, first the dorm elevator, and then the service elevator.

"Elevators don't bother me that much," Tami said. "But I do sleep with earplugs."

"It was the stopping and starting. And guys would come back at all hours of the night, even in the jock dorms." He sniffed again, following her down the hall to her apartment. "What was your college experience like?"

"Oh, the usual, I guess. I went to Seaside, about six hours south of here. Very libertarian school. We CompSci students kept to ourselves. I graduated in three years." She opened the door to her apartment and gestured. "After you."

"Nice," he said, stepping in, and she didn't know whether he meant her college accomplishment or her apartment until he said, "I don't know anyone who graduated in under four years, but we were kind of assembly-line shoved through the school anyway."

"I thought most star players only did one year in college."

He grimaced, ears flattening, and for a moment she felt bad, but they came back up quickly and his smile didn't change. "One, I wasn't a superstar talent. At my school I was one of the stars, but I kept hearing from scouts that I'd be a fourth round pick, and the money there is okay, but…" He wiggled his paw. "Two, my mom and dad are pretty well off and mom insisted I graduate. And by the way," he said as the door closed behind them, "I got picked in the second round by the Firebirds, so take that, scouts."

"What's your degree in? Football?"

He laughed, tail swishing. Tami scraped her paws over the mat, and Ty followed suit. "Communications. I wouldn't mind being a commentator after my career's over."

"Oh, okay. Is there such a thing as a football degree?"

"No. Well, I guess you could major in physical education? This is a nice place, by the way." He nodded toward the two bookshelves. "I think that's more books than everyone I know owns. Have you read them all?"

Tami raised her eyebrows. "Twice, some of them. But those there are textbooks—the bottom two shelves of that one—and then the ones above that are books I've accumulated professionally. You said you read a playbook every week, so you've done a lot of reading. That's all this is."

"Hah." He swished his tail and went over to look at them. His ears were taller than the top of her bookshelf. "I like that. 'Waterfall Programming Challenges and Benefits.' You program waterfalls?"

Even in the simple act of bending over to inspect that title, Ty showed a fluidity and grace in his body that Tami had never felt in hers. She was hit with a moment of realization: this guy was in her apartment, had accepted her invitation to come up. And seeing his body in the confines of her living room gave her a greater appreciation for it.

Either that or it was the fact that she anticipated soon seeing him un-clothed. The memory of his bare chest swam back into her mind, only this time her paws were on it. How had Jason's chest looked, the last time she'd seen it? Not that good, that's for damn sure. And his arms, and that nice foxy tail… She cleared her throat and walked over to the bookcase. "Waterfall is a type of coding team management. When you have a bunch of people all working on a project, you have to coordinate them. Waterfall is one way to do that: you get one stage done, like all the project requirements, then move to the next." She made a wavy motion with her paw. "Like a waterfall. That's oversimplifying, but…"

"Good enough for me." He straightened and looked around. "Nice TV, little selection of movies there. I see at least a few familiar titles. Say, uh." He reached up and scratched an ear. "You ever see a movie, um…I forget what it's called, but it has dragons in it?"

"I've seen a couple movies with dragons."

"This one had weasels, like a weasel army…" He trailed off. "Never mind, it's not important."

"I think I heard about that one, but I've never seen it. 'Fire in the Sky' or something like that?"

He nodded, but moved away from the movie shelves, his ears half-down for some reason. Maybe he was embarrassed about liking a terrible fantasy movie? "Yeah, maybe. This is a comfy place. I like it."

"Thanks. I do too." She cleared her throat. "You want something to drink, or…"

"Sure. What do you have?"

"Beer, probably some rum but I don't know if I have anything to mix it with." She padded to the kitchen to check.

"Beer's fine," he said. "Also, mind if I use your bathroom?"

"Through there." She reviewed whether she'd left anything embarrassing out in her bathroom and couldn't think of anything. "I'm just going to send a couple emails while you do that."

So she brought out two bottles of beer and then opened up her laptop. There was Hadley's email, and there was a message from Fatima inviting her to a meeting tomorrow morning with the marketing team. Why hadn't that pinged on her phone?

Right, she'd turned notifications off before coming on the date. She turned them back on and accepted the invitation, adding a note asking if there was anything she needed to prepare and whether it would be okay to loop Devin in on the meeting. Then she pulled up Hadley's code and scanned it to make sure that her solution would work. It seemed like it would, so she cut and pasted a few lines, adding in her thoughts on it.

She was emailing Hadley with the solution when a clink behind her caught her attention. She turned and saw Ty with his paw on one of the bottles, the other holding open a book. "Sorry," she said, "do you want a glass?"

A grin spread over his muzzle. "I'm finished," he said. "I didn't want to disturb you. If you're going to be much longer…"

"No." She glanced at the clock on her laptop screen and scrambled up out of the chair. "Oh my god, it's eleven. You should've told me when you came back in."

His paw landed on her shoulder, stilling her worries. "It's no big deal. The beer was cold and you've got this book of political cartoons that was pretty good."

He returned the book to the shelf, and when he turned back, Tami put one paw on his waist and stood on tiptoe to kiss him.

Ty kissed her back lightly. Their eyes met as Tami pushed her muzzle forward to kiss him more deeply. It took him a second to really get into the kiss, and then he put his arms around her and held her so securely that she felt she could've let her calves go limp and she'd stay pressed against him, their lips warm together, the scent and taste of him on her tongue with the aftertaste of the beer, his body hard and warm against hers. He was a good kisser, firm and sensitive, moving slightly with her and matching the points of their muzzles.

When they broke apart, he continued to hold her. She moved her arm down his back. "You have a lot of muscles," she murmured, breathing in his scent. Up close he smelled young, vibrant, and aroused, and it was gratifying that she could provoke that reaction.

He chuckled, and she felt as well as heard it, his diaphragm rumbling against her. "Part of my job," he said, but his tail wagged despite the casual tone of his voice. "So…you want to have your beer?"

Her tail wagged as well. "No," she said. "I'm good."

Tami expected Ty to move toward the bedroom, but instead he bent his head to hers and kissed her again. This time their lips parted slightly and she tasted him even more strongly, and below the beer there were undertastes of the meat and the Coke he'd had with dinner. She pressed her paws against the small of his back and sighed at the warmth of the embrace and the kiss.

He pulled back. "Hey," he said, his eyes serious, "are you allowed to kiss someone who eats meat?"

"Yes, that's fine." She smiled and pulled him back down to kiss him again, and this time she took a step toward the bedroom.

He went along with her, holding the kiss for a few steps and then breaking it to make it easier to walk. "I like the scent," he said.

"It's a lilac-vanilla blend, but it's light. I don't like to overuse scents."

"No, that's what I like." He inhaled. "Not that your natural scent is that bad. Quite nice, actually."

"Uh." She didn't know how to respond to that. "Yours too. It feels like I've known you for a while."

He reached back to the bedroom door. "Closed or open?"

"Nobody else is going to walk in." She smiled. "I don't care."

"Okay." His paw came back from the door to her cheek ruffs, and then his eyes looked at something over her shoulder. "Wait, do you have a webcam in here?"

"What? No." She cupped her ears back and caught the hum of her computer's fan. "I have the old desktop in here because I work in here sometimes."

"Ah, okay." He relaxed. "I'm not necessarily opposed to that, you know. Filming, I mean. I have to be careful it doesn't get out, though."

"No, I wouldn't…" She laughed and looked up. "You're teasing me."

"A little." He smiled.

"Come on." She pulled him to the bed and pushed him into a sitting position on it. Even sitting on the bed, his head was almost level with hers as she stood, so she knelt astride his thighs. They were so large that her own thigh muscles stretched and complained, but she ignored them, lowered her head, and kissed him again.

This time he put his paws on her sides and lay back, pulling her down atop him as they kissed. She took a moment to enjoy that this was happening, that this handsome fox was holding her and kissing her, and then she enjoyed the kiss itself.

When she felt his paws slide down her body to her rear, she pulled her head back and smiled down at him. Now that she was lying fully against him, she could feel his readiness against her hips, and her mind raced ahead to the future of the evening. How would he, how would she, what would it feel like? The urge to take his pants off and slide her paws over his erection overwhelmed her, surprising in its strength. Soon enough, she thought, and indeed his paws were not only cupping her rear but playing with the waist of her pants, which were loose enough to let him get his fingers down inside them.

So she slid her paws down his sides, tugging up the yellow Jack B's shirt and running her fingers through the short fur underneath. His body was warm, the muscles taut even around his stomach.

And god, his paws were down inside her pants now, holding her around her hips, and she was already panting. "All right," she said, and shifted so that her fingers could get at the front of his pants. She fumbled at the snap as he waited, and finally she got it undone, pulled them open and pushed them down his hips.

Underneath he wore tight athletic briefs that didn't get pushed down with his pants. Tami couldn't resist running her fingers over the shiny lycra fabric, first along the curve of his hip, and then along the sharply defined bulge of his erection.

It might be rude or unseemly, jumping there so quickly, but Tami was beyond caring. She'd wanted to touch it and there it was, asking to be touched. And Ty lay back with his eyes closed, obviously enjoying it, so there was nothing wrong with it. She lay her paw over it, feeling the trembling readiness, and that itself was enough to make her warm and damp in anticipation.

"Here," Ty said after a moment. "Let me…"

She thought he was going to take the briefs off when he reached down, but he merely pushed his pants all the way off and then lifted the yellow t-shirt over his head. Both fell away to the floor, and the scent of his arousal rose to dominate the room. Then, because she was still kneeling on the bed, he put his paws to the sides of her chest and kissed her again.

It was easier kissing this way, without their chests pressed together, because they didn't have to twist their muzzles as much. It also allowed her paws to explore the hard lines of his chest as he followed the curves of her breasts, starting at the edges and teasing inwards. And then, without breaking the kiss, he was lifting her hoodie off and she was raising her arms over her head. Their muzzles had to separate for the hoodie to come off, and it dragged her shirt most of the way with it, so she helped get that off, too, and then she thought she might as well get her pants off.

During the next kiss, he unhooked her bra, and she again got the sense that *this is really happening*. She barely knew this guy, and here he was with his fingers right on her breasts, playing with them in an inexperienced but nonetheless pleasurable way. But it wasn't the same as the time in college when she'd hooked up with that guy at the bar. Then, she'd been fairly sure she would never see him again (and she hadn't, not unless you counted across the aisle at graduation). Ty she knew only a little better, but this act was all within the plan for their relationship, whatever that was going to be.

And when they broke that kiss, she scooted back on the bed and looked at him, russet and ivory fur trimmed over a landscape of hard curves. He lay back on his elbows, both expecting and enjoying the attention, and his tail flicked back and forth across the bed. "Want to take a picture?" he asked, appearing completely serious.

"That's okay." She laughed, sliding off the bed. "Where are those condoms?"

"Bathroom." He pointed. "And I meant for your friend Devin."

"Axel. Devin's the straight one who likes sports." But still, he'd remembered Devin's name.

"For both of them, then." He smiled that easy smile.

She looked pointedly down at his underwear. "Sure you want to hit pause? I can take the picture after."

"Your choice." He nodded down his chest and stomach. "I can get back in the mood pretty easily."

"I'm going to put myself ahead of Axel this time." She found the paper bag in the bathroom, got the box out of it and a condom out of that, and hurried back to the bed to find Ty pulling his briefs off his ankle. He tossed them to the floor and lay back again.

Tami stared down at his erection, rubbing the condom packaging between her fingers, and then perked her ears up. "All right, then," she said, and pushed her own panties down to her feet and stepped out of them.

"Mmm." Ty's eyes traveled appreciatively over her form, which was nice of him considering the females he must be used to…*no, don't think like that. He's here now, you're here now. Open the condom package and get him ready.*

Tami herself was pretty ready, but still, she took a moment to slide her fingers along him, playing with his length and enjoying his squirming as she did. He surprised her by slipping his paw between her legs and playing with her cleft, and she flicked her ears back and stopped her own caresses so that Ty looked up and asked, "Is everything all right?"

"Yes." With her free paw, she guided his fingers back. "It's nice."

"Not expecting it?" He looked very pleased with himself. "A lot of guys don't think to do that. They just push right in."

"I'm familiar with that." She stroked his length up and down, and he in response increased his explorations of her. "But…ah…right now it feels like we're both ready…"

"Absolutely." He lowered his paw, rubbing fingers down her inner thighs.

So she got the condom out and rolled it down over him (it had been a while but she still remembered how to do that) and then lifted one knee over his legs, straddling him, and then…

And then he was inside her, her memory of sex made real and current and yet different because he was different. His scent was new and the sight of him was new and he fit inside her unlike any of her other lovers—not necessarily better or worse, not yet, but different. And his paws gripping her hips were huge, almost able to circle her thighs, and they held her as he pushed up into her, sank down, pushed up, and Tami closed her eyes.

Not too long after…Ty's fingers tightened, and she knew he was coming even though she was nowhere near finishing herself. She brought a finger to her clit, but even as she rubbed around it, Ty arched his back and made a moaning noise, his muzzle twisting as he pushed his knot all the way into her, hips jerking against the tie.

She kept rubbing as he flopped back, tongue lolling out of his mouth. His eyes opened and he looked up. "Uh. Uh." He panted, smiling, and then noticed the motion of her fingers. "Oh, you…you didn't…?"

"No." His warmth inside her was pleasant, though, and with maybe ten minutes she could. "I don't always."

"I can…" He gulped, collected himself. "Wait."

"It's fine."

"No, I can…do you want me to…?"

"I've got it. It's really okay."

His paws squeezed her thighs. "We'll be tied for a bit, so keep going."

Right, the knot. Jason hadn't been a canine, so she hadn't been thinking that Ty would be stuck inside her. That would give her enough time, wouldn't it?

No, as it turned out. But even if she didn't orgasm, it was an enjoyable ten minutes. She thought about faking it, and if Ty'd been a one-night stand she might've done that to make him feel better. But if this was a bellwether of their future together, she should be honest.

So when he slid out of her, she met his questioning look with, "Still no. But it was good, don't worry about it."

"Next time…" He struggled to sit up, reaching out to put an arm around her. "There will be a next time?"

"Yeah." The word bubbled out of her with a smile.

"Then next time I'll do better. I promise."

"I told you, don't worry. Look, it's been…a long time. It was nice just to have the contact again. And you…" Naked, embracing, it was harder to hide the truths between them. "You made me feel pretty. I know you're twenty-two or whatever and probably just thinking about sex gets you aroused, but…"

"You are pretty." He slid his fingers through her fur, down her side to her rear and along her tail. "I'm not putting on an act."

"I'm not as pretty as your usual girls."

"Maybe not," he said, "by some guys' standards. But like I said…I wouldn't want to talk to a lot of them before or after we had sex. That's attractive."

"Flatterer," she said, half-sincerely and half-sarcastically.

"You don't seem like the type to want empty flattery." He leaned forward and kissed her.

"No." She kissed back and slid her fingers down his arms. "But I like genuine flattery."

"Okay, then." Ty put a finger to the side of his muzzle, mock-thinking. "Hang on, let me come up with something…" He held the pose while Tami waited. "Okay, got it. I really love the softness of your fur. It's clear you take really good care of yourself."

She squinted at him. "Thank you. I appreciate the confirmation of my taste in conditioner."

"Also," he said, "I love that you have all six of the 'Cop Class' movies sitting next to 'Citizen Kane' on your shelf."

"They're…pretty funny." She shook her head and grinned. "Actually they're really dumb."

"Terrible."

"But still…they make me laugh."

"And 'Citizen Kane'?"

She let out a small chuckle. "Not as funny. But a good movie."

"I've never seen it."

"What?"

He shook his head. "Shameful, I know."

"Well…" She flicked her ears. "I mean, it's a great movie, but it's not exactly something where I'd say, 'Hey, let's sit down and watch it this evening for fun.' It's more like a film you ought to take an evening to sit down and watch so you can appreciate it."

"And so you don't have to say you haven't seen it when people ask."

"That too."

They fell silent, caressing each other's sides and arms, until she said, "This was really nice."

"Good." Ty smiled. "Do you want to set up a second date now, or wait for a day or two?"

"I'll have to look at my schedule." The mere mention of her schedule brought her work seeping back into her thoughts, the meetings, the responsibilities, the people she had to report to and manage. One of the very nice things about the sex had been freeing her mind from worrying about any of that for at least half an hour.

"All right. We can wait. And in the meantime, I probably will have to meet some other candidates at dinners. But I'm going to tell my parents that I want to see you again and that you're my favorite."

"So far," she said, to hide how pleased she was.

"So far," he agreed. "But unless one of these Yamatese vixens likes 'Cop Class,' I don't see much real competition."

"Will your parents let you…" She didn't want to say, "marry me," so she finished with, "date me?"

"I'll—I'll make it work. If you—if we—want it to work."

"Give me a few more dates," Tami said.

Ty smiled. "Gladly."

He offered to stay the night, but Tami had to get up early and had also realized as she watched him put his briefs back on that she hadn't finished that email to Hadley. The last thing she wanted was to go back to her work while Ty was here in her bed, so it was better all around if he left.

And when he was gone, she finished the email, worked on her project review, and then crawled into bed. And the bed smelled like him, and she clutched the pillow against her, remembering not the warmth of his organ inside her but the warmth of his eyes and the sparkle in them when he talked about the movies they both liked.

Chapter 18

"I didn't prepare a lot for this," she told Axel the next morning at work, "so how about you tell me how your projects are going and if you have any issues."

His eyebrows rose and his ears perked up. "You didn't prepare, meaning the date went well?"

"You have half an hour," Tami said. "Are you sure you want to spend a few minutes talking about my dating life?"

"I'll spend the whole time if you'll let me." The marmot folded his paws in front of him.

"No."

"All right, a few minutes then. Did you get a picture?"

Tami sighed and slid her phone across to him. Axel picked it up and stared. "Oh my god. Can I keep this open here for the whole meeting?"

"No."

"Can I have a copy?"

"No."

"Tami…"

She reached out and took the phone back. "Yes, the date went well. I'm probably going to see him again. He's…he's a lot nicer than I would've expected from someone who's had everything handed to him his whole life." Though he'd said something about sports being an escape from his family, hadn't he?

"That body and a personality?" Axel fanned himself. "Please tell me he's bi."

"I don't know about that," Tami said. "He certainly appreciates the female form." The memory brought a smile to her muzzle.

"All right. In my fantasies he's going to be bi." Axel shook his head. "Glad you like him."

"Yeah…" Tami tapped her claws on the table. "The thing is, after he left, I started worrying. I mean, his parents are presenting him with this array of proper Yamatese foxes, and…is he only interested in me because I'm maybe acceptable to them but I'm different?"

"I'm sure that's the reason."

"I mean, is he settling?"

"We all settle." Axel spread his paws. "I mean, in this case you're settling for a jock who isn't ever going to really understand the work you do."

"That's cheery. Also maybe not true."

He leaned forward. "What I'm trying to say is that settling isn't bad. You settle to start with, but you can build a loving relationship out of that. Mialo flaked on our first two dates, and he complains all the time that I push him to be a 'clock-watcher.' Would I like someone who can get somewhere on fucking time? Yeah. Would he like someone who," he made air quotes, "isn't a slave to the 'fictional precision of the second hand'? Sure. Do I love him?"

He waited. She raised an eyebrow. "Yes?"

"Hell yes. He's smart, he's sweet, he's funny…so I try not to get upset when he's ready at 6:55 for a seven o'clock movie, and he tries to be ready about fifteen minutes earlier than he thinks he has to. There are other things too, but that's an example. No two people are perfect for each other. But if you even like this guy, this…" He stared wistfully at her phone. "This platonic ideal of a male who is worth millions of dollars…then fucking go for it."

"Thanks," Tami said. "Ready to talk about work yet?"

She salvaged twenty minutes of the meeting, getting Axel's perspective on the problems he was having with one of the database guys, which she would have to go to Roscoe about at the managers' meeting next week. She got back to her cubicle a little after ten to find a cluster of people standing around it: Devin, Gri, and Paul from her team; Janine, the bear from the front desk; Miranda from sales; and Mike, one of the other project leads who sat next to her.

"Hey guys, what's going…" She caught the smell of roses when she was fifteen feet away. "…on?"

Everyone grinned widely. Janine pointed into the cubicle, her little round ears twitching. "Look! They just now dropped them off."

"It took three of them." Devin leaned on the corner of her cube, his arms folded, looking down. "Makin' all the rest of us look bad."

"Nobody expects something like this," Miranda said, a note of jealousy in the rabbit's voice even though she was smiling. "Who is he, Tami? An Amazon millionaire?"

Tami rounded the corner of her cubicle and stared at what must have been six dozen bright red roses in three large crystal vases, the fragrance powerful but not overwhelming. She put a paw to her muzzle.

"And they're the special low-scent variety," Devin said.

"All of them are blooming." Miranda leaned over the cubicle wall. "And those vases are Waterford. This must have cost five hundred dollars. Did he cash in on some startup I've never heard of?"

"Football millionaire," Devin said.

"What?" Janine literally gasped and clutched at the collar of her dress. "A football player? Where did you meet him?"

Tami tore her eyes away from the roses and made a sweeping gesture shooing them away. "Okay, you know what, I have work to do. Why don't you schedule a gossip meeting on my calendar and I'll fill you in on all the details then."

"A *professional* player?" Miranda asked. "What's his name? Does he play for the Manticores?"

"Out," Tami said sternly, and sat down, docked her laptop, and opened her email.

Grumbling, everyone left except Devin, who hung over the cubicle wall. "You know," he said, "I only send flowers after sex."

"Great," Tami said. "How lucky for your dates. You ready for this marketing meeting?"

He made an exasperated noise. "Lunch today?"

"Sure." She didn't look up, but listened as he walked away. And when she was alone, she finally scooted her chair back to look at the flowers.

They were gorgeous. She wasn't really a flower person, especially as most of them were over-scented as far as foxes were concerned, but as her fellow canid had noted, these were the low-scent variety. Presumably more expensive. And the vases were really nice, she had to admit. Better than "really nice"; they were gorgeous. She didn't know crystal well, but these had hundreds of facets that caught the horrible overhead fluorescent light and turned it into something soft and beautiful.

And the roses…even the reduced scent was enough to make her dizzy, so she moved two of the vases to the edge of her desk and sat looking at the

Tami rounded the corner of her cubicle and stared at what must have been six dozen bright red roses in three large crystal vases, the fragrance powerful but not overwhelming.

third, which had the card on it. Before reaching for the small folded paper, she examined the roses. Each one was in full bloom, no dead spots, none losing petals or not quite open yet. And with the scent of them diminished, she could appreciate the loveliness, the texture of their perfume, sweet with a sharp undertone and a promise of excitement that drew a wag from her tail. The stems felt waxy, the thorns sharp against her pads. She reached for the card and held the stiff paper open.

To Tami,
I hope you like rosses.
See you soon.
-Ty

She had to laugh, at the misspelling and the impetuous gesture and all of it. He was adorable, that was for sure. Of course, Jason had been very sweet the first month or so they were going out. And Jason had been able to talk coding with her. But he'd never bought her even one rose, let alone…

She counted them. There were fifty total, split between the three vases (17-17-16, she noted, so the flower place wouldn't even throw in one extra rose to make the vases even). And counting them brought home again how perfect each one was. Her finger brushed the soft petals, bringing a small burst of the fragrance to her nose again.

Throughout the day, people kept coming by and commenting on the flowers, from things like, "those are gorgeous," to more intrusive comments like, "I didn't know you had a serious boyfriend." Tami smiled and kept her muzzle shut in response to all of them, nodding and going on with her work. Even during the marketing meeting, which she wanted to pay attention to because game leads had to know marketing , she found herself thinking about the flowers and about Ty.

Axel joined her and Devin for lunch, and to her surprise, instead of going to the company cafeteria, Devin steered them toward the door. "It's such a nice day," he said, stepping out into the drizzle.

Tami eyed him, but Axel bustled cheerfully past her. "Plus, down at La Taquita, we can sit in a booth and you can tell us privately about your date."

"I don't want to go to La Taquita," Tami said. "They take forever."

"Fine, we can to go Lobster House." Devin turned.

"How about Taverna?" Tami put her hood up over her ears.

"They're slower than La Taquita," Axel said.

"Yeah, but at least I can get baklava."

"Fine!" Devin walked faster, swinging his tail back and forth. "Let's just go."

So they sat in a booth in the back of the Hellenian restaurant and ordered gyros and kebabs. "All right," Devin said. "You slept with him, didn't you?"

Tami looked across the plastic table at the two of them. "I don't think that's any of your business."

"Axel told me you did. So how was it?" Devin asked.

"How was *he*?" Axel leaned forward.

"I did not tell you I slept with him." Tami shook her head.

Devin shook his back in mockery. "Come on, Tami. Even if your non-denial wasn't clue enough, you're so much more relaxed. I noticed it even though I didn't sit with you for half an hour this morning."

She glared at Axel, and the marmot smiled. "Besides," he said, "to get that picture you showed me and then not sleep with him, you'd have to be ace or dead."

"All right, all right." She sighed, and to both of their anticipatory smiles said, "But no details."

"Was he better than Jason?" Axel asked.

The question brought Tami up short. "I mean, Jason at the beginning or Jason at the end? Jason at the beginning was a lot more enthusiastic and attentive. At the end he knew me better but things were…formulaic."

"Jason at the beginning," Devin said. "Fair's fair."

"All right. I don't know if I can remember that far back. It was weird because with Jason, we went on three dates before I slept with him, and with Ty it was technically two but really one. But things are different with Ty for a lot of reasons."

"You never have to pick up the check."

She scowled at the wolf. "Because we met through this weird ritual his parents are putting him through. So we're doing things kind of backwards, you know? I didn't meet Jason's parents until we'd been dating for a year."

"Not really backwards." Axel rubbed his whiskers. "You're taking things as they come up."

"Who initiated it?" Devin leaned forward. "He did, didn't he?"

"No, actually." Tami took a drink of water and brought her ears forward so her slight embarrassment wouldn't be too obvious. "He was afraid of moving things too fast. I said we should get the sex out of the way."

"Well." Axel leaned back. "No wonder he sent you roses."

"Why, because I initiated it?"

"No, no." He waved a paw, flustered. "It was sarcastic. Because you said 'let's get it out of the way.' "

"Oh." She smiled at his discomfiture and relaxed. "I didn't say it quite like that."

"I'm amazed you took enough time away from work to have sex," Devin said.

"I almost didn't." She told them briefly about getting wrapped up in her email. "But he was cool about it."

"Guys will wait way longer than an hour for sex." Devin pointed at her. "So…better or worse than Jason?"

She exhaled. "It's tough to remember Jason because I idealized those early dates and then the memories of later are a lot clearer. But Ty is…he's a fox, and that makes a difference, and even though he has way more reason to be arrogant than Jason did, he's not."

"I meant in bed." Devin folded his arms.

"That's all part of it!" She shook her head. "I know for you guys it's all about how they touch your dick, but for us there's a lot more involved. It's how he acts before and how he holds you and how he kisses you and does he pay attention to you and all that. And I guess he was a little better than Jason."

She wasn't sure that was true. Jason, for all his other faults, had been a capable, attentive lover early in their relationship. But it was what they wanted to hear, and more importantly, it was what she wanted to tell them.

"Good." Axel nodded sharply. "So you'll be getting more pictures?"

Tami laughed. "We'll see. I don't know how much more he'll let me take pictures of."

"And can we meet him?"

She smiled at Devin. "If things go that far, yes."

"All right." The wolf sat back and turned his ears toward the kitchen. "Now what do we talk about for the next half hour until our lunch gets here?"

"How about your dating life?" Tami asked sweetly. "How's Gloria?"

"Oh, busy, same as me." The wolf waved a paw. "Saturday night we're going to dinner at La Conchita."

"I'm telling ya, you should see her Friday nights, too." Axel elbowed the wolf.

Devin rolled his eyes. "You want to bring a girl in with you and Mialo?" He didn't wait for Axel to answer. "Then stop trying to get me in a three-way with Gloria and Frejo."

Axel laughed. "At least spend your Friday nights doing something other than working. You're going to end up as bad as Tami, just when she's starting to realize there's more to life."

"Devin's a good leader," Tami said. "Don't tell him to ignore his work."

"Perish the thought." Axel looked up. "Hey, our salads are coming."

•

The roses made it impossible not to think about Ty for the rest of the day, even through her meetings and project work. But she managed to get a lot of work done, and the smell of the roses made a nice background. It was nice to have them there when she turned her head, too, a reminder that outside the screens and post-its and spreadsheets pinned to her cubicle wall there was a bright, fragrant world.

He didn't text her all day, and it was only as she was leaving around eight at night, having decided to take one of the vases home, that she thought to text him back. *Love the rosses*, she wrote. *Thank you.*

And when she got home, there was a reply. *You're welcome. I'm in another meeting tonight. Not too dull but thinking of you.*

Thinking of you. She set the roses next to her laptop and sat down to finish her work for the day, which technically took her forty-five minutes into Friday.

Six hours later she woke up from a distressing war dream and spent an hour at the computer answering an email from Fatima's boss, Mr. Francis. It had to be just right because this was the guy who was going to appoint the lead for the Destiny's Angel game. Fatima had given her guidance: stick to facts, be direct but not too direct. "As a female," she'd told Tami, "you don't want to be labeled 'emotional'."

The resulting email felt dry and uninspiring, even more so because quoted in Mr. Francis's email were two replies from other project managers, David and Rick, who had made facts just a launching point of gushing confidence in their team, promises that even Tami could tell were unrealistic.

She didn't want to go that far, but surely just a little more than the dry "person-hours available" and "project bugs resolved" that Fatima wanted her to relate.

She got that done finally and headed in to work for another day filled with meetings and politics and too little actual coding. Her mother called her twice to make sure she was going to show up for the dinner, and Tami promised she was going to. And then Marci texted her to tell her that she and Kalia were doing bar night Saturday and she was coming, no ifs, ands, or buts, and she was going to tell them about her football player.

The world's demands were closing in on her again, the world blocking out the beautiful roses. If she went out with both her mother and Marci, when would she have the time to get the slide deck for the project review nailed down? Sure, she could get the basics done in a couple hours, but she wanted to run them past Devin for his thoughts, and if she had a chance, look back at her previous reports to see where this one stood with respect to her past projects.

If she went out with Marci for two drinks tops, she could get back in time. She could keep Marci to that. She'd feed her some juicy details about Ty, enough to satisfy her, and then she'd head home.

CHAPTER 19

Dinner with her mother went easily and quickly. Tami only half paid attention during the biweekly obligation, which consisted mostly of her mother bringing her up to date on the activities of a number of friends she hadn't seen in years. The subject of Ty came up only once, when her mother told her that she hadn't heard back from his parents. "I guess you weren't good enough for them," she sniffed. "It's terrible what a bit of money will do to some people."

"They were all right," Tami said absently, toying with her mushroom stew, which was too creamy and rich. The bread at least was okay.

"Do you hear anything from Jason?" Her mother turned her attention to her chicken pasta.

"No, Mom. We broke up two years ago."

"People stay friends. I just connected with my high school prom date on Facebook."

"Great." Tami swallowed. "Is he single?"

"He's far too old for you."

Tami looked up to see her mother smile. "I'm teasing. No, he's not single. He's married to a vixen, actually—oh, don't give me that look just because I don't hang my independence on a silly word—and they have three cubs, two foxes and a koala."

"What?"

"He's a koala, did I not mention? Their cubs are adorable and he's a vice president at an insurance company, and his wife is the chief financial officer of a company that makes spreadsheets or some kind of sheets, I'm not really sure which." There Tami zoned out again, thinking about her project and Jaden's QA report on the latest build, which had come in that night at 6:30 pm and would need to be incorporated into the deck.

She spent most of Saturday working on the deck for Monday, made more complicated by the fact that new bugs kept coming in from the publisher even on Saturday. Fortunately, most of them were small and Tami could reasonably estimate the time to fix—in one case she thought it would be fixed before the meeting. By the time Marci called to make sure she was coming, it was in reasonably good shape. "I'll be there soon," she said.

When Marci called again, she was tightening up the wording on the fifth slide. "Hey," she said. "I told you I'd be there—"

"By seven, yes, it's quarter after now."

"It is?" Tami stared at her computer's clock. "Oh, shit. Sorry. I'm leaving now."

"It's all right, I didn't call until now so I'd be sure of winning my bet with Kalia. But seriously, get here soon or we'll be too drunk to hear about your football player."

The roses had lost very little of their bloom or scent. She looked at them again and smiled as she hung up the phone. He hadn't contacted her in a while, but for some reason she wasn't worried about it. She inhaled their light perfume and impulsively texted Ty: *How'd your meeting go?*

Her phone beeped as she was getting into her car. She took it out and looked.

Want to hear about it in person?

She hadn't seen Marci since the night after her and Ty's "meeting," but she was sure Marci and Kalia would tell her to go for it. *Sure*, she wrote back. *Where?*

You pick the place this time.

For a moment she was tempted to bring him to meet Marci and Kalia at the bar, but she wasn't quite ready for that yet. So she picked a place Axel had told her about, where she'd been impressed with the clam chowder. *Lorora's Fish House?*

While waiting for him to reply, she texted Marci and told her *Last-minute date, sorry to bail.* And as she'd expected, Marci wrote back that booty comes before booze, "and not just in the dictionary."

The one on 4th? Ty wrote back. Tami affirmed, and set off on her way.

Lorora's wasn't a fancy place, but it was a step above "buy it at the counter and sit at a plastic table." The wooden beams were hung with fishing nets and plastic fish, and the planks in the floor were thick and solid like the timbers of a ship. The waitstaff wore blue aprons and jaunty blue hats, and the whole place smelled like fish oil and chowder.

When Ty walked in, he spotted Tami at her table right away, even before she looked up to see the six-foot-four fox looming over the five foot otter at the host stand. "Never mind," he said, and moved easily across the restaurant to the empty seat at her table. Ears perked and heads turned to follow his progress, at which Tami felt an odd combination of self-consciousness and enjoyment.

Tonight he'd worn a casual polo shirt, red on the top and white on the bottom, with some navy blue stripes of various widths at the boundary. The shirt was tucked into his jeans, which Tami noticed flattered his butt nicely below his long, flowing tail. "Nice place," he said.

"I've only been here once, but the chowder was really good, and Yap says the swordfish is great."

"Who's Yap?" he asked, and she had to tell him about the crowd-sourced restaurant review app in between ordering drinks.

He asked how her work had been going and she found herself chatting away. It was easy to talk to him about work because she didn't have to watch what she said the way she did even to Devin and Axel; a comment about management or about one of their co-workers could come back to bite her. She could talk about her frustrations with Paul, about how the publisher sent bug reports without adequate documentation and expected them to be fixed anyway, about how she had to write up a new report every week and it was all the same. And Ty listened, ears perked forward, as intently as if she were talking about something he knew or cared about.

When their chowders arrived, she let out a long breath. "It's good to get that out. Sorry for going on."

"Don't apologize." Ty picked up his spoon and blew on the chowder. "I'm glad to hear about it. Reminds me how much I'd hate having an office job."

"Ugh. Athletes." She rolled her eyes and grinned. "So what's been going on in your life? How'd that meeting go?"

"Ah." He tested the chowder with the tip of his tongue and jerked it back. "Her name was Miyuki and she lived up to it. Clearly she thought that meeting me wasn't worth her time. When she talked, she answered as curtly as possible. My parents adored her because she has," he made finger quotes, "'traditional Yamatese bone structure and perfectly proportioned ears.' But they'd only have to look at pictures of her. They wouldn't have to live with her. Anyway, her father was clearly all about the money and she was barely even there. No, Mom likes Hideyo and Dad is kind of going along with her, although honestly Dad is fine with whoever I pick."

"Are you out of candidates already?"

He ducked his head, his ears going flat. "Sort of. We went through the first tier. One to go, I mean, but Mom already doesn't like her because they've rescheduled twice and she says, 'if everyone else could make time to plan their daughter's future, they should be able to.' But that's Mom."

"Maybe their daughter is really incredible and that's why they're making you guys wait."

"Maybe." He tried his soup again and this time sipped it. "I don't know that she could beat you, though."

The words hung there. At first Tami wasn't sure she'd heard correctly, so she laughed. "I'm sorry, what?"

Ty wiped his muzzle and grinned. "I'd like to hang out with you and date you even if our parents weren't conspiring to make it happen. That's not something I've felt with any of the others, even the one who'd spent hundreds of dollars making her fur glossy before our dinner." When Tami didn't respond, he said, "Not that I look for glossy fur. I look for personality. I mean, when I'm dating."

That reminded her of his history of one-night stands, and she glanced away, down at her soup. She was what, six years older than he was, and yet he'd had more sexual partners in the last two years than she was likely to have in her life.

But, she reminded herself, he was here with her now and trying to tell her he liked her a lot. "I like you too," she said, and her laugh came out nervous. "That's the only l-word I'm comfortable with right now."

"Mmf." He swallowed his soup and put his spoon down with a clatter. "For sure, for sure. I wasn't saying—I just meant—my parents are pushing and they really want this to happen this summer, and I want this to be over."

Her ears folded down. Ty stopped and said, "Fuck. No." He slid his chair around the side of the table, squeezing in between that one and the one next to them (which was fortunately empty), and he put his paw on Tami's wrist. "I'm bad at this."

"People are looking," Tami murmured, aware of the attention on them after the scraping of his chair. She was reminded of stopping to watch a couple who seemed to be fighting, one time when she was out with her mother, and her ears burned.

"People are always looking." Ty held her wrist and she didn't pull it away. "What I was trying to say wasn't that I want to pick you just so everything's over. I was saying that I want to pick you because I'm pretty sure I'm not going to find anyone better. Why keep looking? And look, I know you might not feel the same, but that's why I'm putting it out there like this. If you don't, I understand."

Tami's mind spun too fast for it to settle on any one thing to say. "I don't know how I feel," she got out. "I didn't know I was going to have to decide this fast."

"You don't." The shadow of Ty's ears on the table came back up, and she lifted her head and looked into his smile. "We don't have to decide anything now."

"Okay." Her poise was returning slowly. "Because it sounded an awful lot like you were asking me to marry you."

"Oh, no." He laughed, and then stopped. "I guess I'm asking you to think about taking the first steps toward that. But it's not the commitment part, not yet. We should talk more about it, what our expectations are and so on."

"I always thought that marriage would be a long-term goal in a relationship, where I'd meet someone, we'd slowly fall in love over years, and then he'd ask me to marry him. Not in a big romantic way, necessarily, but also not as, you know," she waved a paw, "the third date."

Ty nodded, his expression serious again. "I'd got the impression you'd be open to this. I was up front about it. But if you really want something else, then I can…I can ask them to hold off a bit longer."

"You were up front." Tami breathed in, chowder and Ty mingling in her nose. "I got that from our first meeting, and I was okay with it, theoretically. But it's all…more real now."

"Okay." He gave her an encouraging smile, released her wrist, and slid his chair back around.

All around them, the other patrons had gone back to their dinners, probably disappointed that there was no big blowup. And why was Tami so concerned about what they were thinking, anyway? Hey, she told herself, we exist in a society and it's perfectly normal to take into consideration what the people around us think of what we're doing. Like, what would my mother and friends think about me agreeing to get engaged to this fox I've just met?

The thought of doing something that would surprise her friends and family was scary and unexpectedly thrilling. Tami with the plan, Tami the sensible one. But of course she shouldn't do something shocking only for the sake of doing something shocking.

"Can I have the rest of the weekend to think about it?" she asked.

"Oh, sure." He smiled. "This next meeting is Monday night, and after that the folks and I are going to sit down for a review." His muzzle wrinkled in a grimace. "I'm really not trying to suck all the romance out of this, but I haven't really had a normal dating life."

"I've been trying to date for ten years and look where it's gotten me." Tami smiled. "Maybe I need to try something else."

Ty laughed and shook his head. "You know, my friends live in my house and spend a lot of their time partying, except for Paul. None of them date. My teammates live such weird lives that they end up with marriages that are long-distance half the time, and what they want in a wife is someone who'll raise their family and who they can live with when their career is over."

It was hard for Tami to picture herself in that role. Staying at home, letting someone take care of her, raising cubs. If that's what he was asking her to sign up for, then maybe she should reconsider. "I haven't really thought about cubs," she said.

"Oh, me neither! Not much. Oops, sorry!" He'd sprayed soup and crumbs out on the table in his hurry to answer. "No, that's one of the things we could talk about."

"Don't your parents have ideas about that? I know my mom does."

"I'm sure they do, but once we're—once I marry, they can't *force* my wife to have cubs."

Tami thought that was rather optimistically naïve, but she let it slide because Ty was young and she didn't want to challenge his optimism. "What have you thought about?"

He pushed his soup away, finished with it. "I mean, I want cubs, but it doesn't have to be right away. It'd be nice to have someone to hang out with in the off-season. Some of my teammates talk about traveling places, but I hate doing that kind of shit alone. And…it'd be nice to have someone to talk to during the season, who'd watch my games. And someone who'd have a life I could check into as well."

So he had thought about cubs, at least a little. That wasn't a deal-breaker. "I don't have a lot of time to travel."

"Okay, well…I mean, I can pay for you to get extra time off."

She shook her head. "Time off isn't the problem. The problem is if I leave, the work doesn't get done, and then I come back and I still have to do all the work I missed."

He frowned. "Isn't there someone who can take over while you're gone?"

"No. I mean…" Tami set her fingertips together. "There is, sort of, but I do things a certain way, and I like them done that way. So if I come back and someone else has started doing things their way…"

"I…guess I can see that?" But his ears were tilted to the side and he was clearly struggling.

Tami sighed and set her paws down on the table. She met Ty's dark amber eyes and said, "Here's the other thing, really the main thing. I'm afraid that if I leave for a week or god forbid two, someone else will do my job as well or better, and when I come back they'll replace me." Ty's ears came up, but he didn't say anything, and she went on, "I know that's stupid, but—"

"No no!" He laughed and reached over to grab her paw. "That I get! You know how many guys go down with a knee sprain or ACL tear—" Here he paused to grin at her. "Anterior…something ligament. Dammit. Anyway, they break something and someone else takes their place. This year every time I tweaked something I didn't tell anyone about it because I'm a rookie. I was terrified they'd take me out of the lineup and I'd never get to start again."

A rush of warmth filled Tami's chest. She lay her other paw over his. "I thought you were really good."

"I am." Ty grinned.

"So what are you worried about?"

He kept his paw on hers. "If I really screw up my knee, I might not ever get back the burst." She flicked her ears, puzzled, so he clarified. "That initial burst of speed when the play starts is really important, and you have to have a hundred percent confidence in your legs. Also for cutting." He made a zig-zag motion with his free paw. "You've got to plant and change direction. Being able to fool the cornerbacks is really important, and if you're worried about your knee buckling, you're not going to be as precise with it."

"Oh, okay." She rubbed his paw. "Lots of players don't get hurt, too, right?"

"Oh, yeah. You have to take care of yourself. But sometimes you can't do anything about it. Guy on our team got gashed in the leg by a boar. He missed a bunch of games."

"Did they replace him?"

"No." He smiled. "But he got a couple concussions when he came back and he just retired. And Dev, that buddy of mine, he got his starting job when the other guy who was starting got stabbed with some antlers. That was his own fault, though. He grabbed them, ripped the caps off." Ty took his paw off hers and made a gesture like seizing bars, then turned them and jabbed an imaginary point into his arm. "You're not s'posed to tackle the antlers because of that, but he got beat and was trying to make up for it."

"You're allowed to grab antlers? That seems unfair."

Ty spread his paws. "Anything that's part of a player. Tails too. So when we run, we keep 'em curled back against our legs." She caught the flick of his tail as he curled it under his chair.

"I got my tail grabbed in college. Sprained it pretty bad."

He tilted his head. "What were you running from?"

"Uh-heh." She picked up her drink. "That's another story. I'm not sure I'm ready for that one yet."

"Mmm." His ears straightened and his smile lengthened. "We need to get closer?"

"Just a bit." She held her fingers a little apart.

"There's a hotel around the corner. I've got a room there for tonight."

Her eyebrows rose. "You hated my place that much?"

He didn't lose the grin. "Not at all. I'm open to that. But I figured a hotel room is a little nicer, more like a vacation, and your work isn't there. If you want. If not, your place is fine."

"Where are you staying?"

"Either the hotel or your place tonight." His nose wrinkled, and now the grin faded. "Otherwise with my parents. I have my own room, but…"

"You haven't bought yourself a house yet? Aren't you a millionaire?"

He rolled his eyes, not exasperated at her but at life, maybe; at least, it didn't feel directed at her. "I mean, kind of? If you put all my assets together, then yeah. But I paid off my parents' house and they didn't want a new one, and I did buy a house but it's in Chevali. I don't really want to buy a house here. It feels like too much to keep track of. The one in Chevali I've got friends living in and taking care of, and my parents live in the one here, so I've got a place to live." The grin came back. "I can afford nice hotel rooms, though."

"I get the hint." She laughed, relaxing under the flattery of him wanting to sleep with her again. "The hotel room sounds nice, but I'm not promising to tell you the story."

"Aw." He settled back in his chair. "If you're okay with the hotel room, though, you don't have to stay non-alcoholic." He pointed at her Diet Coke with his nose. "Want to add some rum to that?"

"Actually…" Tami rolled the taste around the inside of her muzzle. "That's not a bad idea."

It wasn't that she needed to relax, or even that the taste of unadulterated Diet Coke wasn't that great. It was that maybe the alcohol would loosen her up and let her think about this future that was being shoved in front of her with a ticking clock on it.

So they got rum and talked about their friends, their families, their childhoods for a little while until dinner was a satisfying sensation in their stomachs. When the check arrived, Ty reached for it.

"Hey, no," Tami said, and reached for her handbag. "Can I chip in?"

Ty produced a credit card and stuck it into the check. "I'm a millionaire, like you said. Least I can do is buy dinner."

His attitude reminded Tami of the feeling of getting her first credit card in college, so she smiled and sat back. His youthful energy was appealing, matched with a maturity that no doubt came from being thrust into a professional career at the highest level at the age of 22. It was as if Shirokaze had hired her and, based on her college education, immediately handed over the reins to Destiny's Angel and expected her to run the title.

Though maybe that wasn't fair; it wasn't like Ty had to navigate complicated personal and business relationships, understand a dozen different markets worldwide, know the broad history not only of this title but of video games in general, and feel comfortable with the economics of video game development. He had to run fast and catch the ball when it was thrown to him.

Not that simple, she remembered. He'd told her about different plays he had to memorize, and when she was directing a project, there wasn't someone actively trying to stop her from succeeding every time, even if it did occasionally feel like it. And she wasn't doing her job in front of millions of people.

All this went through her head in the time it took for the waitress to take Ty's credit card and come back with it. Ty, either lost in his own thoughts or respecting hers, signed the slip and stood, holding out a paw. "Shall we?"

She stood and took it, her heart beating a little faster. Ty, too, stopped when he took her paw, the warmth and pressure of that simple touch becoming a reminder of what had happened and what was about to. The fish smell in the restaurant made it impossible to pick up on subtle nuances of Ty's scent, but in the strength of his paw, Tami felt his excitement like an electric charge, and without thinking she squeezed back and a smile blossomed on her muzzle.

The height difference made it awkward to keep their paws linked as they walked out, but neither of them wanted to let go, so they managed it. Outside it was a little easier even on the crowded street, and through the light drizzle their arms swung back and forth, linked by their fingers. Tami wasn't sure what to say on the walk; it felt awkward to articulate that this felt natural and comfortable, that whatever the long-term plans, their interests followed the same path at this moment.

Or, she reminded herself, they were both eager to fuck again. Maybe don't over-romanticize this. Even the marriage semi-proposal had felt more like a business arrangement than a romantic gesture.

That didn't feel as weird as it had originally when he'd mentioned it. After all, people had lived with arranged marriages for a long time, right? And she'd known this was what was coming when she sent him that email in the first place. But she hadn't been thinking about it then; it had been a lark, something to do to make her mother and friends get off her back about needing a guy.

Not thinking about the consequences of her actions wasn't like her. But really, writing that email had felt like buying a lottery ticket. What were the odds that some random guy would actually write her back, a football star (Almost-star? She had no idea.), and that they would arrive at this moment where he was talking seriously about marrying her? If Axel had offered her thousand to one odds on it she wouldn't have taken the bet.

And she was considering it. He was nice, courteous, and had a fantastic body (she kept coming back to that and it felt shallow but, she told herself, it meant he took care of himself). He was a little inexperienced, a little casual with money, but he showed interest in her life, at least for now. It'd be nice not to have to worry about money, and though she was sure she wouldn't ever have to work again if she married him, she had no desire to quit her job. Shirokaze might be a slog sometimes, but she was making games she was proud of and she had a boss who understood her. Her future there was bright whether or not she got Destiny's Angel (but it would be so much brighter if she got it).

"Hey," Ty said. "What'cha thinking about?"

"Oh, my job."

Only when he laughed did Tami realize what she'd said. He looked down at her ears. "I guess taking you out of the apartment didn't work."

"No, I mean—in a larger sense. Like, my place at my job and everything."

"Oh! So, like…the future."

"Yeah. Kind of." She squeezed his paw. "What were you thinking of?"

His ears went back and he squeezed her fingers in return. After a moment, he said, "About the hotel."

It was adorable. She inclined her nose toward him to try to catch the scent of what he'd really been thinking about, but either he was wearing Neutra-Scent underwear (he hadn't been last time, but he also hadn't been expecting sex last time) or the scents swirling around her were too strong. She didn't really need the scent to confirm it, though, because a moment later his other paw tried in what he probably hoped was a subtle way to adjust the front of his pants.

The hotel was a swanky Elements hotel, the kind that didn't even have a self-park, the kind where no matter what you looked like, a perfectly courteous pine marten in a crisp brown uniform had the door open before you even got there and another offered to take your umbrella once you were inside. The leopard who walked in ahead of them handed his umbrella over and walked on without waiting for a claim check or anything.

Tami pondered whether that was a hotel umbrella or they just knew the leopard while trailing Ty up to the front desk. The large black bear behind it smiled, reached under the counter, and brought out a small folio. "Your keys, Mr. Nakamura. Everything is ready."

"Thanks," Ty said, scooping it up.

"Will you be needing your car later tonight?"

"I don't think so." Ty smiled down at Tami. "Will I?"

She brought her attention back from the umbrella check-in. "No. But—oh, shoot." Her tail wrapped around her leg. "I don't know if the garage I left my car in is overnight."

"Which one?" The bear clerk addressed her directly.

"It's the one on Third and Hansom."

He nodded. "It closes at 11 but opens again at seven. Overnight parking is permitted. You'll be fine."

The amazing thing was that he did that without even looking at a computer. "Oh. Thank you."

"My pleasure. Will there be anything else for either of you?"

She shook her head, but Ty said, "Do you have a dessert that's light and sweet?"

"Of course." The bear spoke as naturally as if Ty had asked the names of his children. "We have an orange-lemon mousse on a crispy Florentine wafer finished with white chocolate shavings. Or if you prefer, we have a trio of sorbets: blood orange, guava, and honey lavender."

Ty turned to Tami. "Either of those sound good?"

"Both of them. I'm less of a sorbet fan…"

"The mousse, then." Ty held up one finger. "We'll share."

"Excellent. It will be up in ten minutes."

Ty kept hold of Tami's paw to the elevator. Once the doors had closed, Tami said, "This place is a level of swanky I didn't even know about."

"I like this chain, but they don't have them in all the cities." Ty smiled. "I haven't stayed in this one before, but they have a database of all their customers across all locations, with pictures and stuff."

"I guess that's only a little creepy." She held his paw up to the tenth floor, and down the hall to their room. Only when he reached for the key did they let go.

The room, after all that, was not particularly large, though it smelled fresh and clean: Neutra-Scent with a hint of orange blossom, just the right level for foxes to detect. The king bed sat between two end tables, each with an elegant green glass lamp, and over the bed hung a pointillist painting of a garden scene. A second chair had been added on the end of the desk, and on the desk itself, two champagne flutes stood upside down beside an ice bucket that held the champagne itself.

"Does the champagne come with the room?" Tami asked as the door closed behind them, trying to establish a baseline for this level of luxury.

"They offered and I accepted. We don't have to drink it, but it was easier than picking out a wine. And I like a little champagne sometimes." Ty gestured to the window. "I asked for a view of the Sound. You like it?"

At night, the pier's lights glittered like jewels and their reflections danced in the water. "Yeah," Tami said, and slid her arm around his waist. "Thank you. This is really nice."

"Well." Satisfaction and pleasure radiated from his voice. "I wanted to make it a really nice second date."

"Third, technically."

"Third, then." He leaned down and she tilted her muzzle up, and they kissed. It started light, grew deeper, and then Ty pulled her against him and she loved the warmth and strength of him, his physical confidence a contrast to his earnest worry about making her comfortable. If only her mind would stop reciting all the reasons her job and her life wouldn't be right for him.

His paws held her sides and she slid hers down to his rear, already happy that this kind of intimate contact was familiar between them. Having someone to share this with: that was something she'd missed in the weeks after the last time with Jason. Only it had been harder then because she hadn't realized the last time was going to be the last time. If she had, then perhaps she'd have done something different, maybe wouldn't have snapped at him when he'd finished early like he so often did.

Then again, if she hadn't snapped at him, maybe it wouldn't have been the last time.

A week after the breakup she'd held a pillow to her, wishing it were warm and solid. For a few days and sporadically after, the longing had been bad. But work made it go away as it always did, gave her life focus and purpose. And she had—well, not forgotten, exactly, but grown numb to the need of not just sex, but intimacy; not just closeness but familiarity and trust.

On their last date, his touch had been exciting, and it still was, but now there was more than just the thrill of a new experience. There was—

There was a knock at the door.

Ty broke the kiss with a smile and went to fetch the dessert, and Tami had time to tell herself to stop thinking about everything and enjoy the moment. And then Ty returned with the mousse and two spoons, and he poured some champagne, and Tami found it much easier to relax over the dessert. The light, sweet mousse melted to a citrus cloud on her tongue, and the cracker provided a dry crunch to complement the texture. It went well with the slight sweetness of the champagne.

When they'd licked their spoons clean, they looked at each other, and then Ty inclined his head toward the bed and said, "Shall we?" and Tami got up and pulled his shirt off, and while she was doing that his fingers worked at her pants, and in the middle of the clothes coming off, they sat on the bed, kissing as they undressed each other. When they were down to underclothes, Ty stopped but Tami didn't, pushing his boxers down and wrapping her paw around his already stiff length. He moaned and lay back, letting her stroke him, and she used this permission, this familiarity, looking at him as her black fingers slid along his pink skin over his cream-white fur.

He collected himself and applied his fingers to her bra and panties, pausing at the lace to finger it and murmur, "Nice," into her ear. She rubbed her muzzle back against his, tail wagging against the bed; the panties had been a gift from Jason and she'd worn them hoping Ty would like them too.

Off they came, and she pulled her naked body to his. He brought up a paw to her breasts and she kissed his shoulder at the touch. Now, finally, she surrendered to the moment and thought of nothing but his touch on her, his body under her paws. He reached for the condoms on the nightstand, wanting to enter her too early; she put him off for a moment and brought his paw between her legs, teaching him what she liked. He caught on quickly, she'd give him that. If he learned his football plays this quickly, no wonder he was considered very good.

And he stayed ready when she was ready, still hard and warm when she rolled the condom down over his shaft. She positioned herself on her back and he slid into her, and this time was better than the last. He came quickly again, a shudder of clenched muscles and a moan through his teeth, but then he kept moving, thrusting into her as much as he could with his knot tying them together, until Tami too felt the surge of warmth spreading outward from their tie. She gasped and lay back, wrapping her arms around him, and Ty stopped, lowering his muzzle to nuzzle her ear. "Good?" he murmured.

"Good," she gasped back.

Still tied to her, Ty worked his arms under her shoulders and held her. "Whatever other problems we might have," he said, "I think the sex works okay."

"Yeah," Tami gasped. "Yes. Very okay."

He laughed and kissed her, and she pulled his muzzle against hers, wanting to find some way to pour back the pleasure she was feeling into him. In this moment they felt right together and her worries about the future seemed as distant and irrelevant as their clothes, strewn on the floor.

CHAPTER 20

Waking in the morning next to Ty was confusing at first. The scent of male fox made her think of her first boyfriend from junior high school, and she wondered muzzily why he was here in her room when she had to get up for math class. Then she remembered math class had been ten years or more ago, and then she remembered Ty, and lifted her head to look at him.

He slept on his back, limbs splayed out with careless abandon as though he'd been tossed onto the bed and had stayed where he'd landed. His chest rose and fell slowly, and his muzzle rested to the side, smiling even in sleep. His tail flicked under the covers, brushing her leg, tickling a little.

What would it be like to wake up to him every morning? Of course, she wouldn't be waking up with him every morning. He would have practices and games and would be away half the year or more. Most of her life would go on as it was now, except that she would have this young husband, who would text her maybe from time to time. She'd have to watch his games and cheer when he did well, send him texts or call him.

"Have to" might be too strong. They'd want to talk, wouldn't they? They had at least some things in common now, and growing together they would have more. It would be work, another project to take on, but one she could enjoy. Especially if it had nights like the previous one.

(Although, she knew, romance tended to disappear as relationships went on. She and Jason hadn't built up anything to replace their romance except arguments, and ultimately the arguments had won out.)

She slipped out of bed to get a glass of water from the hotel bathroom. When she returned, he was lying in the same position, but his eyes were open, sienna gleams in the russet of his muzzle. "Morning," he croaked, and then cleared his throat and said it again.

"Morning." She sat at the edge of the bed, uncertain whether to get back in or not, and then he shifted to accommodate her and she swung her legs up and pulled the covers over the two of them.

His arm slid under her shoulders and rolled her against him so that her muzzle landed on his shoulder. "Sleep well?" he asked.

"Uh-huh." She rested her paw on his stomach and traced his muscles with her fingers. "You?"

"Yeah." He nuzzled her ears. "When do you have to go?"

"Oh, uh." The clock read 8:19. She'd slept for eight hours? When was the last time that had happened? "Probably in a little bit. I have…"

"A lot of work, I know." He nipped her ear and she squirmed, laughing.

"I'm sorry! I'm not used to…not thinking about it. I can't shut it off like you can."

His long fingers stroked down the fur on her side, under her arm, pleasantly close to tickling but not quite. "I know, I know. I can't shut football off during the season either. Well, sometimes I can, but those times are, uh, over quickly."

Her paw, tracing small circles on his stomach, encountered the tip of his erection. Her fingers jumped with her surprise and he shivered, exhaling across her ear. But he didn't object, or move, so she reached for it again and slid her fingers up and down. Fully hard, first thing in the morning; she'd forgotten that that happened to guys.

"Times like this?" she murmured.

He kissed her ear. "Uh-huh. What about you?"

She hadn't been particularly in the mood, but the feel of his arousal and now the scent making its way to her nose stirred some warmth in her. "Give me a few minutes and then probably."

Ty smiled and then rolled her onto her back. "Then I know how to spend those minutes."

Her fingers slipped from his shaft as he scooted down the sheets, and she realized what he was going to do a moment before his breath warmed the fur between her legs. "I'm not very good at this yet," his voice came muffled by the covers, "so tell me what I need to do."

And then his fingers rested on her thighs and his tongue moved between them, and she spread her legs and closed her eyes. This wasn't something Jason had done often (he claimed his teeth got in the way, although it was easy enough to find squirrels giving oral sex online if you looked), and when he had, it hadn't been better than…than…

She gasped and arched her back. Ty might not have known what he was doing, but he knew enough to keep at something that was getting a reaction. His tongue kept washing over her clit, and her stirrings grew quickly into a heat that spread throughout her body. She pressed one paw to her breast, gripped the sheets with the other, and breathed harder and faster.

Ty lifted his head. "Was that enough minutes?"

She could hear the smile in his voice. "Keep going," she panted. "Please."

"Mmm." He lowered his head again.

She came in a long, slow wave of pleasure rippling through her, drawing a low moan from her throat and a tightening of her muscles. It took a long time to subside, and as it did she gasped, "All right. All right. Thank you."

Ty rested his head on her stomach, looking up at her. "That sounded a lot more impressive than last night. Should my cock be jealous of my tongue?" He trailed his fingers along his erection, now covered with a condom.

"Uh." She reached down for his shoulder and pulled him up to lie atop her. "Looks like you're ready. Give him another try. Him? It? Does your cock have a name?"

"No." He wriggled his hips, situating himself. "Not my style."

"Mmkay." She reached down, getting her paws on his rear and pulling him up closer, which left her muzzle against his upper chest as the tip of his erection teased at her.

He entered her quickly and finished quickly, clutching her tightly against him, groaning as he shuddered and pushed his knot inside. When he sagged down atop her, his weight drove her down into the bed until he braced himself on his elbows. His breath steamed into her ear, and then he kissed it.

"Huh. Huh." He rolled carefully onto his side, staying locked to her. "You okay?"

"Uh-huh. That was nice."

"Yeah." He nuzzled her between the ears. "And still time for you to get some work in."

She nipped his chest and he wriggled. "I wasn't thinking about work."

"Oh good," he said. "It works for you too."

When his knot went down and he slipped free of her, he kissed her nose and they stayed in each other's arms. "You can shower first," he said.

"Mm." She stroked a paw down his side. "In a minute."

"Okay." He trailed his claws down her spine to her tail, rubbed at the base and then along the tail itself, making her shiver.

She held him and closed her eyes. Their paws caressed and stroked, slow and easy, until Tami felt herself dozing again. Ty's eyes, too, were drooping. "I guess I should get going," Tami said.

"Mmm." Ty nuzzled her again and didn't move.

She stroked along his rear. "I could seriously stay here all day. But I probably shouldn't."

"Okay, fine." Ty grinned.

So she showered and got dressed, and Ty slipped out of bed still naked and hugged her, and his fur was still sticky and smelly and she got a thrill out of it anyway.

"See you again soon," he said.

"Good luck with the last meeting." She kissed him.

Back at home, she sat down in front of the computer and pulled up the Powerpoint for the project review, but after staring at it for an hour she still hadn't made much progress. She kept thinking about Ty, about waking up with him and about how big a project the marriage would be. Did she have the time to take it on? Would it interfere with her video game career?

It was ridiculous really to base a marriage on one meeting and two dates and two orgasms. Maybe two and a half. But marriages had been arranged on less; that was the whole point of the way Ty's parents were going about it. He didn't have time to meet a suitable girl the regular way, and Tami didn't have time to meet a suitable boy the regular way either, when it came down to it. So what was wrong with doing it this way? They both had their own lives, and they would be married so they had each other to fall back on.

Only if they ever wanted cubs, that would all fall on Tami. The pregnancy, the raising of the cubs, years of her life. And Ty wanted cubs—that dancing around had likely been for her benefit.

"I don't see what the problem is," Marci told her when Tami called her at lunch. She was too busy to sit down for lunch, but had time to chat on the phone while driving from the gym to her afternoon meeting. "You like him now, marry him. You don't like him later, divorce him. It's how things are done."

"I…never thought of that." But Tami recalled the stiff formality of the dinner. "I think I'd have to get both sets of parents to approve if I wanted to divorce, though. Even if he wanted to as well."

"You don't *ask* them, dear." Marci's voice grew fainter and then clearer again. "But if you have moral objections, then don't marry him."

"But what if I never find someone?"

"You've never struck me as the sort who mooned about wanting a husband more than anything. You're very content with your job. It's one thing I love about you. I don't understand why you're dithering."

"Because I don't know what I want." Tami sighed. "It's complicated."

"No. This case I'm working on, a question of property rights, this is complicated. If you want a husband, and he proposes, then accept. If you don't want a husband then don't."

"I told you—"

"And don't tell me you don't know. You know. You might not know how to find out, but you definitely know."

"You're not helping."

"All right, let me ask you this, then. Don't think about the answer, just tell me: do you like being alone?"

"Yes. No. Wait, what kind of question is that?"

"Apparently not the right one. I'm at my building, dear, I'm sorry, I'm already late for this meeting."

"All right, fine." Tami sighed. "I'll figure it out."

"I'll leave you with this: I've never known a problem you couldn't figure out. So go get 'em."

"Thanks, Marci." She pressed the phone to her ear. "Wait, did you say 'them' or 'him'?"

But Marci had already hung up. So Tami went back to her computer and opened a new project called "The Marriage."

An hour and a half later, she had a long list of items and still no conclusion. So she went back to Jumbo Bubbles X and worked on that, trying to let her subconscious figure out the marriage thing.

Devin texted her that evening. *Just checking to see if you need any help.*

Do I ever. But you probably mean about our project.

:) What else is going on?

Let me email you what I've got so far. You up for Skype?

So she emailed him the project (the Shirokaze one) and then got on Skype with him. "It's the football player," she said.

He was sitting at the desk in his apartment; behind him she saw the poster for Federal Treasure: Treason, the first game they'd worked on together. "Nakamura?"

"Yeah. He's nice. He's really nice. And he likes me. But he wants to get married quickly, like maybe this summer."

"Whoa. To you or to the first one who says yes?"

"Me, ideally."

Devin was quiet for a while. "That's a big deal."

"It is." Tami rested her chin on her paws. "Is it crazy that I'm thinking about it?"

"You are?" She nodded. His ears flattened. "So would you quit?"

"No!" She shook her head. "He doesn't—I don't want that. We'd have our jobs and our lives and then—well, that part is what I'm trying to figure out. When he's not working, playing, whatever, he'll be here, I guess. He wants to take vacations."

"Vacations." The wolf snorted and grinned. "That'll be a change."

"I told him it's hard for me."

"'Hard.' So you undersold it."

"I was thinking, if it's between titles. Like not now, obviously, but in a few months when we ship…"

"And we're ramping up on Destiny? Or whatever other title we get stuck with when they assign them?"

She sighed. "I know, but…you could handle the ramp up. For a week or two? And my mom keeps saying I should get away, think about more than work."

"And you keep saying she doesn't understand how jobs work in our industry."

"You and Axel told me that a couple weeks ago. That's partly why I emailed him."

Devin raised a finger. "We told you to date. We didn't tell you to take a month off work."

Tami lowered her muzzle into her paws and rubbed at her eyes. "I know. Fatima goes on vacation, though. She has a family."

"People can do it, sure. I'm just not sure you can."

"Maybe I need to figure out how." She looked up. Devin was half-smiling, but still serious. "I mean, what happens if JBX tanks and Shirokaze cuts our group?"

"We'll get a job at another studio. Come on, Tami, we've talked about this."

"We talked about taking opportunities, too, didn't we? Like if Dramatica called and wanted to hire us. What if this is an opportunity for me? A nice guy, a stable marriage, *maybe* cubs down the line…"

"Whoa. You want cubs now?"

"Not now…"

"No, I mean…*now* you've decided you want cubs?"

"Maybe down the line, I said. I don't want to rule it out completely." Of course, with an arranged marriage, cubs would be expected, but the parents would be satisfied for a while having a marriage with the promise of cubs, and Tami was adept at putting off her mother's inquiries about her private life.

Devin steepled his fingers in front of him. "All right. But at least read up on football wives, okay?"

"What do you mean? Are they some kind of society I need to know about?"

He laughed—well, more like smirked—and shook his head. "I'll send you a couple links, but you can search on your own. One of Nakamura's teammates is having family problems. That just broke this week. But there's others. There's like, domestic violence stuff."

"Oh, Ty's not like that."

Devin raised his eyebrows. "Sure, not when he's out with his parents or trying to impress you. I'll look up his college. You should talk to his coaches, maybe some of his friends."

"He said he lives with some of his college friends down in Chevali."

"Well." The wolf tilted his head. "Maybe that's where your first vacation should be."

It wasn't a bad idea, actually. Tami cared a lot more what kind of friends Ty had than what kind of parents. And Ty seemed like the sort who would enjoy introducing her to his friends. She brought out her phone to text him, and then the links from Devin came into her inbox.

So she read about Gerrard and Angela Marvell, about how he was living in an apartment and Angela wouldn't make a statement on why he'd been kicked out of the house, but how this coyote named Palla Corrason in Hellentown claimed that Gerrard had fathered her cub and Gerrard wouldn't comment on it and Angela wouldn't comment on it. The cub looked rather like Gerrard's cubs, but of course that wasn't conclusive at all;

unlike foxes, who had myriad coat variations, coyotes were all pretty much of a kind.

There was another link, a Pelagia player who'd been arrested for domestic violence and then released. His case was pending, and his girlfriend hadn't made any public statements since the arrest except to say that she supported him. And the last link was about the culture of football wives.

That was a long read. Tami went and got a Coke to read through it. The stories presented in the article were troubling, one a deer who'd been hit several times, one a bear whose husband had thrown a chair at her, and another whose husband had punched her after she'd accused him of infidelity.

None of them had brought charges. All of them said the team had encouraged them to stay quiet and support their husbands. All of them wished they'd spoken up at the time.

Of course, all their accusations were alleged. Nothing had been proven. Nothing ever would be, either. Tami licked at the sour taste the Coke had left behind in her muzzle. She wasn't going to be like these wives, though. She had her own life, and if Ty so much as raised a paw to her, she'd report it to every authority she could think of. She felt bad for the wives, of course, but maybe if she got to know some of them…it sounded like they did have a society of their own. They probably talked to each other about their husbands. Maybe she could talk to some of them, help them with their problems.

And it was only three wives, though they did say that others were afraid to come forward. There were hundreds of professional football players, and if half were married, that was still hundreds of wives. It wasn't like she was signing up for some kind of Blackbeard story.

Further research discovered some of the happier wives, those using their husbands' money to start a clothing line, or (very commonly) charitable foundations. The wife of a prominent coach was a lawyer, and other football players had married professionals as well: an actress, a writer, a mechanical engineer. No video game project managers, though. That made Tami smile.

It's a strange world, she wrote back to Devin, *but maybe that's the challenge.*

Chapter 21

Monday morning she woke an hour before her alarm went off, convinced she'd slept through the meeting. Several agonized seconds of reorienting herself ended with checking her phone to make sure that the meeting was still for 10 a.m.

With her heart settling back to normal, her mind turned back to the wedding. She tried to imagine Ty sleeping next to her, understanding her anxiety about the meeting. He'd be anxious himself some times of the year, about…about learning plays? About performing?

He was a good guy. That wasn't too hard to imagine. She pictured him stirring sleepily, saying, "Can't sleep?" She'd shake her head, say she was nervous about the meeting. He'd reach out and hold her. It would feel nice.

Maybe this marriage thing wasn't crazy. Or at least, not as crazy as she'd been worried it was.

On the other paw, she thought in the shower, maybe she was idealizing. Maybe Ty would get tired of hearing about her interminable meetings. Sure, he loved video games, but so did a lot of her friends, and none of them wanted to hear about her meetings to determine how late the updates to the Plink engine would be.

And the fact that she was so unsure about it meant that she didn't know him that well. But that was the point of an arranged marriage, right?

Cripes, she was going around and around on this. Maybe she needed to refocus. Get through this meeting today and she could think about it more tonight.

She got into work at ten to eight and settled in to answer the emails she'd looked at over breakfast. One of them was from Devin, asking if she wanted to get together before the meeting. She asked him to come by around 9:45 to run through everything.

To her relief, Devin was prepared and ready to back her up on her talking points. He'd also talked to two of the people on the project teams over the weekend to get updates on the most recent bugs that had come in, even one from that morning.

Fatima welcomed Tami and Devin into the conference room, guiding the fox and wolf to seats at the front next to the projector. Tami plugged her laptop in, and her display came up flawlessly on the screen. One less thing to worry about.

Three other people sat around the table besides her boss the otter: a polar bear and a red wolf, both in shirts and ties, sat on Tami's side: the other project leads under Fatima for Jumbo Bubbles X. At the other end of the table, a field mouse wearing a Shirokaze t-shirt under a blazer checked his Blackberry: Mr. Francis, Shirokaze's VP in charge of intellectual property, Jumbo Bubbles X specifically.

Tami'd met him a few times, and was at least sure that he knew her name from the emails they'd exchanged. Fatima handled most of the executive communications, but Mr. Francis had shaken her paw and called her by name at the kickoff meeting, and he'd been on a couple email chains with her.

He didn't say anything as they went through the current status of Tami's side of the project. At a couple points she asked Devin to jump in with the information from the people he'd talked to, both because he'd done the work and knew it better and because it was important to Tami to make Devin look good as well. Fatima asked a couple questions, which Tami and Devin answered, and then the otter looked down the table. "Anything else you need to know, Mr. Francis?"

The field mouse shook his head. "Just wanted to know why the project's yellow. I assume we'll hear more about that from the next two?"

"Of course. Thank you, Tami," Fatima said, and Tami unhooked her laptop as the red wolf came up to the front with his.

She and Devin texted under the table as the other reports were going on, assuring each other that their presentation had gone well, that it wasn't as important that there were risks—every project had risks—as it was that they were aware of and addressing them. And indeed, Mr. Francis didn't show any more interest in either of the following reviews. At the end, he said, "Thanks, Fatima, Tami, Royce, Sean, and…" He lingered on Devin.

"Devin," Fatima said, gesturing to the wolf.

"Devin. Nice work, everyone. Fatima, you'll forward all the decks to me?"

"Of course."

"Thanks." And he was gone, leaving them sitting in the sterile conference room.

Fatima kept them a little while longer to give her feedback and assign action items to everyone, and Tami couldn't help keeping score in her head. The other two leads had three things to take care of each, while she only had two. And Fatima spent more time talking to the other two about how their teams were doing.

When she did come around to Tami, she asked for updates on the bugs that had come in most recently, so Tami let Devin field the questions while she listened and put in information where she could.

When the meeting broke up, Fatima asked Tami to stay behind for a moment. So Tami sat, heart speeding up as she reviewed what she'd talked about. Had anything gone wrong? But when the otter closed the door and turned around, she was smiling.

"I wanted to let you know that Mr. Francis and I talked before the meeting. He's said he's going to go ahead with my recommendation and make you lead on the next Destiny's Angel title."

"What?" Tami jumped up from her chair. "Are you—really? He decided?"

Fatima smiled broadly, nodding. "We talked just before the meeting. Congratulations. You've earned it."

For a second, she couldn't feel her heart at all; it had been racing and now it stopped cold. And then it started again, all at once, and she had to put her paws to either side of her muzzle and feel her whiskers to reassure herself that this was happening. "Can I pick my team?"

"We'll see. You might be able to pull one or two people over from other projects if you want. Destiny's going to be a top priority here."

"I know. God." She reached out a paw to Fatima, but the otter drew her into a hug.

"Don't let me down," she said to Tami's shoulder, and then released her. "I won't."

She hurried out to where Devin was waiting for her, her mind already abuzz with plans.

"Everything okay?" he asked.

"It's great." Tami realized Fatima hadn't told her whether she could tell anyone, so she bit back the impulse to share the good news. "Thanks for filling in the gaps."

"Anytime." He smiled and lowered his voice. "Hey, did you think more about the marriage thing?"

She was doing well here, she was important, she was going to be in Fatima's position on the next Destiny's Angel, the sequel to the best game Shirokaze had ever done. She'd done all that without a husband, and where would Ty fit into all this? He'd be nice to spend nights with, sure, and he was someone who'd been fun to talk to. He was a gateway to a different world and that was exciting, thrilling. She could go to football games and meet the other wives. And he'd certainly make her friends look up to her more; heck, he'd already done that. Not that that was important, or should be. But she'd be lying if she didn't admit to herself that she felt good about that as well.

"Yeah." If she had to make a decision right now, right in front of Devin's hopeful eyebrows and raised ears? She knew what the correct answer was, even if it didn't feel right. "I...I think...I don't know if there's room in my life. You know?" She waited, half hoping he'd talk her into it.

The wolf tilted his head. "You're hesitating, though. Did you talk to his friends?"

"No, but...I can't just call them up. I'd want to meet them in person."

"So go."

She shook her head and curled her tail around one leg as they brushed a cubicle wall. "I'd have to go, like, next week. This is all happening too fast. That's another reason." But if she already had the position of Destiny's Angel lead, could it hurt to take a couple days remotely? To make sure this decision was right? Besides, the game wasn't really going to kick off until mid-summer, and that was right around when Ty was going to get busy with football. She'd have months until he'd be asking her to go on vacations and such.

"Go on Wednesday." He saw her start to object and raised a paw. "You'll be here for the team review Tuesday, you can do your one on ones remotely, and I can handle anything else that comes up."

"You can't," she said, but he pushed the paw at her and she quieted.

"You're not going to be doing any of the coding on the bugs coming back. All you might have to do is move around resources, and you can do that over email, and honestly, I can do it without you. If something blows up, really blows up, you can hop a plane and be back here, but what are the chances? We know this process, we know this game. Work remotely for a bit if you want, but look, you have to make this decision, right? And you need all the information to do it." He put a paw to his chest. "I would not forgive myself if you missed out on the chance to get me championship tickets because you weren't sure if this guy was right for you."

She laughed. "It's all about you, isn't it?"

His ears flicked back and his smile dimmed, so she said, "Kidding!" and patted his arm until his ears came up.

"Of course it's about me," he said easily. "I mean, when the championship rolls around again, just remember that I helped you out."

"I won't forget," she promised, and at that moment Fatima came out of the conference room. "Thanks, I'm going to go ask Fatima before I change my mind."

"Good luck!" Devin's tail wagged as Tami hurried back.

Fatima didn't mind as long as Tami checked in daily. "And you're sure Devin can cover for you if you're out of pocket?"

"Absolutely." Tami smiled. "Thank you so much. I guess I should make sure I can actually go, right?"

The otter raised her eyebrows. "This is a last-minute trip and you have not consulted the person you're going with?"

"It's a long story, but I have to make a quick decision about getting married." Tami laughed. "I know how that sounds. This is what happened…"

As quickly as she could on the walk back to Fatima's office, she told Fatima about Ty and their whirlwind courtship-slash-arranged marriage. "That's interesting," Fatima said. "My marriage was arranged as well, did you know?"

"I didn't!" They had arrived, and Tami waited at the door while the otter stepped inside. "You'll have to tell me about it sometime."

"I would enjoy that. It isn't viewed very positively here, but it can work out very well indeed. You must enter into it with the expectation that you will have to work, but knowing that you are both committed to that work makes a huge difference."

"That's good to hear, thanks."

"But it is still important to do your research before the marriage. Normally your family would do it, but…"

The statement ended as a question. "The parents introduced us," Tami said, "but we're kind of getting to know each other just on our own. Plus…I can't ask my mom to meet his friends for me."

The otter nodded. "I understand. So go, find out, and I hope it results in a positive trip."

It felt good to be doing something again, moving toward resolution of a problem rather than going around in her head about it. Of course Ty's friends would only say good things about him, but Tami could read people pretty well.

Not that she had any experience, but after a lunch with Axel and Devin, she had a better idea of what kind of questions to ask. "And smell around the place," Devin advised. "If he has a lot of girls over, you'll be able to smell it."

"Also if he's doing drugs, you'll be able to smell it."

"He hasn't mentioned drugs," Tami said, and then, seeing their expressions, "but of course he wouldn't."

"And you'll be able to tell from his friends," Devin said. "Guys stick together like that, they all do the same thing. Pot, coke, meth."

Axel snorted. "Like you know from coke and meth."

"There was a lot of meth in my high school." Devin wrinkled his nose. "Once an armadillo brought some to school and he got caught when a teacher smelled it. It smells weird."

"I don't know what it smells like." Tami flicked her ears. "Can you describe it?"

Devin shook his head. "It's chemical and the smell of it makes you feel a little woozy, like a quick headrush. I dunno, I've never smelled anything else like it. You'll be able to tell."

"All right. I'll keep a nose out for meth." She grinned. "He's got money now, I doubt he has to get cheap drugs like meth."

"You'd be surprised. People get a taste for something, they don't want to change."

Axel shook his head. "I don't think that works with meth. People use meth because it's cheap, but it's shitty. If you have money you move to coke or something."

"Look," Tami said, holding up her paws, "I don't want to know how you guys know all this."

"Fraternity brothers," Devin said.

"Movies," Axel said. "And TV."

"All right, thanks for the advice. I still have to call him and make sure it's okay with him."

•

Ty loved the idea. "I'll come back with you," he said. "I haven't seen the guys in a while and I could use a break."

"The idea is for me to ask them about you," Tami said. "Won't you being there make that awkward?"

"I won't be around all the time. I'll go out with Kellen while you talk to Paul, or something. Besides, it'll let us see how we travel together."

It made sense that her research trip would include further research on how she and Ty would get along. And, she added in her head, she'd probably get laid a couple more times on the trip. Assuming Ty had his own room.

The other benefit of traveling with Ty was that he insisted on paying for her ticket. She could afford the last minute flight, especially on PelagiAir, but Ty without even thinking bought two first-class tickets on Union Air and seemed surprised when she commented on it. "I need the leg room," he said. "And I like the free drinks." She didn't point out that a coach seat was cheaper enough that he could buy drinks for his entire row and not make up the difference. Ty was used to a certain way of doing things, and if she was to marry him, she'd probably have to get used to it as well.

So Tami spent the next two days and most of the next two nights getting things in order for her to leave. "I'll check in and be working for a few hours in the morning," she told Devin and Fatima on separate occasions, and both of them told her that that would be fine. The thing that she wouldn't be able to do was code reviews, but Devin assured her and Fatima that he could do that.

She got to the airport Thursday morning with a bag packed for a four-day weekend and only about half the normal work thoughts in her head. The rest of the space was taken up with thoughts of Ty, watching how he moved through the world of travel and regular people.

He did not seem to be observing her as closely, though of course she didn't know quite what was going on in his head yet. Being first class passengers entitled them to a certain level of treatment with which he was very comfortable: he told her she could have a drink before the flight attendant had even offered one.

They had two seats together to themselves, more roomy than any seat Tami'd been in on a plane ever. The pre-flight cocktail wasn't bad either (a mimosa since it was early) and so she was more relaxed than she would've thought possible by the time they got in the air.

"Three hours," Ty said. "Did you bring a book? Or some work?"

"A little work." Tami left her laptop in the carry-on for the moment, though. "But we can talk for a bit too."

"Good." He smiled. "I should tell you about the guys."

"Oh. Yes." She adjusted her tail even though there was plenty of room in the seat for it. "I was thinking we could talk about us, too."

He tilted his head. "I thought this trip was so you could figure out if you wanted there to be an 'us.'"

"Sure, but that's not the only factor. We've talked about the marriage but I want to hear a little more about what you think our life would be like."

"Uh. Okay." He leaned back. "I imagine you having your job, and I'll live up here in the off-season. And during the season, I'll be at training camp and then in Chevali or wherever and if you can come down on the weekend that'd be great. But I know your job is busy so you won't be able to come down every weekend." He looked sideways at her. "Maybe I'll end up playing on Pelagia someday and I'll be able to live at home."

She liked the way he said "home," but it wasn't exactly what she'd been looking for. Maybe part of the problem was that she didn't know what she was looking for. "I mean, we're getting married—we *would* be getting married—mostly because your parents, and my mom, kind of, want us to. But we should also know what we want a marriage to look like. What are your long-term goals? After you're done playing, I mean. Mine are…I want to produce a video game. I want to be responsible for it from beginning to end. I've been in the industry for a few years now and I've seen the mistakes people make. I know I could do a good job."

"Okay," he said. "What about after that?"

She flicked her tail. "What?"

"After that." He stretched his legs out. "It sounds like you'll get to run a title, if not this one, then some other one soon. So what happens after that? Like you just asked me, what do I want to do after my career. What do you want to do once you've made a game?"

"Make another one?"

"Just keep making them until they won't let you anymore?"

"Yeah. I guess." When he put it that way, it sounded poorly thought out, but Tami ached so much to get that first game under her belt that she hadn't worried about what would come after. "What about you? You mentioned announcing?"

"After I'm done playing?" He grinned. "Yeah, maybe. But I figure that's years away and I'll have a lot of time to explore the things that I like. Some ex-players get into announcing, sure, but some have another career. Some become coaches. I think it's okay for me not to know right now."

She nodded, and he leaned over to her, his muzzle brushing her ear. "I think it's okay for you not to know, too."

"I don't like not knowing." The flight attendant came by then to ask if they wanted more mimosas. Ty said yes, but Tami got a plain orange juice. "I guess I thought that when I got that first title under my belt, I'd get to do more, maybe…"

When she paused, he leaned over. "What?"

"Well…it's silly." Only it wasn't silly, it was ambitious, that was all. "I've never told anyone."

"So. Can you tell your fiancé?"

He smiled, joking, but she felt like she could tell him, this young fox who could do anything. "I'd like to own my own studio someday."

His ears perked. "Studio? Is that like a company?"

"Sort of. I mean, the company I work for is a studio, technically, but they've gotten really big, so they have a lot of titles going on at once and they have a whole business arm devoted to distribution now so they don't have to go through the console companies and…" She sighed, laughing. "Sorry, I'm boring myself now."

"No, it's interesting. I never thought about how those games got made. I just like to play them. Oh, by the way, you're going to get along great with Kimi. He's trying to write his own game, too. Morshin plays them all the time, but I don't think he's ever thought about how they get made. Kellen can't be bothered usually, and Paul's always got his nose in his books."

She let him guide the conversation to his friends. "How did you meet them all?"

"Oh, huh. Paul and I were friends in high school and we went to the same college and stayed friends. Kimi and Kellen were on the football team in college but weren't good enough to get drafted. And Morshin…" He scratched behind one ear. "You know, none of us remembers how we met him. He's just always been around, ever since college."

"So what do you all do when you're not playing football?"

"Go to parties." He shifted his tail. "Play games. Watch movies."

"Do any of them have girlfriends?"

He shook his head. "Kimi and Kellen aren't ready to settle down with anyone, Morshin might be except he doesn't leave the house all that much, and Paul—well, Paul did have a girlfriend for a while, an otter from one of his classes. But she stopped coming around. He said they broke it off, decided it wasn't right."

"What species are they all?"

"Oh yeah! Kimi's an otter, Kellen's a swift fox, Morshin's a goat, Paul's a red fox."

"Another red fox?"

"That's why we were friends in high school. We were the only two foxes."

"Really? What high school is this? There were at least twenty foxes in mine."

He leaned his head back. "Our class was mostly otters, muskrats, wolves and bears. I went to Lake Bell. Well, I transferred there in tenth grade once I was good at football. We placed third in the state my first year and second my senior year. I mostly hung out with the football team, but Paul was in one of my classes and we became friends my first week there when he came up and offered to show me around."

"Something to be said for same-species friendships." Tami smiled. "Though with girls it's a little different. All the female foxes in my high school had their own independent groups of friends because they didn't trust each other. Except me and Janine, who just liked video games. I wonder what happened to her."

Ty laughed. "There weren't any female foxes in our class. But I was popular because I played football, and Paul was popular, sort of. As much as he wanted to be. He liked going around to parties and stuff. He's always been the friend who kept me…" He gestured with a paw, trying to come up with the word. "Grounded? Something like that. Who reminded me that no matter what happened, I'm still me, for better or worse."

"It's good to have someone like that." Tami exhaled. "My best friend Marci…I'm not sure what I am to her. Maybe just a reminder that there's something outside her job and her husband. We met on a double date after college, and we both broke up with the guys but stayed friends."

"That's a great story." Ty gave her that bright smile again. "How did you know you were going to be friends?"

"Oh, well." Tami leaned back in the seat. "Marci's date was this ocelot who kept tapping his plate, making this clinking sound, and my date was his friend, also an ocelot, who called me 'babe.' So we went to the restroom together and Marci said, 'It's been nice having dinner with you, babe,' and I tapped my claw against the sink, and we just knew."

"See, that's neat, when you meet someone like that." He went on, but Tami was thinking about Ty texting her during the dinner with his parents, how right it had seemed then.

When the flight attendant came by to take their lunch orders, the conversation flagged, so Tami took her laptop out to check on work over lunch. She'd been looking forward to trying out the new in-flight WiFi service, but to her surprise found that a first class seat didn't come with free WiFi. She paid without telling Ty, sure she could expense it through her job, and happily worked on the slow, spotty connection. By the time she'd finished answering emails (she couldn't resist sending one to Axel and Devin saying, "I'm sending email from a plane!") and catching up on the project status, the plane had started banking into its descent, so she closed the laptop and put it away.

Ty put down the magazine he'd gotten (Sports Illustrated) and looked out the window. "Check out that desert."

Indeed, the view out the window was mostly ochre sand bounded by the occasional arrow-straight road. Off in the distance, Tami saw the glittering city of Chevali approaching. "It looks pretty from up here."

"Lots of things look better from a plane." Ty shook his head. "Trust me, when you land, remember this is still March and it gets hotter for four or five months before it cools down."

Tami stuck out her tongue. "As long as we drink lots of water, I'll be okay."

"Yeah." Ty hesitated for a minute. "Hey. About what we were saying earlier. The marriage and all? Well, I think we're compatible, but different enough to make this fun. And worthwhile. Like, I'll help you put a lot of your plans into effect. And you'll help me figure out how to make plans. I think we could work well together."

"Sounds good." Tami smiled.

"But that's not the main thing." Ty took a breath. "The main thing is that I never met a girl before that I *wanted* to take to meet my friends, that I wanted to spend time talking with. I know I said that before, and I know that maybe that means I'm more eager to do this than you are, but I think it's worth repeating. I don't know how many guys you've met like that. Probably more."

"You'd be surprised," Tami said. "I mean, my two best male friends are in relationships, and I work with them so even if they weren't it'd be not a great idea. Outside of work…I don't meet that many people, to be honest."

"I'm glad you sent me that email, anyway. Even if your mother made you."

Tami laughed with him, but two thoughts had sprung to life in her head. First was that she really should introduce Ty to Marci and Kalia, Axel and Devin. They would all like him, she was sure. But second was that she had been thinking of this trip as her own fact-finding trip to learn more about Ty. It hadn't occurred to her that he would also be watching how she got along with his friends.

And then every negative thought she'd had about herself bubbled up to the top of her mind: she couldn't talk about anything but work, she was shy, she didn't know how to meet new people, her range of interests was severely limited, she blurted out the wrong thing sometimes…and what if his friends were all these fun-loving early twenties guys, like fraternity types? She had no idea how she'd relate to them.

What if they hated her? What if Ty changed his mind and withdrew his offer? She wouldn't be much worse off than where she'd started, true, but… the thought made her terribly sad, so she pushed it away.

Chapter 22

Ty had a car service waiting at the airport for them. "Your friends can't come pick you up?" Tami asked as they got in the back of the car. A clear divider separated them from the driver, a cougar in a spotless blue uniform.

He tilted his head. "Why should they? The team pays for this. They don't want us driving around. Dangerous. We might get in wrecks. Although Ford—that was one of my teammates, but he got traded last year—he had some muscle cars and he had it in his contract that he was allowed to drive them." Ty leaned his head against the window, almost a rusty-orange silhouette against the bright blue of the sky and the yellow of the buildings rushing by. Even in the rather large car, he seemed oversized, his knees drawn slightly up and his ears folded over against the ceiling when he had them perked like he did now. "You like cars?"

Tami shook her head. "They get me from one place to another, but I never had that thing that boys get about them. Do you?"

The other fox smiled. "Ford took me out in one of his cars once. It was pretty great. I'd like to get a nice Lambo one day, find a place where I could open 'er up. I like to go fast."

"Seems reasonable."

He flashed her a grin. "Wide receiver stereotype?"

"Or a fox one. Or both. Do all the wide receivers own fast cars?"

"Rodo has a motorcycle, I think, though he's only allowed to ride it when his antlers aren't in." When Tami frowned, Ty rubbed the top of his head. "The helmet can't go on otherwise."

"They don't make helmets for antlered people? I'm sure I've seen some."

"Oh, they do." Ty nodded. "He wears a football helmet during the season. But on a bike, you're going so much faster, there's the risk that if you get thrown, your antlers will catch on something and twist your neck around and…" He mimed the motion with his paws around his own neck.

"Ugh." Tami shook her head. "I get motorcycles, but you know the statistics of how many people are injured riding them?"

"People are injured playing football, too," Ty said. "Sometimes you gotta ignore the statistics and go for it."

Well, Tami thought, staying quiet, that was something they could discuss if it ever became an issue. Not just the motorcycle thing, but any statistics-based decision. If it got to the point where they were making decisions together, if his friends liked her.

She itched to call Marci, just to get the reassurance she knew the rat would give. Then she thought, isn't Ty the one who should be reassuring me? So she asked him, "Do you always ignore the statistics?"

"Nah. But you gotta balance the risk versus the reward. Like, I wouldn't go climbing mountains or anything. Don't care about heights and that shit is dangerous. But riding a bike? Driving a fast car? That's pretty cool. That's a rush."

"I guess…" Tami tried to think of the sensations she loved, but most of them were tied up with getting a difficult piece of code to work. "I think the most risky thing I've done lately is email you."

He turned away from the window to smile at her. "And was the sensation worth it?"

That smile was working on her more and more every time. "So far," she said, trying to match his smile with one of her own.

His ears went up far enough that they pressed hard into the car's roof, so that appeared to have worked. She reached out a paw and took his, and they talked like that the rest of the way to his house.

He lived in a normal-looking house in a normal-looking neighborhood. Well, Tami's standards of "normal" were probably skewed a bit; this neighborhood had a lot of green lawns, which when she thought about it probably meant a lot of piped-in water and therefore a lot of money. And the houses were large, but there was a lot of room out here in the desert. Nice hills up behind it, brown but dotted with scrubby Joshua trees and brush, and the smell in the air was fresh and clean.

Ty caught her nose-lift as they approached the house. "That's mostly the lawns you smell," he said, although the front of his house had a rock garden dotted with cacti and a border of succulents rather than a grassy lawn. "House has an advanced filtration/ventilation system so us foxes don't choke living with Morshin." He hefted her bag over his shoulder and shifted his grip on his own. "Speaking of which, you probably want to stay out of the basement."

"I'll keep that in mind." She rested an elbow over her purse and followed him to the porch and the front door. "And where am I going to be staying?"

He turned, key in the door. "With me. If that's okay?"

She thought about the box of condoms she'd packed in her bag. "That's perfect." When he opened the door and gestured for her to precede him, she walked inside.

The cool blast of air conditioning, nicely ocean-scented, and the sound of video game battles greeted her. In the spacious foyer her paws landed on a soft colorful rug, "Hey guys!" Ty called, dropping their bags and walking forward into the wide open space in front of them. The carpeted floor dropped down two stairs into a sunken living room, where a pair of right-angled couches framed a coffee table and an immense television on a wooden entertainment unit.

The TV showed a split-screen battle in progress, a game Tami recognized as "Executive Order," a protect-the-President FPS. A goat and a swift fox sat on opposite couches, leaning forward with controllers in familiar stances. The goat played casually, his fingers doing all the work, while the swift fox put his body into the game, twisting the controller in the air. "Goddammit!" he yelled as one side of the screen flashed red. "Get the fuck behind—no!"

The swift fox threw his controller to the ground as the words, "YOU HAVE DIED" flashed on the red side of the screen. "Stupid fucking controllers. I hit the button, it just didn't register."

"Sure, dude," the goat said. "Hey look, I'm shooting your corpse in the head. Now I'm gonna go skullfuck your president."

Ty cleared his throat. "Hey guys, I'd like you to meet Tami."

Both of them half-turned on the couch, and then the swift fox scrambled to his feet. He was maybe half a foot shorter than Ty, wore knee-length athletic shorts and no shirt, and he brushed down his chest and stomach fur as he walked around the couch, tail flicking behind him. "Oh shit, sorry," he said. "I lost track of time."

From the couch, the goat, also shirtless but wearing what looked like baggy pajama pants, raised one hand without letting go of the controller. "Hey," he said. "I'm Morshin."

"Kellen Grindle," the swift fox said, extending a paw with a wide smile. "It's a real pleasure to meet you."

Ty cleared his throat. "Hey guys, I'd like you to meet Tami."
Both of them half-turned on the couch, and then the swift fox scrambled to his
feet. "Oh shit, sorry," he said. "I lost track of time."

Half a foot shorter than Ty still left him half a foot taller than Tami. She looked up and smiled back as she clasped his paw. "Tami Tachibana. Pleased to meet you, too."

"Sorry about Morshin," Kellen said. "He's great with video games and that's about it."

"Truth," Ty added.

"Sour grapes, foxes." The goat pulled up a start screen. "You wanna go again?"

Tami released Kellen's paw. "I didn't know 'Exec' had a versus mode."

The swift fox's ears perked up, and Morshin turned their way again. "Yeah," the goat said before Kellen could answer. "He's shitty at it but I like playing the terrorists."

"It's the controller," Kellen said tightly. "You keep the best controller for yourself."

"Wanna switch?"

Kellen focused on Tami. "So how long are you in town for?"

Ty put an arm around Tami's shoulders. "The weekend. Mind grabbing us drinks while I toss our bags in our room?"

"Sure." The swift fox kept his eyes on Tami. "What do you drink?"

"Don't let me interrupt your game."

He laughed. "Please. Giving me literally anything else to do would be terrific. Drink?"

"Pretty much anything." She glanced toward the kitchen. "Diet sodas if you have them."

"Light beer?"

"Sure."

"Right." He padded to the kitchen.

Tami followed Ty back to the foyer, snatching her bag before he could. "It's no trouble," she said when he reached for it.

"All right, all right." He laughed. "Come up. Up the stairs to the left, the master bedroom is mine."

The master bedroom was larger than Tami's first apartment out of college. It was actually a master suite, it looked like, because the first room she walked into was furnished with a couch, entertainment center, and a desk with a computer on it. The thick wine-colored carpet sank under her paws, soft enough that she dragged her feet over it as she walked in. It smelled faintly of Ty, an old odor that was in line with how long ago he'd last been here, and more strongly of the new carpet itself. No female scents.

One side of the room was dominated by a wide window with a door that gave out onto a small deck overlooking a back yard. Tami peered down past the varnished wood. "Nice deck," she said, looking into a scrubby yard of cactus and more succulents, beyond which was a paved driveway with a basketball hoop overlooking it. A basketball lay against the base of the hoop, and just beyond that a black and a red truck were parked side by side.

"Kimi planned the backyard." Ty came up to stand beside her. "He took an ecology course in college and heard about how wasteful it is to have lawns around here. So he went and found a bunch of native plants, and we had the whole lawn torn out. It was expensive but it's a lot better for the environment, plus in another couple years it'll pay for itself with the savings in water use. We're hoping that some of the neighbors pick up on it."

"Have any?"

His ears flattened. "Not quite yet. But Kellen talked to the armadillos next door and took them on a tour of the backyard, and he said they seemed interested."

"That's good. It's pretty."

"In a month, Kimi says it'll be flowering."

"Hope I'll be around to see it."

He smiled and wrapped an arm around her shoulders. "Bedroom and bathroom are over here."

Opposite the glass windows there were two doors in the wall, both ajar. Through the left-hand one, she saw gleaming white and blue tile, and through the other, more of the wine-red carpet and a wood cabinet and mirrors. "Bags in the bedroom?" she asked.

"Yup." Ty walked toward the right-hand door and showed her into the bedroom, dominated by a king bed made neatly with red and gold sheets. A big wooden dresser and wardrobe stood against the far wall; the mirror on the wardrobe was what she'd seen.

"Nice furniture." She set her bag down against the foot of the bed.

"Oh, Kimi picked it out. He's got an eye for design." Ty tossed his bag onto the bed. "I didn't have time to do any of the furnishing. He picked out the Firebirds-colored sheets too. At first I was like, 'really?' but it turned out to be a neat thing I can tell people in interviews. My fans love it."

She laughed and brushed the sheets. "Don't they make sheets with a logo?"

'That would be tacky." He grinned back and stepped toward her. She leaned her head up and he put his paws on her shoulders, then leaned down to kiss her. "I'm glad you're here. I want this to be a fun weekend."

She kissed back, letting herself relax. "What did you have in mind?"

"Oh, I figured it'd be chill. We can watch some movies—I got a bunch— or we can play video games, or hang out on the deck and talk. There's some good places to eat, there's movie theaters we can go out to, there's, uh, GameSpot if you're into that."

"Sounds fun."

"What do you usually do with your weekends?" He held up a paw. "Besides work."

"Let's not talk about that." Tami sighed. "But I want to spend time with your friends, too."

"Oh yeah, that's the point. I texted Kellen to organize things and he said if we play video games, we can hang out with Morshin; if we go out to a club we can hang with him and Kimi. I bet they'd be up for chilling at movies too, here or out. And we'll drag Paul out of his room once in a while."

"Great."

He slid his paws down Tami's arms. "Want to head back downstairs?"

The invitation was clear, and Tami was tempted to roll around on the big king bed, but she'd never had sex in the middle of the day and she still felt a bit stiff from the plane flight. And yet, and yet…

She slid her arms around his waist and felt his muscles shift and tense. "I think let's go hang out and see what you have here for lunch. But I'm looking forward to trying out this bed later."

"Mm, good." He leaned down to kiss her again. "Lunch sounds great."

•

Lunch was leftover Xaiqinese food, for which Ty apologized and Tami sincerely told him not to worry. Morshin didn't eat but Kellen joined them and Kimi bounded down the stairs when he smelled the food from the microwave, skidding to a halt on the kitchen tile. The otter, like everyone else, didn't wear a shirt, but looked in better shape than the swift fox even, with muscular arms and a taut stomach over powerful legs visible below his board shorts. "Yo," he said. "You're the fiancée?"

"Tami." They shook paws; his grip was more powerful than Kellen's. "Love the backyard."

He blinked and then smiled. "Oh, thanks. Yeah, it's like totally way better plus we cut down on water bills and we got a letter from the city water department congratulating us."

"We did?" Ty leaned across the table.

"Oh yeah. It's on the desk in the office. It's no big deal, like a PR campaign or something. Top ten percent of houses with lowest water usage in our neighborhood."

"Which is amazing considering the showers you take," Kellen chimed in.

Kimi extended a middle finger. "You should try it sometime, musky."

"Guys," Ty said.

"No, it's okay." Tami smiled. "Up in Pelagia, water's not a big deal. It falls out of the sky a whole bunch there. Have you thought about getting solar panels here?"

"Yeah!" Kimi's face lit up. "There's a program we applied for, but it's taking a while to go through. Local government, you know, there's a lot of shit to do, red tape, papers to sign."

He told them more about the solar panel program and about his attempt to lobby the local government to start recycling. Tami didn't have a lot to contribute to that but listened with interest, then turned her attention to Kellen when he broke in to say that of course Ty's gal didn't want to hear about recycling all day and asked Tami instead what movies she'd seen recently.

Of course she mentioned the Dark Knight movie, while in the back of her head she was thinking, "Ty's gal?" And Kimi had said, "Fiancée."

And then as though he'd heard the thought, Ty leaned in. "She's not my gal yet, and I'm not her guy yet. We're still working it out."

Of course it had been only an expression, but it was nice that Ty'd realized she'd be bothered by it. Or maybe her ears had flicked back. Her mother would've killed her.

And they talked about movies while Morshin played "Executive Order," eventually settling on going out that evening to a showing of a buddy comedy that they all knew was going to be awful, but it was March and there wasn't much in theaters worth seeing.

All three of his friends told her over and over what a great guy Ty was. She'd expected that, and she wasn't looking to hear that. What she was interested in was what kind of people his friends were. She liked that Kimi was so into recycling, and he told her later that he was trying to write a video game as well. He'd played football in college, like Ty had said, but, he told her, his experience had been a lot different from Ty's or even Kellen's.

"Those guys, they were on scholarship," he said. "Kellen was a third-string QB, sure, but he got some reps in. I walked on as a backup safety and I mostly showed up for the other guys to practice against. I met Kellen after a practice and he introduced me to Ty. We all got along because we weren't all that interested in the football player life, you know? Ty, we knew he was special, but he always said he'd rather hang out with us than go to those big parties like the hotshot players."

"So how did you get into video game design? Were you studying computer science and playing football?"

"Ah, no." The otter ducked his head. "I got my degree in Interactive Media."

"Still. That's not a cake degree."

"No, I worked hard." He grinned. "I didn't work so hard on the football though, but you gotta sleep sometime, right?"

"So what are you going to do with it?"

"Ah…I'm trying to make this game, it's like a platformer with an otter ninja. See, he's attacking a castle…"

He went on to describe the game in a little too much detail. Tami listened patiently, appreciating his enthusiasm for the game. "So how much do you have done?" she asked when his description wound down.

"Not a lot." His whiskers fluffed up when he smiled; kind of cute, actually. "It's really hard to plan these games out. I guess you know that. I'm watching tutorials online, but also we're supposed to keep an eye on Ty. Like, he told us to keep him from getting spoiled with football money."

"Really."

"Yeah, there was a thing at the rookie symposium that told them to make sure their friends were invested in their well-being, so we go to parties with him but one of us always makes sure to stay sober so we can drive him home, and we don't let him stay out late before practice even, let alone a game, and we don't let him do any serious drugs…" He trailed off, his whiskers sagging and eyes widening. "I mean, not that he'd do any of that shit anyway. Ty's real responsible. More than me and Kellen sometimes."

"It's all right." Tami laughed. "I already know I like him."

"Good. He likes you, too."

"He does?" Despite her nonchalance, her ears went up.

"Oh, sure. You can tell. He never brings girls here to the house."

"Ah." She didn't tell him that this visit had been her idea. But Ty had agreed to it, and at least that answered the minor question of how many other girls had shared that big king bed.

She spent a few hours tending to work, but here in this energetic house of young guys, distractions abounded. Usually she was pretty good at shutting out the world, but she was here to hang out with Ty's friends, so she didn't want to put on earphones or move to another room.

Then a flurry of bug reports came in that she had to deal with, and soon after, an email from Fatima asking her if she could get on a quick call in half an hour, so she excused herself. "Work problems," she said.

Ty, talking with Kellen about some new album that had just come out, looked up. "Everything okay?'

"It's fine. Or it will be. Sorry, I have to go talk to a few people. Half an hour at most."

"Go up to my room," he said. "It's pretty quiet with the door closed, even when Morshin turns his video games up."

The goat extended a middle finger back at Ty without breaking concentration on the game he'd switched to, a slower-paced puzzle game. Tami smiled. "Thanks."

Fatima had seen the bug reports and wanted to make sure Tami had the necessary resources for them. Tami restrained her annoyance; she had already allocated the bug fixes and had been in the middle of writing up a report when Fatima's email had come in. If Fatima had just let her… but this happened a lot and Tami swallowed her annoyance, repeating to herself, "Destiny's Angel, Destiny's Angel," over and over. Devin was also on the call, and Tami told Fatima that he was keeping an eye on things if Tami didn't get them assigned in time. Which she had, but she didn't say that part.

After the call, Devin said, "Hey, Tami, can you stick around a couple minutes?"

"Sure," she said, and after Fatima and the others disconnected, she said, "What's up?"

"Not much, I just wanted to see how it was going for you. Are the natives friendly?"

"They're fine, yeah."

"Sorry to interrupt your vacation so soon."

"No, it's cool. I'm glad we got it taken care of. Everything else going okay there?"

He hesitated. "Yeah."

"What's wrong?"

"No, it's nothing. Things are fine. There's just—well, I got an email from that VP. Mr. Francis? I guess he asked Fatima about me and he wants to sit down with me tomorrow and talk. Fatima says he might want to move me to another team."

"That's great! I mean, I'll be sad to see you go, but that means more responsibility. You think it's the Space Race team? Marent hasn't been pulling his weight for a while."

"Maybe. I really don't know. Anyway, we told him you were on vacation but he might email you tomorrow to ask about me. I just wanted to prepare you so it doesn't come out of the blue."

"I'll talk you up. Hey, my tail's wagging for you, Devin. Good job."

"Thanks. Mine's wagging too." He gave a nervous laugh. "I hope it goes okay."

"You'll be great. Just be you."

When she hung up, the peace of Ty's room was so compelling that she pulled up her email. Just the two most urgent messages, she promised herself, but it was almost an hour later that Ty knocked on the door.

She started, then got up from the desk. "Sorry. What time—I got caught up in emails."

"We were gonna go out to this Etruscan place whenever you're ready."

"I'm ready now." As soon as he mentioned food, her stomach growled. "Really ready. Etruscan sounds great."

So they went out, even Morshin (with some coaxing) and had a lot of tomato-sauced pasta, fresh bread, and good wine. The dimly-lit restaurant felt right out of a mob movie, with Sinatra playing in the background, pictures of local celebrities and Catholic luminaries on the wall, and the green and red and white décor in between the pictures and around the dark wood beams.

The conversation remained light, and though Tami still felt like an outsider, it was nice that most of the group (besides Morshin) made an effort to include her. The most embarrassing part was when they asked what her favorite video games were and she had to confess that she hadn't played many games in years. "Not alone, anyway. We have parties at the office when a new game comes out, but mostly a couple people play them and the rest of us sit back and comment on them."

"Video games at work, though, that'd be pretty cool." Morshin spoke while chewing a piece of his spinach ravioli.

"You have to have a job first," Kellen said sharply.

"Don't see any of you at a nine to five."

"Paul will be."

"Yeah, well," Kimi put in, "Paul's special."

"Where is he?" Tami asked to cover up the fact that she'd forgotten about Ty's fourth roommate.

"School. He studies in the library most weeknights, comes home late, goes in early. You probably won't see him 'til Saturday." Kellen dabbed bread around his empty plate.

Ty leaned into Tami's shoulder gently. "You'll like Paul," he said. "He's really smart and he's fun, too."

"Used to be fun," Kimi put in. "Before law school."

"I can sympathize," Tami said.

The table fell quiet for a moment and then Ty said, "You're fun."

"Oh, you know…" She looked around at him and his friends. They all watched her, curious. "My friends say I was more fun before I got this new job. It's stressful, but I'm really proud of what we're doing. These games often go way over time and over budget, but this one is only a little over time and over budget, so…yay."

Ty laughed and the others joined in. They asked her about the game and she told them what she could, and the rest of the dinner went well. She felt, if not comfortable, at least approaching comfortable with the group, even if her mind still buzzed with worries about the various bugs in the game and in her conversation (did you have to talk about work so much? why haven't you done more fun things?).

That wasn't the end of the night, not by any means, but Tami was getting tired by the time they got home. So she declined the beers, joined in a little of the conversation, and then excused herself to go upstairs, with the thought that she might check in on her email before heading to sleep.

"I'm pretty tired too," Ty said. "See you in the morning, guys."

He followed Tami upstairs, and as he closed the door of the suite of rooms behind them, he said, "Are you really tired?"

"I am, sort of," she said, but with a smile. She fought the urge to go open her laptop. "But I think I have enough energy to stay up for a little bit."

He moved toward her and she slid into his embrace. His muzzle brushed her ears. "Good," he said. "Me too."

She liked the view of the night sky outside the large window over the deck, but she also liked the warmth of Ty's body against hers and the smell of his arousal as hers rose to match. So they shuffled together toward the bedroom, undoing each other's clothes along the way, and then fell on the bed together, Ty on top. He nuzzled down her muzzle to her neck and collarbone, then pulled her t-shirt off and ran his paws down her sides and up her breasts. She sighed and closed her eyes and let go of work.

The sex was good again, maybe even better. Ty still made love with a joyful energy that inspired Tami to match it, and she climaxed in a lovely cascade of pleasure that left her sighing happily in his arms when it was over. They lay together under the red and gold sheet and she fell asleep to the rhythm of his breathing.

•

The next day, Tami managed to sneak in half an hour to make sure that everything back at Shirokaze was going well. Devin had emailed her with a rundown of progress on the existing bugs, and miraculously, only two had come in that morning. So Tami closed her laptop to take a walk with Kimi and then had lunch with Kellen. Both of them said glowingly nice things about Ty and, more importantly, seemed to be very nice people themselves. Morshin was less forthcoming, and she didn't get much of a read on Paul in the five minutes she saw him before he ran off to class.

That night, Ty asked if she wanted to go out to a club, but she said she was more in a movie mood. The guys offered to let Tami choose the movie, but she'd said she wanted to see what they picked, and Kimi said, "Whoa, it's a test."

Tami stressed that she wanted them to pick something they'd like to watch. Kellen made margaritas for everyone while they were discussing it, and at first Tami declined. The swift fox seemed to understand why. "Look," he said as Kimi took a glass over to Morshin, "if you're worried, I'll make sure Ty keeps up with you."

"I'm not sure what my tolerance is," Tami said.

"Oh, probably half his." Kellen smiled. "So I'll make sure he drinks twice as much as you."

It was not unpleasantly like being at a college party. Tami had only been to a couple, and what she hadn't liked about them was the fierce, almost desperate need to either hook up or get drunk as fast as possible, or both. What she'd liked was the time in the first couple hours of the party when everyone had had a couple drinks and the conversations were going easily. This evening felt more like those first couple hours, and besides, maybe a few drinks would help her forget about work.

Work. She should go upstairs now and check in on Devin before things got too late. No—she was on vacation and he had her phone number if he really needed her. She'd checked in that afternoon; nothing would have changed since then. Logic fought with emotion, but in the end logic won out.

So she nodded to Kellen, and he held out a wide bowl glass with a stem, full of a limey-strawberry crushed ice drink with the sharp tang of tequila spiking it. As she took it, he winked at her and turned to Ty, who was staring at a message on his phone. "You done with that one yet, big guy?"

"Huh?" Ty looked up.

The swift fox gestured at his glass. "Come on, you're falling behind."

Ty shook his head. "You're supposed to be looking out for me." But he lifted his glass and drained it, then passed it to Kellen. "Thanks."

"Sure thing."

Tami watched the swift fox go back to the kitchen and fill Ty's glass, and then add another shot of tequila. She wasn't sure how she felt about getting her fiancé drunk, but as long as she got drunk too, maybe it was fair. She wouldn't get too drunk, though. She could tell Kellen to stop at any time.

The group eventually decided on a terrible action movie by means of Kimi putting it in the DVD player and announcing, "Movie's starting!"

Drinks in paw, Tami settled in next to Ty on the big couch with Kimi on her other side and Kellen and Morshin on the other couch. Paul agreed to watch the movie with them from the kitchen bar so he could have his books out and do some studying.

By the end of the first movie, Tami was well into "loosened up" territory, and the idea of getting Kellen to stop had long since vanished. They snarked at the movie together, and when everyone laughed at Tami's cracks, she felt good, part of the group. And then there were a couple moments when the guys all laughed about something and she didn't quite get it, but then they'd known each other for years.

Then there was the time Morshin pointed at the screen and said, "Hey Ty, did you stay near there?"

The closing credits scrolled by over a helicopter shot of the lovely city of Yerba, with the wharf prominent in the foreground. "Uh, sorta," Ty said quickly. "Hey, what are we watching next?"

Paul followed the goat's finger. "When were you there?"

Kimi responded when Ty didn't. "That time he was fed up with all the girls his folks were taking him to see and he spent a weekend there." The otter saluted Tami. "Thank god that's over, huh? No more getaways to Yerba."

"Yeah." Ty's ears folded down, but he perked them up quickly.

"What'd you go to Yerba for?" Tami asked, buzzed enough to ask in front of everyone.

"Oh, just to get away. Uh, Dev was there with his…anyway, I had dinner with them a couple times." He grinned. "You'll have to meet Dev. He's a great guy."

This was a vibe she hadn't gotten from Ty very often, but she recognized it from Marci, whenever the rat was talking about a case and Tami asked the wrong question about it. With Marci, it was usually followed by, "Sorry, I can't talk about that part of it." Ty just changed the subject, and she forgot about it quickly.

During the first half of the second movie, Tami stopped worrying about whether what she was saying was going to be funny. They were her jokes and made her laugh, and anyway these guys weren't exactly Late Show monologue material.

Nobody seemed to mind. Ty laughed really loudly at most things she said and tried to explain one of her remarks when Kimi said he didn't get it.

That turned into a fifteen-minute conversation which only ended when the hero's airplane crashed into the terrorists' airplane in the movie.

Later on, the hero, an elegant black-and-white skunk, grabbed the black-and-white skunk female lead and kissed her. Tami, who had previously ranted that of *course* he was going to choose the skunk over the leopard because these movies promoted the same-species couple status quo, gathered a breath to say, "Here we go," and found Ty's muzzle pressed to hers, their tongues already sliding against each other.

The time had jumped slightly; she didn't have any feeling that he'd pressed himself on her. Nor did she mind his paw on her breast as they kissed. His mouth tasted like tequila and fake strawberry like hers, cold and warm at the same time.

The otter and swift fox made drunkenly appreciative noises while the goat said, "Hey, this is the good part."

"Mmm-hmm." Ty pulled back from the kiss. Tami touched her nose to his and smiled. "Hey guys," he said, "I think we're going to skip the rest of the movie, huh?"

"Ohh yeah," Kellen said. "This movie sucks anyway."

"Hey." Morshin pointed at the screen. "This is Damian Danforth's third best movie."

Ty and Tami laughed all the way back to the bedroom, keeping their balance pretty well by leaning on each other. The hallway was tilted more than Tami remembered, but she only banged into the wall once and it didn't hurt at all. Ty kept his arm wrapped around her, keeping her safe as they got to his bedroom and fell down on the bed.

•

In the morning the sun was at least twice as bright as usual. Tami's head throbbed as she shielded her eyes from it, and beside her, Ty grumbled something at her movement. She was naked, as was he, and they'd remained entwined in each other's arms through the night. With the shifting of the covers came the smell of sex and the memory of the night before.

She remembered it hazily, but it had been good, and she clung to that memory. There was a frantic moment of *had he used a condom?* even though she wasn't in season. Only one empty condom wrapper lay on the nightstand; had they cleaned up the one they'd used the night before? "How you feeling?" Ty asked softly next to her ear.

The moderate panic tangled up in light nausea in her stomach. This was why you didn't get drunk and have sex. But she didn't want to say anything about that to him. "Nnf. There's too much sun."

He chuckled and kissed her ear. "Stay here. I'll get you a hangover cure."

"I'm not hung over," she protested, and then tried to get up and pain lanced through her head. She fell back to the bed. "Ugh. Maybe a little. How are you?"

"Me? I'm fine." He pressed a paw to his head. "A little dry maybe."

"Yeah." She rubbed her sandpaper tongue along the roof of her mouth. "Water would be a great step one."

"Already on it." He leapt from the bed, all lithe and muscular and showing every bit of it under his close-shaved fur, and padded to the bathroom.

Christ, even his tail looked fine after an evening of drunken sex. Tami hated to think what hers looked like. And drunken sex? That wasn't like her at all. It had been enjoyable, though, she remembered that much. Plus, the parts of her body that weren't hung over had that pleasantly spent feel that a night of sex gave her. Tentatively, she tried to determine by the feel of her fur whether Ty'd used a condom or not. The results were inconclusive.

She closed her eyes and pressed a paw over them. The memories were clear in patches: the sex itself, for instance, and parts of the undressing. She focused on them, trying to bring back one of putting on a condom.

Ty's scent returned to the room with the cool, clear scent of water. "Here," he said, and a cool glass pressed against her fingers.

She sat up and drank. "It helps a little," she said. He'd gotten sweatpants on, which annoyingly didn't make him any less attractive.

"That's not the cure." He smiled. "It'll take me a few minutes to whip that up. You okay here or want to come watch?"

"I'll stay here." The water cooled her mouth and throat and then the glass was empty. Ty reached for it, but Tami said, "I can get myself more."

"All right then." He kissed her between the ears. "I'll bring it up."

"Hey," she said, hating herself for mentioning it even though it was a legit concern. Ty stopped and waited, watching her. She pressed a paw to her forehead. "Did we, uh…" She gestured to the nightstand and the lone condom wrapper.

His ears flattened. "Ah, shit. I don't know. I think so? I mean, I—I don't remember exactly. But you're not in season, right?"

"No." She shook her head.

"Okay, well. I'm clean. I get tested pretty often." His ears came up. "If I didn't—sorry."

The nausea had receded slightly. Tami nodded. "Me too. I mean…I get tested." She'd been tested after Jason, and what few guys there'd been since then had all used condoms.

He smiled and kissed her head. "Let's get you feeling better and then we can discuss it."

While she was refilling the glass in the bedroom—walking wasn't too bad once she got used to it if she kept her paw in front of her eyes—she recalled one more detail from the night before. Ty fumbling with the buttons on her shirt and pulling her shirt off to stare at her breasts. "See," he said, "these are amazing. I should be able to have both."

He'd slurred it a bit, and at the time she'd laughed and pushed her chest at his face, and told him, "Course you can."

Now, in retrospect, it seemed like an odd thing for him to have said. Sure, he was drunk. Maybe he was wanting another mouth? Maybe he wanted breasts himself? The words had stuck with Tami because she'd never thought of her breasts as particularly impressive, and the compliment made her glow.

She still appreciated the compliment, but the wording made her curious, and it was something to focus on to distract her from the shame over having had unprotected sex (maybe). Returning to bed, she sat cross-legged and leaned against the headboard, turning the memory over. By the time the smell of bacon filtered up to her, she'd made no more sense of them, and her stomach took over most of her thoughts at that point until Ty returned.

"Gimme," she said, reaching for the plate he held that was producing the heady aroma that prevented her from thinking about anything else.

He held the plate up over her head. "First off," he said, "there's veggie bacon on this side, and some meat bacon for me. Make sure you don't get confused."

Veggie bacon was fine for calm, sunny brunch mornings, for polite conversation and accompanying sweet potato hash and orange juice, maybe a mimosa. But her nose told her that what she wanted was on the other side of the plate, so she took two of the veggie bacon strips to be polite and then grabbed two of the others.

"Hey," Ty said, and she shook her head.

"I'm allowed to cheat once in a while. Bacon for a hangover is on the list." That was one thing she didn't regret from her relationship with Jason, at least.

Ty picked up the remaining meat bacon as Tami stuffed all four strips into her mouth and bit down. Hot and crispy greasy salt exploded in her muzzle, everything that was right about bacon. "Oh god, this is amazing," she moaned.

"I learned to make bacon in college," he said. "Nobody else was going to because we had this great diner a few blocks away, but every time we went there we got toast and pancakes and lots of carbs." He patted his stomach. "Not good for my diet."

As she recovered a little energy, she thought about asking Ty about what he'd said the night before, both about her breasts and about Yerba and Dev, but the hangover wasn't exactly conducive to a conversation that wasn't about bacon. Given the rest of what was going on with his team, maybe it was another kind of soap opera. Dev was Dev Miski—right, the gay one. That boosted the possibility of soap opera drama by an order of magnitude. Maybe Ty was privy to some secrets and didn't feel like he had the right to tell them. Tami certainly wasn't one of those people who believed that spouses should reveal all their secrets to each other.

Spouses. She licked her fingers and watched her fiancé crunch bacon strips. Prospective fiancé?

"And I could resist eating them, but they all smelled so good and I decided I'd rather cook at home." He flicked his ears. "Or, my terrible little off-campus apartment."

What more was Tami waiting for in a husband? Someone more mature, maybe? That was maybe the only area she could think of where Ty was lacking, and someone more mature wouldn't be quite so exciting. She could use more excitement than maturity in her life, when it came right down to it. Even Marci and Kalia, her drinking buddies, were more mature than exciting these days.

"Weren't you a big star in college?" The bacon was good even when it wasn't hot. Tami's headache and light sensitivity had already gone down. It occurred to her that there was a way to take the mistake of unprotected sex (if it had happened) as a message. If she trusted Ty enough while drunk to skip the condom—which she had never, never done—didn't that say something? She hadn't checked in to work in almost fifteen hours, and when was the last time that had happened? Even thinking about it now, there wasn't a knot in her chest that something might be going wrong.

"Not that big, but anyway we're not allowed to take money, so I had to be thrifty. But I like cooking bacon. I can get it the way I want it now."

"It's good." She swallowed and put the plate on the bed so she could reach out to take his free paw. Their fingers were both greasy and smelly. "I'll marry you."

He froze in the process of licking his fingers, and then a delighted smile burst over his muzzle. "Are you serious?"

"Yeah." The smile was contagious; her own spread wide.

His fingers squeezed hers. "Is it because of the bacon?"

She laughed and fell against him, and he wrapped an arm around her. "No," she said, "I realized that I'm waiting for some sign or something to tell me not to do it, and you know, your friends are all nice, and you're nice, and it feels like we can work things out if there are problems."

"That's a lot of thinking for first thing in the morning with a hangover." Ty nuzzled her ear.

"The bacon helped a lot." Tami rested her muzzle against his bare chest.

"See?" He licked her ear. "I knew it was the bacon."

•

At first, Tami didn't want to tell everyone, but they agreed that she and Ty would call their parents, and then they would go down and tell his friends. And from what she heard, her conversation went better than his did. Her mother was ecstatic, and her main complaint was that probably the Nakamuras wouldn't let her participate in the wedding planning.

Ty sounded like he was spending much more time convincing his parents that this was a good thing, but when he hung up, he turned to Tami and said, "They're excited."

She arched an eyebrow. "Really?"

"For a wedding, at least." He took her paws. "But they'll love you. Let's go tell the guys."

"Can we shower first?" Tami asked, and so they cleaned each other off and spent a little more time than they needed to, and then got dressed and went downstairs.

"I'm gettin' married!" Ty announced to the room, which consisted of the goat and otter, and Morshin paused his video game, which Tami already knew was a momentous occurrence. Because Ty had gotten to tell his friends, she took a break to run to her laptop and email Devin and Axel.

The rest of her visit turned into an engagement party. Kellen, when he heard, ran out and got wine, and Paul took a break from his studies. Ty took her out to a beautiful canyon where they talked about the near and far future, and that night they made love without being drunk (and with a condom), which was also pretty good. She lay next to him afterwards, warm and content, and thought, *I could do this for some years. Or a lifetime, maybe. I guess we'll see.*

.

Chapter 23

Her flight Monday got her back to work right around lunch. At the airport, she checked in to work and found fifty bug reports summarized in three emails from Devin, all assigned. Thirty of the bugs they'd already gotten or known about were done. His last email said that the project was still well on track and that he might even move it back to green. Tami nearly missed her flight while composing a reply telling him that she thought it was probably green as well but she wanted to keep it yellow just to be safe for another two weeks until they had the complete list of bugs from the publisher. By the time she got into the office, she already had an idea of how much work she was going to have to do.

I'm engaged, she thought, and made a lunch date with Devin and Axel, although they couldn't meet until Tuesday because Devin was busy. Axel still wanted to have lunch, and Tami said fine, but she wasn't going to tell the stories from the weekend twice.

So she cut lunch with Axel short. "Answer me one thing," the marmot said. "Are you happy?"

"Yeah," she said. "You know, I wasn't sure about it, but he's a really nice guy. We get along, and he's…he's really down to earth considering the world he lives in."

"So are you going to quit and live off his money?"

"Hell, no," she snorted, and leaned in. "Look, keep it secret, but…I'm gonna be running Destiny's Angel."

His eyes widened. "Seriously?"

She nodded. "Fatima told me last week. But it's not official yet, so you can't say anything."

"No," he said, "of course not. That's amazing! Congrats!"

She returned to work with a glow that did nothing to help her productivity. Jumbo Bubbles X felt like nothing more than a series of obstacles set in the way of a goal she didn't really care about anymore. Not that that mattered; she had never really loved the game, but she'd worked her tail off for it. It was a stepping stone to the next stepping stone, and it brought her one stone closer to the goal she did care about.

Every so often she remembered the feel of Ty's paws on her, or the quiet of sitting with him by the canyon he'd taken her to on Saturday, or the disorientation of being drunk, the crunch of bacon, the laughter of his friends. This wasn't conducive to powering through the pile of work she had to get done, but she was enjoying the feeling of missing Ty, so she didn't worry about it too much. Ty was going to work out details with his parents and present a selection of dates to her and her mother, and he assured her that she would have very little to do except answer questions from his mother. "And that will be plenty," he'd laughed.

Around three, Fatima asked her to come in for a meeting that wasn't on her schedule. Tami asked if it could wait until Tuesday, when she thought she'd be all caught up. *I'd rather get this addressed today*, Fatima wrote back, which was typical, so Tami finished up an email and walked through the cubicles to the otter's office. She could take the opportunity to tell her boss about her engagement, that the weekend had been a success.

"Close the door, please," Fatima said when Tami knocked and came in.

That wasn't as typical. Tami closed the door and took the chair in front of her boss's desk. In the back corner of the office, a fountain burbled down into a small pool with a mat in front of it; Fatima often rested her feet there while on calls. "What's going on? JBX is still yellow, but we'll get it green in two weeks. It's not in danger."

"This is not about Jumbo Bubbles." Fatima laid her paws on her desk and her whiskered face took on a grave, almost sad expression. "I'm afraid Mr. Francis has changed his mind about promoting you to the Destiny's Angel project."

The floaty, happy feeling Tami had been enjoying all morning vanished like a popped bubble. "Wha—why?"

"I don't know." Fatima stared down at her paws. "He informed me this morning."

"So who—I mean, am I fired?"

"Oh, no!" Now the otter lifted her head. "No, I'm certain you'll be a project lead. There will be more titles coming up next year and you'll be on the short list for any one of them."

"Like what titles?"

Fatima sighed. "Tami, these things happen. It was never official."

"Then why did you tell me?"

"Because Mr. Francis told me."

Tami's claws dug into the side of the chair. She knew they made a noise when scraped across the plastic, but she was about two seconds from not caring. "And did he tell you it wasn't official? Did he say he was leaning that way or did he say I got it?" Fatima shook her head, but Tami went on. "Is this change unofficial too, or is this one more final?"

"I don't know. You'd have to ask Mr. Francis."

"Maybe I will." Tami got up. "Thanks."

She felt bad about leaving so abruptly, but Fatima would understand. She'd just opened the door when the otter cleared her throat. "Tami. My advice? Don't cause a fuss."

"Why? Because it would hurt my chances later?" The office door was a foot open; outside, the low buzz of the office carried on as it always did, and Tami wanted to lose herself in it, forget about what she'd had briefly and lost.

"You know how difficult it is to be female in this business."

Yes, she knew. Despite what she'd told Ty, she knew there was a different set of rules if you were female. If you protested too much, you were "shrill" or "demanding" or, heaven forbid, "bitchy." If you didn't protest, though, you got overlooked. She'd been warned about that but shielded from it for most of her career, lucky to work for people who'd appreciated her coding. As she approached higher echelons of the company, those problems she'd been told about rose up more and more.

Here was another one. If she went to Francis, undoubtedly he would say that he'd only mentioned to her boss that he was thinking about it, that he hadn't intended for her to tell Tami, and he wasn't responsible for office gossip.

Now she was getting herself worked up over something she was imagining Mr. Francis saying. He might be completely reasonable. Maybe there was an explanation for it. Maybe it had to do with her leaving this weekend.

Logically she knew that that probably wasn't it. She'd had coverage for her meetings and had stayed on top of her project. What else had changed?

Back at her desk, she couldn't focus on her work. It was only 3:30, so she walked over to Axel's desk. "Hey," he said, and his cheer became concern the moment he turned. "What happened?"

"Let's get some coffee."

"I can't." He gestured at his screen. "Mialo and I have dinner reservations and if I don't get this done tonight I'll be up until one a.m. Tomorrow morning?"

She exhaled. "Yeah. Sure."

"If you really need to talk, I can take like ten minutes."

"No," she said, "this is a longer conversation. It's okay." She put a paw on the marmot's shoulder. "I'm not feeling great anyway. I think I'm gonna take off early. I'll wrap up my work at home."

"Okay." He patted her paw. "Feel better, okay?"

That might take a while. She packed up her things and walked out of the office early. Of course people raised their heads to look, but she didn't meet their eyes. She felt like someone who'd been let go, whispers trailing in her wake until she pushed open the door and walked out into the silent lobby.

She got home slower than she was used to; of course there was more traffic at four in the afternoon than at seven or eight in the evening. All the way home her thoughts ran in circles, and when she logged in to her email, she still couldn't focus.

She couldn't call Axel or Devin; Marci and her mom would still be at work. So she dialed Ty's number.

"Hey, beautiful," he said. "I was missing you too."

"I didn't get the project," she said.

"What?"

So she explained the whole thing to him, keeping it very short, and he stayed quiet until she was done. "Oh, jeez," he said. "That sucks. I'm really sorry. So what are you going to do?"

"I don't know," she admitted. "This just happened. I guess I'm going to finish out Jumbo Bubbles and see where they put me next. Keep doing the best I can."

"Tell you what. I'll fly back tomorrow and we can talk about it tomorrow night. How about dinner at Aquitaria? Or is that too formal? Jack B's?"

"All right," she said, "either of those." To her surprise, the simple fact of knowing she would have a friend to talk about the situation with allowed her to relax and get back into work that evening. The game still felt pointless to her, the work numbing and boring, but she pushed herself to do it.

Going to bed that night, she couldn't find her toothbrush. She looked through her bags and then realized that while she remembered brushing her teeth in Ty's bathroom, she didn't specifically remember re-packing her toothbrush. So she called Ty again to ask him to bring it, but he wasn't answering his phone.

Ty had given her the number of the house, so she called that up, and Kellen's sharp high voice answered. "Hi, it's Tami," she said. "Can you ask Ty to bring my toothbrush when he comes back tomorrow? He's not answering his phone."

"Oh, he's home already, sorry. But I can send it up to you. Where'd you leave it?"

"Sorry, he's home?"

"Yeah, he took off this morning a bit after you did. Said he was going to start planning the wedding. Maybe he didn't turn his phone on again after getting off the plane. Try his parents."

"I will." Tami paused. "It should be in Ty's bathroom. Blue and white toothbrush."

"Hang on." A pause, scuffling of movement, just enough for her to wonder, where is Ty? Then Kellen was back. "Got it. I'll express it tomorrow."

She thanked him and hung up, then checked her phone. Ty's home number was in there too, but she hesitated before calling. Had Ty said he'd come over tomorrow or that he'd fly back? He'd said "fly back," she was pretty sure.

Calling his parents felt like checking up on him. Did she want to do that? Just two days into their engagement she was turning into a stereotypical wife? Hadn't she thought that spouses didn't need to tell all their secrets?

There was a reasonable explanation. There had to be.

•

Devin begged off lunch again—"just super busy right now"—and so Tami went to the Greek place with Axel because it was going to be slow and she knew she would want to vent about the job. But Axel started off asking her to fill in gaps from the previous day's lunch, and she told him the story of getting engaged to Ty while naked in bed eating bacon, which had the nice side effect of putting off when she would have to tell him about Destiny's Angel.

"That's maybe the best engagement story I've heard," the marmot said. "Glad his friends were cool."

"They are, although I think relying on Ty's money has most of them… aimless maybe? Except Paul, who's killing himself to get through law school."

"Probably wants to prove he's not relying on Ty's money."

She nodded. "His one friend is working on a video game, supposedly, but I don't know that he's done much more research than play a bunch of them. Another one sits around playing video games all day—literally. And I don't know what Kellen does except watch out for Ty."

"Everyone needs someone like that." Axel lifted his water glass to her in a toast.

"I'm glad I have you and Devin." But that reminded her that Devin was busy, and that she was still waiting to find out what had been going on with Ty.

"So when do we get to meet him?"

"Oh, soon." She scratched her ears.

Axel opened his mouth, closed it, and then visibly shifted topics. "Okay, what happened yesterday that you wanted to tell me about?"

At that moment the server came back with their drinks and asked if they needed anything else, and told them their lunches would be "right up," and all through it Axel tapped his claw against the table and stared at Tami. When finally the server left, he leaned over and said, "What? Am I not on the Destiny's Angel team? Look, it's okay, I know you tried. I won't hold it against you."

"No." She inhaled a breath, held it, and let it out. "*I'm* not on the Destiny's Angel team."

"What? You told me yesterday—"

"I know—"

He shook his head, angry at himself, and reached out to her. "Sorry. You know you told me. What happened?"

She let his paw lie atop hers. "I don't know. Fatima told me Mr. Francis changed his mind. I don't know what happened. Was it that I left for the weekend?"

"That doesn't seem right." Axel frowned. "You're not behind, and besides you logged in from Chevali a couple times."

Like five times, but the precise number didn't matter. "What else could it be? He doesn't know I'm engaged. Nobody does except you and Devin."

"Oh." Axel's frown deepened. He withdrew his paw from hers. "Fatima does."

Tami tilted her head. "No, she doesn't. I talked to her yesterday and she didn't say anything about it."

"She does, though." The marmot drew out the words as though they were painful. "She came by first thing Monday morning to ask if we knew when you'd be back and Devin said that you were going to be in later but to cut you some slack because you were engaged."

Tami's ears felt warm. She folded them down. "He told her?"

"Yeah." Axel nodded. "I thought it was out of line, you know, that's your news to share, but Devin was excited…I guess."

"What did Fatima say?"

"She didn't really say much." Axel took a drink of his Coke. "Something like, 'oh, how nice,' and then she took off. I told Devin he shouldn't have said anything and he shrugged and said that you'd already talked to Fatima."

"About the weekend, yeah, about the possibility of getting engaged. Not that it had actually happened."

"See, I didn't know that."

"Don't worry, I'm not blaming you. But…you think that's it? That I got engaged?"

"Maybe?" The marmot rubbed his whiskers back. "I mean, it could be one of those things, right? Maybe someone else came up and Francis's boss said 'you have to let this guy run Destiny's Angel.' The timing could be coincidence."

"It could be."

"It would be really fast."

"Yes. But then…why didn't Fatima say something about my engagement?"

Axel shook his head. "Because she was waiting for you to tell her? Because she didn't want to bring it up in a meeting where she had to tell you something painful?"

"Maybe. That's probably it." Tami scraped a claw along the side of her glass.

"Course it is. Look, what did you tell me? Stand up for yourself but don't stand on a chair and shout? I think it's totally okay for you to go to Fatima and say, you know, 'why was the change made and what can I do to be a better candidate in the future?' "

"I tried." Tami sighed. "I tried, Axel. She wouldn't say anything. Said she had no idea."

"All right," the marmot said, "so go to Mr. Francis."

Eating lunch helped. With a full stomach and a day's perspective, Tami could acknowledge the depressing reality of the situation and still consider her options. Going to see Mr. Francis wasn't a bad idea. She'd met him enough times that she felt comfortable walking over to his office after lunch.

She and Axel had talked for a while about how exactly to phrase her question. Tami had to be careful not to act as though she were entitled to the job, and to acknowledge that Francis had the authority to appoint whomever he chose to the position. But she also had the right to know what would make her a better candidate. And if Fatima wouldn't answer her, then Francis should.

Still, it took her until around three to work up the nerve to walk by his office, and then he was on the phone. He didn't have as nice an office as she'd imagined; it wasn't larger than Fatima's, although the otter did have the fountain and pool in her office, and Mr. Francis had a lot of greenery up on the shelves. His office smelled much better, in her opinion, even though none of the greenery was flowering.

She stopped by Gri's cubicle to help with a problem they'd asked her about, and on the way back saw that Francis was off the phone. So she knocked on the open door, and the field mouse waved her in. "Ms. Tachibana, what can I do for you?"

"Ah…" Should she close the door? She left it ajar and came in. "Do you have a minute?"

"I have a call at four, but I have a few minutes. What's on your mind?"

"Well." She sat down. "I wanted to talk about Destiny's Angel." His posture straightened and his ears and face stiffened when she said that, but she pretended she didn't notice. "Fatima told me you were leaning in another direction for the lead, and I wanted to ask what I could do to make myself a better candidate. For that job or for another one if—when it comes up in the future."

Mr. Francis removed his glasses and set them on the desk. "I'd really prefer you have this conversation with Fatima."

"I tried, but…I mean, I suppose I could go back. I was a bit emotional when she told me."

As soon as she said that, she cursed herself. Emotional, just like a female? Ugh, she might as well have told him she was in season or something. But if Mr. Francis was thinking anything like that, he didn't let on. "I mean that I was initially leaning in your direction, but Fatima changed her recommendation. I believe she was concerned about an upcoming life event? She wasn't more specific, but I assure you that from what she's told me, you'll continue to be a strong candidate for future projects here."

"I'm getting married," Tami said softly.

The mouse held up a paw. "I didn't know and don't want to know. I mean, congratulations. But I didn't make a decision based on that."

"Could you still…" Tami snapped her jaw shut in mid-sentence, paralyzed by the worry of how her question would be perceived.

Mr. Francis shook his head. "We want to get the team in place soon. But if you'd like to be involved, I'm sure Mr. Dinaska will be glad to find a place for you that can accommodate your schedule."

Mr. Dinaska? "Devin? I'm sorry, what?"

"In fact," he went on as though he hadn't heard, "given your close working relationship with him, if you feel you can assist him, your experience… Oh, I'm sorry. I thought Fatima would have told you."

"Devin's going to lead the game?"

"Yes." He cleared his throat. "Why don't I let Fatima explain the decision to you? I don't really know what was behind it. I only know that I have a very high opinion of you both."

"Thank you." She got up. "I'll go ask her."

Fatima wasn't in her office, and Devin wasn't at his cube. So Tami went over to Axel's cube and sat on his desk. "Devin," she said in a harsh whisper.

"What?" The marmot looked up from his laptop.

"They're giving it to Devin."

"Giving what—oh." His eyes got big and round. "That? Seriously?"

"Uh huh."

"Did they say why?"

"Because I'm getting married."

His eyes got wider and rounder. "He said that?"

Tami sighed. "Actually he specifically said that he was *not* saying that. But what else could it be? Fatima changed her recommendation."

The springs in Axel's chair creaked when he leaned back. "What did Fatima say?"

"I haven't found her yet."

He pointed. "She just walked back to her office."

"Oh!" Tami's ears, folded down, had been tuning out the office buzz. "Thanks. I'll go now."

"Wait." Axel grabbed her arm. "Are you going to quit?"

"Quit? No…" But would she? If the alternative was being second to Devin on a project she loved? She was still going to be on the project, and yes, subordinate to a guy who'd leapfrogged her, but that was okay. She was still getting to make games.

Right?

"Okay." He let her go. "I don't want you to do anything rash."

"What, like deciding on a project lead for a billion-dollar game and then changing your mind over a weekend because the person you decided on is getting married?"

Axel leaned back in his chair again and looked up at her. "Point," he said. "All right. But if you quit, I get your second monitor."

That made her laugh. "I'll bring it over myself."

She hurried through the cubicles. In the back of her head she knew that bug reports and progress reports were coming in all day and none of them had been attended to in the last half hour. She was going to have to be up late again that night to finish work—oh crap, and Ty was coming in. Oh well. Maybe she'd be out of a job and wouldn't have any work to do.

"Fatima?" Tami poked her head in the otter's office. Fatima was sitting with her feet in the pool, laptop on her lap. She turned, and Tami stepped in and swung her tail inside, then closed the door. "Can I have five minutes?"

"Oh…" The otter lifted her feet and shook them off, then pressed them down on the bath mat before setting the laptop on her desk. "Yes, of course. What's going on?"

"Mr. Francis said you changed your recommendation. He said you recommended Devin."

Fatima folded her paws in front of her. "Yes, I did."

"Why? You know I have more experience, I'm ready for the job, and I've told you a million times I wanted it."

"You're getting married," Fatima said.

"You knew I might be. I told you."

"Yes, I thought perhaps an engagement, a wedding in a year or two. But your fiancé's family wants you to marry this summer, during the critical ramping-up period—"

"They're taking care of all the details. And how did you know that? Did Devin tell you?"

"Listen." Fatima put her paws up. "I know you think you can do everything. But I have been through a wedding before. You will lose time. You will be distracted. I cannot hand over this project to someone who will not be able to give one hundred and fifty percent of their time during the first six months of the project."

"Wow." Tami shook her head. It was hard to pick out the right thing to say, the thing that matched how she felt but also didn't ruin her chances of future employment at Shirokaze. "You didn't even ask me."

"Because I know you. You believe you can do it all. I admire that. But there are times when it is not realistic."

"You're female just like me." Tami tapped her chest. "And you gave the job to a guy, because he wasn't going to have a personal life. I have news for you. Devin has a personal life."

"He won't let it affect work," Fatima shot back. "You're marrying a rich athlete, and it's an arranged marriage. There are visits to relatives, arrangements to make. You will be very busy, believe me. I am doing what is best for the company."

"If I were male—"

"If you were male, the demands of a wedding would not be as great. That is not discrimination, it is a reality of the world."

"I'll be interested to know if HR sees it the same way."

Fatima got very still and composed. "I have already spoken to HR, but if you believe you have cause, you may lodge a complaint against me. The fact is that Devin does not have nearly as many responsibilities in his personal life, and the ability to work overtime is a major consideration for this position. In addition to which you left this past weekend with very little notice to decide whether or not you were going to become engaged."

"Everything was covered. You've never had a problem with me working remotely before."

"I will continue to support you," Fatima said. "Once you are married, I'm sure your personal responsibilities will lessen."

"Oh my god. Do you hear yourself? I feel like I'm in an eighties docudrama about working females."

"I am a working female too—"

"That's what makes this so terrible!" Tami stood. "You're basically throwing me under the bus without even consulting me."

"I'm sorry you feel that way."

"And you picked Devin!"

"I know it can hurt to have someone promoted over you." Fatima's tone remained equitable. "We do hope you'll continue on in your present position on Destiny, but if you don't, I'm sure we can find another project for you to work on."

Tami left then, because she was five seconds from telling her boss to screw off, and that wasn't going to be good for her career no matter which way you looked at it.

Ignoring the weight of the reports piling up unassigned in her email box, she roamed the floor and this time found Devin at his cubicle. "Congratulations," she said without preamble.

The wolf turned in his chair and half-rose. His ears were back and he didn't meet her eyes. "Oh, hey, Tami."

"Hey," she said. "Sorry, are you busy preparing to take the title I've wanted to work on for two years?"

"You can still work on it." His ears came up about halfway.

"Jesus Fox," she said. "At least feel bad about what you did."

"Hey!" He grabbed her arm as she started to walk away. "I didn't—I didn't tell them what to do. I made my case to Fatima."

"And you told her I was getting married."

"What, you thought you could hide that?" He stood, meeting her face to face. "Would you rather lose out on Destiny now, or get taken off it halfway through because you're distracted with wedding planning?"

She shook her head. "Fuck you."

He shushed her, but already heads were turning around the cubicles. "Listen," he said, "you would have done exactly the same in my situation."

"Except for one thing." She held up a black finger. "I would've told you that I was interested in the job. I wouldn't have gone behind your back."

Devin arched his tail, and his ears came all the way up. "You knew I was interested. You think you're the only one who stayed up every night for a week playing the first one? I love that game. Look, I'm happy for you. You're getting a husband, access to a whole bunch of things. He can buy you a game studio!"

Around them, people had stopped working, unabashedly watching. "You think that makes it okay?" Tami snapped. "You can forget about championship tickets."

Around them, people had stopped working, unabashedly watching. "You think that makes it okay?" Tami snapped. "You can forget about championship tickets."

The wolf sighed. "Yeah, I expected you wouldn't be able to deal with it, but I hoped—"

"Oh, what? What did you hope? Tell me! You hoped I'd just, what, lower my ears and say, 'Gosh, Devin, I guess the better *male* won, let me work under you now'? Did you want—"

"It's not about male and female," he said, frowning. "It's about—"

"It is exactly about male and female," she snapped.

"Well, I don't see it that way."

"That's because you're male and you don't have to." Pressure built behind her eyes; she willed it back. "You don't have to watch how you say everything, you don't have to worry that if you decide to get married or have cubs or take up a hobby or just express your goddamn opinion that someone will bring your gender into it. You don't have to choose between being passed over for shit because you're passive and don't say anything, the way they want you to behave, or being passed over for shit because you speak up and you're 'shrill' and nobody likes a 'bitch.'"

His ears stayed up. "Hey," he said, "I've never judged you that way."

"No, maybe not." She drew in another breath. "You were a good friend. I thought."

He put his paws up, pads out. "Okay. You think what you need to think. But maybe you can't have everything."

She let that go because she had to walk away then. She was tired of the feeling of being brought to the brink of cursing at or punching people she'd used to consider friends. There was only really Axel left at work; everyone else she worked with had joined her team in the last couple years. Not that Gri wasn't nice, or Paul, or Hadley, or any of them, but she had only gotten to know them. She hadn't gotten to trust them yet.

CHAPTER 24

Once again she packed up to go home early. On the way home Ty called her to tell her he'd made reservations at Aquitaria, and that reminded her of the questions she had for him, too. Was anyone in her life what they appeared to be?

Settle down, she told herself. She knew Ty, maybe not as well as Devin but still well; whatever he was doing was a secret, not a betrayal. Still, she wasn't sure she was going to want to stay with him at the hotel room he'd reserved.

She called Marci for advice—about Shirokaze, not Ty—and the rat clucked in sympathy at Tami's vague description of her problem. "If you want to threaten legal action, I'll help. Honestly, you probably don't have a case, but you could probably scare them into a settlement."

Her mother said that she should suck it up, though not in those words. "People will take advantage of you all the time. Take comfort in the fact that you're a better person than they are."

Neither answer satisfied her. She didn't want to sue Shirokaze or even get a settlement from them, although the idea had a kind of vigilante justice appeal to it. Devin and Fatima were the ones who'd betrayed her, not the company, and she didn't want some legal drama to prove to them that they'd been wrong. She wanted them to acknowledge and admit that what they'd done had been wrong. And she didn't think she could continue to work with Devin even on Destiny's Angel, although she was willing to admit that that was a feeling that might not endure past the shock of betrayal. So she shelved both solutions and went off to have dinner.

Aquitaria was as lovely as she remembered, and even though she'd dressed up even more (she thought), she still felt underdressed. But Ty had dressed down, in casual pants with a shirt and tie—no jacket—and that made her feel better. It reminded her of the dinner at Jack B's, and that gave her enough warmth to smile as she hugged him.

"Nice to be here without the parents," Ty murmured as the host showed them to a small table with an elegantly simple centerpiece and a short candle that smelled miraculously of nothing, not even wax. Did Neutra-Scent make candles, Tami wondered? "You want another Negroni?"

"Um, sure." Tami wasn't sure how to bring up her questions, and a cocktail seemed like it might help.

Ty started off by telling Tami that his mother wanted her to come over sometime in the next week to review plans for the wedding, playing up his mother's enthusiasm to be more than it was, Tami was sure. It wasn't until about halfway through her Negroni that the conversation lagged, and Tami said, "I appreciate you coming back early."

"Oh, well." He flashed her a smile. "We're engaged. I'm supposed to do that." His ears folded down a bit. "I mean, when I can. It's the off-season…"

"I know." She nodded quickly. "Phone calls will be fine when you're playing." The reassertion that they were going ahead with the wedding felt like something she could cling to, a hope that whatever he was going to tell her wasn't going to be important.

"So what happened?" he asked.

"Um…I want to ask you something first."

"Sure." He perked his ears.

"Where were you last night?"

How he reacted was important too, so she watched. His ears flicked back. "I stuck around Chevali."

At least he appeared to feel guilty about lying, so that was a good sign. "Funny," she said. "I called because I forgot my toothbrush there."

The ears went down now. "You could've called me again."

"I did. You didn't answer. So I called the house, and Kellen said you'd left soon after I did." She took a breath. "He thought you were here at home with your parents. I didn't call them to ask."

"Look," he said, and she raised a paw.

"I'm tired of people telling me to 'look.' Just tell me the truth. If it's something that makes me not want to marry you, then I'd rather find out now than afterwards, when I have to do a lot of paperwork and have a lot more invested in it." The similarity to Devin's argument gave her a queasy feeling in her stomach, but she powered through it. "A lot of people have been going behind my back and lying this weekend apparently."

"Ah, jeez." He lifted his beer and sipped it. "I don't have to…" He stopped himself and his frown lifted. "I'm sorry about that. I promise, it's not anything bad."

"Then why are you hiding it?"

It took him several breaths to put the beer down with a decisive thunk. "Okay, but not here."

Tami frowned. "Why?"

"Because." He flicked his ears to the sides. "It's...not entirely mine to tell."

And there were big-eared people around, people who might hear him and write about him. Tami had forgotten about that aspect of his life, but Ty never could, and she was going to have to get used to it. "Fine," she said.

"And so it's not uncomfortable sitting through dinner waiting," he said as he reached to her paw, "why not tell me what else has been going on?"

So she spilled the story for him in low tones, not mentioning Destiny's Angel by name now that she was as aware as he was that people might be listening. He held onto her paw through all of it, and though she had been tempted to pull away at the beginning of it, by the end of the story the reassurance comforted her. He kept his ears cupped toward her through the whole story and made 'tch' noises at the appropriate times.

"So I don't know what to do. I can work on the title I've wanted to for years—reporting to the guy I have more experience than, who went behind my back to get the job. Or I can decline and work on the next shitty bubble game or something. Or..." She sighed. "I can quit."

Ty rubbed his whiskers. "How much does it cost to start a game studio?"

Tami shook her head and laughed shortly. "Devin said you could buy me one. No, it takes hundreds of millions."

"Yeah." He laughed. "Sorry. I'll work on my endorsements, but that's not something we can plan for next week. I might be able to make some calls, but..."

"No, no." She turned her paw over so she could grip his fingers. "I need to figure this out."

"I can help, though." His ears splayed in kind of a cute way as he thought. "You know...you don't have to work. All the time, I mean. I don't mean you shouldn't work at all, but if these people are being douchebags, you can walk away. Maybe we can't start a game studio, but you can find a better job and I'll support you while you wait."

She'd been thinking something very similar, and yet this option didn't feel any more right to her than her mother's or Marci's: let her husband take care of her when everything didn't go her way at work. But what else was there? Keep working, quit, or threaten to sue: those were her options. If none of them felt right, maybe there weren't any right options here. "The problem is Devin," she said, trying to articulate further. "Fatima a bit, but Devin…I really trusted him and he went behind my back. I might be being dramatic when I say I don't know if I can work with him again, but I could never trust him. Like…I would always be imagining that he'd be taking credit for my stuff or laying some blame on me."

Ty tilted his head. "I could get some guys to beat him up if you want."

She stared. He kept the mask of seriousness up for a minute longer and then dissolved into laughter. Tami laughed with him. "I won't deny it's tempting," she said, and exhaled as the coil of tension inside her unwound a little.

After that, the dinner was mostly pleasant except when she worried about what he was going to tell her. How bad could it be, though?

The hotel room was gorgeous, of course. He'd picked an old hotel whose decorations dripped with gold flourishes, from the elaborate paisley-upholstered chairs to the artfully tarnished mirror and the gold tassels on the curtain pulls. The bed, a four-poster canopy, looked soft and inviting, and Ty pointed out the box of condoms on the nightstand but insisted that they sit at the table in the living room area first.

"I'm still committed to marrying you," he started.

"That's promising," she said, even though that was the last thing she was worried about. Scenarios ran through her mind: he had another family, another girl, a gambling problem? If it was a girl, well…athletes fooled around on the road, right? It was not okay that he'd run off to her right after getting engaged, but at least they could work through it. She was pretty sure.

He took a breath. "I haven't told anyone else about this, okay? And it's taken me the whole evening to get up the nerve to sit here with you."

"All right." She folded her paws together, and then, because he'd reached out to her, she reached out and took his paw.

He squeezed her fingers back lightly. "There was this night a few months ago, Dev's boyfriend took us to this club in Yerba."

"Uh-huh." That wasn't how she'd expected this story to start.

"And there was this wolf."

So it was a girl. She tightened inside and then breathed, preparing to tell him that it was okay.

"And we danced together for a bit. Really good dancer."

She nodded. Ty took a breath. "And that weekend, I was depressed about the game. We...kinda hooked up."

"So you went back to Yerba to see her." Tami nodded. "And that's where you were that week that Morshin was talking about? I'm hurt that you went back after getting engaged. That doesn't make me feel good."

"Yeah, I get that." His ears had folded down. "I shouldn't be keeping it secret."

"I don't need you to be a hundred percent faithful," Tami said. "We haven't really talked about this. But I need you to be safe and I'd really prefer you didn't have cubs with someone else. I know with a wolf that's not an issue, but still."

"I thought you didn't want cubs."

"Not now. But you clearly do, and we haven't really talked about that either, just kind of assumed it would work out."

"I don't want them right now. I'm only twenty-two. But in four or six or eight years, yeah, I think so. I mean, you probably have a lot of Yamatese traditions in your life, right?"

"Not so many." Tami leaned on the table, her tail swaying behind her. "My mother tried, but...I was all over the place, and my brothers were a lot to manage, and Dad wasn't any help in the few years he was around, so it was all she could do to teach us some basic phrases and a few things about our grandparents."

He nodded. "We have a lot of little ritual things that I really loved and I want to do for my cubs. I want to teach them history but also about how to get along in the world. But I want them to be ours." He met her eyes. "And if you don't want to get pregnant, we'll have a surrogate or adopt or something. They'll still be *ours*."

"Would your parents agree to an adoption?"

"Sure. My Uncle Lucas isn't Yamatese but they consider him part of the family. I'm sure we could talk them into it."

His confidence reassured and settled her. "All right. And you're being safe?"

"Very."

"Then..." Tami squeezed his paw. "Just tell me about these things in the future. I know it might be weird, but I'd rather know than have to find out some other way."

"Yeah, okay." He clasped her paw between both of his. "Thanks."

"And also," she said as they got up, "remember that if you can hook up, so can I. And you can hear about that or not, as you like."

He stopped, still holding her paw. "Uh."

"It's purely theoretical now."

"I'll think about it," he promised.

"So…are you all sexed out or do you still want to use that bed?" She raised an eyebrow at him.

He tugged her toward it. "Why don't I show you?"

•

She woke in near-darkness and the warmth of Ty's company that she was becoming very familiar with. He didn't stir when she rested a paw on his arm, feeling the fur and the muscle that had been wrapped around her the night before.

There had been a dream or something that had woken her, but it was gone already. Still, she slid out from under the covers and went to stand by the window.

Dawn whispered in pink tendrils through the Pelagia skyline. Tami watched long enough that the pink crept up the sides of the buildings and glowed against the clouds. A light rain pattered against the window; another beautiful day in Pelagia.

There were nicer places to live: the desert in Chevali had been beautiful, unsarcastically beautiful. But she had family here and the job scene was good here for a video game project manager, so she put up with the rain.

Family; job. Could she have it all, as Devin had accused her of wanting? If she broke off the marriage to Ty, would Fatima reconsider? Would Tami even want her to?

Her tail swished. And if she quit the job, let Ty support her for a while, how long would it take her to find her dream job? Would she get complacent when she didn't have to worry about her bank account?

So many questions, so many uncertainties. If her life were a project, she would be calling them 'risk factors' and trying to figure out how she'd gone from green to yellow so fast.

The sure thing, the safe thing, would be to work for Destiny's Angel under Devin and marry Ty. If she did her job, she'd get paid, and now that she knew she couldn't trust Devin, she could work around him. And Ty had his secret girl in Yerba, but that was over, or maybe it wasn't. He actually hadn't said it was over, hadn't said it was just a hookup. And there had to be a reason he'd been secretive about it, even from his friends.

So maybe she had to look at what her life-project goals were. Financial security? Destiny's Angel? Something else, something less tangible?

Yellow and orange had joined pink behind the buildings. She rested her nose against the glass, her breath fogging it, and watched the sun come up.

A short time later, her ears flicked back at the sound of movement in the bed, and Ty's sleepy voice rumbled across the room. "Morning, gorgeous."

Her tail swished at the compliment and her heart tightened. "Hi."

"Thinking about your job?"

"Thinking about a lot of things."

He was quiet, and then he patted the bed. "Come tell me about it?"

She wavered then. He was a good guy, and maybe she was making more out of this than it merited. But she'd thought Devin was a good guy, too.

So she sat on the edge of the bed. "I think I'm going to quit Shirokaze. Not right away, but I'm going to turn down the job on Destiny's Angel and I'm going to look for something else while I finish up the bubble game."

He opened his mouth and closed it again. She could see him figuring out what that meant. "Tami…"

"I don't think I can marry you." She hurried the words so she wouldn't be tempted by his flat ears and hurt eyes to take them back. "Not this summer."

"I thought we worked that out," he said softly.

"First, there's the cub thing. You definitely want them, and I'm not sure, and you act like you can just throw money at the problem. I appreciate not having to go through a pregnancy, but even if we adopt or use a surrogate and then hire someone to look after the cub and raise him or her—I'm still a mom. That's a responsibility, and I need to think about it. But I'd want to do it with someone I trust, and…"

"You can trust me," he said quickly, and in that moment she had no doubt that he meant it. But still.

"You met this wolf in Yerba during the season sometime. Then you went back after the season. Then you went back again the day after I accepted your proposal, the day you should've been thinking about our engagement. You haven't told your friends about her. That's not just a hookup. That's—there's something else there." She didn't want to follow these logical steps, didn't want them to be true. She liked Ty, dammit, and she felt like the heroine in one of those dumb romantic comedies Marci used to drag her to. But if that were true, then this would be the middle of the film, an obstacle, and Ty would come back with an explanation that made all the sense in the world and she would feel a rush of relief and everything would be all right.

"But I left early when you needed me. I came right back."

"And what if she needs you? Will you rush off to Yerba sometime? I know we were looking at this like a business arrangement, but we're going to be married. We need to be able to depend on each other."

"That won't happen." His voice lowered, rougher now. "Rushing off to Yerba."

"But how can I be sure of it?"

"It's over."

Her ears flattened. "It's over, but you 'left early' to come see me?" She shook her head. "I'm sorry, but I'm really hurt right now and I can't—I can't." She caught her voice when it threatened to break. Of course this wasn't a dumb movie and he really did love someone else and she was surprised at how much that hurt. He wasn't ever going to be exclusively hers, but the cheating was supposed to be all physical, and here she was down to maybe one or two friends she could really rely on and she couldn't, just couldn't bring herself to marry someone she couldn't trust.

He reached out for her paw, and she let him take it. "What can I do?"

At least that was the right question. "Nothing," she said, and then swallowed. "I don't know. If you want to—if you want to keep dating for a year or so, have a proper long engagement so we can get to know each other, then maybe…if we both still want it…"

The room fell silent and stayed that way. She knew that his parents wanted a marriage settled quickly and would likely not go for a year-long engagement with an 'if' at the end of it. She wasn't sure she would, either, but he was right here and she couldn't leave him with no hope.

"I…" She leaned over and kissed his nose.

He pulled her in and kissed her properly, and she let herself enjoy it, kissed him back, and then she sat back and released his paw. "I should go," she whispered.

Ty sat up in bed and watched her get dressed. "I'll stay in touch," he said.

She managed a smile and raised a paw, and left the hotel room.

PART 3: Ty

CHAPTER 25

The first thing he did was call Kellen and yell at him. It was seven in the morning, so the swift fox was barely awake for Ty's rant. "Whoa, what's going on?" he said the second time Ty took a breath. "I do have your back. What are you talking about?"

"Fucking hell," Ty snarled. "Just get out. You don't live there anymore."

"What? Are you serious?"

"You said something to Tami and now she doesn't want to get married."

"What? What did I say? I swear, I had no idea. Come on, fox, don't—I'll apologize to her, whatever it was. What did I say?"

If he told Kellen, he'd have to confess that he'd lied about where he'd been, and would then have to confess where he had been. And it wasn't Kellen's fault. It was his. So he hung up the phone.

The hotel had a breakfast, but although Ty was hungry, he didn't do more than pick at it. His anger kept bouncing off people, at Kellen, at Tami, at himself, at Arch, at his parents. He didn't get angry often; he'd been angry in college when he'd been demoted from a starting spot for a game because he'd been late to a practice, and when one jaguar he'd slept with didn't want to sleep with him again. Stuff like that. He'd gotten over it quickly, of course: he got his starting spot back and scored three touchdowns, he met another girl and slept with her.

But here he was the problem, he was the one who had fucked it up. And sometimes he could see that, sometimes it was crystal clear, and then it would slip away.

"Tami doesn't want to get married right away," he told his mother when he went home the next morning, sitting at the counter in the kitchen where he'd eaten so many bowls of cereal before school. She sat on the stool next to his with a glass of orange juice, another morning ritual (she had offered him one and he'd refused, feeling more in a Bloody Mary mood).

"Fine," she said. "Who was number two on your list?"

"She thought we might date for a while." His ears stayed flat when he said it, knowing what her answer would be.

Her voice sharpened. "Date for a while? What more is there to find out?"

"I don't know." If he knew what he could do, there wouldn't be a problem. "I think it was too fast for her, that's all."

His mother clicked her teeth together the way she did when she was displeased. "This is what happens when you go outside of my recommendations. I warned you about her. So what, we wait on her pleasure now? None of the families I chose for you would allow their daughter such liberties. What if you date for another month and then she says no?"

"She was thinking more like a year," Ty said.

"Ha." His mother took a drink of her juice, shook her head, and the last fading hope that things would go ahead with Tami ended with the clink of glass on the table. "I will contact Hideyo's parents and express our interest in moving ahead with the marriage to her."

That tone held a familiar finality. Ty had to fight his instincts so he could keep talking. "But Mom. I want to try…" Try what?

"There are many vixens who want to marry you, why should you chase one who doesn't?"

Why indeed? Why for that matter should he be still thinking about a gay wolf in Yerba, too? He barely knew either of them, had only known Tami for a couple months and Arch a few before that, and what was his philosophy? Easy come, easy go. So they'd come, and now they were gone.

His phone rang, and it was Kimi's cell. Probably the otter wanted to know what the hell was going on. "Yeah," he said, hitting Ignore, "join the club."

"What?" His mother was already looking up a number on her phone.

"Nothing," Ty said, getting up. "I'm going back to the hotel."

That stopped his mother. "Don't be silly," she said. "You have a room here."

"Yeah," Ty said, "but you guys are going to be planning and I don't want to get in your way."

She followed him to the front door, but after he'd closed it behind him, he realized he couldn't remember a single thing she'd said.

•

The problem with Pelagia was that he didn't know anyone here anymore who wasn't family, only a couple guys who'd been friends in high school like five years ago. Nobody he could talk to, nobody even he could go out and get drunk with. He knew a couple guys on the Manticores who'd been at the rookie symposium with him; they'd gotten drinks together but it was in a group of twenty people. Worth a call anyway maybe. Later.

The bar opened at eleven. He extended his stay for one more night and then ordered lunch and the Bloody Mary he'd been craving.

His phone rang a few more times that day, twice from Kimi and once from his parents. He ignored all of them. The news repeated itself every half hour, the same headlines and commentary over and over again, until around 2:30 when two of the TVs switched to a basketball game on the east coast, and Ty lost himself in that. What he wouldn't give, he thought, to have a game coming up on Sunday, to have a defense to prepare for and coaches to tell him where to run and what to look for.

At six a female fennec fox came on duty at the bar, with a name tag that read "Leah." She sniffed at his glass. "Goose Island?"

Ty nodded; he'd switched to beer after lunch, nursing them so he didn't get too drunk. "Keep 'em coming," he said.

"Yes, sir."

She brought him a full glass, then came back to bring him another an hour later. "What do you think about the Keystones this year?" she asked, nodding up at the TV.

"Terrible. You from there?"

"Went to college there. My family's from central Goldenwater and I was sick of the desert."

He nodded. "I grew up here but I live in a desert now. I like it. Wish I was back there."

"What are you doing here? Family?"

"Yeah." He drained the first glass and slid it to her, picking up the full one. "Mom's arranging a marriage for me."

She stopped halfway to the sink. "Seriously? Are you Bharatan?"

"Yamatese."

Her whiskers and nose twitched. "Huh. Wouldn't have guessed."

"Not native born. Second generation. Grew up here, like I said."

"No, I mean…" She nodded at him. "Not too many Yamatese foxes built like basketball players."

He'd been ignoring the signs of interest, but at that point his ears perked up. "Football, actually."

"Oh?" She smiled. "Professional?"

"Chevali."

"Right, you said desert."

Ty sipped a little more beer and smiled. "So is your name pronounced 'Lee' or 'Lee-uh'?"

Her shift was over at two a.m. For the next eight hours, she chatted with Ty at the bar when she could, and he watched basketball when she couldn't, until about eleven when the games ended and he watched sports recaps.

And at two a.m. Leah came with him back up to his room, cleaned of all Tami's scent. He already had the condoms.

The sex was good in a physical sense, and Leah enjoyed herself. But while she was cleaning up in the bathroom, all Ty could think about was that this was the first person he'd fucked in weeks—months—who wasn't Tami or Arch. That should make him feel good, or liberated. But it just felt weird.

"Hey," Leah said, pulling her shirt on over a pair of nice breasts, "it was really nice to meet you. How long are you at the hotel?"

Ty sat up in bed and leaned against the headboard. "Probably going home tomorrow."

"Home Chevali or home family?" She held up his tail brush. "Mind?"

He waved permission. "Uh…good question. Probably home family for a bit and then Chevali."

"All right, well. I'll keep an eye out for you on the field in the fall. Number 88, right?" She swept the brush through her tail a few times and then set it back on the bathroom counter.

"Yep." He managed a smile and waved as she let herself out. And the thing was, he didn't even want her to stay.

And then he fell back on the bed and exhaled. So this was his life now, back to random hookups until his mother married him to Hideyo and he had to have sex with her enough times to have cubs. Random hookups on the road if he felt like it, nobody he was going to want to curl up with for the night.

"Aaaaargh," he groaned. Feelings were stupid and he hated having them. He'd just picked up a bartender and fucked her, easy as that. And she'd been cute, too; there'd been two other guys hitting on her at the bar. Tami wanting to know where he'd been and picking the one thing he wasn't ready to tell her about yet; Arch telling him how his engagement was going to change him, all of it was confusing and frustrating. Why hadn't there been a rookie symposium on dealing with girlfriends? Apart from the one that warned them to carry condoms all the time and not to fuck random girls while drunk (one for two on that one tonight, though he hadn't really been more than buzzed anytime the whole day).

Maybe he should look up a gay club, try to pick up a guy. Even as he thought it, though, he knew that while he would happily get off with a guy, it wouldn't be any more satisfying than the sex he'd just had. And even his cock wasn't jumping at the idea (give it a few minutes, though, and it probably would). Besides, if he got spotted with a female, it would be unremarkable, barely even news. If he got spotted with a guy…or, worse, if the guy went to social media with his story…

Arch had said that a couple times, assured Ty he wasn't going to publish the photos on his blog or anything like that. Come to think of it, Ty hadn't actually looked up Arch's blog. The wolf had said it wasn't anything special and didn't get updated often, but Ty had thought he might like to read it. Now, of course, there'd be no point.

He hadn't even expected Arch to text him again, the way he'd left things last time in Yerba. Walking out of a hotel room too, the same way Tami had. But then Arch had sent him a photo of a paw wrapped around his cock and the message, "Miss you," and Ty had sent back a message saying, "What part of you misses me again?" and had gotten back a photo slightly out of focus that Arch had clearly taken by reaching his little flip phone under his tail. So he'd said he could swing by Yerba on the way home, and he'd gotten a hotel room, but while they were at dinner, Tami had called with her emergency.

So Ty'd told Arch he was going to have to go, and they'd argued about that a little, but it wasn't really a full argument because Arch knew how it was going to be. And they'd had sex, and it was good, but again it was a little sad and neither of them had said much. Afterwards Ty had reached out to hold Arch and the wolf had snuggled against him and said, "I'm sorry I sent that picture."

"Don't be," Ty had said.

"I won't do it again."

And Ty didn't have any response to that except to hold the wolf more tightly amid the smell of wolf and fox and sex.

When he'd left that morning, Arch had said, "Bye. It was fun," and Ty had nodded and waved, knowing what he meant. He'd spent the plane flight angry that he'd had to say good-bye but knowing that it had to be that way. At least, he'd told himself, he was going to be able to marry Tami.

In the morning, with Leah's scent still in the sheets, Ty showered and left the hotel. Staying with his parents was not going to be productive or enjoyable, so he went home, packed his things, and told them he was returning to Chevali. "Let me know when the wedding is," he told his mother. "I've got to get back to working out."

There was that wide receiver camp in Taysha somewhere that Ford had invited him to, a workout class for a bunch of wide receivers. It didn't start for another two weeks, so he called and asked if the invitation was still good and Ford said of course it was, so Ty booked his tickets then and there. Throwing himself into football, that was the answer. That was something he could still control.

CHAPTER 26

When he got to the house in Chevali, Kimi met him at the door. "What the hell is going on?" he said. "Kellen's half packed even though I keep telling him he doesn't really have to move out, and you won't say more than your flight times when you call."

"I told you Kellen doesn't have to move out." Ty hefted his bags, and Kimi didn't offer to help. The otter bounced alongside him, not missing a beat.

"I told him that but he wants to hear it from you. So go in and tell him and then tell us what's going on."

Ty sighed. Even in March the sun beat down on him here and it was a relief to get into the cool tile floor and plaster walls of the house. "Tami broke off the engagement," he said.

"Kellen said something about that but I thought it was just an argument. You two seemed so great together." Kimi fidgeted for a moment, rocking back on his thick tail, and then said, "I'll go get Kellen."

The swift fox came down the stairs with his ears flat and tail wrapped tightly around his hips. "Hey," he said.

"You don't have to move out," Ty said. "Sorry I said that. I was mad. Tami broke it off."

Kellen's ears came up and his eyes widened. "Shit, dude. I thought it was just—"

"It's fine." Ty waved a paw. "Easy come, easy go, right?"

Even to him, the words sounded hollow. Kellen's ears flattened. "What did I say? Shit, was it because I got you guys drunk?"

"You didn't get us drunk. And no, it wasn't something you said." The half-lie was easy to tell because of the truth behind it. "It's just—girls, you know?"

Kellen's eyes narrowed. "She didn't seem like one of those 'girls' though. You sure you're okay?"

"I'm fine," Ty said. "I'm gonna go to my room now, if that's okay?"

"Yeah. Sure. Uh…wanna go out later?"

"Maybe." He absolutely did not want to hang out with people, or go to a bar, or pick up another girl somewhere. Not tonight.

Nor did he want to do it for any of the other nine nights he was at the house, though he did go out once when Kimi pestered him into it. He didn't get drunk because he was afraid he might yell at Kellen again, or talk about something he didn't want to talk about, and the others let him nurse his single drink quietly. He ached to get back to football now, to be running a route and waiting for that ball to drop into his paws so he could take it to the house, because the ball couldn't stop you halfway down the field and tell you to put it down because it didn't trust you.

His withdrawal became an accepted norm in the house until he left for the camp. His mother called to tell him that Hideyo's family had accepted an offer to marry, and it took him a moment to remember who Hideyo was. "The short one," his mother said. "Who was going to college? Your father was quite taken with her."

Then he remembered. Well, good. She could help run Mom's foundation and Ty wouldn't have to do anything except produce some cubs. "Sounds great," he said. "Let's throw a party."

He didn't tell his friends about his new engagement—or impending engagement, he wasn't sure at this point. But when he checked his email for instructions about getting to the wide receivers' camp, he found an email from his uncle Lucas:

None of my biz, I know, but what happened with Tami? I wanted to grab dinner with you but you took off before I had a chance, and your mom doesn't know or isn't saying. Give me a call when you get a chance.

Lucas would be good to talk to, but Ty kept coming up against the wall of telling people about Arch. So he sent back a quick note saying he was really busy with football right now but he'd try to call when he got back.

Lucas didn't reply, and a day later Ty flew off to Taysha to meet up with Ford.

CHAPTER 27

Ford Vavilov wasn't running the wide receivers camp, but he was friends with Mustafa Ayyam, the Hall of Fame red fox wideout who'd founded it, and he'd gone every year for the last five. It was Ty's first year and he had no idea what to expect other than a bunch of wide receivers, mostly foxes.

Ayyam had rented out a gorgeous workout facility and had brought a couple former coaches from around the league. Twelve red foxes, one fennec, and seven non-foxes came to the introductory meeting in a large classroom like the ones Ty had his position meetings in, only much cleaner smelling. Neutra-Scent had partly sponsored this camp because it was founded by a fox, and one of the things Ayyam told them was that if there were any unpleasant smells anywhere, they could notify one of the staff and it would be taken care of. "Not like when you're playing," he laughed, and told them about one year when he roomed with a bear who farted constantly. When he'd got them laughing at that, Ayyam introduced the coaching staff and laid out what the next two weeks were going to entail.

Sitting next to Ford, Ty listened to most of it, though he figured someone would be telling him where to go and what to do as the days went on. They were all there to get in shape and get better at their jobs, but also to meet each other and network. Even though he was the only Firebird there, there was a pretty good chance that he'd end up being teammates with one of the other guys before his career was over.

So after the meeting, they all went out to the field, which smelled of clean grass and wafts of ammonia from the sparkling bleachers around the track. There were fewer seats at this track than anywhere Ty'd worked out since high school, and when he commented on that, Ford said, "Yeah, there are two high schools that share this field in the fall. Usually around the end of the camp he brings the cubs out to meet us and do a few workouts."

Two tables held nutrition bars and energy drinks, to which they were encouraged to help themselves. One in each paw, Ty walked around and introduced himself to everyone.

The reception lifted his spirits. Most of the guys knew him, and if they didn't recognize him right away, they knew him as soon as he said his name. "Ah, you guys played a great championship," a red fox from the Tornadoes told him, one of the few there Ty didn't recognize. And a coyote from the Fraters named Jeff said, "Loved that touchdown you caught in the semis."

"You were great in your game, too," Ty said. "And in the championship last year. Maybe you can teach me that jiggle-step you used to break that run in the third."

Jeff's ears flicked back, pleased. "Glad to. You got a trick for learning routes? Still gives me problems when we have a lot of them."

"We'll talk."

That kind of conversation repeated itself with variations throughout the afternoon. Jeff was the friendliest; a lot of the others followed up with things like, "Yeah, but did you see me against the Manticores? Double juke, the corner bit, and even though Kendrick underthrew the ball I got to it and almost scored."

Ty got caught up in that a little, too. It was the wide receiver mindset: you always have to be pointing out how great you are because you're not going to get the ball all the time like the quarterback. Maybe they don't throw to you so much in one game, your stats look bad, people start to think maybe you're not worth all that money. So you have to say shit like, "I can't score unless you get me the ball," and then people talk about how you have this me-first mentality.

The thing Ty got drilled into him in college was that when the ball isn't coming to you, you do three things: One, you act like it is. Defenses can tell when you're slacking off. Two, you block for the guy who's getting it. Because when you get it next play, or the one after, you want him blocking for you. And three, you keep alert and if the play stretches out, you get yourself open so your QB can dump it to you if he's in trouble. Don't slack off, support your brothers, support your QB. Do those things, his college coach had told him, and you'll have a long career in the UFL.

But you can't brag about blocking for another guy's spectacular catch, or about keeping the safety occupied so the left side of the field was free. You can't brag about being a safety valve on a busted play unless you actually get the ball and do something with it. You've got to bust open the big plays to earn the big bucks. That was something Ford had taught him, and the guys in the camp were basically measuring their dicks against each other by going over their best plays.

Ty was lucky; a touchdown in the playoffs his rookie year was a pretty good card to hold. But one or two of the guys remembered his last play, the one where he couldn't get a return through, and they brought it up. "Don't feel bad," a meerkat named Hasan told him. "Kickoff returns for scores are like one in five hundred."

The point was for them to bring it up, to remind him that along with his success had been a failure. The flip side of being a wide receiver was that your failures were rarely as big as your successes. You dropped a pass? Fine, as long as it wasn't in the end zone. Misran a route? Probably didn't even get the ball, and you could blame that on the quarterback. Ty had had his paws on the ball in the last seconds of a championship game with the world watching.

But this camp wasn't about making big plays. This camp was about being in shape, about fundamentals, about route running and blocking and all the things you were supposed to have a handle on by the time you got to training camp. And even the guys who were dicks were pretty cool once you got down to the workouts. There it was all about how you did, and you could measure times, measure weights, look for precision in your foot placement.

Arch would like hearing about all the buff guys in the skintight workout clothes, Ty thought one night, and Tami might too. Tami would also like the benchmarks in the workouts and the way they measured progression and success, the way they were being taught to work together as a team. Arch would make some comment about Ty's work being a lot more fun than his, and Tami might too, or more likely she would ask him how it was going, how he was getting better, not because it meant a bigger house or car for her but because she wanted him to be the best.

He didn't dwell on these thoughts, nor did he check his email or pick up his phone. They intruded nonetheless, especially at the one part of the camp Ty didn't do particularly well at: the evening socializing. It was supposed to be a time for guys to bond and get to know each other better, and what most of these guys wanted to talk about was all the sex they'd had. This horse and that bunny and that vixen, and Ty found himself starting to correct Hasan, who was the one talking about vixens. They want to be called foxes, he thought, and stopped himself before he could say it. Hasan was going on about her tits and how hot she'd been for his cock and it was clearly not a politically sensitive moment.

The one saving grace was that in this group of prima donnas, you had to force your way in to tell a story, and if you didn't, nobody really noticed. Ty had a couple—the waitress at the strip club, the bartender at the hotel, the mink at the party—and he tossed them into the mix in an offhanded way, because there wasn't much interesting to him. He'd been horny, the girl had been there, they'd fucked. The other guys there kept recounting details of the encounter even when they were clearly exaggerated ("I fucked her twice and then I fucked her friend in the ass while she watched and then she wanted my dirty dick again so we went one more time"—Ty's record was three times in one night, and that was in college when he basically walked around with a perpetual erection and came at the slightest touch).

But the other guys liked hearing that the waitress had sucked off Zillo before fucking him, and that he'd shared the mink with his friends, so he played up those parts. They were pretty baller, after all. Some of their stories were as good or better, and a few of them involved illegal drugs (worse than pot), which Ty knew better than to get involved in, though the element of danger made the stories pretty cool.

Jeff, the coyote, was married, and Ty did manage to corner him one night in the training room as they were both stretching to cool down. Ty knew a few coyotes, but Jeff was the suavest, most self-possessed one he'd ever met. Most of them were more like Zillo, always twitching to look behind them, or else they swaggered around with chips the size of a stadium on their shoulder like Gerrard, constantly proving to someone invisible that he was the best at football.

But Jeff had gotten past all that. At thirty, he was here to keep his body and mind sharp, he said. He'd talked about missing his wife, so that night as they loosened their muscles on the machines in the training room, Ty asked him about her.

"Ah, she's great," Jeff said. "Takes care of the cubs and the house and she manages my charities, too."

"So I gotta ask…do you fuck around? During the season, you know, on the road or whatever?"

The coyote paused. He gave Ty a look. "I ain't gay."

"Hey," Ty said, "don't flatter yourself. I want to know 'cause I had an engagement broken off."

Jeff's ears went up. "Shit, dude. But if it was 'cause you were fuckin' around on the side, you're better off not marrying her. Any wife expects her pro athlete husband to be faithful is an idiot and your cubs'll turn out to be retarded or something."

He laughed, and Ty laughed politely even though it wasn't very funny. "So your wife knows about you sleeping around?"

"I mean, we ain't talked about it or nothin'. But she told me once 'don't go having cubs with any other bitch out there,' so I feel like anything else is A-OK. Anyway, I'm pretty sure she's fucking the neighbor. He's a jackal, in investments or some shit, 'works' at home. It's cool, yanno, I'm gone months outta the year, can't always be there to keep her wet and happy, so as long as she doesn't catch some disease or get pregnant or something…" He shrugged. "Whatever."

"Yeah, that's what—that's what my ex said." It actually hurt to call her his ex, because the term felt so final, like she'd been excised from his life.

"Dames." Jeff rolled his eyes and laid his ears back as he reconfigured the machine to work his hamstrings and reclined on it, one leg going up almost perpendicular to the other. "They change their mind a lot too. Get used to that. Go get yourself another one and don't be a fuckin' pussy about it."

"So if your wife left you, you wouldn't be upset?"

"Sure I'd be upset. Divorce, custody, that shit's expensive and a hassle." He grinned at Ty. "Oh, what, you want me to say I'd miss her? Hell yeah I'd miss her. She's a sweetheart and I'm gonna take her around the world when I retire. I could find someone else to shack up with but it'd take time to get used to her and to get her used to me and that'd be a pain in the ass. But that's the thing. There's always someone else. So get over your ex and get on with your fuckin' life."

"My mom's picked out another fiancée for me already," Ty said, switching from chest to back stretches.

"So what are you complaining about?"

Good question, Ty thought, but outwardly he laughed. "You're right. It's hard being the one to get dumped, that's all. Like she's going to find someone better?"

"Ha, yeah." Jeff shook his head. "I get you, it stings, but you gotta put it behind you and move on to the next one. Sometimes, you know, it's not your fault when you miss one. Could've been a great play and you did everything right but it was just a bad throw."

If only. That was one thing Ty loved about football, that most successful football players he knew loved about football: that as long as you could play, there was always another game, always another pass. You could wipe out your mistakes and start again. There were exceptions, sure: one Freestones cornerback had blown his coverage and given up a touchdown to the hated rival Devils, and he'd been let go at the end of the season. But even he had kicked around the league for a couple more years.

And the flip side of that was the specter that shadowed them all: what if this was the last pass, the last play, the last game? Some players got to leave on their own terms; many left when the work offers dried up. You'd see them around training camps, the guys in their mid-thirties with the hunger in their eyes the only thing remaining from their heyday. They were a step slower and always seemed to be fighting through an injury.

Ty wasn't close to that point, but there was a very real possibility that he wouldn't get back to another championship game. So in a sense, that last play of the championship might have been his last. That was something he had only a limited amount of control over. Look at Lightning Strike. Dude was ridiculously talented and he'd only been to two championship games in his career. Lost them both. If one guy could make a difference, that guy would have three or four rings by now.

Relationships, to the extent Ty had thought about them in college, had been a lot like that. You hooked up, it went well or not, you moved on. Sometimes if things worked out you hooked up with the same girl a couple times, but it was always low-stakes, easy. There was another one coming next day or next week.

He'd thought Arch was that way too: an experiment, a guy he loved to dance with who made him feel good in bed. But when Arch had texted him, he'd been so happy that the wolf missed him that he'd jumped at the chance for one more time.

And he'd blown that in trying to be a good fiancé to Tami, but it turned out he'd blown that one too. And now he felt like he had after the championship game, sitting among a bunch of people telling him it was just another game, that he'd have another chance, and in football that was true. In life…games weren't scheduled, practices weren't watched.

So Ty would have to live with three fumbles now rather than just one. But a good wideout had to be able to do that. All the guys around him who were successful had done that. And as he immersed himself in this world, it became easier and easier to leave those fumbles behind. There'd be another chance or there wouldn't; he couldn't control that. What he could do was make the best of those chances when they came around.

•

For the rest of the camp, he relegated his love life to the same part of his mind as the championship game, and he finished the two weeks feeling more positive about himself than he had since Tami had liked his bacon. There were some little competitions, because of course twenty guys playing one of the most competitive positions in the most competitive professional sport would want to compete. He was the fastest of the twenty, though not with the handicap they'd made him take because he was also the youngest. In the catching competition he'd come in ninth, which he would have to work on, but in route running he'd been judged seventh, ahead of a bunch of guys who'd been in the league longer, which made him proud. The only competition in which he'd finished in the bottom half of the participants had been the obstacle course, and he didn't care so much about that.

As much fun as the competitions were the evenings after, ribbing each other over light beers. Spending a couple weeks with a bunch of guys really did bring them closer together, and Ty got a lot of tips on football life from them, everything from how to sneak out of (or into) your hotel late at night to what brand of anti-fungal spray to use on your feet after showering.

And for the first time, he was excited about the coming season, which was a nice change. He should get in touch with some of his teammates, start reconnecting and working out with them. Hadn't Dev said something about Gerrard doing workouts?

It had been such a nice two weeks that he didn't really want to open his email, but he had to do it sooner or later, so he checked in from the hotel on the last night of his stay. Ford and one of his current teammates were also staying and had invited Ty to dinner and dancing at the hotel's rooftop club, but before he did that he went to the hotel's business center and logged in.

There was an email from his mother asking him to call her, and then another email saying that she knew he'd told her to contact him via email only but she'd left him a voicemail and could he listen to it, and finally a third email telling him that because he hadn't gotten back to her she'd assumed he would be free this coming weekend and had scheduled the engagement party he'd requested for him and Hideyo at the Plaza Hotel in Bellefort Beach, a suburb near their house with a large Yamatese population.

That he'd requested? He couldn't remember saying anything about that, but fine, whatever. It would be great.

She'd attached all kinds of details about what he would have to wear, and that if he didn't want to get a tuxedo himself he could send her his measurements, and that maybe it was better for him to do that anyway so she could match the colors to the decorations.

He should have been excited about the ritual. His parents had told the stories of their courtship and engagement enough times, and Ty had always thought, someday that'll be me with my future wife. Now he was being pushed into this ritual and he felt like the time when he was nine and he'd found the store where they sold his birthday tea. He'd made himself a cup in secret and drank it, but rather than feeling that birthday happiness, he'd been acutely aware that he was doing this at the wrong time.

He read through the instructions again and felt like his mother was dressing him for his high school prom. Tami would have enjoyed that comparison, would have made fun of it too even as she bemoaned having to be part of it. And Arch, like Ty, would have been frustrated at the pageantry of it all. He would've mocked the habits of rich people.

But he didn't have them to talk to. So he wrote his mom saying he'd be there, and then he went out with Ford and the other guy, also a red fox, and he told them about his engagement party.

"Yeah," Ford said, "but fortunately you only need to go through that shit once."

The other fox, whose name was Lagape and who was in his late twenties, agreed. "I got photographed with this vixen a couple years into my marriage. My wife was gonna leave me until I bought her a new car."

"Oh yeah." Ford lifted a beer. "New car is way cheaper than getting married again."

Which made sense to Ty. And these guys had a pretty good life, it sounded like. They both enjoyed the time they spent with their wives as long as there wasn't too much, and they both had the freedom to do what they wanted on the road as long as they were discreet. In Lagape's case, it sounded more like "what she doesn't find out won't hurt me."

That sounded a lot easier to him than worrying about the right thing to say all the time. So that'd be his life: exactly like it was now, only with someone else to handle his charity work and his parents and, eventually, his family.

CHAPTER 28

His family had decorated the Plaza for his engagement party with traditional paper lanterns and crepe streamers in burgundy and white. "They are April's colors," his mother explained when she presented him with his tuxedo, white with a burgundy tie and cummerbund. "For the wedding we will use red and white," of course.

Fragrant cherry blossom branches adorned each of the high tables; this was to be a cocktail hour rather than a formal dinner, though there was a dinner in the banquet afterwards. "How much is this all costing me?" Ty grumbled good-naturedly to his mother.

"It was your idea," she said, "and Hideyo's parents are paying for most of it. Some of it. The cherry blossoms bring luck. Your father and I were engaged in a cherry orchard, but that one was torn down and the closest one is two hours away. You can't expect your grandmother to drive two hours to your engagement party."

"Wasn't my idea," he said, but he let it go.

At least there were drinks at the party. He wished Kellen were here to keep him from drinking too much. Then he spotted a tall fox looking very handsome in a grey and burgundy (or maybe cherry) suit, and made his way over to his uncle.

Lucas beamed as Ty approached him. "Hey, nephew. Congratulations!"

"Thanks." Ty flashed a tight smile. "Hey, can I ask you a favor? Can you, uh, keep an eye on my drinks and help me stick to one an hour?"

"Sure. But hey, it's a happy occasion. I'm sure people will forgive a little tipsiness from the prospective groom."

"Right. So how are you doing?"

His uncle's ears perked up. "Don't be so gloomy. Marriage isn't all bad."

"How would you know?"

The other fox laughed. "I talk to people. Besides, if you're home as much as you were this last year, you'll barely have to deal with her at all. So what happened with Tami?"

Ty scanned the room and found his parents. "Ah, it didn't work out. Easy come, easy go. Hey, I'd better go see where I have to stand and if I have to say anything."

"Don't you have to propose?"

"Dunno." He shrugged. "I'll go find out."

So he crossed the room, slower than he would have liked as his parents' friends all wanted to stop him and congratulate him, and the people he didn't know (Hideyo's parents' friends, he assumed) wanted to meet him. By the time he'd navigated the tables, the scent of cherry blossom throbbed like a headache in his nose.

"We're all foxes," he said to his father. "Why did we get smelly flowers?"

"Not everyone here is a fox." His father reached up to straighten Ty's bowtie.

The bowtie was fine, but his father had to feel like he was doing something, so Ty stood still for it. "What do I have to do?"

His father checked his watch. "In forty-two minutes, we'll all stand here." Next to them was a small temporary stage that hardly seemed large enough for three people, let alone six. Two hotel employees were arranging a large white lattice and weaving cherry blossoms through it under the direction of his mother. Ty could already smell them.

"Ugh," he said. "What do I have to say?"

His father seemed surprised. "Nothing. Didn't your mother tell you?"

"I told him," his mother said without turning around. "He listened like he always does."

"Anyway," his father said, "this was your idea, Ty."

Ty rolled his eyes and walked away. "I'm going to get some fresh air," he said. "I'll be back here in forty-two minutes."

"Forty-one," his father said.

His mother hurried after him. "You're not leaving this room, are you?"

"That's what 'fresh air' means."

"It's raining outside. You'll ruin your clothes. And besides, you have to greet all the people who came to see your engagement."

"None of them are my friends. They're all yours. You greet them."

His mother's ears swept back. "If you'd invited your friends, maybe they would be here."

"If I'd known about it…" Ty felt the argument curling back around on itself. "Fine," he said, "I'll go be sociable."

"I don't know why you're in such a bad mood," his mother called after him. "You're getting engaged to a lovely vixen and you don't have to go on any more of those dinners."

That was a fair point, all things considered, but Ty thought he would appreciate it a lot more with one more drink.

As the cheetah bartender was making him a mojito and Ty was trying to figure out why his cologne smelled familiar, Lucas appeared at his elbow. "This is your last drink until after the ceremony."

"I'm fine," Ty said, "but thanks."

The older fox leaned on the bar and smiled. "Just looking out for my favorite nephew. I'll have a mojito too, when you're done," he told the bartender.

Ty snorted. "I have to go 'be sociable.' Which means talking to a bunch of bankers about whether I think the Manticores can win the championship next year."

"They want inside information. Anyway, they're not all bankers. Some of them are investment consultation professionals."

His uncle grinned, and Ty felt an answering smile creep across his muzzle. "Those guys are even worse."

"Sure, but are they worse than Nolan Jenkins?"

"Oh my god." Ty accepted the mojito the bartender slid across to him and stepped back to allow his uncle to take his spot while his was being made. "Jenkins tackled me once and it was over. It didn't go on and on for forty minutes."

"Tell you what," Lucas said, "I'll walk around with you. You can tell me about the football camp, and I'll help lubricate your conversation."

"This is already doing a great job of that." Ty sipped the mojito.

"Then tip." Lucas indicated the small glass with a few bills in it. "If Joel here did a good job, show your appreciation."

"I don't have my wallet in these pants." Ty's ears flushed warm and he set them down. "It's in my hotel room."

"Cubs," Lucas said to the bartender, fishing his own wallet out of a pocket. "You can give them all the money, but you still have to teach 'em how to use it. There." He dropped a bill into the jar and turned to Ty. "You owe me twenty."

The cheetah smiled. "Thank you very much, sir."

They walked away from the bar with their drinks. "You're a good tipper," Ty said.

"No, you are." His uncle sipped the mojito. "This is pretty good. Not great, but you can afford twenty bucks. These guys don't get paid shit. Always look out for the guys doing a good job for shit money."

"I know, I know." Ty sighed. "I bought our equipment staff new iPhones."

"Oh?" His uncle patted him on the shoulder. "Good."

"Got the idea from Strike. It wasn't that much. There's like ten of them so it was, what, six thousand? Something like that. My agent took care of most of it."

They set their drinks on one of the high tables facing the rest of the room. "Okay," Lucas said. "That's really nice of you."

"The other guys were doing things for the training staff. Seemed like a good idea." The mojito went down cool and minty with the richness of rum and the right amount of burn. Ty closed his eyes and looked out at the room. "So who do I need to talk to here?"

For the next half hour or so, they circulated around the room and Lucas guided Ty through variants of the same conversation: *Thank you, it is a wonderful day. I know, it would have been better if I played for the Manticores. Hideyo is beautiful, yes. I honestly don't know many guys on the Manticores, so I don't know what their plans are for next year. Yes, I'm so happy to be getting engaged.*

And then his mother called him on the phone from across the room to tell him to get over to the stage. "Good luck," Lucas said, clapping him on the shoulder.

As it happened, Ty didn't have to stand on the stage. His mother and father stepped up there with a microphone, and Hideyo's mother joined them. Ty's mother started with a long speech about uniting their families, about all the wonderful things Hideyo's family had done and how smart and successful their daughter was. Hideyo's mother went next with a speech that was almost identical except that she praised Ty, which she ended with, "Their cubs are going to be beautiful."

That sent Ty down a track of thinking about being a father. The thought of having his own cubs, maybe one day being on a stage introducing his daughter or son's prospective spouse, held some appeal for him. But it wasn't Hideyo he pictured next to him.

As the cheetah bartender was making him a mojito and Ty was trying to figure out why his cologne smelled familiar, Lucas appeared at his elbow. "This is your last drink until after the ceremony."

Then Hideyo's father led her out and she looked lovely, in a white kimono with a dark cherry-red flower print, her fur immaculately groomed and her natural scent enhanced with—of course, cherry fragrance. Ty took a deep breath and held it in as she joined him, standing in front of the stage.

If only he had the stamina, he would've held his breath for the entire interminable thing. His father made the actual proposal, and Hideyo's father accepted it, and all the while he and Hideyo stood holding paws and looking into each other's eyes. Ty didn't know what Hideyo did or if her neck hurt after craning it back to look up at him for all that time, but he was counting the petals in the flowers on her shoulder or else thinking about the wide receiver camp and some of the things he'd learned there.

When it was over, everyone applauded, and Hideyo turned to them and bowed. Ty turned a moment later, unsure what he was supposed to do, and behind him his mother hissed, "Bow!"

So he bowed, and everyone laughed because he did it awkwardly and late, and his ears flushed but he kept them upright. "Is that it?" he said over his shoulder to his mother.

They were all climbing down from the stage and the crowd's attention had left them. "That's it," his mother said. "Now you can go get drunk if you want."

"I hope you won't," Hideyo said. "At least not here. I can't control what you do anywhere else."

"Thanks," Ty said. "Nice to know we're equally excited about this."

"I am excited." She stood straighter, smoothing out the lines of her kimono. She had an attractive enough body, and when she touched it like that, sure, it turned him on. That was good to know. At least sex wouldn't be a chore. "I'm going to get to go to Plainfield business school."

"Because you got engaged?" He cast an eye back at her parents, still chatting with his. "Did they hold that over your head?"

"No." She smiled up. "Because you're paying for my schooling."

"Oh." Then his ears did fold back.

"Oh." She mimicked him. "What did you think, I was going to run your foundation and bear your cubs and that's all? I have ambitions too. Anyway, it won't cost more than a hundred thousand or so. You'll hardly miss it."

"Sure," he said. "You're welcome."

"I'm going to study marketing and non-profit business, so I'll be very good for your foundation. We're going to do a lot for the world."

"Great," he said. "That sounds awesome."

"Just keep scoring those touchdowns."

"Yeah. Excuse me," he said, "I'm going to grab another drink."

"Your uncle told me to keep an eye on what I serve you," the bartender said when Ty got up to the front of the line. "But you still seem okay, so what can I get you? Another mojito?"

"Sure." Ty exhaled.

"I make a pretty good Manhattan, if you want to try that."

"Never had one. Does it take a while to make?"

The cheetah laughed. "It can."

"Do it, then." He caught the name tag and remembered his uncle using the bartender's name. "Thanks, Joel."

As the cheetah brought out some bottles and measured them into the glass, he called out behind Ty, "Anyone just want a glass of sake or wine?"

Several people came forward, so he said, "Mind if I pour for these folks first?"

Ty shook his head. "Go on."

The sake and wine pours took about ten minutes, during which Ty looked around the room again. The bartender, he concluded, was the guy closest to his age in the entire room, except for maybe Hideyo.

"There," Joel said, and wiped his paws on a towel. "The rest of you want mixed drinks?"

Three older males remained behind Ty, all of whom answered in the affirmative. "All right. I'm gonna make a Manhattan here. What do the rest of you want?"

The others came up and put in their orders, and Joel mixed all four drinks in order, but gave Ty his drink last. "I still don't have my wallet," Ty said in a low voice as the other three left tips and walked off.

"That's okay." Joel lowered his voice too. "Do you know Dev Miski well?"

"Pretty well." Ty brought the drink to his lips and sipped. This was definitely better than the mojito.

Lucas came up behind him, a smile teasing at his whiskers. "Is that your first drink since the ceremony?"

"Yes," Ty said. "It took a while to make because he's really good. Try it."

Lucas took a sip and nodded. "Not bad, not bad. Can you make me one too?"

"Of course," Joel said.

"And by the way," Ty said, "I owe you another twenty dollars."

The cheetah smiled as Lucas fished another twenty out of his wallet and stuffed it into the tip jar. "All right," Lucas said, "but you can only owe me another sixty, so keep the drinking to a minimum."

"I'll keep an eye on him, sir," Joel said, and smiled at Ty.

It clicked with him then that the cheetah's cologne was familiar from the gay club in Yerba and nowhere else. Of course. He'd asked about Dev, and he wore a silver cuff on one of his black and white ears. Not that the ear-cuff was a sure tell that the guy was gay, but it sure didn't say that he wasn't.

Ty had picked up the bartender at the hotel; he could probably pick up the bartender here. If the guy wasn't too picky about going off with the guy who'd just gotten engaged. But hey, if Ty didn't care, why should he?

Three tedious conversations about football later, Ty's mother announced that dinner would be served in fifteen minutes and that everyone was moving to the restaurant. Ty downed the last swig of his Manhattan and made his way back over to the bartender.

"Can you make one more to get me through dinner? This one was great." What would he say if he was hitting on a female bartender? "You've got a really nice touch."

The cheetah shot him a look, which Ty answered with a smile. "Coming right up, sir."

Lucas came by about halfway through the drink mixing, fishing for his wallet. "This guy better be making amazing drinks," he muttered, laying another twenty on the bar.

"He is," Ty said. "Go on in, I'll be there in a minute. Save me a seat."

"You're sitting next to the—oh, ha ha." His uncle shook his head at the joke. "Don't make that drink any stronger than it needs to be," he warned Joel as he left.

The room had pretty much cleared out by the time Joel slid Ty's drink over to him. The fox left it sitting there. "Got a pen?" he asked, and Joel produced one quickly. "I'll probably be at dinner for a couple hours. But after that I'll be staying here at the hotel." Ty scribbled his room number on a napkin and set the pen down on it.

The cheetah's eyes widened. Ty picked up his drink. "Maybe see you later," he said, and walked away without waiting for an answer.

•

His parents had reserved a private back room in the restaurant, with the family members all together at one long table and the rest of the guests seated at two others. Ty refused the offer of another drink under the eye of his uncle two seats down, though he would've liked a little more to help him through the conversation.

The arrival of the appetizers gave him something else to focus on. His parents kept asking him how he liked the food, from the appetizer (some kind of small game bird with a maple glaze) to the salad to the main course, steak with vegetables in a buttery cream sauce and flecks of green in it, potatoes, bread, all the standard things you had at a dinner. "It's good," he said, though he couldn't really recall the taste of any of it as soon as he'd swallowed. Sometimes, to mix it up, he said, "Really good."

At one of those points, Hideyo leaned across him and said, "I really like the way the chef has built the flavors to complement each other. You can tell they're a real artist."

His parents ate that up. Good, Ty thought, at least they're getting one cub they can relate to. At least here he was mostly, save one of Hideyo's relatives, insulated from the people who wanted to ask him what the odds would be on the Firebirds going back to the championship, or worse, if he knew such-and-such player. Ty always thought he knew a lot of players in the league until he talked to someone outside it, and then they could rattle off the names of players he'd never even heard of: the Manticores' backup wide receiver, or the gazelle they'd drafted out of Columbia State.

Of course Hideyo sat beside him, and they jumped in on each other's conversations, play-acting at two people who liked each other. "Training camp starts in a couple months," Ty said to the relative who'd asked about football.

Hideyo leaned over. "So we want to have the wedding in early June. I'm going to take some summer sessions to get up to speed for business school in the fall, so I'll probably be as busy as Ty is."

"Spending money, not making it," Ty muttered under his breath, but Hideyo's ears perked up and he knew she'd heard him.

"Business school?" Hideyo's aunt, across from them, hadn't heard Ty, at least. "So you're going to have cubs later?"

"Maybe." Hideyo waved a paw. "We can afford to pay for surrogates and nannies, so we could have cubs anytime. It depends on how much time their father wants to spend with them."

Of course it did. Ty put on his best public relations smile and said, "I'll spend as much time as I can get away from my job."

"Job." Hideyo laughed. "It sounds so formal and intense when you put it that way."

Ty's parents were deep in conversation with Hideyo's parents, so he shot his uncle a despairing look and his uncle shook his head, warning him to stay on his good behavior. He took his phone out to text his uncle under the table: *Can you believe this shit?*

But his uncle didn't answer. The texting reminded him of the dinner with Tami, so Ty put the phone away and turned his mind elsewhere. He picked up his Manhattan and sipped it, thinking about the cheetah. Would the guy come to his hotel room? (Probably.) What would they do there? (Whatever they wanted.) Would they fuck, or just jerk each other off maybe? (Whatever felt good.) Ty didn't have condoms, or lube for that matter. The cheetah had seemed like a nice guy, though, and maybe he had a good sense of humor. Ty hadn't really seen what his body was like, but gay guys kept themselves in shape, right? (As far as he knew.)

Finally, finally, the last coffee had been served and people sat around talking as the staff cleared plates. Ty's phone told him that the couple hours he'd told Joel had elapsed, and though he kept himself mostly calm on the table, twice he realized his tail was twitching and had to stop it.

"This has been really nice," he said at a lull in the conversation. "I'm looking forward to the wedding and all."

"I hope there won't be a lot of football players there," Hideyo said. "It is going to be a formal affair."

"There'll be me," Ty said.

"Well, of course." She sniffed.

"And most of my friends are football players. If they're free, they'll come."

"Of course your friends are welcome." She smiled as though he'd not understood her meaning.

"Good." He stretched his legs out under the table. "You know, I'm still sort of beat from that camp I went to. Mind if I take off?"

"Of course not," Hideyo said.

His mother had opened her muzzle to object, but at Hideyo's words she nodded and said, "We'll come back here in the morning to collect you. Sleep well."

"You're staying at the hotel?" Hideyo's voice became sharp.

"Yeah. I came here straight from the airport so I already had my bags and everything. It was just easier."

"Hm." She gave a quick nod and then turned back to her parents and whatever their conversation was about, something to do with politics.

Ty stood up. The tables fell quiet, so he said, "Sorry, I'm really tired. Going to turn in. Uh, thank you all for coming."

The room murmured a response. He pulled his jacket from the back of his chair and draped it over his arm as he left the restaurant, heading for the door as quickly and precisely as if he were waiting for a quarterback to get him the ball there.

In the elevator, he sagged back against the wall and relaxed, pulling the damn bowtie off his neck. There'd be the wedding and then maybe a couple charity functions a year, and otherwise he wouldn't have to deal with shit like this anymore. That would be really nice, to be able to hang out with football players and be part of his football world and not worry about what all these people he didn't really care about thought of him.

And, from time to time, get laid by a new, exciting person. He sniffed the air of the hallway when he stepped out, but didn't smell the cheetah's cologne. Good, so he wasn't too late. He hurried back to his room, where he threw his jacket onto the chair and soon followed it with the useless cummerbund, the bowtie, and the stiff cotton shirt. He paused at the pants; better not to answer the door mostly naked. Although if the cheetah did come up (and Ty believed that he would, unless he'd misread all of Joel's signals), he certainly knew what he was getting into.

He turned the TV on to ESPN and tried to let sports make him forget about the other hotel rooms and the other people he'd waited for in them recently. He was mostly successful, and fortunately it wasn't even ten minutes before there was a knock at the door. Ty put his eye to the peephole, though he'd already caught the smell of cologne.

"Glad you came up," he said, opening the door to Joel.

The cheetah had changed out of his red bartender's vest and formal white shirt into a black t-shirt and black cargo pants with a whole bunch of silver rings and snaps around the waist. He stepped into the room and curled his tail around his leg as Ty closed the door, then let it flow behind him. "Are you kidding?" he said. "You're a football player, right? Wow, you're in great shape." He reached one paw out to Ty's bare abs and then stopped. "May I?"

"Sure." Ty tensed his abs to make them stand out under his trimmed fur, then leaned back against the wall, stretching his arms over his head.

Joel traced the lines of his stomach muscles with warm, gentle fingers. "Mm, nice. I'm not gonna look that good, I'm afraid, but I can make up for it."

"Make up for it?" Ty had already noticed the slight bulge around the cheetah's waist, not like he cared.

"I have it on good authority that I give a damn good blow job."

Ty laughed and crossed to the bed. "I guess that answers my question about what we're going to do."

"Sit down," Joel said. "I'll take care of the rest."

The fox obeyed, leaning back on his elbows as the cheetah sank to his knees at the foot of the bed. Then he remembered a discussion he'd had with Arch. "Hey," he said, "are you going to want me to blow you after? Cause I don't think—"

"Nah." Joel smiled. "Don't worry, I like giving head."

"Okay." He'd only been about to say that he didn't think he was very good, but if Joel was going to let him off the hook, he wasn't going to question it.

And the cheetah was pretty good. He opened up Ty's pants and got his sheath out, already hard of course because Ty'd been thinking about this moment for a couple hours. Joel had a shorter muzzle than Arch, but he used it well, and it also allowed him to get his throat muscles or something involved. Whoever had told him he was good at blow jobs had not lied.

Ty'd been worried that he'd be uncomfortable with a guy who wasn't Arch, the masculine scent and everything, but Joel had a nice scent and Ty relaxed easily into the sex. "Ah, yeah," he said, and just at that moment there was another knock at his door.

He started up from the bed. Joel kept his muzzle down on Ty's shaft and then slowly drew back. "Naughty, naughty," the cheetah said with a smile. "Did you set up a threesome and not tell me? Is it Vance?"

"No," Ty said, and lurched off the bed. He reached for his pants and then hesitated; if he pulled them up, would that signal to Joel that the blow job was off? His cock dripped onto his paw, and automatically he licked his fingers clean. "Give me a sec," he whispered, and went to the door.

No scent tipped him off. He put his eye to the peephole and saw his uncle Lucas standing outside, looking back and forth down the hallway. "Hi," Ty said. "Uncle Lucas?"

"Ty, if you're not asleep, can I come in? I just wanted to…" His uncle's nostrils flared and then he coughed. "Hey, maybe we can meet for a drink in the bar in a little bit?"

"Uh, yeah, sure. Like half an hour?"

"Sure." His uncle turned from side to side again and then seemed about to say something. Ty waited, eye pressed to the door, until Lucas walked away down the hall.

"Sorry," he said to Joel, coming back to the bed. "Lot of family here, and—oh, okay."

Joel had pushed him gently back to the bed. "It's fine," he said. "Just means you get a little bit more time."

Not a whole lot, it turned out. Ty gasped and came within three minutes of sitting down again. He fell back onto the bed, panting.

"Heh." Joel sat back on his heels, licking his lips. "Pretty eager there."

"It's been a couple weeks." Ty struggled to sit up.

The cheetah's eyes widened. "Since you got off?"

"Oh, hell no." Ty laughed. "I was at this football camp and I had a private room, so I jerked off every night."

"Ha ha." Joel licked his lips and shook his head. "I remember being twenty."

"I'm twenty-two." Ty grinned. It was a little weird talking to this guy on this floor with his glistening shaft bobbing between them.

The cheetah nodded. "Same thing, more or less. You went to football right out of college, so I guess you're pretty good?"

Ty raised an eyebrow. "I thought you'd heard of me."

Joel shook his head. "Nah, sorry. I mean, they told us it was some football player's engagement, uh…" His eyes drifted down to Ty's cock. "But it wasn't until today that someone said you were with the Firebirds. I got a few friends who are all into Dev Miski and I was pretty sure that was the same team." He cocked his head. "So…are you gay too? Or just like getting your dick sucked? You didn't seem to spend a lot of time with your fiancée, is why I'm asking, and I've bartended a bunch of engagement parties."

"I guess I'm bi?" Ty's cock retreated into his sheath slightly. He held up a paw and slid off the bed. "I'm gonna clean up, but you can stick around a bit."

"Oh, you're 'bi,' okay." Joel seemed amused. "I was bi for a little while, too. I guess if I was a public figure I might still be."

Ty wasn't sure what that meant. "I'm not crazy about this fiancée. She's my second choice. Actually, she's my parents' choice."

"What happened to the first? She find out about your love of cock?"

"I don't…" He dampened a washcloth and cleaned his shaft off. "No, we had a fight and she backed out."

"Huh." The cheetah's tone went from amusement to perplexity. "She didn't want to marry a football player? This one sure doesn't have a problem with that."

"What do you mean?" Ty came out of the bathroom, rubbing himself dry with a towel.

"Oh…" Joel glanced to the side, then down at his paws.

Ty leaned against the door. "You won't be telling me anything I don't already know. She spent most of our conversation talking about all the things my money was going to buy her."

"Yeah. Her relatives said a lot of the same shit." Joel lifted his head. "That's kinda why I came up. Figured as long as I wasn't taking money from her, she wouldn't care if someone else blew you."

"Probably not." Ty pulled his pants up. "You got here at the perfect time, too."

"Yeah, well." Joel got to his feet. "I might've been chilling in the lobby for a bit after my shift to see when you left the restaurant." When Ty grinned at that, the cheetah said, "Hey, I've never blown a football player before. Wasn't going to pass that chance up. Dunno what I would've said though. Glad you made a move."

"Appreciate it." Ty swished his tail, watching the cheetah walk past him. "Hey, do you dance?"

"Nah." Joel lifted a paw. "But I'm in a band. You want to come to one of our shows sometime, that'd be cool."

He produced a worn business card from his pocket and gave it to Ty. "We play like a fusion of 80s ska and disco. It's pretty cool."

"Thanks." The band name seemed to be "That Midtown Sound," or maybe that was the description of their music. Hard to tell from the card. He shoved it into his pocket. "Maybe I will."

"Okay, well. Seeya." Joel opened the door and walked out into the hall.

Like the waitress or the mink, or Leah the other bartender, the cheetah was in and out of his life, and that was the way it was going to be. Better that way: no attachments to get Ty tangled. He could be at Hideyo's side when she needed him, and even better, she wasn't looking to need him anytime soon. He left to meet his uncle in the bar, and the room door slammed behind him.

CHAPTER 29

The hotel bar gleamed with brass finish and polished wood so much that the huge TVs showing basketball seemed slightly out of place, though at least they were muted. Ty picked a small group of plush chairs around a low marble-topped circular table and sat down. Within a few moments, a young white-tailed deer came up to him and stood patiently.

"What do you have on tap?" Ty asked, watching the basketball game on the TV.

"Sorry, I'm not—uh, you're Ty Nakamura, right?"

Now he looked at the deer, a skinny young kid with huge eyes (even for a deer), wearing a loose collared shirt and jeans and fidgeting from one leg to the other. Ty shifted into public persona. "That's right," he said. "You a Firebirds fan?"

"No, uh. Manticores. But you're really cool. Congratulations. I saw the announcement. I mean, it was—"

He kept tripping over his words. Ty smiled and reached for one of the cocktail napkins on the table. "You want an autograph?"

"Yeah, sure!"

So he scrawled his name and "#88" on the napkin and handed it to the deer, who smiled like he'd just won a championship of his own. "Thanks so much, Mr. Nakamura!"

"No problem. But you have to root for the Firebirds this year when we're not playing the Manticores, okay?"

"Sure! Yeah!" And the deer ran off, weaving around chairs and tables.

"Nice," Ty heard behind him, and his uncle's scent reached his nose. Lucas plopped into one of the adjacent chairs. "You've got the 'public face' thing down pat."

"It's easy when there's only one." Ty leaned back.

"I guess so." Lucas signaled the waitress, a snowshoe hare in a gold vest, and ordered a martini. Ty asked for the beers on tap and selected a light one.

He waited for his uncle to say why he'd wanted to meet, but the older fox looked at the TV and said, "Good game?"

"It's okay."

They watched the TV without saying anything. At a commercial break, Ty asked. "So what's up?"

Lucas turned from the TV. "Ah," he said. "I was originally going to ask if you were doing okay, excited about the engagement, had anything you wanted to talk about. Now I'm trying to figure out how to ask you why you were having sex in your room with someone I'm assuming was not Hideyo less than half an hour after leaving your new fiancée at your engagement dinner."

There wasn't any use in denying it; Lucas had smelled him through the door. Ty shrugged, watching the commercial. "Because I can."

His uncle let that remark sit for the remainder of the commercial. "Okay, so you don't have everything down pat about being mature."

"Whatever." Ty scraped his claws along the fabric of the chair. "I'm engaged, okay? I'm going to be married. I never agreed to be exclusive, and she sure as hell doesn't care if I mess around. She told me: keep scoring touchdowns and don't have cubs anywhere else."

"She said that about the cubs?"

No, that had been Tami. Ty cleared his throat. "One of my teammates' marriage broke up because he had a cub with some other coyote, so I guess people are thinking about that."

The hare brought their drinks over and left. Lucas sipped the martini. "Passable," he said, and set it back down. "Still, it's not exactly polite to go hooking up at your engagement party."

"Maybe for normal people," Ty said, and took a drink.

He set down the beer glass hurriedly because his uncle was leaning over the arm of his chair. "Don't you ever let me hear you talk like that again. You're special, yeah, there's no denying it. But that doesn't mean you don't have to treat people with respect. And respect means not doing something you kinda want to do because it might hurt them. You got that?"

"Yeah," Ty mumbled, ears flat against his head.

Lucas sat back in his chair. "We—your parents brought you up better than that. You always had pretty good perspective on your success and what it means. I thought you had your head screwed on right, but I'm starting to wonder. Were you trying to sabotage this engagement?"

Ty sulked back in his chair and played with his tail. "No."

"So what were you trying to do?"

"Get laid. Since it didn't seem like it was going to happen any other way."

"Did you ask your fiancée?"

He snorted. "She'd probably have asked me to buy her a new business suit or something."

"Ugh." Lucas exhaled. "Leaving aside that you are not getting married in the fifties, did you think for a moment that maybe the way to build a relationship is to extend some trust and vulnerability yourself? That if you tried to be a good friend as well as a business partner, she might surprise you?"

"Then what?"

His uncle blinked in surprise. "Then you have a nice life together and enjoy each other's company? Help me out here, son, what are you looking for?"

"Doesn't matter. All I want to do is play football, okay? Mom's the one insisting I get married now, right away. I don't even know why."

"Because she wants you to have a family to take care of you when you stop playing football. You can't play your whole life, you know. You've got maybe ten years. Fifteen if you're really good and take care of yourself, which comes back to respect, which is another reason I'm worrying about you."

"Don't worry about me," Ty snapped, and then moderated his voice. "I'm doing fine."

Lucas nodded slowly and took another long drink. They watched the basketball game for several more minutes in silence, and then Lucas said, "What happened with Tami?"

"It didn't work out."

"What did she do?"

Ty frowned. "She said she didn't want to marry me."

"Oh." Lucas tilted his head. "From the way your mother said it…all right, then, what did *you* do?"

"Don't want to talk about it." Remembering what he'd done then, in light of what he'd just done tonight, made him certain that Lucas would judge him, maybe yell at him again.

"I can't make you, but I wish you'd tell me." Lucas finished his martini and set the glass down, his ears half-lowered. "You should see the difference in you between when you were with Tami and now. I know it sounds like a dumb movie, but you were happy then, excited. You talked about her and her job. And now that you told me *she* broke up with *you*, I'm wondering if you're punishing yourself for something you did. In which case, if you tell me about it, maybe we can work through it."

Ty side-eyed his uncle. "You're not a shrink."

"No, but I watch a lot of 'Frasier.'" Lucas chuckled. "Come on. I never told your parents about you smoking in tenth grade. And remember the Christmas presents?"

"All right, all right." Ty took a breath. "Promise not to yell at me."

"I won't promise that."

"Talking it out doesn't mean yelling." Ty glared at his uncle. "I did something dumb, okay, and I know it was dumb already, so I don't need to be lectured about it."

Lucas smiled crookedly, which made his whiskers fluff out on one side of his muzzle, a move that had always made Ty laugh. Even now he smiled before he could help it. "I'll be the judge of that," his uncle said. "Go on."

"Ugh, fine." Ty set his beer down. "You know we were in Chevali the other weekend and she met my friends and everything? She flew back Monday to work and her work went to shit so she called me and I said I'd fly home to be with her." He took a breath. "Only I'd told my friends I was flying home Monday. And she called them and they told her that."

"Was she checking up on you?"

"I don't think so. She forgot something at the house."

Lucas nodded. "So where were you?"

"Yerba."

His uncle's eyebrows shot up. "Like, the city?" Ty nodded. "Why?"

"I was…visiting someone."

"Ahhh." They had already been talking in low tones, but here Lucas dropped his voice still further, for Ty's ears only. "And she found out that you sleep with guys?"

Ty froze. His paws squeezed his tail and his jaw worked without making a sound. Lucas reached out and laid fingers over his wrist. "It's okay," he said. "I don't love you any less, and I'm not gonna tell anyone. Definitely not your parents."

"I'm not—"

"Please." Lucas wrinkled his nose. "Your friend's cologne isn't exactly strident, but it's also not exactly feminine, and I spent enough time with you at the bar to remember it. It was the bartender, right?"

"No, it was…" Ty dropped his eyes. "Yeah."

"Hey. It's nothing to be ashamed of, though I know why you have to hide it. But shouldn't you be more excited about this marriage, then? If Hideyo doesn't care whether or not you share her bed?"

"But I'm not gay. I mean, I like both." There was something terrifying and yet relieving about telling his uncle. Ty could hardly imagine his family taking the news so calmly, so positively.

"I get that." Lucas chuckled. "I won't say I've been only with females my whole life."

"Uh." Ty stared at his uncle. "Seriously?"

"Well, I never left an engagement party to be with a male, much less my own. I certainly didn't do it twice. You did get engaged that weekend in Chevali, right?" Ty nodded. "So, do you see a pattern here?"

"It's not like that. The, uh, my friend in Yerba, they texted me over the weekend and said they missed me, and I wanted to see them again too, but not until my time with Tami was over. And when she called I booked the next flight back to be with her."

"Whoa." Lucas's smile faded and his ears came up. "This wasn't just a fling? This sounds like a relationship."

"I guess it sort of was."

"Was?"

"They broke it off."

"Ah, Ty." Lucas squeezed his wrist. "You got dumped twice in the same week?"

"In two days."

"Damn." His uncle let go of him and sat back, thinking. "Why?"

"Oh, they…they didn't want to be just 'a thing on the side.' And they knew there wasn't a future." Mostly Arch's words.

Lucas flicked his tail and his eyes focused somewhere beyond Ty. He thought for several seconds and then raised his paw. "What?" Ty said.

"You're going to tell me about it," he said, "so I'm going to get another drink."

Ty got a water, and when they'd both been served, he gave his uncle a summary of his two breakups. The one with Arch hadn't really been a breakup, more like a post-breakup hookup at the end of which Arch had said that he didn't want to keep doing this especially when Ty was married. And he skimmed through the conversation with Tami, then went back through it when Lucas asked for more details.

It took him the rest of his beer and half his glass of water to get through it all, and when he was done he said, "So yeah, I figured I'd lock in a wife and then get laid whenever I can. You got a better plan for me?"

His uncle finished his second martini and set the empty glass down. He flipped his tail over the arm of his chair and shook his head. "If I had any sense, I'd leave you to deal with the disaster area you've made out of your love life."

"I resent that," Ty said, raising a paw to order another beer. After that story he was going to need to get his buzz back on. "There wasn't any 'love' in it."

"Ha." Lucas shook his head. "You might not have said the word, but there was love all over it. You know, you got pushed into this grown-up world so fast. You've got kids coming up asking for your autograph, you're performing in front of millions of people, you're away from home at this job that takes you into a whole other world with its own rules, and you've learned those rules and you're good at them. It's easy to forget that you're only twenty-two. Jesus Fox, I remember when you were running around crashing your head into my knees. When I was twenty-two I'd just graduated from college and I decided to go fuck around in the woods for three months. I certainly wouldn't have trusted myself to hold down any kind of pressure-filled job."

Ty narrowed his eyes but kept quiet. His uncle went on. "But here's the thing. It's not just that you were happier with Tami. I mean, maybe you weren't; I only saw you a few times and I'm comparing that to tonight. But when you were with her, and with 'Yerba,' I guess, you were the kind of guy who would fly to another city when one of them said they miss you, or that they needed you. You wanted to be there for them. And it sounds like you cared enough that you were going to give up one of them for the other." His eyes softened, warming. "That's the Ty I love."

Ty folded his ears back because they felt very warm. "And I don't think you've been that Ty since then," Lucas said. "You've behaved kind of like a shit tonight. Or—like the bad stereotype of the professional athlete, if you prefer."

"My friends aren't…"

"Yeah, I know." Lucas waved a black paw. "Your friends on the team are great, they're not asshole athletes. Good. And look, you don't have to care what I think, or anyone else, really. You've got enough money to be insulated from the world for the rest of your life. What's important is: which Ty do you like better? Which one do you want to be?"

The buzz from two beers was not strong at all, but it gave Ty the feeling that this was a momentous question, that right here in this hotel bar with the taste of beer in his mouth and his uncle's words in his ears and the warm memory of a cheetah's muzzle between his legs, he had the opportunity to take his life in one way or another. But to admit that he wanted to go back to Tami, that he'd made a mistake—that was hard. He wanted to move forward. You didn't replay games; you improved and did better next time.

"The thing about athlete-Ty," his uncle went on, "is that you have this entitlement complex. You've gotten the best of everything and you think you can still have whatever you want. You got laid 'because you can.'"

"I don't think I deserve it. I work for it," Ty objected, glad to have the decision put off.

"How hard did you work to get that bartender in bed?" Lucas raised his eyebrows. "Huh? Did you get to know him? Make an effort to do things he liked, find out what movies he likes and talk about them? Or did you just tell him, 'I'm a football player.'"

"I didn't tell him," Ty mumbled.

"No, but he knew, right?" His uncle nodded. "Yeah, thought so. So you have this idea that you can get whatever you want. But when it comes to something you really want, the smallest obstacle makes you give up. Because it's not easy."

"Hey!" Ty raised his voice. "I just spent two weeks busting my tail to get better my job. I'm a starting wideout in the UFL and there are only maybe fifty of those in the world. Don't tell me I don't work hard for things."

"So you didn't want things to work out with Tami?"

"She broke it off. What am I supposed to do? Stalk her like in one of those movies? Didn't you tell me those are great instructions in what not to do?"

Lucas shook his head. "Don't stalk her. Did you hear what she said to you? Did you listen to the words you repeated to me just now?"

Ty played the words back in his head. "What, that she'd want to date me for a year or something? That was to make me feel better. She knows

Mom wants me to get married this summer. And what if we date for a year and she doesn't want to marry me at the end of that? Then I've wasted a year and I'm back here only with a worse selection of vix—of wife candidates. I might not love Hideyo…" His uncle's raised eyebrows stopped him. "Okay, I might not even like her. But she's smart, she'll take care of things, and she's willing to have cubs. That's not bad. Tami didn't even know if she wanted cubs."

"Do you?"

"Do I what? Cubs?" Ty shook his head. "Yeah. Someday."

"So," Lucas said, "Doesn't that seem like something you and your wife should talk about?"

"What's the point of all this? Huh? You want me to go back to Tami and beg her to take me back?"

"I don't think you'd have to beg."

"Anyway." Ty gestured around at the hotel. "I'm engaged to Hideyo already. Did you miss that part?"

"Don't see a ring on your finger."

Ty looked at his paw, at the long fingers and the short, unbounded black fur. "That's a formality."

Lucas smiled. "You were engaged to Tami, too. Engagements can be broken."

"Jesus Fox." Ty rolled his head back. "Imagine me going to Mom and telling her I don't want to get engaged. She'd kill me."

"I can help with that, I think."

Ty snapped his head back. Lucas was smiling, his head tilted slightly but his ears up and whiskers bouncing. "Seriously? Why—how—?"

His uncle held up a paw. "Let me worry about the how. But tell me: if I told you I could do it, if I told you I could get you a second chance with Tami, would you take it?"

A second chance? But she wouldn't even talk to him again, would she? Then again, he hadn't tried… He scraped claws along the chair's armrest. "What if she doesn't want to?"

"Forget that." Lucas leaned forward. "If I could get you a second chance, would you take it?"

He'd had so much fun hanging out with her, he'd been able to talk to her, his friends liked her, and the sex had been better because he knew her and enjoyed making her happy. This here was his decision, he realized.

Maybe he didn't quite love her yet, or maybe he did, but either way he was closer to real love with her than with anyone else he knew, except maybe one other person. "Fuck yeah I would."

"Okay." Lucas patted his shoulder. "Then let's go for it."

"Wait wait wait. What do I say to her?"

"You're going to have to figure that out." His uncle relented and smiled. "All right, all right, don't give me those eyes. Look, the problem was that you broke her trust, right? So…try being completely honest with her."

"Uh…"

"Yes. Even about that."

Ty swallowed. "You really think…"

"Hey." Lucas settled back in his chair, arms over the armrests. "If it's not that important to you…"

"All right. Yeah. I'll…I'll figure it out."

"Good boy." The older fox squinted at him. "No…good guy. You're grown up now, like it or not."

"Huh." Ty's heart pounded and his fingers shook slightly as his head spun with scenarios of what he would say to Tami. "Is this what that feels like? Because I have to say, I'm not a big fan."

"Yeah, it sucks sometimes." Lucas smiled at him. "But there're lots of rewards too."

"One more thing." Ty brought his tail into his lap and combed through the fur. "Why are you doing this?"

"Cause I love you."

"Mm." Ty tapped Lucas's paw, the black fur there broken only by a college class ring. "Someday you'll have to tell me if there's a story in your past like this one. Did you not go after the girl and regret it?"

Lucas's ears flattened and his mouth parted before snapping shut again. He composed himself. "You watch too many movies."

"So what makes you think I'll get Tami back?"

His uncle shook his head. "I don't know if you will. But I know you'll regret not trying."

It was possible to regret trying, too. Ty had thought he could field the kick and run it back at the end of the championship game—a one in five hundred chance, like that guy at the camp had said. Failing at that haunted him. But how much worse would it have been if he'd seen the ball coming and stepped aside, let Strike get it, because he'd known he would probably fail? He'd tried, after all, and there was something important in that.

"I'll probably regret this too," he said to his uncle. "But okay. Give me the ball."

CHAPTER 30

"We've both been drinking," Uncle Lucas told Ty's mother on the phone, "but we'll be sober by the time you get here." So they waited in the bar with club sodas and bowls of nuts and crackers, though Ty felt personally that just the threat of talking to his mother had spiked his adrenaline enough to sober him up.

"What do I even say to her?" he asked his uncle.

Lucas looked evenly at him. "I think you know all the things you need to say. I'll help out where I can, but it's got to come from your heart, so don't rehearse it."

"Thanks." Ty licked the wedge of lime in his club soda to wince at the burst of sourness. "You know, the coaches give me a playbook and everything."

The other fox laughed. "Not everything is football, Ty. I think you know that. All right, all right. I'll give you one tip, the only one I really think will help."

Ty leaned forward, ears perked. His uncle gestured at him with a paw. "Parents always see their cubs as cubs for longer than they should. Your mother may not fully realize that you're grown up."

"You just told me I wasn't grown up yet."

"Heh heh." Lucas shook his head. "We're none of us really grown up. We just get to a point where people can't put our mistakes down to age anymore. Take that excuse as long as you can. But really, show your mother that you're serious, thinking about this with your head and your heart and not just your dick."

Ty tossed back the rest of his soda and grabbed a bunch of crackers. "Please don't ever say 'mother' and 'dick' in the same sentence again."

Lucas laughed again and nodded. "You got it."

When Ty's mother walked in, she scanned the bar and walked over to them, very obviously stifling a yawn as she did. "It's quite late," she observed, and touched her muzzle to both his and Lucas's, sniffing for alcohol as she did. Ty said a quick thank-you to Joel for not asking for a reciprocal blow job, and then turned his attention to his mother as she sat.

"It is late," Lucas said. "Sorry about that. Ty has something he needs to tell you, and I think you should hear him out."

His mother's ears flicked in his direction, remaining upright although her whiskers curved downward. "Very well. Go on."

Speak from the heart. Speak from the head. He didn't have a route to run, no coach to tell him where to put his feet; he had to trust his instincts. "I don't want to marry Hideyo," he said.

His mother gave an exasperated sigh. "I thought—"

Lucas held up a paw. "Please."

Miracle of miracles, his mother stopped talking, inclined her head, and listened to him. And now here it was, here was his chance. "She doesn't care about me. She just wants to be part of this life, access to my money. But I don't think that's enough. Tami—" His mother remained formally, politely impassive, but the tip of her tail twitched at the mention of the name. Ty forged on. "Tami cares about me. She—she makes me responsible for my mistakes and she pushes me to be a better person. She doesn't care if I make a lot of money for some foundation."

Lucas made a heart shape with his paws. Ty shook his head. "I don't know if I love her yet. I mean, I'm not even sure what love feels like. I think I'm close to loving her, though. I miss her a lot." He clenched a fist and tapped his chest. "Right here."

His mother gave no indication of her feelings. "Is that all?" she asked.

"I want to date Tami. For a year, for however long it takes for us to figure it out one way or another. If it doesn't work out, then at least I tried. I won't have any regrets." All three of them sat in silence, and then Ty said, "That's all."

"Very well." His mother looked at Lucas, then back at Ty. "I have heard you. I understand the feelings of a young heart. But what do you think has just happened here? Agreements have been made, futures have been planned. What do you think will happen to Hideyo if you abandon this engagement?"

"I assume she'll get a loan for business school," Ty said. His mother frowned, and he went on. "Seriously. I mean, I think that's the biggest thing she'll be upset about. Maybe her parents will be angry, or feel they've lost face, but look, blame it on me. Say I insisted on backing out. I'll pay for her to go to school anyway."

"Tell them Ty hired a prostitute tonight," Lucas offered.

"I don't think there's any need for—" His mother saw the cant of his ears. "Oh, Taiyo. Why?"

Lucas, having thrown him to the sharks, rescued him. "We don't have to go into why or how close that even is to the truth," he said smoothly. "It's a story that would let Hideyo's family back out, 'saving their daughter' from the shame of this marriage, and Ty's willing to go along with it."

"I am not willing to go along with it," his mother snapped. "His actions reflect on me as well. What would people think?"

"The real question is…" Lucas leaned forward, both paws clasped together. "Do you want to make your son marry someone he doesn't love, and leave behind someone he does love, for the sake of tradition and how it would make your family look?"

His mother stared between both of them, off into the distance. "It is still possible for him to have a happy life," she said finally.

"It's not the fifties anymore," Lucas said. "It's not even the eighties."

"Mom." Ty slid forward to the edge of his seat. "I don't want to do this without your blessing. I could have—" Lucas tilted his head warningly, but Ty forged on. "I could have just gone and married Tami and left you to clean up the mess. But I think when you get to know her, you'll know why I think she's a better choice. For one thing, she knows how much I have to learn and she wants to take her time. She wants this marriage to be about both of us. And about our families."

"She did not seem to have much interest in tradition at the dinner."

"But her mother did. Tami's smart, she's Yamatese, she's really funny, and she's prettier than Hideyo."

His mother raised her eyebrows. "I have met them both."

You haven't seen Tami naked, Ty wanted to say, and fortunately was not drunk enough to actually say it. The feeling of getting past the last defender, end zone in sight, grew in his chest. "Please, Mom," he said.

For several moments, the only sound was the basketball game in the background. Then his mother got to her feet and smoothed down her dress. Ty started to get up as well, but she waved him back to his chair. "I believe we can come up with a better story than a prostitute," she said.

Ty sprang out of his chair then and wrapped his mother in a hug, sending her staggering two steps backwards. Through pressure in his throat, he said, "Thanks, Mom. Thank you."

She hugged him and then stepped back and wagged a finger at him. "I am still angry. About the trouble we are going to have to go through."

"I meant it about paying for her business school. If that helps."

"And about the prostitute. Or whatever it was." There he dropped his muzzle and flattened his ears. "Though I suppose I'm not surprised." She turned to Lucas. "You know what he did at a friend's birthday party when he was sixteen?"

Lucas chuckled and Ty gaped at his mother. "You knew about that?"

She gave him a satisfied smile. "His mother called me and told me."

"You've known for six years? Why didn't you say anything?"

She raised her eyebrows again. "There was no need to talk about it."

"But there is now?"

"As I said." She smoothed her dress down again. "I am angry. It seems appropriate to remind you that you can't keep as many secrets as you may think. Good night, you two. I will speak to you both tomorrow."

Ty collapsed back into his chair. When his mother had left the bar, Lucas leaned over to him and said, "Good job. Now comes the hard part."

•

They watched the end of the basketball game, and Lucas asked Ty if he had a way to get in touch with any of those players, and Ty told him that he'd met a couple basketball players at a charity event but didn't have a lot of friends in the sport. And when they finally parted, his uncle hugged him and said, "Let me know how things go with Tami."

Back in his room, the smell of Joel's cologne lingered in the air. Ty sprayed around some of the Neutra-Scent the hotel had provided and lay back in his bed, playing out the conversation with Tami in his head. Finally he turned to the clock on the nightstand. 11:13. She'd still be up. And if he wasn't going to do it now, then when?

Visualize yourself doing it, his college coach had taught him. This was about running routes: know where your feet go on each step, count the seconds in your head, know where you'll be every second. Visualize it and then do it.

This was easy. Get out your phone, go to "recent," where Tami's number was still listed. Tap it. Pull out the mic and put the phone to your ear. Four steps, about six seconds.

Phone.

Recent.

Tap.

Mic.

Ear.

The phone rang. Maybe she wouldn't answer. Maybe she'd look at his number and say—

Click. "Hi."

He exhaled. "Hi."

"Congratulations, I guess."

For a moment, he thought she meant on having the courage to call her. "Oh, it wasn't—I had a talk with my uncle and I wanted to call you."

"Didn't you get engaged tonight? It was on one of the news sites. Marci sent it to me."

How the hell did people find these things out? He'd been so pleased there weren't reporters tonight, too. "Uh yeah, I guess."

"You guess?" Her wariness sharpened, turned to slight anger. "If you're looking to cheat on your latest engagement with your last one—"

"No! No. This isn't…" He stopped and closed his eyes. "I want to see you."

"Why?"

"Why? Because I want to." He heard the words as he said them, and how similar they sounded to his uncle's "typical athlete" language. "That's not what I mean. I mean…I miss seeing you. And," he said before she could respond, "I want to apologize."

"You can't do that over the phone?"

"I guess I could, but I'd really rather not. I've got a lot of stuff to say."

She thought about that and sighed. "Fine. But not at my place and not in your hotel room."

"I'm not going to try to seduce you," he said, annoyed.

She laughed. "That's not what I'm worried about."

"All right," he said. "Tell me where. I'll take a cab."

"Where are you?"

"At the Plaza in Bellefort Beach."

"Fancy. All right, how about Jack B's?"

"Are they open?"

"Until midnight."

He glanced at the clock: 11:22. "I'll be there in twenty minutes."

CHAPTER 31

She had no idea why she was going out at eleven-thirty at night to meet up with a guy who'd broken her heart the way Ty had, but she suspected it had something to do with Marci lecturing her and the realization that Devin's betrayal had hurt her more than she'd thought. Maybe she needed to hear an apology from someone. Maybe a tiny part of her hoped it would be a good enough apology to mend the relationship. Besides, he'd called her, so it wasn't like she was desperately trying to get him back.

Jack B's was busier than she'd expected. The waitress, a tall sea otter, showed her to a table. "Food or just drinks, hon?" she asked.

"Just drinks for now. Diet Coke, please." Her stomach rumbled at the smell of the fried food wafting around from the kitchen. "Oh, and an order of fries, I guess."

"Coming up."

She wasn't in the same booth they'd sat in for their date; that one was occupied by a pair of spotted skunks leaning against each other, sharing a milkshake. How cute, how cliché, she thought. Ty probably wouldn't have a milkshake because he wanted to keep fit.

He came in around quarter to midnight, hurrying through the door and looking around the restaurant. He had on a fancy white collared shirt and expensive-looking white pants that were clearly part of a tuxedo or elegant suit. When he saw her, he smiled and padded quickly across the tile floor, ignoring the hostess who'd nearly run back to her station.

"Every time I come here, I'm overdressed," he said, and unbuttoned his shirt.

The waitress came hurrying over. "Sir, please keep your shirt…um." She stopped dead as he held out a fifty dollar bill.

"Can I have an extra large t-shirt from your front? Sorry, I forgot mine from last time."

She stared at his exposed chest. "Um. Sure. Yes. I'll be right back with that."

Tami couldn't help her smile as Ty slid in across from her. "Did you come here just to flirt with the waitress?"

His ears flattened. She put up a paw. "Teasing. I'm sorry. You wanted to tell me something."

"Yeah, uh." He lifted his ears and scratched behind one of them. "Let's wait until I'm dressed."

The waitress returned with a shirt and held it out. "We're, uh, we're out of extra large. Hope a large will fit."

"I think I can squeeze into it." Ty shrugged out of his shirt and pulled the t-shirt over his head. It did fit, but bunched tightly around his broad shoulders, unable to fully cover his biceps. "It'll be fine. Diet Coke, please."

"Mm. Yes, sir." The sea otter stared and then hurried away from the table.

There was the annoyance of someone else ogling Ty paired with the smugness that he'd chosen her to be with—no. Tami tried to shoo away both emotions. He wasn't hers, so neither the possessiveness nor the pride had any place here.

"So how've you been?" he asked. "What'd you end up doing with, uh, with Shirokaze?"

"Oh." She lowered her nose. "I'm going to finish the project I'm on, and I've got resumes out to some other companies. Some of them aren't in this area, but we'll see. I decided I couldn't work with my friend—my former friend—" She caught herself before going into a rant. "I didn't want to be shuffled onto another one of their B titles."

Ty nodded. "That sounds like a good compromise, I guess."

"It was the best I could think of." As the news leaked out, other people were coming to her to tell her how unfair it was, and so far she hadn't broken company loyalty and told anyone the whole deal (except for Axel, who was emphatically on her side), but it was getting harder and harder. There was also the complication that Devin was still technically working under her on Jumbo Bubbles, but she'd had a formal meeting with Fatima where she asked that Devin report directly to the otter, and Fatima had been gracious enough to expedite that.

"Did your friend—ex-friend—ever apologize?"

"No." Tami lay her ears back. "He said it was 'just business.' He said I would've done the same thing."

"That sucks."

That clearly wasn't what he'd come to talk about. When he'd gotten his drink, they sat in silence while he gathered himself, and then he said, "Whoof. Okay, here goes. Um. First of all, I'm sorry for lying to you. I didn't do it because I was trying to deceive you…no, I mean, I guess I was, but I didn't mean to harm you…like, I wasn't doing anything to hurt you."

"The lying hurt me." She kept her voice steady.

"Right. Yeah. I'm really sorry."

He didn't seem to know where to go from there. Was there going to be more? Had he wanted only to apologize to her? She opened her muzzle to talk, and that spurred him to keep going. "But I want to explain—to tell you about it, and maybe you'll understand."

She nodded. It was strange how this was the first time she could remember seeing him as the young fox he was. He'd always seemed so self-assured and confident that she wouldn't have thought it would make him more appealing to be unsure.

He took a breath. "So, the wolf in Yerba. I met them during the season, and it wasn't serious. I mean, we both knew it wasn't going to go anywhere. It was fun, that was all, and the dancing was great. But then I was so annoyed with the dinners that I went down there again after the season. And then…I thought it was done, I really did. But then I got a text the weekend we were in Chevali."

The pronoun avoidance pinged her curiosity, and she thought she knew what was coming. Ty took a breath. "And it was…it really was just one last thing. I thought I could squeeze it in before coming back here for the engagement. And it would've been over, I promise."

She didn't say anything, but he took a drink of his soda and his eyes flicked down to the table. "I thought it would've been over. I guess…if we played in Yerba again, I might've…I mean, if I'm being totally honest…"

"Okay," she said. She was tempted to ask about the gender of this mysterious partner, but waited to see if he would reveal it himself.

And indeed, that was what he was working himself up to next. "So this wolf…I mean, the thing is…" Here he lowered his voice to a fox-whisper. "He's a guy."

Again her perception of him shifted, and again, not in a bad way. "I work with a gay guy," she said.

"I'm not—" He caught himself. "I'm bi. But that's why I didn't want to tell anyone. If it gets out…"

"You work with a gay guy, too," she pointed out.

"He knows. I ran into him—we ran into him." Ty ran his paw back over his ears. "That was a bit embarrassing."

She had to cover her mouth and laugh at that. "That's how he found out? He *caught* you?"

"Yeah…" He met her eyes with an abashed smile. "I mean, it turned out okay."

"The thing is…" Tami put her serious face on again. "It doesn't matter that it was a guy and not a girl. I understand the secrecy, and it's a tough situation, but it still hurt."

"Right. I'm sorry about that."

He looked down at the table and clasped his paws together. Did he have still more to confess? What other things had he done? She said, "I really appreciate you coming here to apologize."

He took a breath. "Yeah, thanks for listening and not judging. And for not letting me off the hook." His smile twisted a bit. "But I also wanted to go back to something you said then. You said you'd be willing to date me for a year or so. You just don't want to get married this summer."

"No, I don't, but…hang on. Didn't you just get engaged?"

"Well, uh." His ears splayed out. "About that."

She gripped the table because the world felt about to spin even though she'd had nothing stronger than a diet soda to drink. Ty went on. "I talked to my uncle for a while tonight." His ears splayed to the side and he lowered his voice. "Um, okay, so since I'm being totally honest, uh. The night after you took off, I hooked up with a bartender at that hotel. And tonight I hooked up with a bartender."

It stung her a little, that he'd gone right out and had sex after she'd left him, but at least he'd also done that after today's engagement. Had he showered, she wondered? Her nose wasn't picking up anything. "Okay."

He held up a finger on each paw. "One guy, one girl. So my uncle kinda caught me and—yeah, he knows too. He said I was happier with you, but also that I was acting different. And he asked me to think about which me I liked better: the stereotypical pro athlete who did whatever he wanted. Like go hook up with random people just because he could whenever he felt hurt or down. Or the one who was, uh." His ears had come back up and now they folded down. "The one who was nicer."

She hadn't expected that. "I don't think you're a typical athlete."

"Sometimes I am. I can be that. I have to be, with my job. I went to this camp and it was really good. I made friends, bonded with the guys there. They all—well, not all, but a lot of them talk about girls like they're interchangeable. For a lot of my life I was sort of like that because that's how I met them. You know, I'd meet a girl at a party, hook up, probably never see her again. I had female friends, but they were different, and then when I started interviewing wives, they were another category, like my agent or something. But you were the first one who was all of that. No, not all, but parts of all of it and more, and better."

"And you made me feel different when I was with you, too. Girls blew me off before, but when you did, it stuck with me. I felt really bad about what I'd done. And you cared enough that when I screwed up, it really affected you. I want to be with someone who, I mean, someone where I need to be the best me."

He stopped to take a drink. Tami kept her paws around her glass, the cold of the drink seeping into her finger pads. She wanted to tell Ty that she missed him too, that the past few weeks had been miserable, but she wanted to wait for him to finish.

"So, uh." He sat up straight and took a breath. "We talked to my mom. And we called off the engagement."

By this time she was prepared, and so she replied evenly, keeping the rising tide of emotion down as if she were in a work meeting. "I haven't agreed to anything yet."

"I know. I didn't want to be married to Hideyo. That's over no matter what we do." He reached for her paw and then stopped and let his paw rest on the table, pads up.

Would she take him back? This wasn't like the Devin situation at all. Truth be told, she had been wondering whether Ty would get in touch with her again. Okay, truth *really* be told, "hoping" was a better word than "wondering." She and Axel had gone out to lunch and although the marmot had not condoned Ty's actions, he'd made an observation that sounded remarkably similar to what Ty's uncle had told him.

Into her silence, Ty spoke, rushed, a little nervous now. "If you want, I'd like to date you again. Maybe for a year or whatever. I want to get married sometime, but I know we have to get to know each other better and I need to regain your trust and, uh, and maybe more stuff you'll tell me?" He tilted his head and smiled.

Tami rubbed her fingers along the glass. The restaurant noise faded around her and there was only the guy in front of her: Ty, a young fox but not so much younger than she was, a pretty sexy guy who also wanted to be a good guy and do the right thing, and his major crime had been that he was in love with a guy and was afraid to come out with that.

She reached out and took his paw, intending to say yes, but found herself asking another question. "How do I know you won't go to your guy in Yerba and ask him to start up again?"

"Oh, uh." His eyes widened. "I don't—I mean, he ended it."

"Like I did. And you thought it was done before. What if he texts you again?"

He nodded. "I know it's this pro athlete mentality to think I can have everything I want, but I'm trying to break out of that. If he texts me, I'll—I'll tell you, okay? And I can tell you I'm tempted or something and we can talk about it."

"What if you're away, like you're going to be most of the year?" She didn't like this suspicious part of herself; she wanted to trust him, but it would be so easy when they were apart. After all, she'd only left Devin for a weekend and look what had happened.

"Then I'll…" His ears flicked and he reached for her other paw. "I don't know. I want to talk to you about everything. I'll do my best."

"I want to meet him." She surprised herself with those words, but she'd been thinking about Devin, and the intersection of that with this situation had popped a thought into her head.

Ty stared. "What?"

"Okay, maybe that's…" She shook her head. "But if you're okay with it, I'd like to. I mean, he means a lot to you, and so if I get the chance… I don't want to fly to Yerba next week or anything, but…"

His smile stretched back. "Does that mean you're saying yes?"

"Oh." She met his eyes and smiled. "Yeah. I guess I should've said that."

He let go of her paws and slapped the table with a report that made Tami jump and drew the attention of everyone else in the restaurant. "Woo!" Ty cried, and then reached forward to grab Tami's paws again, his eyes shining. "Thank you. I promise I'll do better."

She laughed, her own spirits rising with how happy he was. And she'd done that, simply by saying she'd go out with him. "I'll try to do better too. You know, I was in a really bad place that night. I felt like I didn't have anyone to turn to. There were a couple times I wanted to call you since then."

"I had my phone off while I was at the camp."

"I didn't try." She held his paw. "I was still mad at you, but I was also afraid I'd call and that you would say you'd moved on, or that you were mad at me."

"I was mad a little bit," he said. "But mostly at myself because I knew I'd screwed up. Hey, can I tell Uncle Lucas you said yes? I want you to meet him."

She let his fingers slide out of hers and go to pick up his phone. "I want you to meet Marci and Axel, too." She watched him text. "And it doesn't have to be a year, but I think whenever we both feel it's right."

"Mmm." He finished his text. "I mean, in a couple months I'll be going to training camp and then there's the season, so it can't be much less than a year, really."

"Right. Okay." She gave a nervous giggle and reached for his paws again. "I stopped thinking about football schedules for a couple weeks."

"Sorry," he said. "Again."

"No, no." His fingers felt good against hers, a solid anchor that she hadn't realized how much she'd missed until she was holding them again. "A lot of couples break up and get back together. I mean, Marci and Djardino broke up and got back together twice and they've been together four years now."

"Four years?" He snorted. "We can beat that."

She laughed. "Let's start with a few months first, Mister Competitive Athlete."

"Right. Right." He shook his head. "I wish you'd called me."

"I kind of do too. But I'm glad you called me."

"Yeah. And I was the one who screwed up so it was on me to call." Ty sounded like he was working it out in his head, talking it out. "I don't know, I've never been through this before. My uncle helped a lot."

"I want to meet him, too," Tami said. "I want to meet everyone."

He squeezed her paws and then brought them to his muzzle. "You will," he said. "I promise."

Chapter 32

This might be the stupidest thing he'd ever done. Justin wouldn't have said that. Justin said that the stupidest thing he'd ever done was to tell the football player to get lost. "With that body and the fancy hotel rooms? Wolf, you hit the lottery and you're giving back the ticket!"

"You haven't even seen his body."

"I smelled him and he smells awesome, and I looked him up on the Internet and he's like six and a half feet tall and built like a football player. You know how many guys would kill you, literally kill you, just to see him naked?"

When a wolverine said, "literally kill you," it felt a lot more real than when, say, a mouse said it, especially since Justin had a habit of baring his teeth when he said "kill." Arch smiled back and said, "I know, but I can get a good lay most nights if I want it." The formula was easy: go out dancing, pick the hottest guy who could dance well, if he wasn't interested, move on down to the next one until you found the one thirsty enough to say yes. Lather, fuck, repeat.

"Not like that one, right?" Justin grinned. "You kept going back for more."

"It wasn't about his body. Not just about his body." Arch sighed.

"Yeah, yeah, you're in love. It'll happen a bunch of times in your life. Use it and get some fantastic sex out of it. Don't throw it away because he isn't in love with you, too. Love is over-fucking-rated."

"This isn't one last booty call."

"No, but you can use it to get one last booty call. And then one more last booty call."

"His fiancée wants to sit there and hear me tell him it's over," Arch said.

"You can say one thing with your muzzle." The wolverine reached up and grabbed Arch's sheath through his underwear. "And another with the thing he listens to."

Justin had been cross-legged on the bed when he'd said that, but he was at work now, and Arch was buttoning up his collared shirt in the empty apartment and staring at himself in the mirror and wondering where exactly he'd gone wrong. Was it that last text he'd sent, the half-joking one that said, "Miss you more than I thought I would"? Or was it the one before that, the picture of himself sucking Ty's cock that he'd kept on his phone, the one that he'd stumbled over that made him remember all the things they'd done? Or was it going down to Crystal City to meet him? Or was it all the way before then, when he'd spotted a fabulous dancer at the Floor and had gone over to dance with him?

More importantly, if he really thought he'd gone wrong, what was he doing looking through his dresser drawer for the cufflinks he hadn't worn in six years?

He finally found them and spent another fifteen minutes figuring out how to put them in, which at least distracted him from being nervous. Then he had to figure out how much pride jewelry to wear, if any. Ty wouldn't want him to wear any out because what if someone took a picture, so it'd be a passive-aggressive asshole move to do it. More so because Arch didn't like jewelry that much anyway; it was an accessory to pick up guys with. But here, would it emphasize his identity to this mysterious girlfriend-fiancée? He weighed the bracelet and then left it on his dresser.

Ty had offered to pick him up, but Arch declined the offer. The wolf preferred to make his own way to the lounge so that he could leave whenever it became uncomfortable.

As it turned out, the first time that happened was the moment he stepped into the building. Because of course Ty had picked a lounge on the rooftop of a luxury hotel in the middle of the tourist district, and the moment Arch walked into the plushly-carpeted lobby past all of the navy blue and gold of the crisp, trim hotel staff, he felt like an outsider. All the guests lounging in the lobby seemed so comfortable in their clothes and their fur, while his clothes hung awkwardly on his shoulders and he walked stiffly and too quickly, he thought, across the lobby.

He had to ask at the elevators for how to get to the rooftop, and a cacomistle in the same crisply pressed navy and gold uniform pointed him to an elevator around the corner. "It goes directly there, sir," he said.

"Thanks." Arch fought back the urge to say, "I'm not a 'sir,'" and went on up to the lounge, his heartbeat racing with every floor the elevator rose.

His phone buzzed. Maybe it was Ty calling off the meeting, maybe he could go home and go back to his old boring life and finally stop comparing every guy he hooked up with to an impossible ideal.

But no, it was Justin. *If you need an excuse to leave, tell them this text is your sick mom.*

Twenty floors to go. Arch smiled and typed out a quick response. *Thanks. Ok for now.*

Ty knew that he wasn't in touch with his family anymore, if he'd bothered to remember anything about Arch. And if the meeting got too uncomfortable, the prospect of getting up and saying, "I don't want to see you anymore," while sad and awkward, held with it a little bit of satisfaction.

Because they'd had fun together, not just the sex but the dancing and the shopping. Arch had known it couldn't turn into anything serious and maybe that's why he'd broken it off, because he'd started to want it to and didn't see the point in torturing himself any further. Anyway, even if Ty didn't have to marry some girl to satisfy his parents, he wouldn't start up a serious relationship with another guy, not as a football player. Maybe it was okay for his teammate Dev, but Dev, for all that he was being held up as a hero to the gay community, hadn't really chosen to come out. He'd been backed into a corner. And nobody was going to back Ty into a corner.

So what was the point of this meeting anyway? Ty had only said that his girlfriend—not fiancée anymore?—wanted to meet Arch and that he'd told her about their relationship. Which sounded ominous; Arch had a vision in his head of the vixen from *Dangerous Liaisons* sitting in her formal gown looking down at him and saying with a cruel smile, "You have no more claim to him; he's mine now."

Ridiculous, but the thought still made him fidget against the confines of the elevator. Of course he had no claim to Ty; he never had. *I'll always be his first cock, though. That'll never change.* That was no foundation of a relationship, though; Arch's first cock had been Dick Juarez back in high school, about which the less thought the better.

And yet the fox had come to Yerba when Arch had messaged him, had booked a hotel room and they'd spent the night together.

And then he'd rushed off in the morning when his fiancée needed him.

The wolf pressed his paw to his eyes and shook his head. Be cool, he told himself. Go out there, smile, shake paws, do whatever he needs you to do. Erase that photo from your phone if you have to.

(It's saved on your computer anyway.)

And then if you feel like you need to get back at him for running out, if you need to get back at the fiancée for putting you through this, then you can make a little bit of a scene. That would help Ty anyway; it would say for sure that things were over. Even if making scenes wasn't really Arch's thing. Justin, now, Justin would stand up in the middle of a restaurant, stare down at his mortified dinner companion, and wait until everyone in the restaurant was staring at them before he hissed, "You bitch," threw wine onto the unfortunate, and stormed out. He had actually broken up with two semi-regular boyfriends that way. The first time it had been spur-of-the-moment, but he'd enjoyed it enough that he'd done it again months later, almost exactly the same way. "Just going with what I feel," he'd told Arch, and the wolf had said, "what, you feel like the star in a bad daytime soap?"

The elevator doors opened onto muted conversation, the clink of glasses and the salty aromas of olives, nuts, and bar crackers over a haze of different alcohols. The floor, a carpet of circular patterns in maroon, rose, yellow, and other colors curved around a glass-topped bar to a magnificent semicircular window with a kind of spiderweb pattern framing the view out past a few more rooftops onto the shimmering darkness of the Yerba Bay. Yellow couches held pairs and trios talking and laughing in low murmurs; a row of people sat at the bar, tails hanging down behind them (except for the rabbit and the doe who were looking at something on the rabbit's phone and giggling).

Arch stopped just inside the entrance and raised his nose to the confusion of scents. Ty's tickled his nose to his left, so he turned that way and saw the two foxes sitting together, both looking out the window.

His fiancée—girlfriend—was really pretty. When Arch found out that Ty was going out with Tami, the video game vixen, he'd pictured her as one of his friends who worked in IT: mussed fur, geeky t-shirts, patched jeans. And indeed, she wasn't wearing a dress, but her jeans were sleek and elegant and she wore a lovely silk blouse that was just the right color to go with her lighter russet fur. Which, by the way, was also brushed nicely as far as Arch could see. He was glad he'd taken the time to brush as well.

Their ears flipped back at the same time as he walked up and they turned a half-second later. Both got up, Ty stepping in for a hug and then releasing Arch to stand awkwardly. Tami extended a paw and Arch shook it and they leaned in to exchange scents and names. Warm, firm grip, and she wore a nice light floral perfume in addition to her natural scent.

He sat on the couch across from them and turned to the window. "Great view," he said.

"We looked up the place online." Ty glanced toward the bar. "You want something? Beer?"

Arch didn't miss Tami's look at the other fox as he rattled off Arch's drink preference. "I'm fine," he said even though both foxes had drinks in front of them.

"Okay, so, uh." Ty looked back at the vixen and then at Arch. "So…"

"I don't normally come to places like this either," Tami said. "But he sort of insisted."

Arch tilted his head. So this wasn't just a "stay away from my boyfriend" meeting, or at least it wasn't turning into one yet. "Oh, I know," he said. "Likes to show off his money."

"Hey." Ty gently pushed Tami's arm. "If you've got it…"

But Tami was smiling. "I know," she said, and her tail flicked against the couch. "It's just funny that we looked at half a dozen lounges and you picked the one with the most expensive cocktails."

"And the best view." Ty pointed at the window.

"Some things are worth paying for," Arch agreed. He hated small talk when the other person knew where the conversation was going and he didn't. "It's okay," he said, "you can get to the point. I won't be offended."

Ty spread his paws and lowered his voice; there was a kinkajou couple on the couches behind them, though they seemed deep in conversation with each other. "Tami wants to be sure it's over between us."

"It is. I told you that," Arch said.

"Why?" Tami asked.

He turned his attention to her, startled. "Why? Because I don't want to be an accessory. I'm twenty-four and I need to start thinking about, you know, my life." Outside, lights sparkled on the rooftops. They were easier to look at, and that way he could watch Ty and Tami's reflections. "I mean, I guess you know we had some fun, but that's all it was. You want me to erase his number from my phone?"

Tami tilted her head. "Do you want to erase his number? I assume if you wanted to, you would have already."

Arch didn't say anything. Tami sighed and took a drink of her drink. "This isn't a warning-off. This is me trying to understand things better. It's what I do. I trust Ty when he says you said it was over, but it also hurt me when he went right from our engagement to you."

"Yeah, well, it hurt when he ran from me right back to you, too," Arch said, and turned to look at her directly.

Her ears folded back and now she looked away, out the window. Ty looked miserable too, and it occurred to Arch that he'd never told Ty that that had hurt him. Good. Something worthwhile happened this evening anyway. He wished it made him feel better.

Ty spoke up as the silence dragged on. "I told you both I was sorry. I won't do anything like that again."

"He's young," Tami said as though Ty hadn't spoken.

"I'm only two years younger than him," Ty said, "and you're still young too. You're not even thirty."

"The point is," Tami went on with a smile, putting a paw on Ty's knee, "that we're going to be spending a little while getting to know each other, and I wanted to get to know you, since you were a large part of his life the past few months and a pretty important experience."

Arch's ears went up and he couldn't help smiling. Ty's ears were down in embarrassment, or maybe sadness? Could be either one. "Well," he said, "I get that. It's a pretty big thrill for a guy like him to meet a wolf who actually works in data entry."

That brought Ty's ears up and he snorted, and Tami actually laughed aloud. "So he said. And then I had to meet one for myself."

Arch spread his arms and leaned back on the sofa. "Live up to your expectations?"

"I'm not sure." Tami studied him. "I haven't seen you dance."

She said it with enough seriousness that Arch sat back up immediately. "Um," he said, looking around the quiet bar. "I mean, do you want us to get up and…?"

"No, no." She laughed and looked at Ty.

The big fox's ears came up. "There's a club down on the ground floor. Should be hopping in an hour or so."

"Okay, but hold on. It's okay for us to dance?" Arch squinted at Tami.

"I enjoyed our friendship," Ty said.

"And I'm not trying to tell him what he can and can't do." Tami rubbed Ty's knee again. "I'm trying to find a compromise that keeps us both happy. This is…this isn't the kind of situation that I'm used to hearing about from my family or seeing in movies or whatever. It's unique."

"Yeah, well." Arch snorted. "I'm used to not seeing my life represented in movies."

"Of course." Tami lifted her muzzle, looking as though she were searching for the right thing to say. "I have a gay friend."

"How progressive."

Tami sighed. Ty cut in. "She didn't mean it like that."

"I really didn't. I mean that Axel says that all the time. And he says that he and his boyfriend have to figure out their relationship themselves. They don't have 'a million movies' and novels to model things after. That's all I meant."

Arch nodded. Tami was proving annoyingly difficult to hate. "It's just a thing I hear a lot," he said, and then grinned. "In movies."

Ty and Tami both relaxed. "So," Ty said. "Dancing?"

"Let's see how it goes." He wanted to, sure. He had other friends who were better than Ty (though not much), but dancing with the big fox was fun for reasons that had little to do with the quality of dancing. He had an enthusiasm and optimism that Arch didn't see too often, and that translated into his body movements. In all kinds of activities.

"All right. Hey, could you grab me a refill?" Tami asked Ty.

"Oh, sure. Same thing?" She nodded, and he stood and walked over to the bar.

When he was out of earshot, she leaned over to Arch. "So why did you text him again?"

This was more what he'd expected. "I mean," he tried to joke, "have you seen him?"

She didn't laugh. "Yes, I've seen him. Naked. He still looks the same. So maybe next year you'll text him again."

"No, I—"

"You told him it was over, then you texted him again."

He held up a finger as his tail bristled up. "I did not tell him it was over. That first time. I told him it was *probably* over."

"And then you texted him the weekend he got engaged. So are you a liar, or did you just get horny?"

"Hey." He stared back at her, responses whirling through his head. She looked intense but not angry, actually. "I'm not a liar."

"I understand getting horny, but that won't stop, will it?"

"No, but…" He took a breath. "I told him once he was engaged, it was over. There's other guys out there, you know. I can hook up."

"You didn't before." When he made an exasperated noise, she clinked her empty glass on the table. "I'm trying to understand what your relationship is with him so I know what to expect."

Like she had any right to know that. Arch fumed and then decided, okay, fine. "You want to know? All right, I'll tell you. You know what, we only spent a few nights together here and there, but it was like getting swept up into a different world. Probably for you too. So okay, we're both people who got to go to this fantasy world, but you know how that story ends: only one gets to stay. It's you. I'm okay with that."

She didn't respond, so he went on. "But before that had been decided… when I could still get one or two more nights with him…yeah, I missed it. I missed him. And I didn't know about your engagement when I texted him." He met her eyes and then lowered his muzzle. "The first time. He told me right away."

"So hooking up with him then, you weren't trying to make him change his mind?"

"No! Honestly, I wasn't…" He took a breath. "I mean, I might've thought, like, wildest dreams maybe he'll…but that was like, like winning the lottery fantasy." Dammit, Justin. "Not a lottery. I know he can't be with me, so every moment is…a taste of what that might be like."

"So if he did say he wanted you instead of a wife, you'd say yes."

Arch frowned. "You said yes."

"Uh huh."

"I mean, yeah, but look, I'm not going to do anything like that. I know it's not possible. If it makes you feel better, I promise I won't come on to him anymore."

Tami shook her head. "I'm not worried about you. I'm worried about a young guy who basically got the world handed to him at the age of twenty-two and is used to getting everything he wants."

"Okay, then, I promise not to be anywhere not in public with him."

"So you still want to go dancing?"

Arch rested his muzzle on his paws. Tami's manner had softened enough that his tail had smoothed down, but he still wasn't completely relaxed. "Seriously?"

"It's fine with me, and I know he'd like it. He says all his teammates are 'U-G-L-Y' when it comes to dancing."

Arch gave a short laugh and was pleased to see her smile. "Yeah, I've heard that." He glanced toward the bar, where Ty was still waiting, talking to the bartender.

Tami followed his look. "Don't worry," she said. "I'll text him when it's okay to come back. You think we're done?"

"You'll text him…oh, you worked that out in advance." He shook his head. "Sneaky."

She smiled and flicked her ears forward, affirming that. "Anything else?"

"Yeah." He pointed at her. "What's your deal? Why are you trying to make sure he and I stay friends?"

"Advice of one of my friends. But also, I had a boyfriend, and he didn't like one of my friends and told me I shouldn't see him, and I don't want to be that girlfriend or wife. You know?"

"Makes sense." His throat was dry, so he took a sip of water. "Did your friend also tell you to be mean to me?"

"Different friend did. One of my friends is a lawyer. I've watched her cross-examine a couple times."

Arch rolled his eyes. "Lawyer friend. Wow. I told him you'd be cool. I didn't know you'd be cool about all kinds of stuff."

"I wouldn't think so either, to hear my friends tell it." Tami rolled her eyes right back at him.

"You make video games, right?" Arch waved a paw. "That should be plenty cool."

"Half my friends do too. Well, maybe not half anymore." She scowled. "Video game industry is full of a lot of politics and stuff just like any other industry."

"I tell you," Arch said, "the data entry game is nearly politics-free, at least as far as I can see. We come in, enter our spreadsheets, and go home. I don't see many people kissing up to the manager to get a different spreadsheet. Anyway, I think our manager is actually an AI. We never see her."

"I didn't know AI was that advanced."

"We figure if they can make one play chess, they can make one that manages data entry."

She laughed, and Arch liked making her laugh, and then cursed himself. You're not supposed to get to like her. She's the one keeping you and Ty apart.

The next minute, he laughed at himself. Keeping you apart? You act as though Ty would run to you if he weren't bound by his family to marry a vixen. Look at how happy they are together, the way they're comfortable with little touches, the way they share inside jokes. They're going to be good together.

"Arch?"

Tami leaned forward.

"Sorry," he said, and gave her a smile. "Lost in my own world."

And Ty came back then, looming over them. He put a drink in front of Tami, and then a pilsner glass in front of Arch. "The bartender said this is the best Hefeweizen they have. It's, um, Blue something?"

"Thanks." He could already smell the malted wheat and a hint of banana flavor. The fox had remembered what he liked.

Ty settled back into the couch. "So what did you guys talk about?"

"You," Tami said sweetly. And when Ty straightened and smiled, puffing up a bit, she added, "and how intolerable rich guys who can buy anything they want are."

"Hmph." He nosed her ear. "I couldn't buy you."

"Maybe you didn't try hard enough."

"How much did you say a game studio cost?"

Arch picked up his beer and poured a generous portion into his muzzle so he wouldn't have to watch this exchange. It would've been more annoying except that right at the beginning, when Ty had said, "Hmph," Arch was almost sure that Ty had glanced in his direction. Which made it slightly less annoying and slightly more heartbreaking.

Only slightly, he reminded himself, because this thing is over and you don't have any claim on him anyway. You want him to be happy and he clearly is.

Tami laughed and said, "Sorry," to Arch. "We really aren't one of those couples."

As much as it annoyed him, he had to admit that objectively, it didn't look like she'd planned it that way. If anything, Ty had started it. So he kept his ears up and said, "You want to start a game studio?"

"Oh, eventually," Tami's ears flicked. "I mean, that's a long way off."

They talked about her career and then she asked about Arch's ambitions. This was a tough conversation, one he'd started having with Justin and some of his other friends this year. He didn't want to tell those friends some of the things he was thinking about, had been thinking about more recently. But here, with Ty and Tami, he felt there was less at stake if they laughed or got upset. "I've kind of been thinking about trying to become a cop," he said.

"Oh, cool," Tami replied.

Ty's eyebrows shot up. "You told me you'd had trouble with police."

"Yeah," Arch said. "Lot of us have. But that's kinda why, right? I mean, you can fight the system or you can become part of it and try to change it. Anyway, the police out here aren't that bad actually. The guys who came out for Justin's ex were cool. Maybe I could protect people, or, y'know, solve murders and stuff." He laughed. "I've been watching a lot of TV dramas lately."

Neither of them laughed with him. They took it seriously, and Tami looked up some resources on her phone that might help him (she had, he noticed, the same shiny new iPhone that Ty had, so money did buy some things at least).

And when that wrapped up, and Arch had finished his beer, Ty smiled at him and nudged Tami. "So…you said maybe dancing?"

She looked across at Arch. "Are you up for it?"

"Sure." He felt at least a little more at ease, and the prospect of one more dance with Ty appealed.

So they made their way down the hotel elevators to a raucous club in the basement, although the raucousness was well controlled here and there weren't any of the more objectionable smells that accompanied the dancing at The Floor and some of the seedier clubs Arch frequented. Pot, though, and whiffs of harder stuff as well over the sweat and beer breath and spilled drinks.

Tami stayed back at the bar, professing herself, "Not a dancer, no way," so it was just the two of them, and with the insulation of the music and the smells out on the floor, Arch didn't have to think about her or about the cold, lonely ride home that waited at the end of this night. It wasn't a gay club, but this was Yerba and there were several gay couples dancing as well, so there was only a twinge of self-consciousness for Arch, and that vanished with everything else into the light and the music and the way they danced together.

He could tell himself that he had friends who were better dancers than Ty, but they didn't dance with him like this, in sync, matching their movements, remembering the dances at The Floor and down in Crystal City. Their dances were the inside jokes they had, a form of communication that Ty would never share with his girlfriend/fiancée/wife. Arch pushed those thoughts aside too, even though a faint hope flickered that maybe they could keep dancing together into the future, if nothing else.

That "maybe" compelled him to push the dancing longer than he normally would go, even though his legs protested and his throat was parched. "One more?" he asked when Ty asked if he wanted to stop, and the fox grinned and nodded.

Finally, though, their last dance was over and they had to go back to where Tami was sitting. She'd ordered a couple glasses of water for them, and Arch gulped down half of his before he'd even sat down. "You two looked great out there," Tami said while they drank.

"Feel great." Ty grinned at Arch.

"Yeah." The wolf panted and finished off his water. He settled back into the chair, enjoying the exhaustion and the coolness of air over his panting tongue. Ty sat too, but pulled out his phone and texted someone. All right, if he was going to text, Arch would talk to...oh, Tami was staring at her paws below the table. Something on her phone, too? Well, he could text too, if it came to that.

He took out his phone, but he didn't really want to text Justin or anyone else. This was turning into a nice night, and Justin would hear enough about it in the morning. Maybe there wouldn't be a last booty call, but the dancing really had helped. Arch had worked out a lot of energy, had had fun with Ty, and found himself strangely optimistic about the future.

And as he was thinking that, Tami put her phone away. She gave Ty a smile. "It's getting late," she said. "I guess we should get back to the room."

"Uh huh." Ty slid off his chair and stood next to hers.

"Okay." Arch put his phone away as well and got up. "Hey, I appreciate you guys coming all the way to Yerba, and it was really nice to meet you, Tami."

That "maybe" compelled him to push the dancing longer than he normally would go, even though his legs protested and his throat was parched. "One more?" he asked when Ty asked if he wanted to stop...

She was looking at Ty, and he was looking back at her, and they were both smiling. Jesus Dog, they were already thinking of fucking. Arch kept his smile up and raised a paw. "All right, I'll see you. Let me know if you want to get together again."

Tami reached out and held his wrist. He turned, surprised, and stopped when he saw her smile. "Uh, so," she said, "want to come back to the room with us?"

He stared at her and then turned to Ty. The big fox had a big smile on his muzzle and his tail was wagging pretty fucking hard. "Hold on," Arch said. "You mean…?"

"Yeah." Ty leaned in. "We've talked about it and Tami's cool with it. If you want."

"Sorry," Tami said. "I know this is springing it on you, but we didn't want to say anything until we were both sure."

Until she was sure, she meant. Arch tried to parse the situation and kept coming up with nothing to say. He couldn't even think past walking out the door (and giving up the chance to fuck Ty again) or going up to the room (and having sex? With a vixen maybe? Or just with Ty in front of someone?).

Tami cleared her throat. "The thing is," she said, keeping her voice almost too low to hear in the din of the club, "I know Ty's used to getting everything he wants. And in some cases he can't have it. But…he loves us both. And I think we both love him. If I tell him he can't see you anymore, he'll be a little more miserable. Maybe a good deal more miserable. It seems like we get along pretty well, so…I mean, I have a friend who shares his girlfriend with another guy. Had a friend." She sighed and rubbed her eyes. "So we don't have to…you know, I mean, we can see how this goes, but if at least you and I can be friends, maybe we can share him."

Ty, who wasn't panting nearly as much as Arch, grinned. "There's a lot of me to go around."

"And he'll be traveling a lot, and maybe we'll have a family eventually."

"Whoa," Arch said.

"No, no." Tami laughed, with a nervous edge. "This doesn't have to be about anything past tonight, just seeing how tonight goes."

"But maybe," Ty put in, and he reached over to take Arch's other paw, "maybe you could be part of something, not just something on the side."

Fuck. Damn him.

No, thanks. That's what he should say, right? He had two friends who'd joined up in threesomes and one of them had ended up out; the other had ended up in a couple with one of the original couple out. Two plus one equals one plus two, that's what everyone said. But there were those guys he'd met last month, the antelope and the armadillo and the squirrel, and they'd been together…a while, he didn't remember how long.

Two plus one, and there was no question here who the one would always be, right? But this wasn't for anything past tonight.

Arch looked back and forth between the two foxes still waiting for his answer. "Yeah," he said, "why not? I mean, my friends said I was crazy if I didn't take every chance to see this guy naked."

"Uh huh." Tami smiled. "My friends said the same thing. Some of them asked for pictures."

"Oh, mine too."

When he still hesitated, Tami said, "And they didn't even know how sweet he is under that fur and muscle. The part that really matters." Gracefully giving Arch more time to think about it.

Arch swallowed. Thinking about it more wasn't going to change the fact that he loved Ty (probably) and liked Tami (definitely) and so… "So, uh, yes. For tonight. And after…"

"And after," Tami said, "we'll see."

They walked to the elevators in silence, Arch's mind buzzing. How had this happened? Where had he gone right? Was it sending that pic to Ty because he couldn't get the fox out of his mind? Was it staying in the hotel room that night because he wanted to sleep next to him? Or inviting the fox back to his place, something he almost never did?

Or was it just the lucky chance that he'd been at a club, had seen a guy who danced like him, and had gone over to dance with him? He didn't believe in love at first sight, and wasn't honestly sure that what he was in now was love. But he knew that he was willing to do some really out there stuff if it meant he got to keep seeing Ty, and that he was happier as they stepped onto the elevator together than he'd been in weeks. Nervous, sure, but happy too.

And that, Arch thought, was enough for now.

EPILOGUE

His room smelled like cardboard more than anything else, so Arch spent most of the morning unpacking. It was a little distressing that most of his possessions could fit into a half-dozen boxes stacked in the corner of an otherwise fairly empty room. Ty had promised a desk, dresser, and bookshelf would be delivered Monday, and Arch had turned down his offer of an entertainment system. He had an iPod and headphones and a computer and that was enough for him. He was going to be pretty busy anyway.

Around noon, the patter of rain on the roof was broken by the sound of a television going on downstairs, and the cadences of a football game became clearer. Arch had gotten through three boxes, so he brought the flattened ones down the thickly carpeted stairs and set them at the bottom of the staircase.

Dim light came in through the windows over the door and in the living room, and on the large couch in front of the 48" television, Tami sat with her laptop open. "Hey," she said. "Tired of unpacking?"

"I wasn't sure if you were up." The wolf smiled. "I slept pretty well myself."

"Haven't been to sleep." Tami sighed. "I made a lot of progress on this project. Axel just got up and we're chatting about it."

Arch shook his head. "You want a drink?"

"I'm good."

He went to the kitchen and grabbed a Diet Coke out of the refriger-ator. "You don't have to solve all their problems your first week," he said, plopping down on the couch next to Tami. The scent of her season was noticeable but not strong, not objectionable.

"They're paying me a lot of money. I feel like I have to give them good value. Anyway, who stayed up until three am last Tuesday night doing a Civics paper?"

"I was packing, too," Arch said.

"Oh, right, which one of your six boxes was that night?"

He grinned and gulped some soda. "How's the game?"

"Um, the announcers are shouting a lot, so I think it's exciting." She squinted. "Peco's up by ten."

"Yes, I too can read the crawl on the screen." Arch pointed. "Hey, that was a good catch."

They watched the replay. "Ty's better," Tami said.

"Sixth real football game and already you know that?"

"Oh, and you've seen, what, two more?"

"Four more." Arch wagged his tail against the couch.

"But I've been to three more practices than you."

He threw up his paws in mock despair. "Curse this education and its schedule."

"Yeah." She leaned in under his arm as it came back down. "You have homework for Monday?"

"No, but…" Arch paused as the Fraters scored. "Oh yeah, I didn't tell you this with all the moving stuff. A guy from the FBI came into our class on Friday. He told us that the FBI really needs agents."

Tami raised her eyebrows and perked her ears. "You want to work for the FBI?"

"They have intelligence analyst jobs. I could be, like, intercepting communications from domestic terrorists and shit. Anyway, it's a Criminology degree just like for the police, but I might have to take a few more electives. It seems like it could be pretty cool."

"That's great. I think it suits you more than directing traffic around parades."

"And they have a bunch of field offices here in Pelagia. Also, I asked the guy specifically afterwards, they don't care if you're gay anymore."

"Do they care if you're sleeping with a football player?"

"Ha." He snorted. "I didn't ask about that."

"Besides," Tami said. "I think technically you qualify as bisexual."

Arch patted her leg. "I think technically I'm still sort of working on that." Because the question of marriage wasn't settled yet, let alone cubs, Ty wasn't even visiting during Tami's season. Arch, by contrast, didn't feel any extra arousal from the scent, which felt rude since Tami was much more interested in sex during her season, and in Ty's absence he felt like he should take care of that even though she said she could take care of herself.

"Oh, right." Tami flattened her ears with a smile. "About that. I picked up something for us to try. Maybe tonight."

"Oh?" Arch turned to face her.

"Yeah, it's…" Tami slipped out from under his arm, picked up her computer, and called up a web page. "Here, this."

"Whoa." Arch saw a mass of leather straps. "I told you, Ty might be getting into bondage, but I'm—oh. Oh. Huh."

"It'll fit most of your toys, when I wear it, and I, uh, bought something for myself, if you want to wear it sometime."

"That sounds like fun, actually." He grinned and leaned back against her. "And that's the game. Peco wins. They're…what? Three and one now?"

"Congratulations," Tami said, "you can read the screen."

"Hush." Arch grinned. "Look, they're showing our boy."

"The Firebirds are three and one so far this year, and one of the reasons is a rejuvenated offense," the TV announcer said.

"He looks so good in that uniform," Tami murmured.

"Uh huh."

She set the computer aside as he leaned into her, putting her arm around his shoulder, which fit just as nicely as the other way around. "This is a little weird, right?" Tami asked. "Did you ever see yourself in a relationship like this?"

"It's only weird if I think about it," Arch said. The scent of her season might not be arousing, but he liked being with her. At first it had been sharing Ty that had brought them together, but since he'd started football again they'd been building their own bonds.

Tami laughed. "I know what you mean. But it feels right."

"I guess we never knew we had it in us." Arch gestured to the screen, where clips from the Firebirds' three previous games played. "You think he knew?"

"I think he felt like he could do whatever he wanted. But he has a good heart and he believed, even if none of us really knew what we wanted."

"That's familiar." He snorted. "I wouldn't be in college right now if not for him. It would've taken me at least another year to get my shit together." He looked balefully up at the rain spattering the windows. "Even if then I would've been in a nice climate."

"He's a good motivator." Tami tapped her laptop.

"Yeah." Arch's tail thumped against the couch. On the TV, the cameras pulled back to show the sunny expanses of the Firebirds' home field as the Tornadoes ran up to kick off. "All right," he said, and rested his head against hers. "Here we go."

Acknowledgments

As with all of my work, this does not happen in a vacuum. I owe many thanks to Carrizo Kitfox and Lynn Hogan, who answered questions about game development process, and to Edwin Aoki and Kevin Frane, who talked to me about Japanese families and customs.

My writing group, Ryan Campbell, David Cowan, and Watts Martin, all offered valuable feedback and critique, as they always do. Neverwolf, in addition to providing wonderful illustrations, also helped with story, as did Rukis.

And of course, Kit and Jack and Kobalt continue to provide this fox with a loving home in which to write these stories, and to them I will be eternally grateful.

About the Author

Kyell Gold took up furry erotica writing after high school, making the team at his small liberal arts college as a walk-on. He was drafted late by Sofawolf and blossomed in the professional league, earning four Ursa Major awards in his first three years as a pro for his novels and short stories. He has since won eight more Ursa Major awards, including one for "In Between," the first Dev and Lee story, one for *Out of Position*, which also won two Rainbow Awards for gay fiction, and one for *Isolation Play*, the second Dev and Lee book.

His various online presences are linked from *www.kyellgold.com*, and you can follow him on Twitter at @KyellGold. In the off-season, he lives in California with his husband.

About the Artists

Rukis is a freelance illustrator and writer who grew up in the Appalachian region, working with animals and on farms from a young age. After earning a Bachelors in Traditional Animation, she started a career in freelance art, writing and illustrating a small collection of comics and novels in the Anthropomorphic fandom. You can see more of her work at *www.furaffinity.net/user/rukis*.

Neverwolf (aka: Never) is a self-taught Canadian artist, working professionally in his field since 2012. When he's not drawing, watching movies or drawing things from those movies, he's learning new skills to further his future endeavours. He has previously appeared in volume fifteen of Sofawolf's long running series *Heat;* and you can find more of his work at *theneverwolf.tumblr.com* and support him at *www.patreon.com/theneverwolf.*

About Sofawolf Press

Sofawolf Press was founded in 1999 to provide a venue to showcase great writers of anthropomorphic fiction and to promote the genre to a wider audience.

Since the debut of its flagship publication, Anthrolations, a literary anthology of short stories, the Press has added to its lineup other magazine-length anthologies, novels, shared-world anthologies, and other novel-length collections, comics and graphic novels, artists' sketchbooks, and calendars. The Press continues to seek out new and creative ways of expanding its offerings of printed creations. Sofawolf's publications have won twenty Ursa Major awards, and in 2012, Ursula Vernon's *Digger* gave Sofawolf Press its first Hugo Award.

Please visit their website at *www.sofawolf.com* for a full list of titles available from Sofawolf Press. Thanks for reading!

www.ingramcontent.com/pod-product-compliance
Lightning Source LLC
Chambersburg PA
CBHW071149020726
47502CB00002B/341